Lon Chaney, Jr.

Lon Chaney, Jr.
Horror Film Star, 1906–1973

by DON G. SMITH

McFarland & Company, Publishers, Inc.
Jefferson, North Carolina, and London

> The present work is a reprint of the library bound edition of Lon Chaney, Jr.: Horror Film Star, 1906–1973, first published in 1996 by McFarland.

Frontispiece: Lon Chaney, Jr., at the height of his career (circa 1941)

LIBRARY OF CONGRESS CATALOGUING-IN-PUBLICATION DATA

Smith, Don G., 1950–
   Lon Chaney, Jr. : horror film star, 1906–1973 / by Don G. Smith.
     p.   cm.
   Filmography: p.
   Includes bibliographical references and index.

   ISBN 0-7864-1813-3 (softcover : 50# alk. paper) ∞

   1. Chaney, Lon, 1906–1973. 2. Actors—United States—Biography. I. Title.
PN2287.C49S65   2003
791.43'028'092—dc20   95-39762
[B]

British Library cataloguing data are available

©1996 Don G. Smith. All rights reserved

No part of this book may be reproduced or transmitted in any form or by any means, electronic or mechanical, including photocopying or recording, or by any information storage and retrieval system, without permission in writing from the publisher.

Cover photographs: Lon Chaney, Jr., in a publicity photo and in makeup in the 1941 film *The Wolf Man*

Manufactured in the United States of America

McFarland & Company, Inc., Publishers
  Box 611, Jefferson, North Carolina 28640
    www.mcfarlandpub.com

To Diana and Cassandra,
who make everything possible

Contents

	Acknowledgments	ix
	Preface	1
1	The Early Years (1906–1931)	4
2	Learning His Craft (1931–1938)	10
3	Of Mice and Men (1939–1940)	24
4	*Man-Made Monster* and *The Wolf Man* (1941)	32
5	The Frankenstein Series	42
6	The Mummy Series	59
7	The Inner Sanctum Series	68
8	*Son of Dracula* and Other Nonseries Universal Films (1941–1946)	81
9	*Abbott and Costello Meet Frankenstein* and Supporting Roles	98
10	Character Gems (1952–1955)	111
11	Horror Films, Westerns, and Television (1956–1962)	129
12	The A. C. Lyles Years (1963–1965)	156
13	Exploitation, Decline, and Death (1966–1973)	172
14	The Summing Up	187
	Notes	193
	Filmography	213
	Selected Bibliography	221
	Index	223

Acknowledgments

Since 1957, when at the age of seven I became a dedicated horror film fan, Bela Lugosi, Vincent Price, and Lon Chaney, Jr., have remained my favorite genre personalities. When I decided in 1987 to write a book on the life and career of Lon Chaney, Jr., several books had already been published devoted solely to Lugosi, and one had been published devoted solely to Price. Chaney, however, had been unaccountably neglected. This book is my way of saying "thank you" to Lon for all the hours of pleasure his work has given me over the years.

Several other "thank you's" are now in order. First of all, I want to thank my wife, Diana, who while running a household, attending to our daughter Cassandra, and taking classes at the university, graciously sacrificed her time in order to give me time to write and do research. She is the true "Wonder Woman." Second, I want to thank my proofreader, Gordon Speck, a scholar and a gentleman, whose corrections are often delivered with a comedic touch rivaling that of Groucho Marx. Third, a special thanks goes to Tom Weaver, who shared with me material he had accumulated during years of research on his own books. Special thanks also go to Blackie Seymour of Pentegram Library for supplying a number of rare stills which appear in the book and for sharing information with me (both published and otherwise) related to Universal Pictures.

I also want to thank the following, all of whom were extremely helpful in the preparation of this book: Forrest J Ackerman, Gary Svehla, Gregory William Mank, Gary Dorst, Bill Littman, Marta Davis of Morris Library (Southern Illinois University), Mon Ayash, Gary Cease, David Miller of M and M Enterprises, Ronnie James, Glen Damato of the Fang Video, Ron Chaney, Curt Siodmak, Virginia Christine, Patrick Knowles, Martha O'Driscoll, Elyse Knox, Aquanetta, Marie Windsor, Russ Tamblyn, Oliver Drake, Myrna Dell, Robert Quarry, Elena Verdugo, Michael Oliker and many others.

Preface

From 1919 when Conrad Veidt walked the expressionistic sets of *The Cabinet of Dr. Caligari* to the contemporary "splatter" cinema of *The Texas Chainsaw Massacre* (1974), *Friday the 13th* (1980), and *A Nightmare on Elm Street* (1984), horror films have enjoyed the largest, most enthusiastic following of any screen genre. Explanations for this phenomenon are varied, but the fact is undeniable. When the lights of the theater go down, shrouding the rows in darkness, the audience becomes part of a waking nightmare. For many, that nightmare touches something deep within them and holds their sometimes unwilling attention with all the power of an ancient mariner's fixed stare. Perhaps the attraction for horror films is so strong because most people experience them first as children, at a time when they are impressionable, open to suggestions of wonder, and eager to face vicariously those childhood "things that go bump in the night." Roger Corman, one of the most prominent directors of horror films, admits that similar considerations formed a foundation for his work:

> I based some of my work...on further theories that I developed, coming to the conclusion that terror was really the re-creation of childhood fantasies. The child is sometimes alone in a house or in a room—in a world he only dimly understands. It's possibly a dark night, it's stormy, there's thunder, lightning—forces that are frightening to him—and he has no way of coping. And they make a very deep imprint on his mind. The parent can later say, "It's only thunder, it's only lightning—these things are normal things," but to the child, I think, these explanations are only partially helpful. The unconscious terror of the dark and the strange noises and lights remains. Therefore, the horror film taps that unconscious and takes one back to childhood fears.[1]

I was fortunate to grow up during horror fandom's most fertile era, a time when childhood fears could be summoned from the subconscious on a regular basis. My parents first introduced me to horror through Grimms' fairy tales, but the fascination became full-blown when they took me at age seven to see

Rodan the Flying Monster (1957). That same year Hammer films released *The Curse of Frankenstein* and they followed a year later with *Horror of Dracula* (1958). At the same time that my parents were taking me to see such films as *The Fly* (1958), *It! The Terror from Beyond Space* (1958), and *The House on Haunted Hill* (1959), a local television station introduced the Shock Theater packages of 1930s and 1940s horror classics. Anyone growing up during those years was exposed to three decades of horror genre history on a weekly basis. Such a fortuitous sequence of events has never occurred since, which is why so many young contemporary horror genre fans idolize Robert Englund (Freddie Kruger of *A Nightmare on Elm Street*), but barely recognize the names of Boris Karloff and Bela Lugosi.

Along with an insatiable desire for the films themselves grows a fond familiarity with and a love for the actors who made the stories live–which brings us to the subject of this book, Lon Chaney, Jr. I do not remember when I first saw him, but I do remember that in 1958 my parents would not let me stay up to watch the first area television showing of his *Man-Made Monster* (1941), thus cultivating in me a desire for forbidden fruit. In the early 1960s, however, television stations began playing the classic horror films early enough in the evening for me to watch them, and I watched every one. On March 26, 1962, I came home from school, ate dinner, and that evening watched *Frankenstein Meets the Wolf Man* (1943). Along with the bleak, atmospheric opening scenes in the Llanwelly Cemetery, the festival of the new wine, and the climactic battle of the monsters, the tortured character of Lawrence Talbot (Lon Chaney, Jr.) impressed me greatly.

Almost a month later I was in Barnes Hospital in St. Louis to have my tonsils removed. As I sat rather nervously in the television lounge on the evening before the operation, I turned the channel to *The Wolf Man* (1941) and reviewed the origin of the Talbot/Wolf Man mythology. While I was anxiously fearing the arrival of morning, I watched several very old and very ill men who shared the lounge with me. I knew that they feared their fates as well, just as Lawrence Talbot did, just as we all do. For fate is unknown, and where the horrors of death and illness are concerned, it is unavoidable. Thus if Freud is correct, the same anxieties that gave rise to religion also gave rise to the horror film. Much that is great in the horror genre addresses these universal fears. All of the great horror performers–Lon Chaney, Sr., Boris Karloff, Bela Lugosi, Lon Chaney, Jr., Peter Lorre, Vincent Price, Christopher Lee, and Peter Cushing– are dear to us at least in part because through their films we struggle to cope with some of the darker and more sinister aspects of the human condition.

As the years passed, I began seriously collecting horror and science fiction film memorabilia, particularly that relating to Bela Lugosi and Lon Chaney, Jr. As my knowledge of Chaney increased, one thing became clear: of all the great horror film stars, both fans and critics afforded him the least respect. While entire books were devoted to the others, Chaney remained neglected.

A typical critical response to Chaney is that of Carlos Clarens: "Chaney revealed himself as a monotonous actor of rather narrow range, possessing neither the voice and skill of Karloff nor the demonic persuasion of Lugosi."[2] But if that accurately sums up Lon Chaney, Jr., why was he the biggest horror film star of the 1940s, and why does the wolf man, *his* creation, still exert such a powerful influence on American popular culture? If he was such a limited actor, why is his portrayal of Lennie in *Of Mice and Men* still considered by many to be one of filmdom's most memorable, and how was he able to sustain a prolific career in films, in television, and on the stage from the 1930s to the 1970s? If limited, why was he cast as both monster and monster hunter, as both cowboy and Indian, as both gangster and sheriff, and as both dimwit and university professor? If monotonous, why was he able to work successfully under the direction of such luminaries as King Vidor, Cecil B. De Mille, Lewis Milestone, Fred Zinneman, Raoul Walsh, Michael Curtiz, Roger Corman, and Roy Del Ruth?

The answers lie within a challenging labyrinth, for Chaney's life and career are fraught with contradictions, and while he is often written off as just good-natured and simple, he was in fact a tantalizingly complex man. At the present time, a cult of personality is developing around him which has led to a heightened interest in his career, an interest largely fueled by the morbid fascination some fans nurture for film stars who lead tragic lives. Examples of this phenomenon are Marilyn Monroe, the unhappy suicide (or murder victim), and Bela Lugosi, the alcoholic and drug addict. Tragedy, contradiction, and complexity are clearly elements in the life and career of Lon Chaney, Jr. Like Lugosi, he was an alcoholic, yet he continued to rack up acting credits to the end of his life. One person who knew him contended that he was sexually confused—bisexual or homosexual—yet he was married to the same woman for 37 years and reared two sons. Many testify to his gentle nature, yet others portray him as a bully boy with a barely concealed taste for violence. Stories of the *Hollywood Babylon* variety abound where Chaney is concerned, but there is more to the man than this plethora of titillating vignettes would suggest.

A few years ago, I concluded that Chaney was important and interesting enough to merit a book devoted to his life and career. Talks with horror film fans around the country have confirmed my conclusion. While this book focuses on his career in horror films, it also examines his larger career, much of which is worthy of attention in its own right, especially his fine television work, which is virtually unknown even to most Chaneyphiles. I hope that this book will aid Chaney's son in climbing to the heights now occupied by his father and others, a height he has earned the right to share.

Chapter 1

The Early Years (1906-1931)

Lon Chaney, Sr., would become one of the greatest stars of the silent screen. But in 1905 when he met and married pretty Cleva Creighton, stardom was still an elusive dream. At that time, he was touring with the Musical Comedy Repertory Company, a small troupe that struggled from one booking to the next. Work was relatively steady, but nothing was certain. Cleva was a choir singer when she applied for work with the troupe and came under Lon's guiding hand. When the new bride became pregnant, she had no choice but to continue working. Unfortunately, the difficulties of travel, the uncertainties regarding income, and the general wear and tear of the actor's life took their toll.

On February 10, 1906, Lon Chaney, Jr., born Creighton Tull Chaney, was delivered prematurely. Weighing only two and a half pounds, the child did not begin breathing as newborns normally do. Chaney explained: "My father, acting as a midwife, delivered me on that very cold morning.... And holding what appeared to be a totally lifeless form, [he] rushed me outside our Oklahoma City shack to a small pond out back where, breaking the ice with his foot, [he] dunked me in the freezing water. This shock treatment started me breathing."[1] The father, elated at the results, still must have quickly sunk back into anxious consideration of how the new family unit would financially survive.

Putting his acting career on hold, Chaney accepted employment as a carpet layer for Doc and Bill's Furniture Store. But when news of a job with another traveling troupe came his way, Chaney packed up his family and again hit the road as an actor.

As a baby, little Creighton's backstage home was a cotton-lined shoebox with holes punched in the lid for air. Later he would laughingly refer to the contraption as "probably one of the world's first incubators."[2] Another sleeping device was a small handmade hammock that Chaney created for his son.

Life was hard for the Chaney family. Always under strain, the parents transported little Creighton from city to city. Doing their washing and cooking in hotel rooms, the performers devoted most of their time to the stage. One time in Chicago, after their show was canceled, the family was down to its last quarter and in dire straits. Later Lon recalled this difficult period with particular fondness:

> As a last resort, Pop could always break into a dance in front of any of them old-time bars and get enough nickels and pennies to buy some food. But this particular Christmas Eve is still clear in my memory. Dad put most of his precious twenty-five cents into the gas meter. Then he started out with me. When we came to the first saloon he sat me on the bar close to the free lunch. Then he did his dances and picked up the small change. Meanwhile I filled my overcoat pockets with pretzels and sandwiches. Do you know what else he did when we got home? After I was asleep, he went out, broke a limb off a park tree, fixed it in a box in our room, and spent the whole night making tree decorations out of a roll of red crepe paper he had bought with a few pennies. He told me afterward he made paste out of cold baked potato and water.[3]

Still the family struggle continued. On occasion the troupe would find itself stranded in a town after its show closed with no work on the horizon. After one such disappointment, the Chaneys headed back to Chicago, their booking headquarters, and back to the poverty of cheap hotel rooms. Sometimes the father and breadwinner resorted to patronizing saloons which served a free sandwich with every beer purchased. He would buy two beers, eat one sandwich, and take the other back to the hotel for Cleva.

Finally Chaney landed a job as stage manager for the play *The Girl in the Kimono*. Shortly afterward, he returned with Cleva and Creighton to Los Angeles, where his brother was a stage manager for a theater. Soon Chaney was on stage again, including a West Coast tour with Ferris Hartman's Comic Opera Company. After the tour, he returned to Los Angeles, where work again became sparse.

While Lon struggled, Cleva used her beautiful voice to gain steady employment as a singer in cabarets. As her popularity grew, professional jealousy crept into the family relationship. Besides her success, Lon also objected to the way she allowed adoring men to buy her drinks until drunkenness ensued. Still, he did not complain until he found an unmailed letter among Cleva's things addressed to a favorite bartender, whom she called her "dearest boy." At that point Lon demanded that she devote more time to taking care of Creighton and less time to performing for men. Argument followed argument as their marriage quickly unraveled. When matters reached a breaking point, Cleva staged a suicide attempt during one of Lon's performances. On this particular evening he was performing as a dancing clown to a very appreciative audience. To the tune of "Little Red Caboose Behind the Train," he lit a large red cigar, blew out a stream of smoke, and whistled like an engine. Suddenly Cleva leaped from the wings into her husband's arms, a stream of poisonous fluid dripping from her mouth. Lon carried his stricken wife to an ambulance and stayed by her side through the night. Newspapers reported that she continually called for Creighton, her "little boy." When her health improved, Lon walked out of the hospital and left her forever, taking her "little boy" with him. For whatever reason, Lon led Creighton to believe that his mother was dead. In reality she was being prevented from seeing her son while undergoing treatment for alcoholism.

Creighton Chaney was now the full responsibility of his father. In order to pursue his theater career, Lon sent the boy sporadically to boardinghouses and schools. As the boy later recalled, "I was put out to live."[3] When Lon discovered that his most recent touring company was booked for the Orient, he made the decision to stay in the United States and find work in that new entertainment phenomenon called the movies. In 1913 he made his first screen appearance in *Poor Jake's Demise*. Creighton was six years old.

One year later, Lon formally divorced Cleva and retained custody of Creighton. Because her voice had been damaged by the suicide attempt, she was unable to continue her singing career. Even though her career was ruined, she said she held no animosity toward Lon, perhaps because she realized that much of what led to the divorce was her fault.[4]

In 1915 Lon married Hazel Hastings, with whom he had earlier toured as part of Ferris Hartman's Comic Opera Company. The marriage, which would prove successful for both of them, provided Creighton with the first real home he had ever known. Still, despite the comfort of consistency, Creighton soon became restless. Years later he recalled:

> Regular schooling wasn't for me. I liked getting around. I never remember not working. I was going to school and then during my vacations I'd hitch-hike my way to the fruit ranches up near Bakersfield and pick apricots. You can't get rich picking apricots. I remember I got three cents a basket–a deep basket–and the rawest sunburn on my neck you ever saw.[5]

The boy would sometimes sit with his father on a wooden bench at the corner of Hollywood and Vine, waiting for the trolley car that would take them to the studio. The spot where the bench once sat would one day sport a marker erected in honor of Lon Chaney, Sr. The boy later recalled the days when his father, after becoming a motion picture star, would drive by that same bench and offer a carload of extras a ride to work. Remembering those years, Chaney later pointed out that his trips to the studio had been few:

> Dad never wanted me to be an actor so he never made it attractive. I watched Dad work out his disguises at home, so it was pretty much a business with me.... In the early days of motion pictures it was not considered a good thing for a star even to be married, much less have a son of my age. Therefore I saw very few of his performances.[6]

In later years, Lon Chaney, Jr., usually spoke lovingly and respectfully of his father. Director Curt Siodmak, however, reveals another side of the relationship:

> The father of Lon Chaney–the old man, Chaney, Sr.–was a very cold man, and he used to beat the boy all the time. Lon told me he had to go into a shed and be beaten with a leather strap, sometimes for things he hadn't done. This *killed* him mentally–he became an alcoholic, and always needed a father figure to tell him what to do.[7]

Although a grandson of Lon Chaney, Jr., calls Siodmak's account "complete fiction,"[8] I believe Siodmak is accurately reporting what Chaney Jr. told him. Siodmak did not provide the account in interviews until the late 1980s, so Chaney Jr. could not have denied the story to his grandchildren back in the sixties or early seventies. In all likelihood, Chaney Jr. simply did not relate the story to his grandchildren, and since it is not a flattering picture of his great-grandfather, the grandson incorrectly considers the account false.

In 1916, Lon Chaney sent his ten-year-old son to live with his deaf-mute grandparents. That experience instilled in Creighton compassion and understanding for the handicapped, qualities that would play a large part in helping his father achieve film stardom. After all, by portraying society's "freaks and monsters," Chaney Sr. would obtain his ticket to Hollywood success.

During the school year, Creighton attended Hollywood High School, an institution that would list among its alumni many individuals successful in the cinema industry. His greatest desire was to make the school football team, but his promising six-foot height was offset by an unimposing 125-pound weight.

Since many of Hollywood High's students looked to the movie studios for possible part-time jobs, Creighton began to eye the studios in a similar light. But when he mentioned to his father that he would like to approach the studios, Chaney's response was emphatically negative. Because of what he had learned from bitter experience, Lon Chaney, Sr., never wanted his son in the acting business. To instill the work ethic, he also never bought his son a car during the boy's years at Hollywood High. As a result, Creighton would not even drive a car until he was twenty years old.

In order to discourage any possible acting ambitions in his son, Chaney Sr. sent Creighton to business college, away from the temptations of Hollywood High. Later, Lon Chaney, Jr., explained:

> His ideal of someone to look up to was the head teller of a bank. He wanted me to become someone like that. Dad never seemed like a star or actor to me. He had a curious suspicion of his newfound success. He always doubted it, always feared it would end. He kept up his membership in the stagehands' union to his dying day, just in case. He was so unassuming that when he died I suddenly realized I didn't have a single picture of him, didn't own a single clipping of him or his work. He wouldn't have any publicity stuff around. Somehow, he always feared it.[9]

Chaney Sr. himself explained in an interview in 1928 that he did not want his son to pursue an acting career because the boy's six-foot two-inch height would hinder him in getting parts. Calvin Beck, however, speculates that Chaney's reluctance might have had another source:

> Perhaps Lon, Sr. was jealous or, since he became Number One in his field, he could not tolerate the thought of anyone, even his own flesh and blood, stealing any of his thunder. Even if he had reason to secretly loathe Hollywood's rat race and overall ambience, it was hardly logical that, having spearheaded a gold mine of his own, he would permit personal prejudice from letting his son have a stake in such an inheritance.[10]

Illogical as Chaney's attitude may have been, it was nevertheless consistent with his character. After all, hadn't he driven his wife off the stage at a time when her income was important to the family's well-being? All the evidence points to the conclusion that Chaney Sr. was a man who could brook no competition, not even from his loved ones.

His acting plans temporarily scuttled, Creighton took after school and summer-vacation jobs in butcher shops and slaughter houses. He also dug ditches, carried papers, delivered ice, and labored in a boiler factory, jobs that added muscle to the once scrawny frame that was cut from the Hollywood High football team. By that time, his father had become a star as a result of great performances in such films as *The Hunchback of Notre Dame* (1923) and *The Phantom of the Opera* (1925). He had also become the first horror genre star in American cinema. Even with this success, Chaney Sr. never adopted an opulent life style, but with the Chaney family unit now financially comfortable, Creighton sometimes accompanied his famous father on promotional tours.

About this time, Creighton found out that his real mother was alive. The anger he directed at his dissembling father led to a period of estrangement during which Cleva was briefly reunited with her "little boy."

In 1927, Creighton married Dorothy Hinckley, who quickly gave him two sons, Lon III and Ronald. At that time, he was working for the General Water Heater Corporation. Because of his father's continuing opposition to the possibility of a film career, Creighton never even considered an exploratory trip to the studios.

In 1930, however, the end came unexpectedly for Lon Chaney, Sr. After finishing *The Unholy Three* (1930), he was diagnosed as suffering from throat cancer. On August 20, a throat hemorrhage landed him in St. Vincent's Hospital in Los Angeles. Blood transfusions allowed the stricken actor to rally, but on August 26, as hospital attendants expressed confidence that Chaney would pull through, another throat hemorrhage proved fatal. On August 28, Hollywood held a funeral for one of its giants. Years later, Lon Chaney, Jr., recalled the day: "I can remember the huge funeral service, the crowds scrambling to get in, the organ playing the theme from *Laugh, Clown, Laugh*. All the major studios shut down for five minutes in homage to his memory."[11]

At his death, Chaney's worth was estimated to be at least a million and a half dollars. His will left to his widow $550,000 accrued from property sales. His life insurance provided for his brothers and sister. John Jeske, his chauffeur, valet, and friend, received $5,000. With a note of sarcasm, he left Cleva the grand total of one dollar. Chaney had previously made a small financial provision for his twenty-four-year-old son.

Helped little by his father's meager financial legacy, Creighton continued to struggle to support his family. To his credit, he finally rose to the position of secretary of the General Water Heater Corporation. Still, the depression made money tight, and two years after his father's death, he again heard the thespian call. This time he would answer it.

Chapter 2

Learning His Craft (1931-1938)

 arly in 1931 Chaney accompanied some of his father's friends to a party where he met an assistant motion picture director. Years later, he recalled the occasion:

> So I sang a song I'd written myself. The assistant director said "Look, why don't you take it around to our music department?" and made an appointment for me. When I went to the studio, I had to pass through the casting office. The casting director looked at me and said, "You're Lon Chaney's son. You ought to be in pictures." That hit me right. I was fed up with regularity and thought he had a good idea.
> "How about it?" I asked. He told me he'd have a job for me in a couple of days.... I haven't heard from that casting director yet![1]

Chaney could smile about the story later, but at the time the rebuff was no laughing matter. Based on the casting director's promise, he had quit his regular job. Seven months later, help came for the financially desperate Chaney. He later explained:

> My pal, the assistant director who took me to the studio in the first place, felt sort of responsible. He took me over to RKO and introduced me to the casting director there. He also said I ought to be in pictures. Only he did something about it and sold David O. Selznik [then head of the studio] on the idea. I got a contract and two hundred dollars a week.[2]

Just before he signed the contract, Chaney granted an interview to Helen Louise Walker, who at the time was working on a story about second generation actors. Walker described their encounter: "It was startling and a little sad to meet him—he is so like Lon. The same strongly chiseled features. The same *searching* expression about the eyes. The young face is as sweet and brooding as the elder one was. The fundamental Chaney traits are there."[3]

10

Chaney visits the RKO studios before signing a contract.

In response to Walker's question about whether he would have pursued an acting career if his father had lived, Creighton quickly replied:

> No. One Chaney on the screen was enough. I'm sure he would not mind—now. We never even discussed the possibility while he was living and I am sure that we never would have done so. He insisted that I be trained to take care of myself, that I learn business and that I experience enough hard knocks so that I needn't be a softy....[4]

In the interview, Creighton also revealed that he had adamantly resisted pressure from RKO to change his name to Lon Chaney, Jr.: "I am *not* Lon Chaney, Junior. If my father had wanted me to have that name he would have given it to me. He called me Creighton Chaney and Creighton Chaney I'm going to remain! ... I shall use my own name—or go back to my old job."[5]

At this early date, Creighton battled against any "help" from his father. He had learned his lessons well, and throughout his life he would resist any temptation to cash in on his father's reputation. RKO finally relented and allowed him to remain Creighton Chaney, but as the actor would soon discover, "the best-laid schemes of mice and men go oft awry."

Chaney went on to explain his strong feelings regarding the proposed name change: "My father was unique! I shall have to feel my way and find out what I can do best."[6] Walker then told Creighton of Boris Karloff's refusal to accept the title of "the new Lon Chaney." Hearing of Karloff's response—"the world doesn't want *two* Lon Chaneys"—Creighton replied, "Nice of him! Awfully nice—to feel like that! I shall like that chap."[7] In years to come, Chaney would indeed come to like that Karloff chap, who had just played the Monster in James Whale's horrific *Frankenstein* (1931).

When Walker concluded the interview by asking her subject if he had always wanted to act in pictures, he replied, "I think I have always known it—somewhere in the back of my mind. But I never should have tried it while my father lived. Now it is different."[8]

Chaney's first screen appearance for RKO was as Thornton in King Vidor's *Bird of Paradise* (1932). The handsome, athletic lad shouts information from the sail of a yacht and does his own dive to save Joel McCrae from a shark. Another bit part followed, that of a chorus dancer in *Girl Crazy* (1932).

About this time, *Variety* (September 30, 1932) announced that Paramount was seeking to borrow Creighton from RKO for the lead in *King of the Jungle*, an imitation Tarzan tale in which a jungle man is dragged against his will into civilization. RKO must have refused because Paramount gave the role to Larry "Buster" Crabbe. RKO cast Creighton in *The Most Dangerous Game*, which starred Joel McCrae and Fay Wray, two of his classmates from Hollywood High. Although RKO edited out his small appearance in that classic adventure film, they subsequently offered him his first starring role—as Tom Kirby in the Western serial *The Last Frontier* (1933).

Based on the novel by Courtney Riley Cooper, *The Last Frontier* is set during the time of the reclamation of the Northwest borders during the period following the Civil War. Chaney found himself heading a cast which included William Desmond, the hero of many Westerns, Yakima Canutt, the famous Western star and marksman who would eventually direct the chariot sequence in *Ben-Hur* (1959), and Francis X. Bushman, himself the son of a famous actor.

Chaney plays Kirby, the handsome young editor of a small pioneer newspaper who also aids authorities by riding incognito as a Zorro-like character known as the Black Ghost. As the Ghost he braves all the dangers typical of a Western serial while capturing a gang responsible for smuggling modern weapons to hostile Indians. At one point, he even does brief triple duty as an Indian.

In his first starring role, Chaney turns in a very wooden performance. As the Ghost, his attempt at a Spanish accent is particularly laughable. While it is only a partial explanation or excuse, one must consider the nature of serials. Usually produced quickly, they called for fast action in which the hero, heroine, and villain passed quickly from one danger to another. Continuity was often ragged, and character development minimal. Directors were interested in speed, not in good acting. Chaney later recalled his first starring role: "I'd never really ridden a horse—not to barge out and jump on one and ride like the devil. And the first thing they had me do was to get twenty feet up in a tree and leap on the villain as he galloped by beneath me....We did a hundred scenes a day."[9] Nevertheless, *The Last Frontier* laid bare Chaney's weaknesses as an actor. While physically promising, he was not a "natural" in any sense of the word.

Realizing that Chaney needed to perfect his craft, RKO cast the actor in several supporting roles in "B" pictures. The first, *Lucky Devils* (1933), was the story of former World War I pilots who become Hollywood stunt men. Chaney found himself as stuntman Frankie Wilde, nicknamed "Imp of the Hooch." He had sparse dialogue in the film and little to do as the action focused on star William "Hopalong Cassidy" Boyd.

Throughout this apprenticeship at RKO, the studio was determined to get its money's worth from the young actor. Near the end of his life he was able to laugh about it:

> I worked under five names. I did extras under one name, stunts under another name, bits under another and leads under my own name. I'd get a call to do a fight, so I'd get on the set and I'd go quick to the assistant director and I'd say, "How long's the fight going to take? And how long am I going to be here?" And he'd say about twenty minutes. "And when are you going to do it?" He'd say about an hour from now. "Okay, I'll see you." I'd run to the next set and work under a different name. And between the three or four sets I'd come off smelling like a rose.[10]

Chaney's next assignment was the Western *Scarlet River* (1933). The plot is familiar. Requiring wide-open spaces to film a Western, a production company featuring cowboy star Tom Keene accepts an invitation to film at Scarlet River Ranch, where Jeff Todd (Chaney) is a scheming foreman. The script elicits a few chuckles at Chaney's expense. In one example, after Keene quickly knocks out the bullying Todd in a fist fight, Judy (the owner of the ranch, played by Dorothy Wilson) comes to check on an injury Todd had received earlier in the day.

> JUDY: I came over to see if Jeff was hurt.
> TOM: [stopping her outside the bunkhouse door] Oh, not badly. In fact he's doing fine.
> JUDY: That's good. [Tom blocks the door as she shows intentions of entering]
> TOM: Oh, wait a minute. [He glances inside at Todd, who lies unconscious on the floor.] In fact, he's asleep right now. I'll just go inside and throw something over him. [Tom goes in, closes the door behind him, and proceeds to empty a bucket of water on Jeff's head.]

Chaney, who has ample screen time, properly receives third billing. Alternately charming and overbearing, he is competent throughout.

RKO then cast Chaney in another oater, *Son of the Border* (1933). Tom Owens (Tom Keene) is working with law enforcement to break a gang of stagecoach robbers. Unknown to Tom, his friend Jack Breen (Creighton Chaney) is among the bandits. Tom discovers Jack's duplicity, but as a token of their friendship allows him to leave the territory. Jack rides into town and tells Tupper (Al Bridge), the leader of the bandits, that he is quitting and going to California. Tupper talks Jack into a bank robbery in order to subsidize his move. Tom shoots Jack as he attempts to escape with the bank's money. On his deathbed, Jack confesses that he is to blame for what has happened and sends for his girlfriend, Doris (Julie Haydon). When she arrives, he tells her weakly, "We're gonna like it in San Francisco," and dies. Jack's young, orphaned brother, Frankie (David Durand), arrives in town, and Tom adopts him. Doris attempts to have a bad influence on the boy, but she finally sees the light when Tom rescues Frankie from a massacre and robbery planned by Tupper, whom Tom brings to justice.

An early RKO portrait

Chaney then appeared in his second serial, *The Three Musketeers* (1933), a French Foreign Legion epic starring John Wayne and including second-generation actors Noah Beery and Francis X. Bushman. In the serial, Legionnaires attempt to stop the activities of gun runners led by the mysterious El Shaitan, chief of the Devil's Circle. Chaney plays Armand Corday, a traitor to the Legion.

True to the direction of most serials, any possible subtlety in the performances is sacrificed at the expense of the obvious. Near the end of the first chapter, Chaney is shot and dies in Wayne's arms.

Chaney's prospects at this time should have appeared promising. The horror cycle initiated by Universal Studios in 1931 with *Dracula* and *Frankenstein* catapulted Bela Lugosi and Boris Karloff to genre stardom. Universal followed with such hits as *Murders in the Rue Morgue* (1932), *The Old Dark House* (1932), *The Mummy* (1932), and *The Invisible Man* (1933). With horror films all the rage, RKO had Lon Chaney's son under contract when they cast *King Kong* (1933). While Forrest J Ackerman suggests that Creighton might easily have played Bruce Cabot's part, it is easy to see why the studio did not gamble. *King Kong* was an "A" picture. Chaney's only starring performance to date, a wooden and weak one, would not have instilled in the studio enough confidence to take the risk. With one more year of experience, Chaney could have successfully essayed the Cabot part, but in 1933 RKO made the correct decision.

While horror stardom was not yet in the cards for Chaney, 1934 did see him star in Monogram's *Sixteen Fathoms Deep*. Here he plays Joe Bethel, a sponge fisherman in love with Rosie (Sally O' Neil). Also in love with Rosie is the villainous Mr. Savanis (George Regas), who floats Joe a loan for a new boat and then attempts to sabotage the young man's fortunes in order to take control of the boat and marry Rosie. Appearing much more relaxed and natural before the camera, Chaney turns in a competent, sincere performance. A youthful, defiant smile crosses his face each time he thinks of a way to overcome the latest sabotage attempt, and he projects a fresh wholesomeness throughout. He also again does all of his own stunt work. Nevertheless, reviews were generally unfavorable.

In *Girl O' My Dreams* (1934), Chaney plays a college track star who barely notices the girls until he wins a senior class election. The scenario even allows him to sing. Chaney, who fancied himself musically inclined, must have welcomed the role. The studios evidently did not believe his musical interlude merited others, and he was never again asked to sing in a film–unless one counts the main theme from *Spider Baby* (1968).

Chaney continued unsuccessfully to press RKO for meatier parts in better films. Finally his persistence gained him a supporting role in the contemporary tragedy *The Life of Vergie Winters* (1934), starring John Boles (the romantic lead in *Frankenstein* [1931]), Ann Harding, and Edward Van Sloan (Dr. Van Helsing in *Dracula* [1931]). Chaney plays Hugo McQueen, a young man who

A merry scene from "Girl o' My Dreams" (1934).

wants to marry Vergie (Ann Harding), only to find that she loves someone else. He is clearly competent in this tearjerker, but the role was not strong enough to gain the attention of critics or studio heads.

Although he had a growing list of credits under his belt, Chaney was clearly frustrated with the status of his career. While he did not see himself as a potential Barrymore, he did believe that if given the chance, he could carve out a distinguished career. Armed with confidence in himself and dissatisfaction with RKO, he abandoned the studio to seek greener pastures when his stock contract expired. What he found instead was parched earth. Studios were polite but generally uninterested. Typecast as a "B" cowboy player, Chaney went through his cash reserves and even verged on having to accept relief. Then a few offers began to trickle in. Unfortunately, between sporadic offers and occasional short-term contracts, life in the Chaney household was difficult. Sources claim that Chaney's predelicton for alcohol was already present in the mid-thirties. That and growing financial worries were creating a troubled marriage.

One harbinger of good fortune was the announcement that Commodore Pictures would star Chaney in a series of twenty-four films over an eight-year period, beginning with *The Shadow of Silk Lennox* (1935). Chaney played John Arthur Lennox, an underworld boss and nightclub owner whose fondness for things that are "fine as silk" earns him the nickname "Silk." Jimmy Lambert

(Dean Benton) and his girlfriend Lola Trimmer (Marie Burton) work at the nightclub. As the police investigate Silk's underworld activities, Jimmy inadvertently provides Silk with an alibi for a bank robbery. When Deacon, the gangster holding the stolen money, tries to skip town, Silk intercepts him at the train station and kills him. Upon discovering that the money is not on Deacon's body, Lefty, another gang member, guesses that Deacon hid it in the express office. Meanwhile, Jimmy becomes suspicious of Silk's activities, and tells Lola that he fears he unknowingly provided Silk with an alibi. When their conversation is overheard by a witness, Silk is arrested. In the police line-up, Silk meets Fingers Smalley (Jack Mulhall), who agrees to open the express office safe. When fearful witnesses refuse to identify Silk in the line-up, he is released and returns to the club. He and Fingers attempt to break into the express office safe, but police arrive in time to gun Silk down. Fingers explains that he is really a G-man named Ferguson.

While the film proved inconsequential, it highlighted Chaney's ability to swagger and create an air of insufferable cockiness. The actor's next Commodore picture was *A Scream in the Night* (1935), which some consider Chaney's first foray into the horror genre. The plot is one of intrigue and suspense:

Deep in the Orient, Bentley, a representative of a large American jewelry syndicate, purchases the fabulous "Tear of the Buddha," a giant ruby reputed to shed real tears. Since dealers, collectors, and thieves all covet the stone, Bentley consummates the purchase in deepest secrecy.

Inspector Green, Jack Wilson (Creighton Chaney), and Yuting, their Chinese companion, pursue Johnny Fly, a notorious jewel thief and dangerous killer. When they lay a trap for their quarry, Wilson does not accompany Yuting for fear that his presence will tip their hand.

Wilson meets Edith, Bentley's niece, in the hotel dining room. Shortly afterward, they discover Bentley in his room, strangled but still alive. Two hundred pounds sterling and some uncut diamonds have been stolen, but Bentley tells Wilson that the attacker was definitely after the legendary ruby. Fearing he had been followed by a thief, Bentley had taken precautions by giving the jewel to Edith, who is carrying it on her person.

When Johnny Fly's lieutenant, Butch Curtain (Creighton Chaney), warns him that the police are on his trail, he has Yuting trapped and knifed. Before he dies, however, Yuting is able to give Wilson and Inspector Green a puzzling clue about a human eye. Meanwhile, though Inspector Green has given Edith a bodyguard, Fly's men successfully kidnap her.

At Fly's hangout, Edith makes Moora, Johnny's girlfriend, jealous when the criminal responds to Edith's beauty. Fly sends Butch to Jahla the pawnbroker to make an appointment for that night to sell the jewel, which he has taken from Edith. But Wilson catches Butch in the pawnshop, and while in police custody the lieutenant unconsciously reveals some of Fly's plans.

Undated rerelease title-card art from "A Scream in the Night" (1935).

Noting the resemblance between himself and Butch, Wilson makes himself up to look exactly like the lieutenant and goes to Fly's hangout just as Jahla buys the ruby.

Fly tells Wilson, who he thinks is Butch, to kill Jahla as they leave and to bring the ruby. Wilson tells the pawnbroker to fake death and tries to locate Edith. Meanwhile, an incredulous Moora tells Fly that someone is impersonating Butch. In an ensuing fight, Wilson overpowers Fly and brings Edith to safety. Inspector Green then arrives to make arrests.

Although the film is really a suspense yarn rather than a horror film, it does contain horror elements, especially Chaney as the disfigured Butch, the first role placing him in the footsteps of his famous father. In fact, the makeup around his left eye resembles that of the elder Chaney in *The Road to Mandalay* (1926). It is significant that *A Scream in the Night* provided Chaney with the chance to play prominently two different characters in the same film, a testament to Commodore Pictures' confidence in the young man. Coincidentally, both Karloff and Lugosi played dual roles in films that same year—Karloff in *The Black Room* and Lugosi in *Murder by Television*. Karloff's performance, one of the best outings of his career, was easily the best of the three. Unfortunately (or fortunately), *A Scream in the Night* was the second and last of the 24 films Commodore planned for Chaney. The rest were never made.

Also in 1935, Chaney made a film for Hollywood Exchange called *A Marriage Bargain,* wherein he plays Bob Gordon, a young and ambitious mountaineer from the backwoods who falls in love with Helen (Lila Lee), the beautiful daughter of Judge Stanhope (Edmund Breese). Of course, her social position and Bob's lack of sophistication make Helen disdain her suitor. When Bob suspects that the building of a railroad in the future will add to the value of some mountain land, he prevents Judge Stanhope from buying the property. Meanwhile, Helen's older sister (Audrey Farris) confesses that she has been seduced but refuses to reveal the man's name. Judge Stanhope assumes the seducer to be young Nelson Williams. When the judge encounters Williams while out riding, he attacks him with a hunting crop, causing Williams's horse to bolt and throw its rider over a cliff. A jury delivers a verdict of accidental death, but Judge Stanhope remains unaware that Williams was innocent, even when his seduced daughter elopes with another man. Meanwhile, Bob finds the judge's hunting crop and demands that Helen marry him in return for his silence. Although Helen still loathes Bob, she agrees to marry him and help him win a seat in the legislature, as long as he will divorce her thereafter. When two drunks heckle Bob about Helen's absence, however, she becomes angry, returns to him, and learns to love him at last.

The film was reputedly based on an actual case in New York in the 1860s involving Count Castaigne, who was wanted for murder in Paris. At any rate, the film opened, to critical silence and disappeared quickly.

If Chaney had a chance to break into horror films at this point on the strength of his father's reputation, Karloff and Lugosi indirectly scuttled it. In 1935, Universal's Karloff and Lugosi vehicle *The Raven* so outraged British audiences and critics that the country banned horror films to all but adult audiences. American audiences were also repelled by the torture and madness in which the film revels. As a result of heavy criticism and decreasing revenues, the first horror film cycle came to an end in 1935, and though studios continued to make some horror films, they would not reach their former level of popularity until the 1940s.

While Chaney's next appearance, in *Hold 'Em Yale* (1935), was small and inconsequential, it gave him the chance to play a football player, a role he would have apparently preferred years ago at Hollywood High. Other roles of little note followed. He landed parts as a heavy in *The Singing Cowboy* (1936) and *The Old Corral* (1936). While two more Westerns would in themselves be nothing to cheer about, these films allowed Chaney to mix it up with the famous Gene Autry.

In *The Singing Cowboy,* Autry, in the title role, goes to the big city to raise money for a paralyzed little girl's operation. Chaney's part as Martin is similar to the ruthless foreman role he played three years previously in *Scarlet River.* Of course, Autry ensures that he does not succeed in his plan to take over the ranch.

In *The Old Corral,* Chaney plays Garland, the right-hand man of Autry's adversary. In the final scene, Chaney suffers in a jail cell as he is forced to listen to a record of Autry singing "The Old Corral." It is interesting to note that the songs for both films were co-written by Chaney's friend, producer Oliver Drake. Unfortunately, in each case the quality of the music makes the soundtracks of Elvis Presley's later films sound like *West Side Story*.

In welcome respites from the saddle, Chaney appears in two noteworthy serials. The first, *The Undersea Kingdom* (1936), is his first science fiction film. Crash Corrigan, athletic star and naval officer, accompanies Professor Norton to the bottom of the sea in the professor's new supersubmarine. Diana, a go-getting newsgirl, goes along for the big story, and unknown to everyone, the professor's son Billy stows away aboard the craft through love of adventure and admiration for Corrigan. While on their journey, they are sucked into the undersea land of Atlantis. Unga Khan, a mad tyrant, is perfecting a tower in which he hopes to travel to the surface and conquer the upper world. Opposing him is Sharad, a high priest of Atlantis who tries to protect his people from Khan.

Under the command of Captain Hakur (Creighton Chaney), robots known as Volkites, a tank called the Juggernaut, and other examples of scientific wizardry trap Corrigan and his allies. Khan "transforms" Professor Norton's mind and turns the scientist into his slave. Struggling from one harrowing rescue and escape to the next, Corrigan finally alerts the upper world to the imminent attack. Corrigan restores Norton's mind to normalcy, and when the tower rises, U. S. naval power reduces Khan's dreams to rubble.

Chaney spends most of his considerable screen time growling orders to those in his command and leading chases after Corrigan and his compatriots. His muscular arms and legs are used to advantage as he emerges as a believable physical foe for the athletic Corrigan.

In the second serial, *Ace Drummond* (1936), the science fiction element is again at work. A mysterious criminal calling himself the Dragon is intent upon driving International Airways out of business. Ace Drummond, G-Man of the air (John King), arrives in Mongolia by clipper ship to solve the mystery. At various times, revolving machines begin to turn by themselves, followed by the mysterious voice of the Dragon, and a ray gun blasts planes from the sky. The film uses Universal aerial stock footage and manages a brisk pace. Besides the many inconsistencies in continuity, the most annoying element of the film is John King's tendency to break into song—and always the same song. Chaney plays Ivan, a henchman of the Dragon, a role reminiscent of his Hakur in *The Undersea Kingdom*.

Chaney also played another henchman in *Killer at Large* (1936), a thriller with some horror overtones. A murder and robbery are committed in the jewelry section of a department store. An engaged couple (Mary Brian and Russell Hardie) try to track down the perpetrator, mysterious Mr. Zero (Henry Brandon), a maniac who owns and operates a waxworks. Police catch two of

Zero's henchmen (one being Chaney) trying to bury a box in the cemetery. Within the box they find the body of Zero's murdered blonde accomplice and the stolen jewelry. Thwarted in his plans, Zero makes several attempts to kill the engaged couple. Zero is finally shot and killed when the couple acts as bait in a trap. Chaney has two or three lines in the film, which deservedly receives little attention today.

As Lon struggled in films in 1936, his marriage was failing. Buoying up the actor, however, was a budding romance with a girl whom he spent some time with during a rain break that occurred while one of his pictures was being filmed. Hoping to kill some time until shooting resumed, Oliver Drake suggested that he and Chaney go see a couple of girls he knew. One of the girls was Patsy Beck, a model. According to Patsy, she and Chaney had known each other for years, having met on the tennis courts of Hollywood High. As his marriage disintegrated, Chaney turned to Patsy for understanding and comfort. When he spoke to Drake about possibly divorcing Dorothy to marry Patsy, Drake tried to scotch the idea. This angered Chaney and initiated a short period of estrangement between the two men.

Ignoring Drake's advice, Chaney followed through on his marital plans. Apparently, Dorothy was only too happy to cooperate as she got a divorce decree from Chaney in Hollywood Superior Court on July 25, 1936, claiming he stayed away from home "night after night" and "drank to excess." Dorothy was awarded custody of their two sons as well as most of the actor's personal property. Then, on October 1, 1937, Creighton married Patsy Beck in Colton, California. Much later, Drake admitted that Chaney had made the right decision, and acknowledged that Patsy indeed turned out to be one of the best things in the troubled actor's life.

The year of his second marriage saw Chaney in a blinding array of films in which he played small roles and often went unbilled. In later years, Chaney recalled the monotony and grind of this early phase of his career:

> I was in a new picture practically every two weeks, always as a heavy. I'll swear I spoke the line "So you won't talk, eh?" at least fifty times, and I'd rather not think about how often I had to say, "Don't shoot him now–I have a better plan!"... Now I knew what Dad meant when he said, "I've taken the bumps." Well...I'd taken them. I did every possible tough bit in pictures. I had to do stuntwork to live. I've bulldogged steers, fallen off and gotten knocked off cliffs, ridden horses into rivers, driven prairie schooners up and down hills–everything."[12]

Wondering if his career was possibly stalled due to a lack of skill, Chaney, deciding to explore every possibility, enrolled in an evening acting school under an assumed name. Quickly realizing that the young man was no amateur, the acting coach told him that he knew as much as he did and allowed the student to teach half the class. When Chaney later sought the aid of a famous dramatic coach, the outcome was the same. Chaney could act. Yet he was mired in a career that was going nowhere. As he later recalled, "I never got anywhere.

Lon and Patsy return from their honeymoon (1937).

I just marked time for years. Only one thing buoyed me up: the gambler's hope that *next* time I'd draw three aces."[13]

The tough California divorce laws had left Chaney broke, however. Frustrated and hungry, Creighton took the step that he vowed he would never take. Near the end of 1937, he signed a contract with Fox as Lon Chaney, Jr. Why did he finally relent? "Because they starved me into it," he explained. "After that, I had a chance, at least."[14] Although Fox repeated the promises he had heard earlier at RKO, he quickly found that they had no intention of advancing his career. As he continued in a depressing series of bit roles, his morale sank to an all-time low.

As though things weren't going badly enough, while filming *Jesse James* (1938) in the Ozarks, Chaney, billed fifteenth, took an accidental tumble off his horse and was trampled by the horse that followed. Used to physical scrapes, the slightly injured actor got up, dusted himself off, and finished his scenes. Fed up with Chaney's nightly drinking, however, director Henry King sent the actor back to Hollywood, where Fox lost little time in terminating his services.

Saddle-sore in more ways than one, Lon ended 1938 with little reason to hope that he would be given a chance to show the world what he could do. Finances ran so low at one point that his car and furniture were repossessed. Unknown to him, however, his big break was just around the corner.

Chapter 3

Of Mice and Men (1939-1940)

At the dawn of 1939, the thirty-three-year-old Chaney could not have been optimistic about the direction of his career. In his first four films of that year he was either not billed or billed anywhere from ninth to twenty-first. One of the films, *Union Pacific*, was a major picture, but Lon was simply a passenger on a train. *Frontier Marshall* saw Lon as Pringle in yet another film exploiting the Wyatt Earp legend. In this one, John Carradine was most effective as the lead menace. *Charlie Chan in the City Darkness* had its following, yet Lon's contribution as another henchman was so slight as to go virtually unnoticed.

Evidently feeling that Lon showed little promise, Fox did not renew his contract, which expired on January 15. The anxiety that Chaney Sr. had hoped his son could avoid set in. Hearing that RKO was going to remake his father's classic film, *The Hunchback of Notre Dame*, he pursued the lead role. After extensive screen tests, however, RKO decided that while Chaney was excellent, they preferred other actors. They briefly considered Orson Welles for the role and then courted the British Charles Laughton. When it appeared that trouble with the American Internal Revenue Service might prevent Laughton from working in America, RKO promised Lon the part if Laughton's services could not be secured. Laughton, however, overcame his tax difficulties and made the picture.

Then, after Lon and Patsy had gone hungry for a full twenty-four hours, Lon's agent informed the actor that he had landed him a tryout for the part of Lennie in the West Coast production of the play *Of Mice and Men*. Five members of the original New York cast had been signed, but Broderick Crawford had deserted the production to pursue another project. As Lon later said, " I can never be grateful enough to Brod Crawford."[1]

Lon reported to El Capitan Theater, where he tested for the part under

24

the eye of producer and actor Wallace Ford. Since Lon had neither read the book nor seen the play, he walked in rather cold and did not do well in the initial test. As he explained, "I was pretty bad the first time I read the lines. The only way I got the part was through the kindness of Wally Ford. He was willing to give me a chance. You can't explain it any other way."[2]

When Lon got the stage role of Lennie, his life changed. Now he had to rise from bed at six every morning to study his lines, and he had to arrive at the theater at two for rehearsals. But after three weeks of this discipline, he mastered the role.

Opening night might have been a horror for anyone else in Chaney's position. The media wrote that Lon's father had been a monumental star, and now it was time for the son to show what, if anything, he could do. Later, Lon said that he did not experience the butterflies that those without his life experience might have felt, noting that "Self-consciousness is one thing hard knocks teach you to squelch."[3]

When he walked on stage that evening, he gave the performance of his life and garnered fourteen curtain calls. The critics cheered, and the play was a hit. Lon Chaney, Jr., had proven to "the business" that he was a good actor capable of good roles–a worthy successor to his father's legacy.

Of course, Lon hoped that his newly found stage fame would encourage casting executives to offer him more meaty film roles. He had missed out on playing Quasimodo in RKO's *The Hunchback of Notre Dame*, but word had it that Lewis Milestone was preparing to direct the film version of *Of Mice and Men* for United Artists. Landing the part of Lennie became Lon's immediate career objective.

Milestone had seen only the original Broadway play, not the West Coast version, so he envisioned a cast that did not include Chaney. Undeterred, however, Lon one day ambled into Milestone's office and asked for a test. Caught off guard by the big guy's openness and nerve, Milestone agreed. The next day the director was testing a girl for the part of Mae and needed someone to read Lennie's lines, so he asked Lon to stand in, promising the actor a separate test later. Lon agreed. Not only did he read Lennie that day, but he continued to read Lennie for all subsequent tests. When it came time to test Lon, Milestone could not see anyone else in the part. Earning the role of Lennie eased any disappointment Lon might have had over losing the part of Quasimodo. Later he remarked:

> I'm not sorry now. It's asking a lot to expect me to come up to my father's performance. I saw a revival of the film just a few weeks ago, and it made me realize more than ever how good he was and what a tough time anybody will have in the part. Anything I might have done would have been a carbon copy.[4]

So in the fall of 1939, *Of Mice and Men* was set to go before the cameras. Since no one could find a suitable ranch, United Artists built the Aguora Ranch set in eight days. The scenario called for Lon's hair to be darkened, so he had his wife's hairdresser die it a brick red, the same color as Patsy's. He also had to wear special shoes that added inches to his already impressive height. The special shoes, while adding stature, were painful in scenes that called for running, but he gained strength from remembering what his father had gone through in creating some of his greatest characters. Between scenes, Lon and Burgess Meredith often passed the time pitching horse shoes. It wasn't long till they could beat any other team on the set.

The plot, based on John Steinbeck's novelette and the screenplay by Eugene Solow, begins with George (Burgess Meredith) and Lennie (Lon Chaney) fleeing from a posse. Having escaped the law, they wander about the rural West in search of work. But this is the Depression era, and while they find odd jobs, they also encounter hostility and distrust. When they finally arrive in California's San Joaquin Valley, they go to work for a ranch owner, who hires them to toil in his barley fields. They take up residence in the bunkhouse, at which point the other workers learn that Lennie is a dimwit whom George has been protecting. It is George and Lennie's fantasy to own their own small ranch someday, and Lennie brightens whenever George tells him about how he can tend the rabbits and stroke their soft, furry bodies. Meanwhile, Curley (Bob Steele), the sadistic son of the ranch owner, taunts Lennie constantly, even though Slim, the foreman (Charles Bickford), tries to protect the gentle giant from abuse.

One reason Curley is so distrustful and full of hate is because his sexy wife, Mae (Betty Field), has played up to other ranch hands in the past, and Curley suspects she might even have been to bed with Slim. When Candy (Roman Bohnen), an aging ranch worker, overhears George and Lennie talking about how they will "live off the fatta the lan'," he begs them to include him in their plans. Later in the film, in a scene foreshadowing the conclusion, Candy tearfully agrees to have his faithful old dog shot in order to put the animal out of its misery.

When Slim asks about Lennie's mental state, George tells him that the big man has a clouded brain "on accounta he'd been kicked in the head by a horse." The powerful Lennie does not know his own strength and is always killing animals when he thinks he is only stroking them. On one occasion, George finds a mouse in Lennie's pocket that he has crushed unintentionally. Later he also crushes a puppy while trying to pet it. Lennie, however, is actually nonviolent and does not comprehend aggression.

When Mae begins flirting with the innocent Lennie, Curley barges into the bunkhouse and starts pummeling the confused giant. Lennie does not know what to do until George tells him to fight. The big man then halts one of Curley's punches in his large hand and squeezes until Curley yields. When the bones in Curley's hand start to crack, George tells Lennie to let the suffering man go free. Later, Mae again comes on to Lennie, who strokes her hair just as he earlier stroked the fur of the mouse and puppy. Unfortunately, Lennie is distracted and ends up innocently killing her. He quickly realizes that "George will be mad at me" and flees into the forest. George, knowing that Lennie will be ridiculed as a freak and executed as a murderer, runs ahead of the posse and decides that he must do for Lennie what Candy did for his old dog. So in the quiet of the woods, George reminds Lennie of how good life will be when they own their own little ranch. As Lennie beams gloriously and stares out across the river as though it were the promised land, George shoots him from behind, allowing Lennie a painless, humane death.

Several things happened on the set to give young Chaney confidence. After watching Lon complete one of his big scenes, the electricians and the rest of the veteran crew burst into spontaneous applause in appreciation for what they had witnessed. A still-photographer who had once photographed Chaney Sr. noted, "Like father, like son, whether he likes it or not."[5]

Of Mice and Men was a financial and critical success. Review after review praised the entire cast, Milestone's inspired direction, and Aaron Copland's excellent musical score. Meredith as the diminutive but intelligent George is a perfect contrast to the large but mentally simple Chaney. Their friendship, while difficult to explain and rather gimmicky, is effective within the universe of the film. Betty Field artfully brings to life the silly, vain, but luckless Mae, and the rest of the cast, especially Bob Steele, is quite good. Lon must have been pleased with the way United Artists promoted him in its publicity. The pressbook cover, for instance, features the title and under it a large head and shoulders drawing of Lennie with a fearful expression. Beneath the drawing we read:

> I'm Lennie... George says guys like us is the loneliest guys in the world. ... Everybody says I ain't got the sense I was born with, but George don't. ... I've known George ever since we were kids.... George says on accounta I'm strong as a bull that some day I'm going to get us into a mess....But I don't want no trouble....I don't want no mess....I didn't want no trouble with Curley's wife, but she made me pet her... And then... And then...

Lon expressed pleasure that "They let me play Lennie my own way" and called Lennie "the biggest, sweetest, most lovable man that ever happened."[6] In an interview, Lon expressed the wish that his work as Lennie would land him more sympathetic roles in the future:

> Whenever they were looking for a big fellow who wasn't the drawing room type, Chaney always seemed to get in the way. I hope I never have to play another gangster or villainous cowboy the rest of my life.... I don't mean any offense to gangsters or cowboy actors. I have a lot of respect for them, and quite a few are my good friends. As a matter of fact, I'd like to play heavies, if they're character parts or sympathetic. That's one of the reasons I was so happy to play Lennie on the screen. He's a heavy, but a sympathetic, understandable, human fellow and, I think, one of the grandest characters ever put on the screen. ... I don't want to be fussy about parts. But there's one thing I hope and pray; Please, no more "bad" heavies.[7]

28 • *Lon Chaney, Jr.*

With Betty Field in "Of Mice and Men" (1939).

While Lon could not know it at the time, just as Lugosi was typecast as Dracula, the part of Lennie would typecast him as someone capable of playing only big dimwits. How many times would the future see him reproduce the baffled grimace, the frightened frown, the backhand across the jaw and mouth, the thumb and forefinger to the chin, and the halting speech and bad grammar typical of Lennie. Just as Saint Teresa of Avila suggested, more tears are shed over answered prayers than over unanswered prayers. Still, *Of Mice and Men* showcases what is probably the defining performance of Lon Chaney's career.

Later Lon looked down at Oklahoma City while flying east and reflected on what had come to pass:

> I looked down and saw it for the first time since that dousing I got the day I was born. I thought of all the things that had happened since. Sure, I crossed up my Dad's wishes. But somehow, I think he'd be happy now. Maybe I can get the name of Chaney back up in the theater lights across America again.[8]

Yes, the young man's future looked bright. John Steinbeck was so impressed with Lon's work as Lennie that he proposed that the actor star in a forthcoming production of his pirate adventure, *Cup of Gold*. Unfortunately, the project was held up and never went before the cameras. In the meantime, Hal Roach offered Lon a key role in his new prehistoric action picture, *One Million B.C.* (1940). The plot was a bizarre reworking of *The Lost World* and *Romeo and Juliet* :

A party of mountain climbers are seeking refuge in a cave during a storm when an elderly scientist tells them the story depicted by the prehistoric carvings on a wall of the cave. Tumak (Victor Mature), a young hunter of the Rock Tribe, is knocked off a cliff during a fight with his father, Akhoba (Lon Chaney), leader of the tribe. When attacked by a wooly mammoth, the bruised and stunned Tumak climbs a tree. The creature uproots the tree and pushes both it and Tumak into a river, which carries the young man to safety.

Drifting into the land of the Shell People, Tumak is found by lovely Loana (Carole Landis) and adopted by her tribe, who nurse him back to health. While recovering, he learns kindness, consideration, and ethics from the Shell People, a more advanced tribe than Tumak's savage kinsfolk. He also learns that the spear is a more effective weapon than the staffs used by the Rock Tribe.

Tumak leads Leona on a journey back to the Rock Tribe and finds that a change of government has occurred. A musk ox has gored Akhoba and left him for dead. During this battle, Skakana (Edgar Edwards), who has aspired to leadership of the tribe, not only refuses to aid Akhoba but attempts to finish him with his staff. Akhoba survives, however, and returns to his tribe a hopeless cripple, merely tolerated by the people he once ruled. Skakana is now their leader.

Tumak fights with Skakana and overcomes the new leader with his spear. He refuses to kill his downed foe but does assume leadership of the tribe, hoping to teach his people what he has learned from the Shell People.

Soon hundreds are killed when a volcano and earthquake assault the land of the Rock People. Loana escapes death and flees to her own people. Tumak follows and finds her. When a huge dinosaur attacks the cave of the Shell People, Tumak's tribe joins their former foes in killing the monster with large

A closeup of Chaney as Akhoba in "One Million B.C." (1940).

boulders. Following the victory, members of both tribes celebrate and dine together in peace and harmony.

Roach's first choice as director was D.W. Griffith, but as arguments and disagreements intensified on the set, Roach and his son took over the reins. Although Griffith's name was withdrawn from all the credits, the film has his unmistakable mark.

At first, Lon was allowed to develop his own makeup for Akhoba. The result was shocking and gruesome, but it was discarded when the producers thought it might mislead the public into believing the film was a horror picture. Anyway, regulations of the cosmetician's union were such that actors could no longer do their own makeup. Bill Madsen took over as Chaney's makeup man and successfully transformed him into the grizzled Akhoba. Particularly impressive is the makeup that took four and a half hours to apply to create Akhoba's appearance after the musk ox altercation.

It was not the makeup, however, that accounted for Chaney's success in the film. Rather it was the pantomime ability that he developed through contact with his deaf-mute grandparents. While the role of the caveman limited Lon's dialogue to a language of grunts, groans, and growls, his knowledge of sign language enabled him to convey a vast range of emotions. In one effective scene, he demonstrates his superiority over the rest of the tribe by feeding his dogs before he allows his hungry people to fight over the burned carcass of a kill. Lon's most effective scenes, however, are those in which he hobbles on a staff after being injured by the musk ox. These scenes are as close as Lon ever came to a meaty "silent" role, and it is hard to imagine his father giving a superior performance.

Upon release, the film received mixed reviews, some writers pointing out that human beings and dinosaurs did not occupy the earth at the same time. Besides some scenes that are just too saccharine, one of the film's greatest weaknesses is the dinosaur special effects. Hal Roach, who had risen to fame producing Laurel and Hardy and "Our Gang" comedies, wanted to diversify the products of his studio, but he did not want to invest the money necessary to make a first-rate film. Of course, as D. W. Griffith knew, what *One Million B.C.*

needed was animated dinosaurs such as those produced by Willis O'Brien for *The Lost World* and *King Kong*. Roach insisted, however, that they save money by simply enlarging pictures of small lizards to make them look gigantic. Knowledge that the results would look phony contributed largely to Griffith's pulling out as director. While the dinosaur special effects could have been better, they were nevertheless good enough to be used as stock footage in many later films.

The special effects crew did, however, construct some fine studio sets, particularly for the very impressive volcano and earthquake sequences. Other scenes were filmed on location at Fire Valley, Nevada.

As *One Million B.C.* toured the theaters, Lon played a Lennie-like role on an "Inner Sanctum" radio program and traveled to New York to do Lennie again for CBS Radio. On the afternoon he arrived in New York, he sat glumly near the bar of the Midnight Frolics and told columnist Louis Sobol that he hated the city. He admitted, however, that he had seen only Fifty-second Street from Sixth Avenue to Fifth, and Broadway from Fiftieth to Forty-second. When nothing else surfaced, he reluctantly accepted the role of a big, friendly, mustached buffoon in Paramount's *Northwest Mounted Police,* an overlong film starring Gary Cooper, Madeleine Carroll, and Preston Foster. As Shorty, Lon plays a Matis, one of a group of people of mixed race who revolted against the Canadian government in 1885. The plot concerns Texas Ranger Cooper searching for a fugitive in Canada. While Lon's scenes are few, he would have other, more successful chances to work with Gary Cooper in the 1952 *High Noon* and *Springfield Rifle.*

Lon's next film was MGM's *Billy the Kid* (1941), which was filmed on an MGM lot and in Monument Valley, Arizona. As "Spike" Hudson, Lon's scenes are again brief as he repeats the cowboy "heavy" role that he hoped *Of Mice and Men* would put behind him. Starring in the film were Robert Taylor as another whitewashed Billy the Kid and Brian Donlevy as Sheriff Pat Garrett.

So, as 1941 dawned, Lon found himself without a contract, without star status, and without any offer of the diverse roles he thought he had earned. Voices were already suggesting that despite his famous father, Lon Chaney, Jr., was a limited actor who could do well only in dullard roles. Then, as the future appeared dark and depressing, the horror film genre that had catapulted his father to fame made a comeback and opened its door to him as well.

Chapter 4

Man-Made Monster and *The Wolf Man* (1941)

A fter the outrage generated by *The Raven* (1935) both at home and abroad, and after Great Britain's adoption of the "H" certificate in 1937 to restrict the age of those allowed to view horror films, Universal Pictures and other studios largely dropped horror films from their schedules. The result was two or three years of genre famine. Then, following a season of financial disaster, Universal noticed that on August 5, 1938, the Regina Theatre, itself in financial straits, gambled on a horror triple-bill of *Dracula, Frankenstein,* and *Son of Kong.* Because of unprecedented crowds, manager Emil Ullman happily kept the films rolling 21 hours a day as the cash register worked overtime. Recognizing the potential for a bonanza, Universal quickly rereleased *Dracula* and *Frankenstein* as part of a national double bill. Overjoyed by the results, the studio chucked its previous ban and prepared for another horror cycle.

First out of the chute was the lavishly produced *Son of Frankenstein* (1939), starring Boris Karloff, Basil Rathbone, Bela Lugosi, and Lionel Atwill. It was followed in short order by *The House of Fear* (1939), *Tower of London* (1939, with Boris Karloff, Basil Rathbone, and Vincent Price), *Black Friday* (1940, with Boris Karloff and Bela Lugosi), *The House of the Seven Gables* (1940, with Vincent Price), *The Invisible Man Returns* (1940, with Vincent Price), *The Mummy's Hand* (1940, with Tom Tyler as Kharis the Mummy), and *The Invisible Woman* (1940, with Virginia Bruce and John Barrymore).

In 1941, Universal was set to shoot a property called *The Human Robot,* a rewrite of an earlier unused script intended for Karloff and Lugosi called *The Man in the Cab.* By this time, however, Karloff had temporarily deserted the big screen for live theater, and Universal had decided that Lugosi could not carry their horror banner into the forties. Needing a new horror star for a new decade, their attention turned favorably to Lon Chaney, Jr.

Man-Made Monster *and* Wolf Man *(1941)* • 33

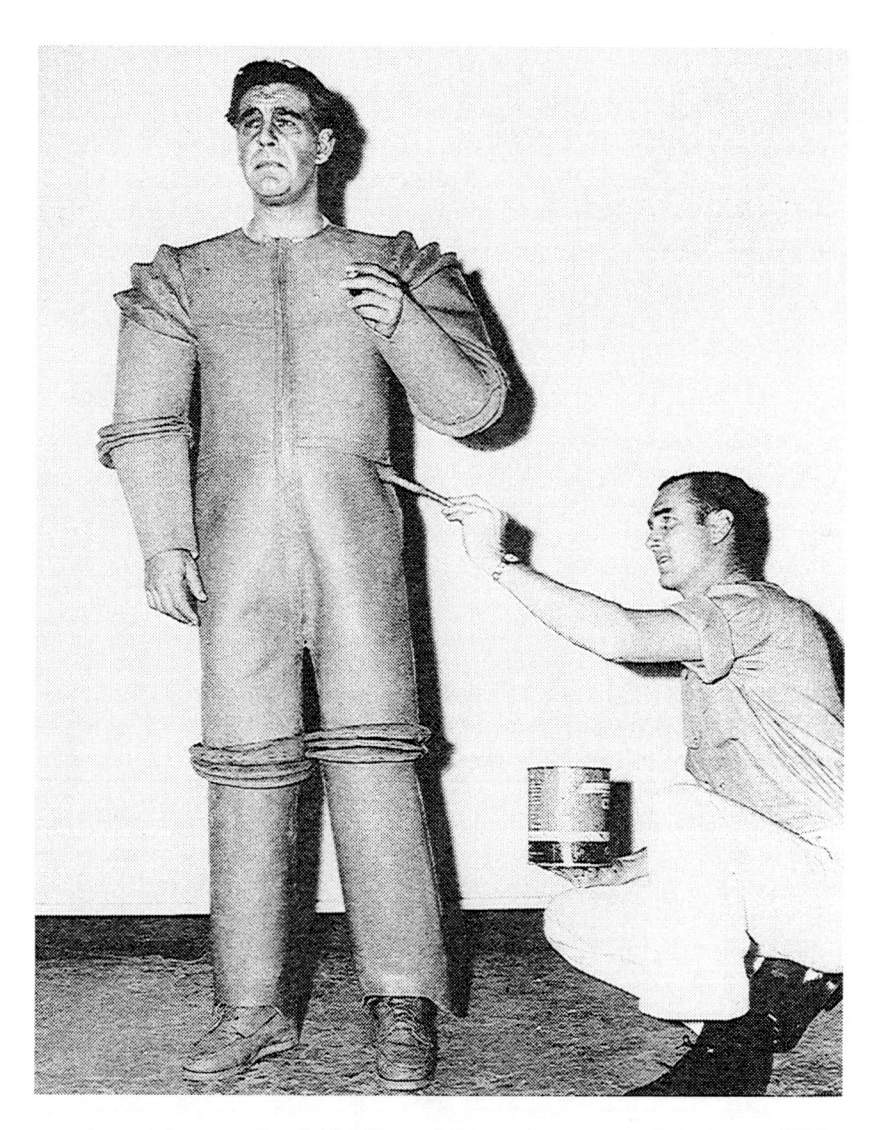

A makeup assistant applies the finishing touches to the monster suit on the set of "Man-Made Monster" (1941).

While the studio was probably impressed with Lon's performances as Lennie and Akhoba, it was undoubtedly the Chaney name that they found most enticing–and marketable. After signing Lon to a contract, Universal tested his drawing power by offering him the lead in *The Human Robot*, which had by then been retitled *The Mysterious Dr. R.* Unwilling to invest very much in Chaney, Universal provided the film an estimated budget of only $86,000.

Before release, the film underwent yet another title change. Finally released as *Man-Made Monster* (1941), it is as quintessential a horror film as one is likely to find:

Big Dan McCormick (Lon Chaney, Jr.), a carnival performer known as Dynamo Dan, the Electric Man, is the sole survivor of a bus crash in which all other passengers are electrocuted. Intrigued by Dan's apparent immunity to electricity, Dr. John Lawrence (Samuel S. Hinds), a distinguished electrobiologist, invites Dan to his laboratory where Lawrence's assistant, Dr. Paul Rigas (Lionel Atwill), is secretly conducting experiments to prove a theory that human life can be motivated and controlled by electricity.

Dr. Rigas, still bitter over a miscalculation that ended his career as a potentially great scientist, resents working as Lawrence's assistant and persuades Dan to submit to his electrical tests. As Dan absorbs more powerful charges, he becomes increasingly both addicted to and immune to electricity. Confused by the change in Dan's personality, everyone in the Lawrence household watches as he becomes a shell of a man.

Rigas performs a final test during which he pours a tremendous electrical charge into Dan, causing the young man's body to literally glow. Dan, his strength enormous, becomes a human robot controlled by Rigas. When Dr. Lawrence discovers what Rigas is doing, he orders his assistant to stop. Undeterred, Rigas orders Dan to kill Lawrence. Afterward, Rigas removes the electricity from Dan's body, returning him to a shrunken hulk. Through power of suggestion, Rigas also makes Dan accept complete responsibility for the murder.

Despite the efforts of June Meredith (Anne Nagel), Dr. Lawrence's niece, and reporter Mark Adams (Frank Albertson) to help him, Dan is sentenced to the electric chair. In the execution chamber, he absorbs three powerful strokes of electricity which return him to a superhuman state. Dan escapes from the death chamber, electrocuting everyone who tries to stop him.

At the Lawrence home, Dan rescues June, whom Rigas is about to subject to his experiments. He kills Rigas and puts on a rubber suit designed to encase his electrical energy. Dan picks up June and carries her out of the house, but he catches his suit on a barbed wire fence. Dan frees June and tries to extricate himself from the fence. During his efforts, however, he tears the suit, releasing his electrical energy into the barbed wire. As Mark and June watch, Dan shrinks to nothingness as the electricity flows from his body.

In their book *Universal Horrors*, Brunas, Brunas, and Weaver zero in on the film's salient qualities:

> *Man Made Monster* is about as basic a horror film as one can get. Perhaps that's why it's such a hard film to dislike. It's fast-moving, unpretentious and entirely predictable. There isn't a single character that isn't a cliche, from the smart-ass newspaper reporter/hero to the lunatic scientist. It's the kind of shocker that Monogram and PRC regularly churned out, yet the style is distinctly Universal.

Man Made Monster fits neatly into the streamlined, modernist mode of the '40s. The Gothic look of the old Frankenstein lab has been replaced by Eric Wybrow's state-of-the-art equipment which would become a fixture in many of the studio's forthcoming horror movies.[1]

As a partial explanation of why he included *Man-Made Monster* in his book *Classics of the Horror Film*, William K. Everson says that while the film is clichéd, the clichés were still fairly fresh and welcome in 1941. Everson quickly sums up Chaney's contribution, saying that he "played his fairly well written role for pathos and tragedy as much as menace, and came as close as he ever would to Karloff's genius for making an audience feel sorry for him even while they feared him."[2] Everson then goes on to laud Atwill, not unjustifiably, as the real star of the show. He also notes, as has practically everyone, that Hans J. Salter's musical score accounts for a great deal of the effective atmosphere in *Man-Made Monster*.

In launching the studio's new star, Universal publicity suggested that history was repeating itself as Lon Chaney's son was making a horror film on the same set as his father's *The Phantom of the Opera*: "There on the identical spot where his father performed in his famed character guises, young Chaney disguised in a gruesome facial covering and encased in a 70-pound rubber suit, played the role of a human electrical man."[3] Universal also claimed that Lon lost sixteen pounds during production. According to publicity, the actor remarked that "After witnessing the torture my father endured in his various makeups, I was more than ready to heed his advice about not doing that type of work. And yet, I suppose the fact that I'm here proves that some people just can't escape their destiny."[4]

Contemporary reviews were generally positive, and Chaney's performance stands up today as a commendable one. His early scenes as the relatively carefree, easygoing, animal-loving young carnival worker are probably his most effective. As he deteriorates under Atwill's control, he arouses audience sympathy, especially with a little help from Hans Salter. Later, as the incandescent monster of the title, he relies generally upon facial expression, makeup, and special effects to elicit the goose bumps. If Universal executives were satisfied with the quality of the film itself, they were undoubtedly troubled by the box office returns. In response they relegated Chaney to supporting roles in four minor productions (see chapter 8). Then, however, they moved full steam ahead, casting him in the title role of *The Wolf Man* (1941), a film that would mean as much to his career as had *Of Mice and Men*.

George Waggner, who directed *Man-Made Monster*, was in the producer's chair for *The Wolf Man*, but this time Universal provided a larger budget than it had for *Man-Made Monster*. First Waggner scouted out a fine cast consisting of Lon Chaney, Evelyn Ankers, Claude Rains, Ralph Bellamy, Patrick Knowles, Marie Ouspenskaya, Warren William, and Bela Lugosi. Then he handed over scripting to Curt Siodmak and undertook directorial duties himself. Siodmak claimed that he wrote the screenplay without reference to Universal's earlier *Werewolf of London* (1935) or to a discarded earlier treatment intended as a Boris Karloff vehicle. The result of hours of research, Siodmak's script introduced most of the classic elements still commonly associated with the werewolf legend. Siodmak's early treatment kept the Wolf Man unseen throughout most of the picture and made Larry Talbot an American mechanic instead of the son of an English nobleman. Universal altered the final product, however, forsaking the subtle approach for visual horror. Regardless, the tale is a classic.

After spending 18 years in America, Larry Talbot (Lon Chaney) returns to Talbot Castle in England, where he is greeted by his father, Sir John Talbot (Claude Rains). Larry takes Gwen Conliffe (Evelyn Ankers) and her girlfriend Jenny (Fay Helm) to a gypsy carnival. While Bela (Bela Lugosi), a gypsy fortune-teller, reads Jenny's palm, Larry and Gwen wander off. Bela sees the sign of the pentagram in Jenny's palm and orders her to leave quickly, realizing that he is about to turn into a werewolf and that she will be his next victim.

Jenny flees but is soon attacked by Bela, now in the form of a wolf. Her screams attract Larry, who returns in time to see a giant wolf standing over the dead girl. Larry beats the wolf to death with his cane, but is badly bitten. Next day, in place of the bite, Larry finds only the faint mark of a wolf's head and pentagram over his heart. According to the legend, this is the sign of a werewolf's victim.

Capt. Montford (Ralph Bellamy) and Dr. Lloyd (Warren William) insist that there hasn't been a wolf in the vicinity for years. In addition, villagers find the body of Bela, not that of an animal. Despite the evidence, Larry continues to insist that he killed a wolf, not a man.

When Larry learns that Gwen is engaged to Frank Andrews (Patric Knowles), he decides not to intrude. But he sees Gwen after she has quarreled with Frank, and Larry and Gwen are strangely drawn together.

Seeking understanding, Larry seeks out Maleva (Madame Maria Ouspenskaya), Bela's mother, who tells him that, having been bitten by a werewolf, he has become one himself. Larry initially scoffs at Maleva's warning, but when a gravedigger is viciously murdered by a wolf and Larry finds wolf tracks in his bedroom, he decides to say good-bye to Gwen and leave. As they part, however, he is shaken when seeing the sign of the pentagram upon her.

When Larry, in desperation, confesses his werewolfery to Sir John, his father dismisses it all as wild imagination and stress. Still, he agrees to strap Larry in a chair while the villagers hunt for the killer wolf.

While Sir John participates in the hunt, a wolf cry pierces the night. Sir John follows the sound and finds the Wolf Man about to kill Gwen. Sir John brings down the beast with the same cane Larry used to kill Bela. Shortly afterward, Maleva arrives to repeat a gypsy ministration over the dying killer. As fog swirls about, the beast returns to human form, and the villagers learn that Larry Talbot was the Wolf Man.

The film went before the cameras on October 27. For his two transformation scenes, each of which took four hours, Chaney accepted the makeup from Jack Pierce's hands that Henry Hull as *The Werewolf of London* had reportedly refused. While the application of the makeup was tedious, Chaney particularly disliked the removal process: "What gets me is after work when I'm all hot and itchy and tired, and after I've got to sit in that chair for forty-five minutes while Pierce just about kills me, ripping off the stuff he put on me in the morning."[5] As the years went on, Lon began to embellish the accounts of his agony:

> The day we did the transformations I came in at 2 A.M. When I hit that position they would take little nails and drive them through the skin at the edge of my fingers, on both hands, so that I wouldn't move them anymore. While I was in this position they would build a plaster cast of the back of my head. Then they would take the drapes from behind me and starch them, and while they were drying them, they would take the camera and weigh it down with one ton, so that it wouldn't quiver when people walked. They had targets for my eyes up there. Then, while I'm still in this position, they would shoot five or ten frames of film in the camera. They'd take the film out and send it to the lab. While it was there, the makeup man would come and take the whole thing off my face and put on a new one, only less. I'm still immobile. When the film came back from the lab they'd put it back in the camera and then they'd check me. They'd say, "Your eyes have moved a little bit, move them to the right... now your shoulder is up...." Then they'd roll it again and shoot another ten frames. Well, we did 21 changes of makeup and it took 22 hours. I won't discuss about the bathroom.[6]

When a reporter suggested that Lon go home and sleep with the makeup on in order to avoid the morning ordeal, the actor replied that he had thought of that, but he was afraid his eyes would glue shut during the night.

While Evelyn Ankers would be Lon's leading lady in many future films, the two did not get along well. According to Patsy Chaney, Lon referred to the actress as "Shankers." Evelyn, on the other hand, objected to Lon's insistence upon sneaking up and grabbing her from behind while in his Wolf Man makeup. As time went on, Lon would give her additional reasons to dislike him.

The film finished on November 25. When the Japanese bombed Pearl Harbor, Universal feared that the horrors of *The Wolf Man* would pale in comparison to the horrors of the real world, or that the public would consider the film in bad taste. But when Universal distributed *The Wolf Man* to theaters in late December, movie-goers made it a top-grosser. The critics, however, were less kind. Typical of their response was that of the prestigious *New York Times*:

> Perhaps in deference to a Grade-B budget it has tried to make a little go a long way, and it has concealed most of that little in a deep layer of fog. And out of that fog, from time to time, Lon Chaney Jr. appears vaguely, bays hungrily, and skips back into mufti. Offhand, though we never did get a really good look, we

would say that most of the budget was spent on Mr. Chaney's face, which is rather terrifying resembling as it does a sort of Mr. Hyde badly in need of a shave.... The fact is that nobody is going to go on believing in werewolves or Santa Clauses if the custodians of those legends don't tell them with a more convincing imaginative touch. And that is precisely where the wolf man is left without a paw to stand on; without any build-up either by the scriptwriter or director, he is sent onstage, where he looks a lot less terrifying and not nearly as funny as Mr. Disney's big, bad wolf.[7]

In his *Horror and Science Fiction Films II*, a more contemporary critic, Donald C. Willis, also sides with the film's detractors:

> The Universal production gloss—terrific lighting for the village sets, and an "A" musical score—is appreciated. But psychology and lycanthropy seem at odds here, as characters offer psychological explanations for Larry Talbot's black-outs, and the film offers no-doubt-about-it werewolf scenes. Among the actors, only Claude Rains and Evelyn Ankers at times start to bring the meaning of the film into focus—Lon Chaney Jr. invariably whacks it out again.... Done better as *Cat People*.[8]

Most present-day critics are considerably more kind, and correct. As though responding to Willis directly, Brunas, Brunas, and Weaver write:

> In spite of the popularity of *The Wolf Man*, it still hasn't received its due in certain critical quarters. To many, the '40s was the decade of Val Lewton, and, compared to his highly imaginative thrillers wherein the focus was on the unseen presence of terror, *The Wolf Man* seems extremely conventional. It's a rather unfair assessment, considering the fact that RKO (Lewton's home studio) didn't jump on the horror bandwagon until *The Wolf Man* drew record crowds. It's worth noting, too, that Lewton's first horror movie, *Cat People* (1942), while excellent, smacks of imitation. In fact, Curt Siodmak's unrevised original script clearly anticipated Lewton's more subtle approach.... But concealed horrors just didn't fit in with Universal's formula. As a result, the werewolf bared his hair, fangs and claws in loving close-ups in the final cut. It's not the most sophisticated approach, but *The Wolf Man* remains an intelligent film that works on almost every level.[9]

Given the passage of time, it is difficult to understand the reluctance of some to give *The Wolf Man* and Lon Chaney their due. The best analysis of both the film and Chaney's performance is the brilliant Freudian critique by R. H. W. Dillard in his *The Film Journal* essay.[10] Therein, Dillard examines the moral texture of the film and explains why Talbot turns into a wolf man rather than into a werewolf on all fours, as Bela the gypsy does. While he lays bare the film's few weaknesses, he concludes correctly that Chaney's performance is exactly what the film needs and that the film deserves far better than it has received from its critics.

The fact of the matter is that *The Wolf Man* is the most important horror film of the forties, as well as a triumph for Lon Chaney. Historically, the Wolf Man remains one of filmdom's classic monsters, sharing the honors only with Dracula, the Frankenstein Monster, the Mummy, Dr. Jekyll and Mr. Hyde, the

Invisible Man, and the Creature from the Black Lagoon. Only time will tell if Freddie Krueger, or the less deserving Jason Vorhees and Michael Meyers, are added to this Mount Rushmore of horror. Any assessments of Chaney's performance ought to be enthusiastically positive.

Dillard describes the essence of Chaney's alter ego:

> Lawrence Talbot... is a physical man, although he is innocent of the full implications of his physical nature. He is a man of the senses, needing to see and touch in order to understand. He is presented to the viewer in terms of activity rather than thought, and when he does find himself forced to think abstractly, he finds it painful and useless to him.... He describes himself to his father as a man who works with his hands, and his hands are expressive of his active emotional nature in other scenes.[11]

In somewhat Lennie-like fashion, Lon expresses his agony by wringing his hands and rubbing them across his face, but Lawrence Talbot is no Lennie. Although he is the son of British aristocracy, Talbot is a product of his years spent in America. He is intelligent, not intellectual, willing in small ways to exploit his social position, yet uncomfortable with aristocracy itself. In bringing Talbot to life, Lon does not just "whack it out." On the contrary, he gives a studied performance largely responsible for the character's longevity in American popular culture.

Some critics have complained of Talbot's self-pity, a quality that dissipates as the sequels unfold. Still, while it may annoy some, self-pity is not out of character here. One can imagine such critics carping, "Come on Talbot. You were an aristocrat with your life before you. Unfortunately you were bitten by a werewolf as you tried to save a girl's life. Now, unless you are destroyed, whenever the moon is full you will turn into a bloodthirsty murderer. But those are the breaks, Talbot. Buck up and take it like a man." Such critics resemble those who mock Hamlet's procrastination, when in reality the prince of Denmark is contemplating the murder of his uncle, the king, whom he suspects, without proof, of killing his father—weighty considerations that only a crude barbarian would rush past in executing revenge. But being human, some critics are themselves self-righteous and crude. More to the point, Talbot is confused, unable to find his way through a maze of perennially significant ideas which include the nature of animals, aristocracy, custom and convention, desire, duty, eternity, family, fate, good and evil, happiness, life and death, love, man, religion, and the soul. At one point, when Maleva can offer him eternal peace only through death, the frustrated Larry understandably cries out, "Oh, I'm sick of the whole thing!"

One aspect of *The Wolf Man* that must have been particularly poignant for Lon Chaney and that undoubtedly added sincerity to his performance is Talbot's strained father and son relationship. Larry Talbot is a motherless son, much as Lon was. When Larry turns to his father as a last resort, Sir John's response is to tie him to a chair in his room in Talbot Castle. Refusing to listen

Chaney in full makeup in "The Wolf Man" (1941).

to his son's explanations, Sir John joins the hunt and rather coldly leaves his son to fend for himself, much as Lon Chaney, Sr., had done with the young Creighton. Before departing, however, Sir John accepts from Larry the cane with the silver handle, the very instrument that Larry knows will protect his father and serve as the instrument of his own death. Lon's unresolved conflicts with Chaney Sr. must have consciously or subconsciously guided and added depth to elements of his performance.

On January 13, 1942, shortly after completion of *The Wolf Man*, Lon demonstrated in a diary entry that his father was still very much on his mind:

> Wish Dad had kept a diary. Remember that he suffered agonies while making some of these pictures. Like to know how he felt about it himself. Finally they called him the man with a thousand faces. Can only remember one, the one with a smile. If he could take it like that, guess I can too. Hope so anyway.[12]

The entry touchingly reveals Lon's obvious love for his father, as well as the pressure he felt to measure up and "take it."

Curt Siodmak, a successful screenwriter and novelist steeped in the psychology of personality, interpreted Chaney's relationship with his father as part of a Freudian etiology accounting for latent homosexuality:

Alive or dead, his father dominated him to the end of his days, endangering his masculinity...

The "macho" image which some male actors portray on the screen is often deceiving. Over six feet tall with a craggy face and a deep voice, Lon conveyed a strong virility. But I couldn't believe his love scenes and therefore never created an ardent one for him in the numerous pictures I wrote for him. Though he raised children and was married to an understanding wife, Lon was sexually confused.... He could not adjust to a sexual preference he was unable to accept.[13]

The above quotation has launched a great deal of speculation regarding Lon Chaney's sexuality. If Lon were a latent homosexual, and if that predilection, as his drinking, had an effect upon his professional career, then it becomes an important factor to consider, as I will do in chapters 9 and 14.

Besides purely aesthetic considerations, one mark of a great film is the number of possible interpretations that the product will bear. *The Wolf Man*, more so than most horror films, speaks to the mind as much as to the gut. Elaborately parabolic, it builds an idea-laden house upon the perennially important Dr. Jekyll and Mr. Hyde foundation. As Dillard writes:

> *The Wolf Man* is...a film worthy of careful consideration. It expresses the horror of a man's loss of self-control and finally his loss of self. Its themes hold their validity, and its images are still able to grip the imagination.... [It is] a carefully wrought if flawed film of considerable integrity and of a haunting darkness which deserves far better than it has received at the hands of its few critics.[16]

Chapter 5

The Frankenstein Series

In later years, Lon Chaney recalled the growth of his popularity after *The Wolf Man*: "The studio received more mail for me during that period than any other star...and they immediately rushed me into a Frankenstein picture."[1] Lon might have been correct about the increase in fan mail, but he was wrong on the other point. Universal did not rush him into a Frankenstein picture on the strength of his Wolf Man performance. In fact, on November 13, 1941, while Lon was still engaged in completing *The Wolf Man*, Universal announced its intention to continue the Frankenstein series. Since Boris Karloff was busy fulfilling stage commitments and had expressed little interest in continuing as the Monster, Universal had to find a substitute. One day later they announced that the new Frankenstein Monster would be none other than Lon Chaney, Jr.

When Eric Taylor's first draft was unsatisfactory, Universal brought in W. Scott Darling, former author of two-reel comedies, for a rewrite. On December 15, the following scenario for *The Ghost of Frankenstein* (1942) went before the cameras:

Frankenstein villagers blame their economic ills on the "curse of Frankenstein." Although they consider the Monster (Lon Chaney) dead, they dynamite the castle to remove its presence from their midst. As the blasting commences, Ygor (Bela Lugosi), the Monster's friend, who has survived bullets and a broken neck, discovers the Monster alive. Its electrical life energy, however, is low.

Ygor takes the ailing Monster to Vasaria, home of Dr. Ludwig Frankenstein (Sir Cedric Hardwicke), second son of the creator of the Monster. Villagers attack and jail the Monster when it is attracted to a child, Cloestine (Janet Ann Gallow). The citizens of Vasaria do not know Dr. Frankenstein's true identity, and Ygor threatens to expose him when the doctor refuses to reenergize the Monster. The prosecutor, Erik Ernst (Ralph Bellamy), asks Dr. Frankenstein to examine the Monster. Enraged when Dr. Frankenstein claims no knowledge of its identity, the Monster escapes the courtroom and is whisked away

The Frankenstein Series • 43

Original title-card art for "The Ghost of Frankenstein" (1942).

by Ygor to the doctor's sanitarium. There, the Monster strangles Frankenstein's assistant, Dr. Kettering (Barton Yarborough). Dr. Frankenstein's daughter, Elsa (Evelyn Ankers), urges him to destroy the Monster, but he decides to place Kettering's brain in the Monster to make the creature good rather than evil.

Dr. Bohmer (Lionel Atwill), Frankenstein's other assistant, who is most jealous of his superior's medical triumphs, agrees to place Ygor's brain into the Monster so that the two of them can rule the state.

Bohmer replaces Kettering's brain with Ygor's, but after the operation the Monster finds itself blind. Railing at Bohmer's miscalculation, the Monster kills the scientist and goes berserk, starting a fire that destroys it, the sanitarium, and Dr. Frankenstein.

Shortly before his death in 1971, Lon recalled the pressures he faced as both Chaney's son and Karloff's successor:

> I remember during *The Ghost of Frankenstein* they had me pose on the old Phantom stage and put a picture of Dad floating in the sky behind me. It used to aggravate me to constantly be compared to him. His style of acting was different than mine. He was from a different era. But by that time I had changed my name and Universal was calling me the Master of Character or something like that. Sometimes you just gotta flow along with life instead of fighting it.
>
> It was tough enough with the "ghost" of Dad floating around Universal, but

> when I had to take over the part of the Frankenstein Monster from Boris Karloff the pressure was on. They didn't have the plastic makeup like they do today and it used to take hours before Jack Pierce had me ready to shoot a scene. It was almost as bad as *The Wolf Man*. Sitting in that chair while they glued on seaweed or whatever it was was probably the worse time I ever had–it smelled, which probably helped the character. But at least I had most of that picture finished without makeup.
>
> For *Ghost of Frankenstein* I had to be in makeup for the total shoot. In the beginning they even had me covered in mud and plaster to simulate dried sulphur when Bela Lugosi found me under the castle. If that wasn't rotten enough I must have been allergic to the Monster's headpiece or the glue, because I broke out in a rash under that gray-green grease-paint and I started to itch–all down my back and around my forehead and scalp. The makeup men refused to take off the headpiece without Pierce's permission and no one else would help, so I tried to take it off myself and part of my forehead came off with it.[2]

That accident earned Chaney a week off for recovery.

Further referring to his trials on *Ghost*, Lon recalled the events leading up to the shooting of his opening scenes in the sulphur pit:

> They cast me as the Frankenstein Monster. It took four hours to make me up. Then they led me to the set. They dug a hole in the cliff and put me in. They stuck a straw in my mouth and covered me up with cement. It took till twelve o'clock to get me sealed in. Then everybody went to lunch![3]

Unfortunately for makeup wizard Jack Pierce, Chaney considered himself Universal's top horror star and refused to "suffer" silently during Pierce's sessions. Increasingly, the ordeals became marked, or marred, by Chaney's temper and impatience. Years later, when asked if he enjoyed working with Lon Chaney, Pierce replied simply, "Yes and no. That's about all I can say."[4]

Undoubtedly, some of Lon's problems were a result of his growing drinking problem. Already studio employees carried stories of the six-foot-nine, 284-pound Monster sneaking belts from a flask between takes. Chaney's mornings were productive enough, but afternoons often courted difficulty. On one occasion, Lon became so confused in Jack Otterson's mazelike corridors that he could not find his way out. Even when aided by the shouts and encouragement of the crew standing less than fifty feet away, it took the tipsy Monster ten minutes to emerge.

Universal added another item to Lon's list of grievances when they dropped the "Jr." from his name and billed him simply as Lon Chaney. As usual, the actor's protests were ignored.

Early reviews of the film were encouraging. The *Hollywood Reporter* concluded that the *Ghost of Frankenstein* "inventively stands on an imaginative par with all its interest-gripping, quasi-scientific predecessors...and Lon Chaney, having dropped the Jr., comes into his traditional own as the giant Monster."[5] The *Motion Picture Herald* thought that the film "maintains a standard of performance, effectiveness and quality exceeding the average for horror films by a considerable margin."[6] Displaying their usual disdain for horror films, however, the *New York Times* asked, "Aren't there enough monsters in this world without that horrendous ruffian mauling and crushing actors? For that, as a matter of fact, is about all he does in this film."[7]

Today, critical opinion remains mixed. According to William K. Everson:

> The last good and reasonably serious entry in Universal's *Frankenstein* series, and the last one to be able to produce a genuine Frankenstein as the scientist, *The Ghost of Frankenstein* is probably the least appreciated of the entire series. Too often dismissed, because it isn't as good as the first three (and there's no denying that it isn't), and because it heralds the reduction of the series to programmer status, it is still vastly superior to the three penny-dreadfuls that followed... *The Ghost of Frankenstein* is in many ways the last of the vintage horror films.... If *Ghost* is already an assembly line job, it's a good, thoroughly professional, and highly entertaining one, an honorable close to a solid decade of first rate chillers.[8]

Although Everson contends there's no denying that *Ghost* is inferior to its predecessors, Blackie Seymour of Pentegram Library denies exactly that. Seymour writes:

> Although the shortest of any of the Frankenstein series by Universal (66 minutes), it was (in our opinion) the best by far, topping the second best, and biggest, "Son of Frankenstein," which it also sequeled. It is the only film of the series, with the exception of "The Bride," to show the monster from the first reel to the last. It was truly the best film concerning the monster itself, even though "Bride" is considered by many fans as their favorite.[9]

Brunas, Brunas, and Weaver give their guarded approval in a conclusion more in line with the "conventional wisdom":

> The *Ghost of Frankenstein* is a polished work, but hardly an artistic triumph.... The film is rife with minor blemishes and inconsistencies, as if someone was asleep at the wheel. But Universal had little reason to grouse. The flaws were easily over-shadowed by Producer George Waggner's knack for packaging attractive, well-mounted horror shows which unfailingly turned a profit. The studio wanted a slick film with plenty of action and that's exactly what was delivered.[10]

Critics have for the most part awarded the cast high marks, correctly applauding Atwill's underplayed villainy and Lugosi's tour de force reprise of Ygor. But in assessing Chaney's performance as the Monster, the critics have been less than kind. Typical is the scornful attitude of Brunas, Brunas, and Weaver:

> Just as he would later demonstrate in his Mummy roles, Lon Chaney believed that all there was to playing a monster was to endure Jack Pierce's torturous makeup sessions. Karloff's interpretation had little influence on his performance and he inherited precious little of his father's gift for mime. Whether he's befriending the little village girl or carting around the corpse of Frankenstein's freshly-murdered assistant, Chaney's stone-like expression remains fixed throughout."[11]

The screenplay indicates, however, that the Monster is sick in mind and body. In fact, the heavy-lidded, expressionless creature that Chaney creates is exactly the one called for by the script. Here are a few scene descriptions drawn from the many which illustrate the point:

> Scene 71: He [the Monster] stands swaying for a moment and then his eyes open as he stares at Ygor. His eyes are dull, lifeless, unseeing. There is no recognition. He tries to take a feeble step forward, but can hardly make it.
> Scene 73: He stares down at Ygor with unseeing eyes.
> Scene 75: The dull lifeless eyes of the Monster show no sign.
> Scene 82: [as the castle explodes] The Monster makes no reaction. He stands staring at the scene below him.
> Scene 112: [in Vasaria with the children] The Monster continues to walk with his slow, plodding strides.
> Scene 131: The Monster brings his eyes around to the child, stares at her dumbly as if he has almost forgotten how she comes to be in his arms.
> Scene 134: The Monster gives her an uncomprehending look, but appears to be struggling to understand her.
> Scene 175: The Monster, with heavy chains on ankles, and a third chain connecting the two, fills the doorway and advances stoically toward CAMERA.
> Scene 187: The Monster is staring at Frankenstein with his usual blank face.

At times the script allows the Monster "almost a smile" or an "expression of pleasure," but the overall intent is obviously to understate the Monster, a clear divergence from Karloff's interpretation in *Frankenstein* and *The Bride of Frankenstein*. Chaney is indeed intended to be the awesome "beast" that the script requires and that the critics decry.

Chaney's performance near the film's finale reflects the fact that the Monster has received Ygor's brain. The scene in which the Monster slowly rises to his feet, exhibiting the chilling, cynical smile of "Crooked Neck," is one of the film's most effective moments. In other words, when the script calls for increased expression, Chaney provides it, but no more and no less.

It is true that a more imaginative or more secure actor might have risen above the script to infuse the role with more emotion. Still, Karloff did little to help the Monster rise above script limitations of *The Son of Frankenstein* (1939), the film that actually precipitates the Monster's decline. In *Son of Frankenstein*, as Leonard Wolf notes: "Sadly enough, though Karloff is still here, the zest with which he played the creature in the earlier two films is gone. The fault may lie with the screenplay in which the creature is no longer presented as 'more sinned against than sinning.'"[12] In fairness to Karloff, when his Monster bends over the prostrate body of Ygor and emits a bloodcurdling scream of rage and grief, he expresses more character and elicits more empathy in that one scene than Chaney does in his entire film.

Still, while critics may lambaste the interpretation of the Monster inherent in Darling's screenplay of *Ghost*, they should not take Chaney to task for almost flawlessly bringing the Monster to life. And bring it to life flawlessly he did, as Ralph Bellamy attested in 1989:

> Lon was a character. He would get so involved in his part that he actually seemed to believe that he had the strength of ten men, as the Monster was supposed to have had in the Frankenstein films. There was a scene that appeared toward the end of the picture where I was to save Evelyn from the Monster. By this time Lon had killed off Cedric and Lionel and he was coming after me, and I was to rush out of the room and lock a massive wooden laboratory door to prevent the Monster from escaping the mandatory torch and pitchfork mob of vengeful townsfolk. As I watched the scene progress I could tell that he was into his character so deeply that he was forgetting his own strength. Lon was a big man, bigger than his father, and he began to smash the laboratory equipment and throw bodies around. I think that's about the only time in the film when I wasn't acting; for I took one look into his eyes as he lurched toward me, was out the door and had it locked in two seconds and without hesitation was through another door just as fast. Sure enough, as I looked out a small window in the second door from out of scene, Lon hit the prop door so hard that it didn't shatter as it was supposed to but ripped completely off its hinges in one piece. Fortunately the bottom hinge held, ever-so-slightly, but had I been a few seconds late in my exit I could have been flattened.[13]

Interestingly, Blackie Seymour, who so challenged conventional opinion in his high praise of *Ghost*, discerned Chaney's ability to convey menace in that film as early as 1966, predating Bellamy's anecdote by 23 years:

> Chaney as the monster was an entirely different characterization than Karloff. He was of course, fuller faced, but in the same token, he was bigger built, which added to his appearance. He seemed more brutal, and in one great scene, crushes his only friend, Ygor (Lugosi), behind the heavy laboratory door. Lon's great facial expression showed right through the makeup job, and when he was angry enough to kill, you needed no one to tell you. ... You knew it.[14]

After casting Lon in a short subject, his first Kharis the Mummy film, and a gangster picture (see Chapter 8), Universal decided to continue the Frankenstein series. *Ghost* was the last good Universal picture featuring the Monster as its centerpiece, but it was not the last good film in the Frankenstein series. At the end of 1942, Universal decided to make a sequel to *The Wolf Man* which relegated the Monster to a supporting role only. Although marred by a few minor inconsistencies and a major postproduction problem, *Frankenstein Meets the Wolf Man* (1943) is one of the most enjoyable films of the entire series. Following up on *Ghost*, Curt Siodmak, who penned *The Wolf Man*, provided a screenplay in which the Monster had both the brain and voice of Ygor. Also consistent with *Ghost*, the Monster was both blind and weak. Since Lon Chaney *was* the Wolf Man and since he had played the Monster in its most recent incarnation, Universal originally intended to let Chaney play both the Wolf Man and the Monster. When the logistics of such a plan became too difficult, the studio offered the part of the Monster to Bela Lugosi. Down on his luck and strapped for cash, Lugosi humbly accepted the role he was too proud to essay back in 1931, before it went to Boris Karloff.

Problems developed after shooting, however, when Universal executives viewed the film and realized that the Monster's Hungarian accent and unintentionally funny dialogue would kill the picture. They immediately cut all the dispensable scenes in which Lugosi spoke and erased his voice from the soundtrack in all scenes that could not be cut. The following scenario went to the theaters in 1943:

Two grave robbers break into the Talbot tomb in order to rifle the "final" resting place of Larry Talbot (Lon Chaney), supposedly dead after being transformed into the Wolf Man by a gypsy curse. When the rays of the full moon fall upon Talbot, he returns to life and commits a series of murders. Realizing that he cannot be killed by normal means and seeking death to end the curse, he goes to Europe to find the gypsy Maleva (Maria Ouspenskaya), whom he believes can help him.

Talbot and Maleva go to Vasaria in search of the Frankenstein diary, which contains the secrets of life and death. During the search, Talbot again changes to the Wolf Man and kills a girl. Pursued by the villagers, the Wolf Man falls into an underground cave, turns back into Talbot, finds the Frankenstein Monster still alive, and befriends him. Maleva discovers them together and persuades Talbot to return to the village. Talbot then ingenuously offers to buy the Frankenstein castle in order to meet Baroness Frankenstein (Ilona Massey) and ask her for her father's diary. She refuses to sell the castle, however, and discounts the existence of such a diary. Soon after, the Baroness and Dr. Mannering (Patric Knowles), who has been searching for Talbot, find him and promise to help him die. Meanwhile the Monster wanders into the village in search of Talbot, and the two make a hasty retreat back to the castle. There, during a scientific attempt to destroy both Talbot and the Monster, Talbot changes to the Wolf Man and battles against the Monster as a villager dynamites the dam overlooking the castle. As a torrent of water crashes over the castle, the Monster and the Wolf Man are destroyed.

It is hardly surprising that *Frankenstein Meets the Wolf Man* has garnered a great deal of negative press. It is somewhat rightfully reviled as the first of the monster jamborees in which two, three, or more Universal monsters combine to spice up the tired proceedings. Leonard Wolf writes: "Here is a film that is important only because it marks the signal decline in film of the compelling *Frankenstein* idea. If the film proves anything it is that one cannot make a fine horror movie simply throwing great old horror regulars together."[15]

Still, aside from the inconsistency of trying to reconcile the time periods of the Frankenstein Monster and the Wolf Man, and aside from the problems arising from casting Lugosi as the Monster, *Frankenstein Meets the Wolf Man* is a thoroughly enjoyable film.

Bela Lugosi, Jr., and Lon Chaney, Jr., on the set of "Frankenstein Meets the Wolf Man" (1943).

As Brunas, Brunas, and Weaver correctly note:
> Chaney dominates the film; forlorn but no longer whiny, desperate but not as panic-stricken, he brings some new dimensions to the melancholy Larry Talbot and evokes yet-greater sympathy as he searches vainly for the secret of death. "Frankenstein Meets the Wolf Man" also boasts some of the best Wolf Man scenes from any of the character's five movies: the opening scene in the crypt, his vicious attack on the Cardiff bobby, the posse in Vasaria and ultimately the roof-raising brawl with Lugosi's Frankenstein Monster.[16]

Gregory William Mank agrees: "It is Lon Chaney ... who carries *Frankenstein Meets the Wolf Man*. His performance is the best of his Universal sojourns, and he creates and sustains a pathos that conveys the tragedy, and not just the melodrama, of the lycanthropic Talbot."[17]

Chaney elicits great empathy in his hospital scenes as he gestures for help, knowing who he is, but not yet remembering what he is. A very athletic and bestial Chaney attacks the Cardiff policeman who earlier discovered him unconscious in the streets and whistled for help. Unlike in *The Wolf Man*, this is a Talbot who has learned from experience, a Talbot who is both cunning and purposeful.

Additionally, Ilona Massey is the strongest and best of all the Frankenstein series heroines, and Patrick Knowles is a better leading man/love interest than he was in *The Wolf Man*. Together they substantially lift the quality of the film. Although he falls short of his classic portrayal of Inspector Krogh in *Son of Frankenstein*, Lionel Atwill is good as the charming but rather puffed-up mayor of Vasaria. Maria Ouspenskaya is every bit as good in *Frankenstein Meets the Wolf Man* as she was in her most memorable film, *The Wolf Man*. Her line in reference to Talbot, "He simply wants to die," is a profound echo of Karloff's "We belong dead," the most poignant line in *Bride of Frankenstein*. The opening credits, which form from the vapors of a test tube, are the best of any Universal horror film, and the atmospheric opening scene in which the grave robbers enter the crypt of Lawrence Talbot is the best of any Universal horror film. The festival of the new wine and the song sung by Adia Kuznetzoff is the best "light relief" in any Universal horror film.

Although *Frankenstein Meets the Wolf Man* is not a good Frankenstein film, it is a top-notch werewolf film, ranking with *The Wolf Man* and *Son of Dracula* as one of Universal's top two or three horror films of the forties. Because Chaney's performance as the Wolf Man successfully rivals that of Karloff as the Frankenstein Monster in *Bride* and *Son*, *Frankenstein Meets the Wolf Man* must be considered one of Universal's finest efforts.

A theme that has never been mentioned in regard to *Frankenstein Meets the Wolf Man* is the Blakeian journey from childhood and innocence to experience. As Baroness Frankenstein says wistfully when hearing the first strains of music from the festival of the new wine, "It takes me back to my childhood." The words of Kuznetzoff's song, "For life is short, but death is long," is a theme of adult experience explored by many writers. This leads us to reconsider Talbot's journey from carefree youth to death-cursed maturity, a journey we all face. The Romantic desire to return to a younger, more idealistic past, symbolized by the journey to Vasaria, is one shared in the film by Talbot, the Monster, Baroness Frankenstein, and the villagers of Vasaria. Freud's death instinct is also a related theme that Siodmak weaves through the character motivation. All these themes will touch the heart of any Romantic and raise the film to even greater heights of artistry for such a personality.

The well-read, well-educated Siodmak endowed these Universal screenplays with philosophical, psychological, and literary themes that deserve even greater scrutiny than they have already received. Perhaps *Frankenstein Meets the Wolf Man* will eventually receive the critical status it deserves.

As usual, Lon garnered the respect of his co-workers. As Ilona Massey recalled:

> I think Lon Chaney is one of the nicest, sweetest people in the world. It was a great deal of fun. You know it took four hours to put on his makeup and when it was on, it was hot under the lights. It was very difficult for him to eat. He mostly had soup which he sipped through a straw and just for fun, we put hot peppers in it! We had a lot of fun.... I never had any difficulty with my co-stars, but Chaney was something special.[18]

As many existing stills demonstrate, Lon also was involved in quite a friendship at that time with his German Shepherd named "Moose." The dog often accompanied Lon to the set and even managed to appear briefly in the film itself. On one occasion the dog bit through Chaney's leather gloves and broke the bones between the actor's thumb and forefinger.

Although it was a money-maker, *Frankenstein Meets the Wolf Man* would have been a fortuitous place to end the sagas of both the Monster and the Wolf Man. Undaunted by the fact that little or nothing remained to be done with the characters, Universal nevertheless made plans in June of 1943 for another sequel. After the concept went through a number of changes, Universal began preparations for the project it was calling *The Devil's Brood*. The brood they conjured up was to consist of a mad scientist, a hunchback assistant, the Wolf Man, Dracula, and the Frankenstein Monster. When the film was released as *The House of Frankenstein* on December 15, 1944, audiences learned that "the more the merrier" did not necessarily apply to monster pictures.

In the film's plot, Dr. Gustav Niemann (Boris Karloff), imprisoned 15 years for following in the footsteps of Dr. Frankenstein, and Daniel (J. Carrol Naish), a psychopathic hunchback, escape from prison during a storm. They join Professor Bruno Lampini (George Zucco) and his traveling chamber of horrors. They kill the showman, however, when he refuses to travel to Vasaria where Niemann seeks revenge against those who sent him to prison. Nieman and Daniel take the show to Vasaria alone. All the while, Niemann promises to give Daniel a new body eventually.

Among their eerie exhibits is the skeleton of the vampire Dracula (John Carradine). When Niemann removes the stake from the skeleton's heart, the bones assume living form. In return for Niemann's protection, the vampire agrees to help the doctor get revenge against those who sent him to prison.

Dracula casts a supernatural spell over Rita (Anne Gwynne), daughter-in-law of one of Niemann's enemies. On the verge of becoming a vampire, Rita is rescued by her husband, Carl (Peter Coe). Dracula is destroyed by sunlight while fleeing his pursuers after Daniel shoves the vampire's coffin from their wagon.

Niemann cruelly murders his enemies in Vasaria and continues with Daniel toward the ruins of Frankenstein's laboratory. En route they rescue a mistreated gypsy dancer, Ilonka (Elena Verdugo), and take her with them.

In the ruins of the laboratory, Niemann and Daniel discover the ice-encased bodies of the Wolf Man and the Frankenstein Monster. The scientist and hunchback build a fire, thawing out Larry Talbot (Lon Chaney), the Wolf Man, who is still alive and wanting to die. The Monster (Glenn Strange), however, is ill and requires further treatment. Niemann immediately becomes obsessed with returning the Monster to full power. Meanwhile, Ilonka turns aside Daniel's love but remains his friend; she prefers the morose Talbot. The jealous Daniel incurs Ilonka's wrath, however, when he tells her that Talbot is a werewolf. Angry because Niemann is spending all his time reviving the Monster instead of giving Daniel a new body, the hunchback whips the prostrate Monster.

Talbot and Niemann search the laboratory for Frankenstein's personal diary, which Talbot thinks can cure his werewolf curse. When Niemann postpones operating on Talbot's brain to continue his experiments on the Frankenstein Monster, Talbot attacks the scientist just as the Monster regains its strength.

To Ilonka's horror, Talbot, the man she loves, changes into the Wolf Man and attacks her. As his fangs destroy her, she kills him with the gun containing two silver bullets he had given her for protection.

Attracted by eerie lights from the Frankenstein castle, a band of villagers go to the castle and chase the monster, who runs into the swamp, carrying along the injured Dr. Niemann. There, Niemann and the Monster sink beneath the quicksand.

Double billed with *The Mummy's Curse* (1944), the film followed in the lucrative footsteps of its predecessors. Unfortunately, it did not follow suit artistically. As many critics have noted, the scenario is too episodic, allowing no interaction among Dracula, the Wolf Man, and the Frankenstein Monster. Following the lead of *Frankenstein Meets the Wolf Man*, the Monster continues in a small supporting role. Although Glenn Strange was coached on the set by Karloff, his interpretation is much closer to that of the slow, lurching Lugosi. Still, Strange's physique ultimately makes his a more frightening and therefore more satisfactory Monster than Lugosi's.

Boris Karloff basically just goes through the motions. As Scott Nollen, author of *Boris Karloff*, writes, "Although Karloff's performance as Niemann is very interesting at the beginning of the film, the character seems completely one-dimensional at the midpoint, after he becomes obsessed with reviving the Monster...."[19]

John Carradine had the potential to be a great Dracula. His physique, facial

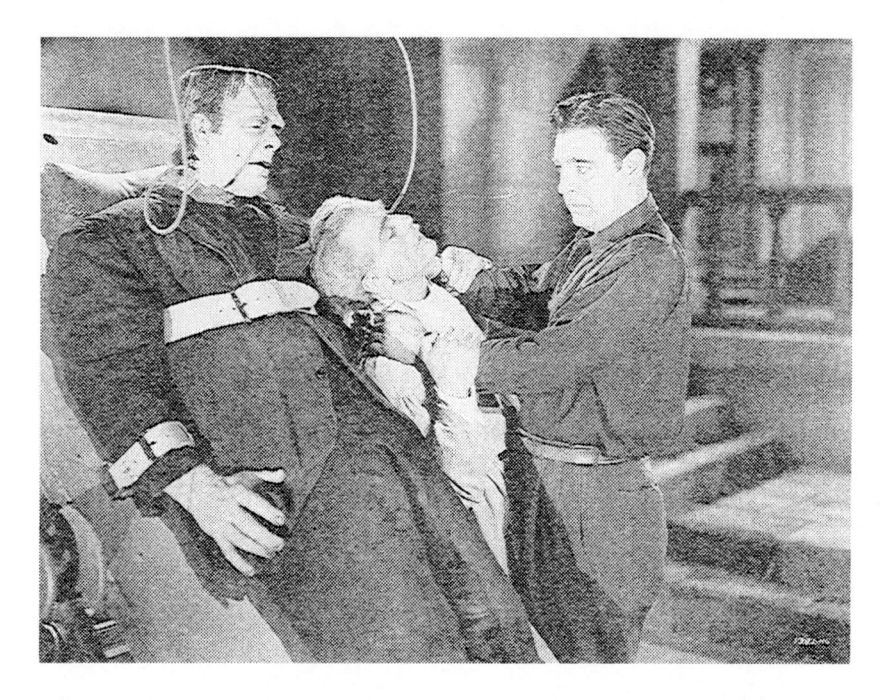

Glenn Strange, Boris Karloff, and Lon Chaney, Jr., in "House of Frankenstein" (1944).

structure, appearance, voice, and height were perfect. Unfortunately, though he appropriately underplays the role, the script of *House of Frankenstein* allows him little more than comic book character development. Carradine's best performance as Dracula would be in the upcoming *House of Dracula*.

The film's strengths are Hans Salter's usual excellent musical score and the superior performances of J. Carrol Naish and Elena Verdugo, who between them steal the show. Although he is playing a "psychopathic killer," Naish emerges as the film's most sympathetic character, and nineteen-year-old Elena Verdugo's flirty vulnerability makes her performance one of the best female ones in a forties Universal horror film.

At this point in the series, Larry Talbot is Larry Talbot, and Lon Chaney simply repeats Larry Talbot in the truncated space allowed by the script. Universal considered his presence important enough to pay him a flat fee of $10,000, more than the $3,500 per week with a two week guarantee landed by Carradine, the $1750 per week with four weeks' work accorded Naish, and the paltry $250 per week for two weeks provided to Strange. Karloff, however, outgrossed everyone with a comparatively whopping $20,000.

Universal publicity obviously hyped the horror, but it also accorded space to Chaney the man. One ad noted his height of six feet, four inches (probably an exaggeration) and his weight of 220 pounds, while another focused on

Chaney the family man, who in September of 1944 purchased a 1300-acre ranch which he appropriately dubbed "Lennie's ranch":

> While scores of American farms are feeling the pinch of the manpower shortage, "Farmer" Lon Chaney isn't pessimistic about finding hired hands for his new 1300-acre cattle ranch in Northern California [near Auburn]. The actor has two sons, both of whom have proven capabilities as farm hands, and pitch in after school and during holidays.
>
> Lon, III, 15 (his dad, the actor, is Lon, II), is 6 feet tall and weighs 175 pounds and ran a caterpillar tractor and a baler on a San Diego ranch last summer, doing the chores of two men.
>
> The younger boy, Ron, 13, is an excellent hunter. He's the "Chaney" of the family, in his father's opinion, while Lon junior is the "thinker and worker." Both boys, obviously, have inherited their fondness for outdoor life from Lon senior, and their late grandfather, the original Lon Chaney, who used to take them on hunting trips.[20]

Those must have been difficult hunting trips for the boys because neither had yet reached the age of two at the time of their grandfather's death.

If Universal publicity had a tendency to exaggerate, *House of Dracula* co-star Peter Coe was straightforward in pronouncing Chaney a likable man who could drink with the best of them:

> I met him when we did *The Mummy's Curse* [see Chapter 8], and we really became friends. He had a ranch up in the northern part of California, the pheasant season had just opened and we went hunting. We were so drunk—I mean *drunk*—it's a wonder we didn't shoot each other! We had a case of booze as we drove up to his ranch—a seven or eight hour drive—and we drank like crazy. Lon was a good drinker, an excellent drinker. We got to the ranch about 9:00 at night and we had to get up early, about two or three in the morning, to go hunting. Lon shook me and woke me up, and in his hand he was holding a glass. I thought to myself, "Oh, tomato juice or orange juice, how wonderful!" I took a sip and choked—it was straight booze! *That* was an eye-opener! We did a horrible thing on this trip. We were in the rice fields up north, it was about 10:00 in the morning and the sun was shining on us, when all of a sudden, boom, it was dark. We looked up and there was a flock, a whole sky of Canadian geese. They landed in a rice field, and Lon said, "We're gonna get some geese, baby!" So we crawled on our bellies holding our rifles, just like in the Army—we got up close and started firing, pow pow pow pow pow. Lon turned around to leave—"Come with me, run!" he said. I asked, "What about the geese?" and he said, "Tonight!" I asked, "Why?" and he held up a single finger: "One goose per hunter!" We had killed 47! We had to come back at night with a truck and load it up.[21]

Elena Verdugo joined Coe in finding Chaney a "great guy":

> Lon Chaney was a lovely, friendly man. I remember often sitting and chatting with him.... For the horror films at Universal, they used to have professional screamers on the sets. For the scene in which the Wolf Man attacked me, they called one of those "screamers" to our stage. This was one of the show's first

shots, and I hadn't seen Lon in his makeup. Well, when the Wolf Man jumped out at me, I was so scared and screamed so wildly that they cancelled the professional screamer.[22]

Glenn Strange had high regard for Lon as an actor. In 1941 Strange played a Lennie-like hired hand in PRC's *The Mad Monster*, and Chaney remarked upon the similarity. Strange recalled:

> Lon Chaney said to me, "What are you trying to do? Lennie in *Of Mice and Men*?" And I said, "Well, I haven't even seen the thing."...There's only one way to do a Lennie, and that's just a big "Da...Da..." You can't do it any other way. But I'll say this, and I've said it many times. We went to see *Of Mice and Men*, and I don't think anybody on the face of this Earth could have done as well, and I'm sure I couldn't have done any better than Chaney did as Lennie. That was a terrific piece of work.[23]

To some extent, the way to the heart of Chaney's fellow thespians was through their stomachs. Lon often displayed his cooking skills in his dressing rooms and invited the others for sumptuous lunches.

An unhappy affair involving food resulted, however, when Universal sponsored a publicity dinner showcasing their horror stars, Lon Chaney, Boris Karloff, Bela Lugosi, George Zucco, and Evelyn Ankers. Chaney, in his cups, began insulting Ankers's husband, actor Richard Denning. Aware of Chaney's condition, Denning ignored him until Lon said, "How come you're in the Navy and still in Los Angeles?" Aware of Chaney's 4-F status, Denning, who was about to begin submarine service, replied, "It's a lot better than not being in the service at all during wartime."[24] Probably still chafing because of his rejection by the service, Chaney smeared Denning's suit with some pistachio ice cream. Thanks to Denning, Lon's face was soon dripping with some of the same. As the green-faced Chaney prepared to hoist hot coffee at Denning, Ankers quickly intervened to reestablish peace. Needless to say, Lon's impromptu dinner performance before the press did nothing to enhance his reputation with the studio.

Unfortunately, Universal was not yet done feeding on the legends of its rapidly tiring monsters. Next in line was *The House of Dracula* (1945), the continued adventures of "The Devil's Brood"–the mad scientist, the hunchback assistant, Dracula, the Wolf Man, and the Frankenstein Monster. While it did little to advance the themes exhausted in its immediate predecessor, *House of Dracula* benefitted from a slightly better scenario:

Dr. Edelman (Onslow Stevens), an eminent European scientist, is tricked into aiding the vampire Count Dracula (John Carradine), who claims to desire a cure from vampirism. The Count, however, soon develops a taste for the blood of Edelman's lovely assistant, Miliza (Martha O' Driscoll).

Meanwhile, Larry Talbot (Lon Chaney), the Wolf Man, solicits Edelman's help in curing him of his curse. Edelman begins cultivating the mold from a tropical plant which he believes can relieve the brain pressure that turns

Talbot into a werewolf during times of the full moon. Realizing that the mold will not be ready before the next full moon, Talbot attempts suicide by throwing himself into the Devil's Cave, where he and Edelman discover the Frankenstein Monster (Glenn Strange).

Ignoring the advice of Nina (Jane Adams), a hunchback who also aids Edelman, the doctor strives to revive the Monster. Dracula, however, has mixed his own blood with Edelman's, causing the humanitarian to transform periodically into a vampirelike maniac. Edelman destroys Dracula and, rather than selfishly pursuing his own cure, redoubles his efforts to cure Talbot. He finally performs the long-awaited operation and cures the Wolf Man of his curse. Later that evening, Talbot witnesses Dr. Edelman kill the servant Seigfried (Ludwig Stossel). Owing his cure to the doctor, however, Talbot does not tell the police.

After strangling Nina, the now mad scientist releases the Frankenstein Monster. The creature soon goes berserk when Talbot shoots Dr. Edelman. The castle burns, and Talbot and Miliza, now lovers, flee the scene of carnage.

One would think by now that the worst news Larry Talbot could receive is that some scientist is again resurrecting the Frankenstein Monster. This time, however, Lon is cured (until 1948, at least) and actually gets the girl. While the screenwriters are cured of episodic script construction, they sin in failing to explain how Dracula and the Wolf Man managed to return from the dead whom they joined in *House of Frankenstein*, as well as in carelessly creating numerous plot inconsistencies. Still, the result is a fairly entertaining melodrama.

Nearly everyone who has scrutinized this film rightly praises the performances of John Carradine, Onslow Stevens, and, to a lesser extent, Jane Adams. Carradine is given more to do in this outing than in *House of Frankenstein*, and he makes the most of it. His scene with Martha O' Driscoll at the piano is both the best scene in the film and Carradine's best moment as Dracula. Stevens is a marvelous mad scientist, totally eclipsing Boris Karloff's performance in *House of Frankenstein*. While Brunas, Brunas, and Weaver belittle Stevens as "inachronistically broad, with the actor chewing the scenery and leering hammily,"[25] surely his leer is one of the most chilling in screen history. Let us say that he out-Slaughters Tod Slaughter. And Jane Adams's hunchback is both noble and pathetic. The film's dream sequence, an impressive montage, is frightening and foreboding. O' Driscoll stands out in her scenes of tenderness with Chaney and in her scene at the piano with Carradine. As for Glenn Strange, he has his best moment ever as the Monster when he grimaces at Talbot following the death of his savior, Dr. Edelman.

This was Lon Chaney's fourth performance as Larry Talbot. Even Chaney's most ardent advocates must admit that Talbot's plight was by now becoming uncomfortably tedious. The performance is flawless, but as Brunas, Brunas, and Weaver correctly conclude, Lon was "clearly on autopilot."[26]

As was becoming his custom, Lon was never far from a drink. Glenn

The Frankenstein Series • 57

The difficult process of taking liquid refreshment on the set of "House of Dracula" (1945).

Strange recalled that when there was a need, Lon could quickly produce a bottle:

> Remember when I was laying in the quicksand in *House of Dracula*, and the opening scene had me with the skeleton of Karloff in the quicksand? Well, I was in there all day long, and that stuff was cold!... Chaney came down with a fifth, and I think I got most of it. He poured it down me and it warmed me up some.... They took the makeup off and by the time I got about half undressed I was so looped I could hardly get up. I got warm, and then I got tight. But I think he just about saved my life that day. I was chilling; I was cold. Well, by golly, he was nice to me, and always has been. I'd like to do another picture with him sometime. He's followed in the footsteps of his old Dad pretty well. He's a good

horror man; you know that. I doubt if anyone could have done as good as Lon as the Wolf Man. He did a good job.[27]

John Carradine, who aspired to greatness on the stage, never took his many horror films very seriously. He later recalled those early years with Lon fondly: "He was a nice guy—a big, good-natured slob. He was a pro who knew his business."[28]

In 1948, Lon would make one more appearance for Universal as the Wolf Man, but in that film he and other classic monsters would join comedians Abbott and Costello in sending up the then tired Universal horror cycle.

Of interest to trivia buffs is the fact that *House of Dracula* represents Chaney's only mustached Larry Talbot performance, as well as the only film in which Karloff, Chaney, Strange, and Parker all appear in one scene or another as the Frankenstein Monster. Hey, what happened to Lugosi?

Chapter 6

The Mummy Series

I n 1942, Lon Chaney was hardly out of the Frankenstein Monster makeup when Universal cast him as Kharis the Mummy in *The Mummy's Tomb*. Universal's first Mummy film was, of course, the 1932 classic *The Mummy*, with Boris Karloff in the title role. The studio later hauled out the bandages for *The Mummy's Hand* (1940), casting Tom Tyler as Kharis. The plot of *Tomb*, a sequel to *Hand*, demonstrates that there was little new for the Mummy to do:

Archaeologist Stephen Banning (Dick Foran), his nephew John (John Hubbard), and John's fiancée, Isobel Evans (Elyse Knox), do not know that Mehemet Bey (Turhan Bey), a cemetery caretaker in Mapleton, is really a fanatical Egyptian priest who has vowed to kill the members of the Banning expedition because it "defiled" an ancient Egyptian tomb. Bey plans to have them killed one by one at the hands of Kharis (Lon Chaney), a living mummy that the members of the Banning expedition thought they had destroyed during their dig in Egypt years ago.

The people of Mapleton are unaware that Bey is hiding the Mummy in a cemetery crypt. First the Mummy strangles Stephen, igniting a police investigation in the quiet little town. Soon afterward, Stephen's sister Jane is murdered. When Babe Hansen (Wallace Ford), fellow archaeologist and member of the Banning expedition, arrives in Mapleton, he recognizes the strange marks left by the Mummy on Stephen's throat. Soon, however, the Mummy also strangles Hansen.

Amidst the turmoil, John and Isobel are secretly married, but Bey orders the Mummy to bring Isobel to the crypt. Meanwhile, John leads a sheriff's posse to the cemetery, where they see the Mummy carrying Isobel away. Bey is shot and killed, and the posse tracks Kharis to the Banning estate.

When the posse traps the Mummy in the Banning residence, John, brandishing a torch, rescues Isobel and grapples with the Mummy as the house bursts into flames. John escapes, and the Mummy is destroyed in the ensuing conflagration. Later, John and Isobel ride toward the railroad station, their bags packed for a belated honeymoon.

The Mummy's Tomb, though filmed just two years after *The Mummy's Hand*, is actually set thirty years later. Far from Egypt, the aging Banning family of *Hand* is now living in a peaceful New England town. A long flashback occupies the first part of the film and is quickly followed by scenes of Andoheb (George Zucco) telling his new recruit, Mehemet Bey, how the bullets repeatedly fired into his body by Babe Hansen in *Hand* only shattered his arm. Bey then turns up in Mapleton, and the Mummy goes on his killing rampage.

Needless to say, *The Mummy's Tomb* artistically falls about as far short of *The Mummy* as *House of Frankenstein* falls short of *Frankenstein*. It also falls short of the modest heights of its immediate predecessor, largely due to the fact that it is a drastically downscaled, unimaginative rehash rather than a sequel. Karloff, for the most part unencumbered by a suit and mask in *The Mummy*, turned in one of the most memorable performances of his career. Tom Tyler, who was fully outfitted in a rubber mummy suit in *Hand* and feigned a paralyzed arm and leg, at least had the use of both eyes, which dart about and peer through the bandages like cold balls of steel. Of Chaney's Kharis, Brunas, Brunas, and Weaver write: "Lon Chaney's debut assignment as the Mummy was merely a contractual obligation which he understandably found arduous and unfulfilling. Wrapped in yards of gauze, Chaney slouched through the part with little shading of character or nuance."[1]

True enough, but it is hard to see from what source Chaney could have produced any shades of character or nuance. For the sake of continuity, he sported the paralyzed arm and leg of Tyler's Kharis. Blackened by the fiery finale of *Hand*, Chaney's Kharis has even lost his right eye. The blame here must ultimately go to Universal Pictures, which had just renewed Chaney's contract before burdening him with the thankless Kharis role. Production stills indicate that Chaney's only pleasure during shooting was the tender moments spent with his dog Moose between takes. Although advertising for the film heralded Chaney as "the screen's master character creator," any actor with the correct physical stature could have performed the role. Chaney knew it and must have felt exploited and cheated.

The film, however, is not without its virtues. Particularly effective is the scene in which Babe Hansen walks from a bar into the windy Mapleton night only to come face to face with Kharis. Hansen runs but is cornered in an alley. As Kharis stalks forward, the doomed man frantically but unsuccessfully tries to scale a high fence. Moments later he dies in the Mummy's grip. That scene, enhanced by Ford's sympathetic portrayal of Babe Hansen, is without a doubt the most suspenseful, atmospheric murder committed by Chaney in his tenure as the Mummy. It is ironic that Lon rightfully counted Wally Ford among his best friends.

Also praiseworthy is the scene in which Kharis carries Isobel through the cemetery gates. The leaves blowing across the ground, the trees rustling in the wind, and the low key lighting create an eeriness rare in the Mummy series.

Most impressive, however, is the fiery climax in which Chaney is trapped by flames on the balcony of the Banning house. Unfortunately for Lon, that well-mounted conflagration would not end the predictable exploits of the Mummy.

On May 2, 1981, Elyse Knox wrote a letter to me in which she recalled working with Chaney: "Even with the rubber mask, his makeup took a long time and was very uncomfortable. Because he had to carry me through graveyards, etc., he was very happy I weighed considerably less than other leading ladies."

Although Lon may have been thankful for Knox's slight weight, his heavy drinking nevertheless caused the actress injury during production. As Lon was carrying Knox through the gates of the cemetery, he misjudged his marks and banged her head against the stone supports. Filming came to a short-term halt while Elyse recovered and the crew widened the gates for the tipsy Mummy's second take.

Undoubtedly much to his displeasure, Lon was back as Kharis in *The Mummy's Ghost* (1944). Although the film itself is full of lapses, it is probably the best of Chaney's Mummy films. The plot returns Kharis to Mapleton and makes no attempt to explain how he survived the climactic fire of *Tomb*:

Kharis the Mummy (Lon Chaney) is loose again in Mapleton, coming from nowhere to strangle noted Egyptologist Professor Norman (Frank Reicher). This time Kharis is under the control of Youssef Bey (John Carradine), priest of Arkam, who was sent to the United States to recover the remains of Princess Ananka, whose sarcophagus was stolen from Egypt. Kharis has already murdered every member of the expedition that carried his princess away. There is more work to be done, however, when Bey discovers that the princess has been reincarnated as Amira Mansori (Ramsey Ames), a student of Egyptology at the local college. Bey sends Kharis to kidnap her, but when the Mummy delivers her to Bey's hideout, an elevated mine shack, the two quarrel over Amira's fate.

A blow from Kharis' mighty arm sends Bey to his death, after which the Mummy carries Amira to the swamp. Joining a mob of townspeople, Tom Hervey (Robert Lowery), Amira's sweetheart, follows the Mummy and his burden to the swamp. There, Amira turns into the mummified remains of the princess and disappears beneath the water of the swamp with Kharis.

Referring to the swampy demise of Kharis and his princess, the *New York Times* begged, "Oh! please, Universal, do not disturb their rest."[2] While the *Times* had reason to fear yet another revival of the Mummy, *Ghost* boasted an unexpected twist, that of reincarnation, not employed since Karloff's original Mummy film of 1932. And this time Universal discarded the convenient rubber suit of *Tomb* and enhanced the Mummy's appearance through makeup. Although the difference is slight, one can see a bit more hatred and emotion

Original title-card art for "The Mummy's Ghost" (1944).

oozing from Kharis' face than emerged before. Carradine is an asset as the high priest, almost overcoming the totally uninteresting performances of romantic leads Lowery and Ames.

Although Kharis was still not Lon's cup of tea, he has several good scenes in the film. The first is his killing of Professor Norman in which the Mummy, with hand clenching and grasping, drags himself toward the terrified professor. Lon even emits some hatred from his still functional left eye. In another memorable moment, just seconds before he kills Ben, an innocent rustic, Lon rears up, arm extended, eliciting fear through his stature and grimace alone. Lon also has an effective moment as he bows his head while Carradine's Youssef Bey evokes the help of the ancient gods of Egypt.

Obviously irritated by his continued labor in the Mummy series and probably lit by alcohol, Lon caused more production problems. In the scene depicting Professor Norman's murder, he gripped elderly Frank Reicher's throat so hard that the actor passed out. "He nearly killed me!" Reicher cried. "He took my breath away." Lon, horrified at his own action, apologized profusely to the old man. Two versions exist of what happened next. In a *Classic Images* "Pentagram Revues" article, Blackie Seymour writes that while shooting the second take, Lon proceeded to brutally strangle Reicher again. Too upset to work any more that day, Lon left the set and performed the next shot a week later when the unfortunate Reicher was gone. While Seymour does not credit director Reginald LeBorg in his review, he told me in a phone interview that LeBorg was indeed his source for the story. LeBorg's later credited versions, however, indicate that Lon simply said, "Pardon me" after injuring the old actor in the first take. When LeBorg cautioned Chaney to be more careful, Lon brushed it off, saying of Reicher, "Aw, he's just a little..."[3] LeBorg then indicates that Lon got the second take right without incident. As the director is now deceased, making a final clarification impossible, I expect that the second version is the most accurate since LeBorg gave it on several occasions and was credited accordingly.

Lon had other problems during production. In the scene in which Kharis shatters a plate glass window in the Scripps Museum, the real glass was supposed to be replaced with a breakaway substitute. When shooting began, however, the substitute glass had not yet been installed. Director Reginald LeBorg asked Chaney to wait, but the actor, knowing that the glass was real, recklessly blasted his hand through anyway. Later, as he nursed the injured hand, Chaney confessed to LeBorg, "I wanted to show you that I had the courage."[4]

In *Ghost*, Lon again suffered for his career. Encumbered by more than 400 yards of specially treated gauze, the actor found little reward to compensate for the misery. The studio resurrected the old ploy of claiming that the actor's gruesome makeup necessitated his taking lunch away from other studio employees. Chaney's exile, however, was self-induced. His dressing room contained a refrigerator that he frequently opened and lay in front of in order to keep cool. What better place to relax and drink lunch.

Although Lon was uncomfortable on the set throughout the Mummy series, he always took time for children. During the filming of *Ghost*, he posed in makeup for publicity shots with one of the Quiz Kids, a group of acclaimed preteen intellectuals with their own forties radio show. On another occasion, the Quiz Kids were touring the Universal lot when Lon rode past in a car. When the kids were told who had just passed, they chased the vehicle till it stopped, at which point Lon got out and signed autographs. Upon seeing the popular horror star out of makeup, one eight-year-old volunteered, "Really, Mr. Chaney—you're quite good-looking. You don't scare me at all."[5]

If kids were not involved, however, Lon was not always as genial on the set. When a United Press reporter visited the set of *Ghost*, Chaney granted a rather unorthodox interview. Sitting before a fan in full Mummy makeup, the over six foot, 220 pound actor complained of his plight with obvious frustration. "This stuff burns to the dickens, if it isn't kept cool," he snarled. " I have to sit in front of a fan to keep it from burning a hole right through my face."[6] The studio used that quotation to emphasize Lon's link with Chaney Sr., but it deleted the actor's additional comment that audiences were nuts for

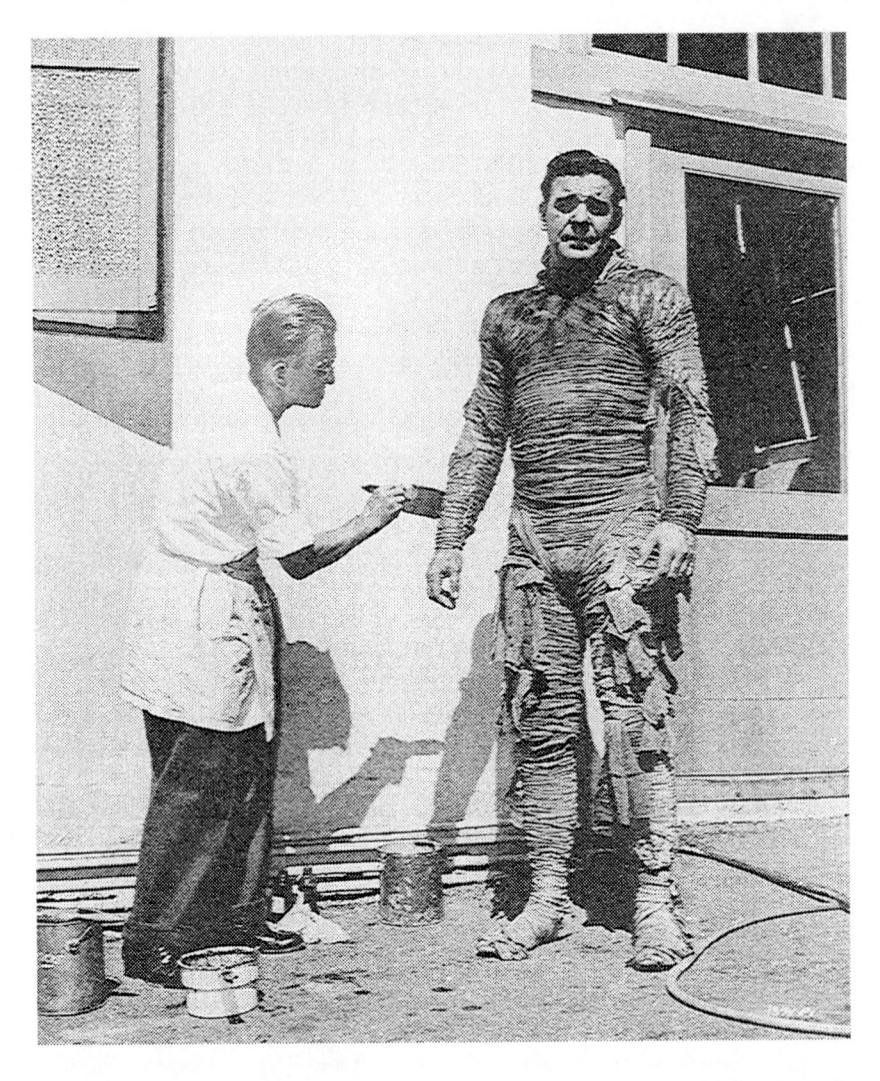

Lon's displeasure is clear as Jack Pierce paints the bandages on the set of "The Mummy's Ghost" (1944).

spending their money to see Mummy films. It was such reckless comments, coupled with alcohol induced "accidents" and "mishaps," that were beginning to sour Universal on Lon Chaney.

Nevertheless, the studio pushed Lon into a third and final Mummy film, *The Mummy's Curse* (1944), announcing their plans for a sequel even before the release of *Ghost*. Again, the screenwriters played fast and loose with continuity. Ignoring the fact that the Mummy and Princess Ananka had sunk in a New

England swamp, they set the new film in the Louisiana bayous with superstitious Cajuns and a stereotypical black. How did Kharis and Ananka get to Louisiana? Nobody knows, and the writers apparently assumed that no one cared. Here is how the plot unfolds:

When Cajun workmen labor to drain a bayou swamp, one of their number is mysteriously murdered. The superstitious Cajuns whisper weird tales about mummies being buried in the area, and the project is temporarily halted. Bossman Walsh (Addison Richards) is annoyed at their fear and further angered when Dr. James Halsey (Dennis Moore) of the Scripps Museum and his associate, Dr. Ilzor Zandaab (Peter Coe), arrive to search for the mummies of Kharis (Lon Chaney) and Princess Ananka (Virginia Christine), believed buried in the swamp. Although Walsh dismisses the stories, his pretty, open-minded niece and secretary, Betty (Kay Harding), becomes romantically interested in Halsey. When bulldozers unknowingly uncover the mummies, Dr. Zandaab secretly meets Ragheb (Martin Kosleck), a workman, who takes the scientist to a hidden monastery.

Zandaab is actually an Egyptian priest, and Ragheb is his servant. Zandaab revives Kharis the Mummy with a brew of tanna leaves. After strangling an old caretaker (William Farnum), the creature stalks off in search of his beloved princess, whom the sun has transformed into a beautiful young girl.

A string of murders ensues, and Ananka, who fears Kharis, hides in the construction camp. Kharis eventually catches up with Ananka and carries her to the monastery. Zandaab is killed by a workman, Kharis and Ragheb are crushed in the ruins of the collapsed monastery, and Ananka returns to her ancient mummy state.

Upon the film's release, *The New York Times* predictably dismissed it:

> The Mummy, that noisome monster which Universal digs up now and then out of the jetsam of a previous picture is at the Rialto again–this time in a wretched little shocker entitled "The Mummy's Curse." And for the benefit of anyone who is interested, we can report that he (or it) is doing the same–exactly the same, for that matter–as he did in "The Mummy's Return [sic]." That is, he is rising from his coffin to clomp about the screen in murderous quest of a vitalized female mummy whom he loved 3,000 years ago. It is all very juvenile and silly, and except for a few hollow laughs, is as dull as Uncle Henry's old jack-knife. It's time to tell that mummy he's a bore.[7]

Yes, the mummy theme was wearing very thin by 1944 largely because Universal, relying solely upon the Mummy in the title to attract the usual audience, did little to give the title character depth or interest. Often showing at the bottom of a double bill with the studio's "A" feature, *House of Frankenstein* (itself hardly a classic), the film was the last in the mummy series. One would hardly want to count *Abbott and Costello Meet the Mummy* (1955), in which the Mummy is mistakenly named Klaris, as part of the bona fide saga.

Even though the Mummy series was at its final stage, Universal managed,

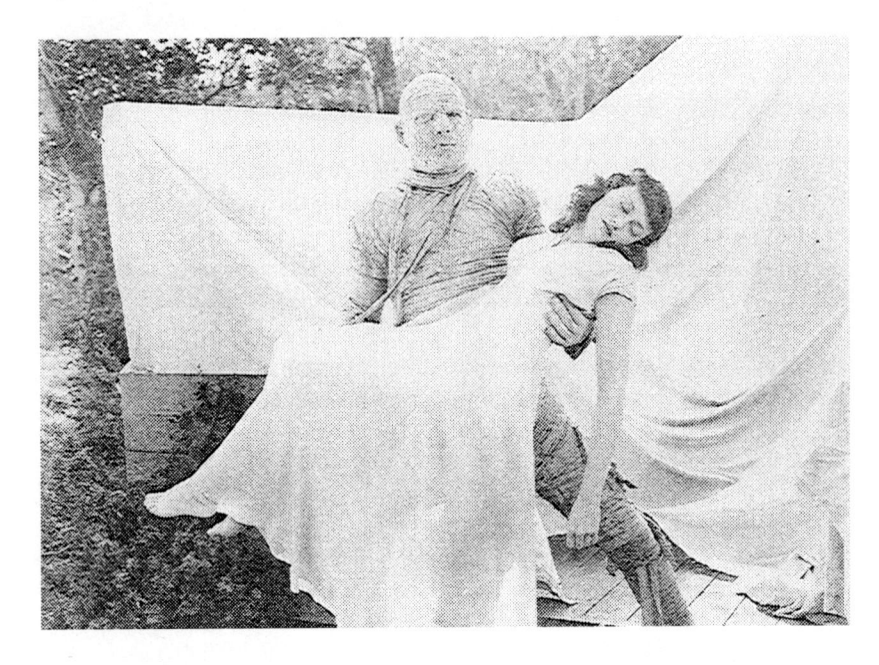

Chaney and Virginia Christine in "The Mummy's Curse" (1945).

as usual, to supply it with several fine moments. Everyone familiar with the film notes the fine performance of Virginia Christine, especially the scene in which she drags herself out of the swamp as a mummified relic and regains her youth and beauty during a walk in the sunlight and a dip in a pond. Also effectively staged are several of the Mummy's murders, particularly those of Tanthe Berthe (Ann Codee) and Cajun Joe (Kurt Katch).

Once again, however, almost anyone could have carried off the role of the silent, shuffling Kharis. In interviews, Chaney always referred to the Mummy as his least favorite role, and rightfully so.

Reactions to Chaney on the set were mixed. On the positive side, Lon's friend Peter Coe recalled how the actor went to bat for aging silent film star William Farnum, who was having trouble remembering his lines and was consequently exasperating director Leslie Goodwins: "He [Farnum] was a friend of Chaney's father–a big star. Both Chaney and I said, 'Lee [Goodwins]–get him a star's chair, otherwise we're going to walk off the set.' Chaney didn't have to do that for the old man."[8] Producer Oliver Drake recalled: "Lon was never hard to work with. He drank about a bottle of bourbon a day. Started in the morning and didn't quit till he went to bed. But he was never drunk on the set. It never interfered with his acting."[9]

However, if Lon's drinking never interfered with his acting, you could have fooled Virginia Christine:

> Lon was a lot like Errol Flynn. He liked the bottle. In the film we were supposed to climb up an old, ancient shrine, located in back of Universal's lot, and the steps were very worn and crooked. The steps were difficult to navigate under any circumstances, but if you're in a mummy suit, had a drink or two, and have a girl in your arms it's worse! Lon was weaving, and I thought, oh, boy. He was a big guy, a very sweet guy, but big. I kept thinking if he falls on me, I've had it. Fortunately, the director, Les Goodwins, saw what was going on and got Lon out of there and put his double in the mummy suit.[10]

As Christine notes, Chaney's bottle proved a problem for director Leslie Goodwins. On one occasion, Lon had to stand in the mummy suit while the crew set up for an outdoor scene. Goodwins noticed that Lon was holding a bottle of bourbon and asked him not to drink too much before the scene could be shot. Uncomfortable and impatient, Lon yelled back, "Why? I have no lines, and I have to drag my butt through the mud."[11]

Based upon experiences while making *Frozen Ghost* (see Chapter 7), Martin Kosleck was one actor who actively disliked Lon Chaney. In one scene, Lon was supposed to turn toward Kosleck, his arm outstretched in the familiar strangler's pose. He was then supposed to drop the arm slowly upon spotting Kosleck's ceremonial robe. In a state of advanced inebriation, however, Lon turned too quickly and bashed Kosleck in the face. Chaney reputedly also relished stalking Kosleck during the film's finale. Recalled Kosleck: "He enjoyed that thoroughly! I remember it well, I was pushed around. Why they had him as a star is beyond me. He was roaring drunk!"[12]

While none of the Chaney Mummy series films were bad, all were repetitious and consistently mediocre. All had their effective and memorable moments and can be enjoyed today as the formulaic, escapist fare they were intended to be, but the series does nothing to enhance Chaney's reputation.

The Chaney mummy films are important, however, to the extent that they chronicle the exploits of one of Universal's classic (though least interesting) monsters, one that remains a part of the American consciousness, and one that can still give children nightmares. With a little more care and respect on the part of Universal, Kharis would have and should have emerged with a greater critical standing than he now enjoys.

Chapter 7

The Inner Sanctum Series

Immediately following Chaney's masterful *Son of Dracula* (1943, see Chapter 8), Universal starred him in the first of their Inner Sanctum series, *Calling Dr. Death* (1943). In order to cash in on the popularity of the well-known radio show and book series, Universal purchased the rights to the Inner Sanctum trademark from Simon and Schuster, and assigned the mediocre Ben Pivar to produce a series of mysteries starring their hottest horror star, Lon Chaney. The resulting six efforts are probably the most critically maligned of any films Chaney did for Universal.

All of the films except *Pillow of Death* begin with the distorted face of David Hoffman informing the audience from within a crystal ball that "This is the Inner Sanctum...a strange, fantastic world, controlled by a mass of living, pulsating flesh...the mind! It destroys...distorts...creates monsters...commits murder! Yes, even you, without knowing, can commit murder!"

Following that lead, most of the films call for Chaney to be the Inner Sanctum's typical "suave mustachioed professional man who is all the rage with the ladies." *Calling Dr. Death*, which was shot in just twenty days, set the tone for the series:

Dr. Mark Steele (Lon Chaney), a prominent neurologist who heals the subconscious complexities of mentally ill patients, is experiencing marital difficulties with Maria (Ramsey Ames), his maliciously unfaithful wife. Steele's assistant, Stella Madden (Patricia Morison), who is in love with the doctor, allows her routine office duties to extend to the management of her employer's private life.

When Maria leaves for a weekend with Robert Duval (David Bruce), Steele finds out and experiences a mental blackout. On Monday morning, Inspector Gregg (J. Carrol Naish), a grim officer, informs Steele and Stella that Mrs. Steele has been murdered. When Duval is tried, convicted, and sentenced to the electric chair, Steele becomes convinced of the man's innocence.

On the eve of Duval's electrocution, as Stella dozes fitfully, Steele dark-

Lon, Patricia Morison, and J. Carrol Naish in a publicity still from "Calling Dr. Death" (1943).

ens the office and hypnotizes her with his pocket watch and chain. Under hypnosis, and within hearing distance of Inspector Gregg, Stella admits that it was she who killed Mrs. Steele.

Lon was happy when given the starring role in the Inner Sanctum series. Hoping to climb out of the monster-of-the-month rut he had fallen into, he accepted the mystery series as a welcome change of pace.

Regarding Chaney's performance in *Calling Dr. Death*, one should first note that the part of Dr. Steele seems specifically written for Lon Chaney rather than for a William Powell type. Steele is a personally troubled man, serious by nature, and anxiously introspective. As Steele, Chaney's nuances of character are nearly perfect. Even the *New York Times*, no fan of forties Universal horror or Lon Chaney, justly concluded that "Mr. Chaney and Patricia Morison play the harried doctor and his nurse with proper restraint."[1]

The *Times*, however, is critical of Chaney's "stream of consciousness" voice-overs, which convey his thoughts to the audience through an interior monologue at various points in the film. This device, which would become a hallmark of the series, has been ridiculed by critics ever since. In recent years, various individuals suspected of bearing responsibility for the effect have fallen all over themselves in explaining why someone else was to blame. The author of the original screenplay, Edward Dein, for example, claimed that he inserted them because Chaney "begged me to put the dialogue on the soundtrack because it was too technical, and although he played a doctor in it, he just couldn't say the words."[2] Director Reginald LeBorg contradicted Dein by blaming producer Ben Pivar, who, LeBorg said, required simplification due to his crudity and lack of intelligence.[3]

The best explanation is that Dein, without any input from Chaney, wrote the interior monologues into the script—and for good reason. The interior monologues would compliment the overall concept of the mind as the inner sanctum; therefore, they were created to bring the audience into the inner sanctum of Dr. Steele. Dein had two unsatisfactory alternatives. First, he could have fleshed out the screenplay with lengthy scenes of exposition designed to give the audience insight into Steele's innermost fears. This, however, would have robbed the audience of direct contact with Steele's inner sanctum. Second, Dein could have had Steele walking about talking to himself at various places in the film. The sight of an eminent neurologist engaged in such activities obviously would have brought the house down in laughter. Despite denials, Dein is probably the one responsible for the interior monologues, and he should not apologize. His clumsy charge that Chaney could not say the lines, however, is as cruelly unfair as it is ludicrous.

Actually, this is a film brimming with good performances. The pain and purposiveness of Patricia Morison are completely believable. When Chaney embraces her early in the film and says that as adults they should stop denying their feelings, her perfectly delivered response—"There's nothing we can do about it"—elicits the desired audience sympathy. Later, as she attempts to keep the convicted murderer's wife from soliciting Dr. Steele's help, her calculating coldness emerges and makes her, along with Steele, a suspect.

Perhaps the best performance in the film is that of J. Carrol Naish as a Columbo-like detective in days before murder suspects had rights. His well-mannered yet decisive harassment of Chaney provides the major conflict of the film—aside, of course, from Chaney's inner conflict with himself.

The screenplay has a few slips, as when the noted neurologist Dr. Steele, after considering the murder suspect's physical features, comments that he "doesn't look at all like a criminal." But the film, which was shot in just twenty days, is clearly not the tedious bore that some critics describe. Those who blindly see Chaney's Dr. Steele as a miscast Lennie fail to appreciate the actor's fine performance. Again, director LeBorg gets Chaney's best acting, which is enough to lift *Calling Dr. Death* at least to the upper levels of average, if not a little higher.

Studio publicity indicated that Chaney interrupted his efforts on behalf of war bonds in order to film *Calling Dr. Death*. The flying tour of which Lon was a part appeared in thirteen cities in ten days and sold a total of $50,911,730 worth of bonds. In one large eastern city, however, Lon became incensed after a stirring appeal had little effect on the crowd. Throwing away his prepared speech, Lon angrily addressed his apathetic listeners:

> I saw you smiling and grinning when Albert Dekker was talking about the most serious business in the world. Instead of grinning, you ought to be marching over to the bond booth and buying all the bonds you can.
> I'm not going to use this speech given to me by the War Department. I have something else I want to tell you. [Chaney then told the crowd about having met two young flyers in the U.S. Air Force who had just returned from Guadalcanal.]
> They had been through hell down there and were complete nervous wrecks. While I was talking with them, I asked if they bought bonds. One of them said that in Guadalcanal he put as high as 94 per cent of his salary into War Bonds. The other aviator seemed ashamed that he only had been putting about 80 per cent of his salary into bonds.
> Then I asked them what other soldiers were putting into bonds. They replied that the boys in the Southwest Pacific were investing an average of 75 to 80 per cent of their salaries in War Bonds.
> Maybe you people can guess how that made me feel. I must have shown how ashamed I was, for one of the boys turned to me and said: "That's all right, Mr. Chaney, you don't need to be ashamed. It seems that the farther away they get from the fighting front, the lower the percentage becomes that is deducted from their salaries for War Bonds."
> Don't disappoint our wonderful boys in uniform who are fighting and dying for you. Dig down in your pockets now, and buy bonds for all you are worth. You in that streetcar, get off and buy bonds before it is too late. You up in those buildings, come and buy bonds, bonds, bonds![4]

According to publicity, not only did the people in the streetcar and the buildings buy bonds, but so did everyone in Chaney's troupe. The obvious question is, did such an event really occur? Pressbooks, as everyone knows, do prevaricate. In this case, however, the publicity is almost certainly true. Chaney was highly patriotic. Because he undoubtedly experienced guilt and anger regarding his own 4-F status, a crowd such as he faced on that day would have made his blood boil.

Along the same lines, *Reader's Digest* reported another ploy used by Chaney, who apparently did not like to read the prepared texts given him by the government:

> During the last Bond Drive at the Beverly Tropics, Lon Chaney, Jr., faced the audience and pulled out a sheaf of papers. "I have here a very long speech which the Treasury Department asked me to read to you. Do you want to hear it?"
> The audience screamed, "No!"
> "Good," replied Chaney, putting the speech back in his pocket. "By gosh, you people better buy all the bonds you can or I'll come back and read it to you!"[5]

Universal immediately followed up their Inner Sanctum opener with *Weird Woman* (1944), based on an eerie novel, *Conjure Wife*, written by Fritz Leiber,

Jr. While the novel treated the supernatural as reality, the film comes down on the side of rationality over primitive superstition:

Norman Reed (Lon Chaney), sociology professor and author of *Superstition vs. Reason and Fact*, returns to Monroe College from an expedition to tropical islands, accompanied by a beautiful bride, Paula (Anne Gwynne). After the death of her archaeologist father, Paula was reared on a tropical island by a tribe of natives and inculcated with their primitive superstitions.

When Norman returns with his young bride, his faculty friends are surprised. None, however, are surprised as much as librarian Ilona Carr (Evelyn Ankers), who had expected to marry the rising scholar. Frustrated and bitter, Ilona spreads the word that Paula is a "witch wife" who uses her powers to ensure Norman's success.

Among those most willing to listen to Ilona is Evelyn Sawtelle (Elizabeth Russell), the ambitious wife of Professor Millard Sawtelle (Ralph Morgan), a mediocre scholar who is competing with Norman for the chairmanship of the sociology department. Ilona's tactics soon play upon the superstitions of Paula, who turns to magic spells for protection. When Norman discovers Paula's activities, he scolds her, pleads with her to leave her island superstitions behind, and breaks what Paula calls their "circle of immunity" from evil.

When Ilona discovers that Millard Sawtelle's plagiarized his new book from a graduate student's thesis, she misinforms the frightened old man that Norman has the information and intends to use it against him. Millard, unable to face professional censure and spousal wrath, commits suicide.

Ilona's plot claims another victim when she plants suspicion in the mind of David Jennings (Phil Brown), a student whose sweetheart, Margaret Mercer (Lois Collier), has been working as Norman's secretary. Margaret actually is infatuated with Norman, but the professor sees her only as a young and sometimes silly student.

When Margaret makes her intentions clear to Norman, he impatiently orders her out of his office. David charges into the professor's office, ready to shoot him in defense of his girlfriend's honor. In the ensuing scuffle, David is accidentally killed. Norman is then jailed and released on bail. Although he begins to wonder if Paula might have been right all along, he soon begins to suspect who is behind his troubles, and, with the aid of Evelyn Sawtelle, lays a trap that makes use of the unbalanced Ilona's own devices of superstition and fear. Terrified that she is about to die as the result of a curse, Ilona hysterically confesses, slips through the slats of a garden catwalk, and is hanged by the vines.

While the *New York Times* pronounced the film "dull,"[6] Brunas, Brunas, and Weaver are on the mark in writing that "for those willing to place their critical faculties in reserve, and approach the movie with their tongue firmly planted in their cheek, *Weird Woman* is an absolute joy...a high camp classic."[7] Reginald LeBorg, at the helm of his second Inner Sanctum picture, gets good performances from Elizabeth Russell, Evelyn Ankers, Frank Morgan, and Grace Gunnison. He allows Lois Collier to overplay the infatuated coed. While critics made the usual charge that Chaney was miscast as an intellectual, this is again a reflection of a widespread refusal to see Chaney as effective in any role but that of a dimwit or monster. As Professor Norman Reed, Chaney is academically serious, cordial to colleagues and acquaintances, and bewildered by the events that unfold around him. As a college professor familiar with other college professors, I find nothing laughable or particularly unbelievable about Chaney's casting. The screenplay, however, undercuts his effectiveness because by discounting the power of the supernatural, it makes Norman appear less than brilliant as he reels from one inexplicable catastrophe to the next. On the other hand, this is where the film provides some of its camp humor. Nothing, however, is more humorous than the last ten minutes, as Evelyn Ankers is terrified by Elizabeth Russell's straight-faced description of how, according to a dream, "the woman who lied" would die in seven days at one minute past midnight. Then we watch in amazement as Ankers becomes increasingly unbalanced at the sight of signs and ads which advertise sales or plays ending in only a few days.

Several cuts above *Weird Woman* is *Burn, Witch, Burn* (1962), a treatment of Leiber's *Conjure Wife* which emphasizes the painful evolution of a rationalist into a believer in the supernatural. Here the power of the occult is real, as it is in the novel.

Chaney's next Inner Sanctum outing was *Dead Man's Eyes* (1944). Again, Reginald LeBorg was ordered to direct, and again the screenplay piddles away the possibilities inherent in the subject:

Dave Stuart (Lon Chaney), an artist in love with Heather Hayden (Jean Parker), becomes terribly depressed when Tanya Czoraki (Acquanetta), his jealous model, accidentally causes him to become blind. Nick Phillips (George Meeker), an old suitor of Heather, reenters the woman's life, thinking that she will now marry him instead of Dave. Heather's father, Stanley Hayden (Edward Fielding), interferes with Nick's suit, much to the latter's resentment.

When Dr. Wells (Jonathan Hale) explains that Dave's sight might be restored by transplanting the corneas from a dead man's eyes, Heather's father makes out a will bequeathing his eyes to Dave. He rejects the offer, and the two men quarrel.

Later, Dave goes to apologize and finds "Dad" Hayden beaten to death. Heather then enters and accuses Dave of committing the murder. Dave denies it, and Captain Drury (Thomas Gomez), a detective, believes he might be innocent. Drury suspects Tanya and Allan Bitaker (Paul Kelly), a mutual friend of all concerned, who is love with Tanya. Meanwhile, Tanya has been acting as Dave's nurse.

In accordance with "Dad" Hayden's will, Dave receives the cornea transplant, but he pretends that it is not successful. When Tanya is about to reveal

74 • *Lon Chaney, Jr.*

Anne Gwynne and Evelyn Ankers with Chaney in a publicity still from "Weird Woman" (1944).

the murderer, she too is killed. Before Allan Bitaker can strike again, however, Dave tricks him into tipping his hand as the murderer.

If there was any doubt about Universal's "throw away" attitude toward the Inner Sanctum series, *Dead Man's Eyes* should have convinced even the most skeptical. With little financial or artistic investment in the series, Universal watched the films turn a profit. That was apparently all that mattered.

So inept is the screenplay that not even LeBorg's direction can inject much life into the proceedings. First of all, Dave Stuart is the most disagreeable, unlikable, and unsympathetic leading man in the Inner Sanctum series. A more deserving recipient of a dead man's brain than a dead man's eyes, Dave is so stupid as to keep acid and eyewash in identical bottles on his shelf. Once blind, he snaps at his friends, bemoans his state in stream-of-consciousness monologues, drinks heavily, and cries and sobs.

Second, the acting of the rest of the cast is mediocre at best, especially that of Acquanetta, who manages to breath not an ounce of life into her character. Third, while the identity of the killer is not telegraphed, the denouncement is wholly unbelievable. All of this considered, *Dead Man's Eyes* is a complete artistic failure. Even the publicity material is rather embarrassing. For example, a story titled, "Actor Defends Horror Movies," has Lon saying, "Horror pictures are often an outlet for pent-up emotions. Far from being harmful, they tend to disperse whatever insane thoughts we may have because we are shown that evil thoughts can become monstrosities. By making the characters ridiculous and the crimes hideous, we revolt the minds of movie-goers against evil tendencies."[8] Well, the characters of *Dead Man's Eyes* are indeed ridiculous, and it is easy to imagine the film revolting its fair share of movie-goers' minds. Although *Weird Woman* is superior, both films represent what happens when colorful ideas are rendered pale gray by the pens of inept screenwriters.

Undoubtedly to his great relief, Reginald LeBorg was not tapped by Universal to direct the next Inner Sanctum mystery. His departure, however, angered Lon. LeBorg recalled: "At the beginning Chaney thought I would be his *pal*, and when after three *Inner Sanctums* I wanted to do a musical...he said to me, 'You traitor! We were supposed to do big things together!' I told him, 'We'll get together again, don't worry.'"[9] That reunion would be *The Black Sleep* (1956).

Lon's fourth Inner Sanctum outing, *Frozen Ghost*, was supposed to have been the second in the series, but script problems and disagreements postponed it until 1945. The director was Harold Young (*The Mummy's Ghost*). The product of at least four screenwriters, the painfully unsuspenseful *Frozen Ghost* is only slightly superior to its boring immediate predecessor.

Alex Gregor (Lon Chaney), a hypnotist better known as "Gregor the Great," performs a stage act with his fiancée, Maura Daniel (Evelyn Ankers). When a drunk (Arthur Hohl) in the audience charges Gregor with fakery, the hypnotist invites the heckler on stage. Before putting the man into a trance, Gregor angrily mutters to Maura that he would like to kill him. When the heckler dies while in Gregor's trance, the hypnotist blames himself—citing murder by suggestion. Inspector Brandt (Douglas Dumbrille), however, does not take Gregor seriously, explaining that the man was a drunk with a bad heart. Nevertheless, Gregor, continuing to suffer from guilt, disbands the act, breaks off his engagement with Maura, and goes to work at the wax museum of his friend, Valerie Monet (Tala Birell), who has romantic designs on him.

Touring the museum for the first time with his friend and business manager, George Keene (Milburn Stone), Gregor takes an instant dislike to Rudi Poldan (Martin Kosleck), a disgraced plastic surgeon whose hands now make the wax figures. Rudi returns Gregor's antipathy when he suspects that Monet's niece, Nina (Elena Verdugo), whom he fancies, is becoming infatuated with Gregor.

When Rudi tells Monet that Gregor and Nina are making love behind her back, she confronts Gregor with these false accusations. An argument ensues, during which Gregor, his eyes twitching mesmerically, stares with hatred at Monet. Falling into a trance, she drops to the floor. Gregor blacks out and goes for an extended walk, returning to find that Monet has disappeared. Fearing that he has killed her just as he killed the heckler, Gregor pours out his guilt to Brandt. This time the inspector begins to take him seriously.

George and Rudi are actually responsible for Monet's disappearance; they hope to drive Gregor insane and acquire his fortune. When Nina finds Monet in a state of "suspended animation," Rudi places her in a similar state. George and Rudi plot to return the women to their normal state after Gregor is safely committed and then to blame the hypnotist for having placed them in a trance. Their plan begins to unravel, however, when Monet dies unexpectedly.

In an attempt to throw some light on the situation, Gregor places Maura in a hypnotic state in order to tap into her psychic powers. Under hypnosis, Maura accuses George, who is immediately placed under arrest by Brandt. Gregor and Maura then rush to the furnace room and stop Rudi before he can consign Nina to the flames.

Brunas, Brunas, and Weaver mercilessly zero in on the film's many flaws:

> *The Frozen Ghost* is slovenly to the point of ridiculousness. Disguised as a wax figure, the "missing" body of Tala Birell is plainly visible to all but the on-screen characters, who blithely walk right by it in their search. The motive fueling the conspiracy is to get Chaney's fortune, leaving the viewer to wonder just how much loot even a *good* stage hypnotist is likely to acquire. It's also stubbornly unclear how business manager Milburn Stone intends to make any profit by railroading his meal ticket into a nuthouse.[10]

On the other hand, Blackie Seymour, who on occasion is overly kind to Universal films, characterizes *Frozen Ghost* as "An imposing line-up of players in a good mystery story...[with a] good atmosphere and a plot that moves along at a nice pace to keep the viewer interested." While the mystery story is slow and riddled with holes and the atmosphere is drab rather than eerie, the cast actually might be labeled imposing. Milburn Stone shines as the amiable villain whom no one would ever suspect. Douglas Dumbrille, who was usually cast as a villain, is surprisingly good as the Shakespeare-quoting police inspector. Tala Birell brings her effective European aura to bear, Elena Verdugo is pert and charming, and Arthur Hohl is alternately distasteful and pitiable as the drunken skeptic. While critics universally panned the film, most had kind words for Martin Kosleck, who carries the film with his smooth, underplayed portrayal of the eccentric Rudi. Only Evelyn Ankers, who was six months pregnant at the time, turns in a flat performance.

To return to Kosleck for a moment, so good is his performance that Lon Chaney evidently felt threatened. According to Kosleck, "The director apparently liked me and I had a lot of close-ups. Chaney always came in and said, 'That's enough.' He *hated* me and I returned it. He was the star and he just wanted me out of the way."[11] The two would be unhappily teamed again, but for the last time, in *The Mummy's Curse* (see Chapter 6).

Lon Chaney is better in *Frozen Ghost* than in *Dead Man's Eyes* because the former provides him with a stronger character. Distressed but not whimper-

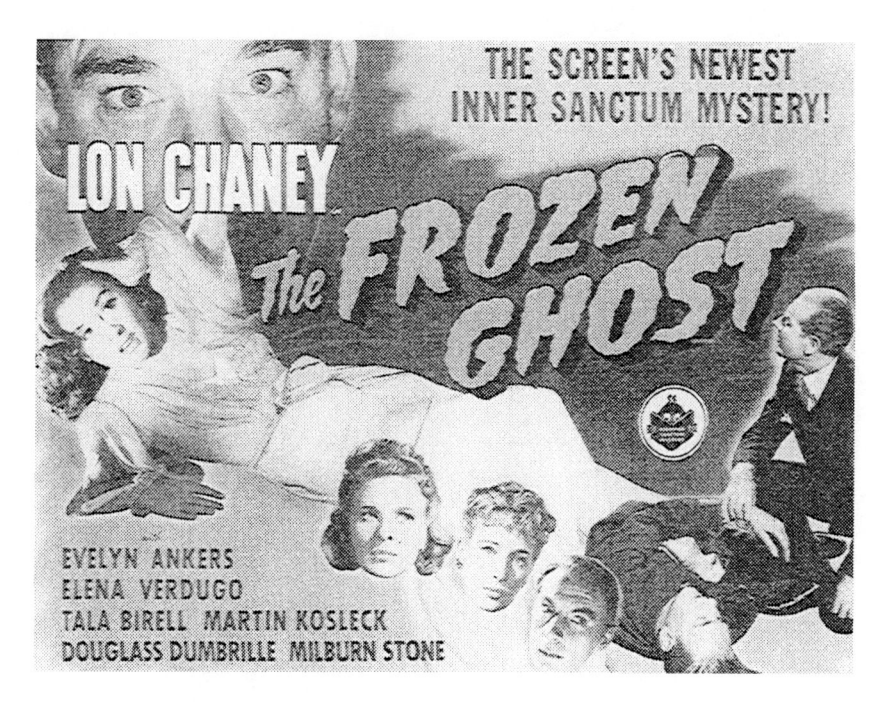

Original title-card art for "The Frozen Ghost" (1945).

ing, Chaney is physically imposing, especially when confronting the likes of Kosleck. Although he is starting to show the bloated, debilitating physical effects of alcohol, Lon plays the sympathetic hero effectively. The scenario must stress some emotional difficulties in order to make him appear persecuted and dependent. In fact, the high point of the film is where, on edge from stress and guilt, Chaney is driven by anger to "mentally" assault Tala Birell. Still, the Inner Sanctum formula was beginning to wear thin, as was Chaney's Inner Sanctum persona. Although *Frozen Ghost* turned a profit, credit Universal with changing the tired formula in their fifth series offering, *Strange Confession* (1945):

Jeff Carter (Lon Chaney), a once-brilliant scientist, brings a bag containing the head of his former employer, Graham (J. Carrol Naish), to his attorney. He then proceeds to explain the events that led a happily married man, pledged to relieve human suffering, to commit murder.

Graham, profit-mad and publicity-mad, loses Jeff as an employee when he insists on marketing an untested drug. Graham blackballs Jeff, who works as a druggist until Graham pressures him to return. Jeff agrees to return when his long-suffering wife Mary (Brenda Joyce) insists that he do so for the sake of their family. Graham, who has fallen in love with Mary, sends Jeff to South America on the pretense of finding a cure for influenza. In the meantime, Graham markets the untested drug and seeks the attentions of Mary.

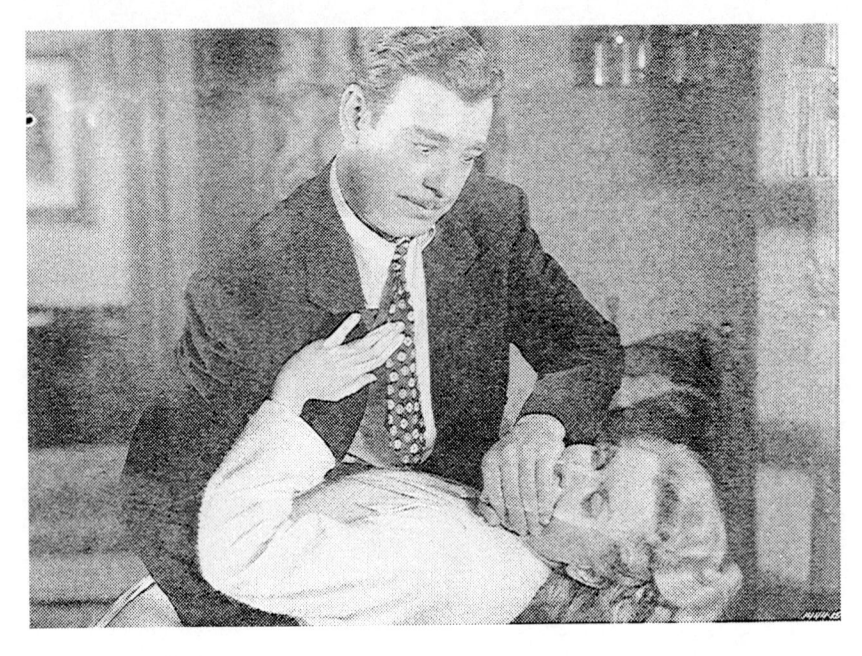

Chaney attempts to murder Brenda Joyce in "Pillow of Death" (1945).

When an influenza epidemic sweeps the country, the untested drug fails. After Jeff's son dies, the scientist returns home and discovers the deceptions to which he and his family have fallen victim.

As Jeff is placed under arrest, his attorney, moved by his client's story, promises legal aid.

Strange Confession, probably the best of the Inner Sanctum series, is a remake of Universal's *The Man Who Reclaimed His Head* (1934), which starred Claude Rains and Lionel Atwill. In that film, Atwill played an editor who stole the political writings of Claude Rains and embarked on essentially the same scenario found in *Strange Confession*.

While giving the film its due as "The penultimate entry in the Inner Sanctum sweepstakes," Brunas, Brunas, and Weaver are uncharacteristically way off the mark in some of their critical pronouncements. First, they claim that the opening scene in which Chaney brings Naish's head to the lawyer's home is fumbled: "Chaney just seems like a simpleton, and when he rambles on and on about strange things that can happen in a brilliant mind, you start to wonder whose mind he can be talking about."[12] Chaney is playing a completely unhinged character at this point—a murderer—and he carries off the scenes believably. The mad Chaney of the opening scenes is designed to stand in stark contrast with the affable family-oriented Chaney of the opening flashbacks. In the same vein, although Brunas, Brunas, and Weaver find the scenes involving

Chaney and his young son unconvincing, I believe they are among the most convincing of the film. In fact, Lon, who loved children, had to act very little to exude a strong and unmistakable fatherly warmth.

While J. Carrol Naish is at his best as the slick, suave, money-grubbing villain, he is still no Lionel Atwill. Brenda Joyce is the best female lead of the series since Patricia Morison in *Calling Dr. Death*, and Lloyd Bridges and Milburn Stone are acceptable in their minor roles.

Chaney must have taken this film more seriously than he did the line of monster and repetitive Inner Sanctum roles Universal was feeding him. Indeed, this Chaney performance is among his top six or seven for Universal.

The film's pressbook reported that a lavish dinner scene was deleted from the script at Chaney's request after dispatches from Nice, France, described riots precipitated by the appearance of a huge plate of caviar in an American film. Claiming that Chaney was a prewar favorite of French cinema fans, the ad went on to describe the actor's concern that an unwarranted display of food might offend his Gallic followers. Brunas, Brunas, and Weaver doubt the veracity of the ad, but given Lon's preoccupation with food (see Chapter 8), it just might be true.

Although Chaney's last Inner Sanctum film, *Pillow of Death* (1945), reunited him with Brenda Joyce, the results fell far short of *Strange Confession*. Harking back to elements of *Calling Dr. Death*, Lon, in love with another woman, is accused of murdering his wife:

At the Kincaid estate, wealthy Belle Kincaid (Clara Blandick) employs the aid of psychic medium Julian (J. Edward Bromberg) in contacting the spirits of deceased Kincaids. Belle's live-in niece Donna (Brenda Joyce) falls in love with lawyer Wayne Fletcher, whose wife, Vivian, is also a medium. When Wayne informs Donna that he is going to ask Vivian for a divorce, he returns home to be informed by Captain McCracken (Wilton Fraff) that she has been murdered by suffocation. When Wayne's alibi doesn't hold up, he is arrested, but he is quickly released on a writ of habeas corpus.

Interestingly, and much to Donna's chagrin, the main person insisting on Wayne's guilt is her own aunt Belle Kincaid. Belle and her cousin Amelia (Rosalind Ivan) arrange a seance at the estate with Julian as medium. Wayne and Donna reluctantly attend. When the voice of Vivian Fletcher accuses Wayne of the murder, he leaves the seance table and pulls young Bruce Mallone (Bernard B. Thomas) from an adjoining room, accusing him of being in collusion with Julian. Bruce admits that he is the boyhood beau of Donna and expresses his belief that Wayne killed his wife. Still, he denies aiding Julian in the seance. Privately, Wayne expresses his suspicion that Julian is either guilty himself or shielding someone else.

Later, Wayne, in a semihypnotic state, follows the voice of his wife to her crypt in the cemetery. The next morning, Belle's brother Sam (George Cleveland) is found suffocated, and Vivian's crypt is found empty. Soon afterward,

Belle herself falls victim to the "pillow of death." When Julian is arrested for the murders, Amelia, mentally unbalanced by the trail of events, traps Wayne and Donna in a closet and attempts to kill them with lethal gas. Fortunately for the lovers, Julian, released from custody for lack of evidence, returns just in time to interrupt Amelia's deadly plan.

When Bruce and Donna find Vivian's corpse in the cellar of the Kincaid house, Bruce admits the deed as a way of tricking Wayne into a confession. Later that night, Donna hears Wayne having an imaginary conversation with Vivian during which he admits to killing the Kincaids to gain their fortune through Donna. When Donna confronts Wayne, Vivian's voice warns him that he must now destroy her too. Wayne agrees and begins to smother Donna with the "pillow of death." McCracken and Bruce fortuitously burst into the room in time to interrupt the murder. Wayne then obeys another of Vivian's suggestions and leaps from a window to his death.

While *Pillow of Death* has a few good touches, such as the scene in which Chaney is drawn to his wife's crypt, it generates little suspense. As Brunas, Brunas, and Weaver write: "Tediously paced and uninspired on every level, *Pillow of Death* pretty much encapsulates the chronic ailments of the Inner Sanctum series: a fairly intriguing tale is demolished by ludicrous plotting, unbelievably bad dialogue, and aimless direction."[13]

The only "surprise" is that Chaney for the first time in an Inner Sanctum film is actually the villain. That, however, does not compensate for Lon's lackluster performance. Even Blackie Seymour, one of the actor's staunchest defenders, concludes that "Chaney is almost stumbling in and out of scenes."[14] Reviews were generally unfavorable.

On December 25, 1945, as *Pillow of Death* ended its run, Lon "remarried" Patsy in Hollywood. To make up for their impoverished 1937 marriage, Lon replaced Patsy's silver ring with a five-carat diamond wedding ring and a platinum and diamond engagement ring. Unfortunately, the studio that had made his economic success possible was about to cast him aside.

Correctly sensing that its second major horror cycle was at an end and fed up with Lon's drinking and general unpredictability, Universal decided not to renew his contract. The studio's decision was a blow to the actor. Although rarely used to best advantage, Lon's films had turned an impressive profit for Universal. Now he would once again face the uncertainties of a freelancer.

Chapter 8

Son of Dracula and Other Nonseries Universal Films (1941-1946)

W hen Universal signed Lon Chaney, Jr., to a studio contract, they first assigned him to two musical comedies. The first, *Too Many Blondes* (1941), gave him an impressive third billing behind Rudy Vallee and Helen Parrish.

In this musical, Dick and Virginia Kerrigan (Rudy Vallee and Helen Parrish), newlywed entertainers, quarrel when friendly blondes keep turning up from Dick's vaudeville days. Although Dick is innocent, Virginia allows Ted (Jerome Cowan), a persistent beau, to talk her into a divorce. Still hoping that Virginia will come to her senses, Dick decides to enlist the aid of Hortense (Iris Adrian), a friendly and cooperative waitress, either to make Virginia jealous enough to reconcile or to give her grounds for divorce. The ruse involves allowing Virginia to catch Dick in the hotel room with Hortense, who does her best to emulate a vamp. Comical complications develop when Hortense's boyfriend, Marvin (Lon Chaney), becomes jealous and protective, and when the hotel manager (Shemp Howard) becomes involved. As in all such films, Virginia and Dick eventually work out their differences, but not before the delivery of several strategically placed songs.

Lon gets laughs as a gauche cab driver who is taking prep-school classes to improve his demeanor. Delivering his lines in stilted charm-school style, he struggles to be a gentleman, even when preparing Shemp Howard for a beating.

Lon's second foray into musical comedy was *San Antonio Rose* (1941), in which he was reunited with the naturally comedic Shemp Howard.

Ex-cons Jigsaw Kennedy (Lon Chaney) and Benny the Bounce (Shemp Howard) confront roadhouse owner Mr. Willoughby (Richard Lane) with his past as a gangster. Willoughby promises the two a hefty profit if they will drive his more successful competition out of business. With a little strongarm talk from the ex-cons, the owner of the rival roadhouse agrees to leave town. When singers Gabby Trent (Eve Arden) and Hope Holiday (Jane Frazee) arrive for their gig, they find their place of employment deserted. When another musical troupe arrives, led by Con Conway (Robert Paige), the frustrated musicians decide to open the roadhouse under their own management. This revival of competition brings a return visit from Jigsaw and Benny. This time, however, they are roughed up by Gabby and sent on their way. Still hoping to sabotage the new roadhouse, Jigsaw and Benny are accepted as headwaiter and bartender. Using their new positions to maximize chaos at the roadhouse, Jigsaw and Benny set off a barrage of slapstick situations that backfire. In the end, both the new business venture and the new romances succeed.

As Marvin in "Too Many Blondes" (1941).

As Jigsaw Kennedy, Lon is a gruff, powerful, but comically inept gangster. Shemp Howard, brother of Moe Howard and a once and future member of the Three Stooges, is the recipient of Lon's Stooge-like slaps and heavy treatment. Lon is at his best when as headwaiter he tries to destroy the roadhouse's reputation. When two couples arrive, Lon greets them with a gruff, "Okay, Okay. Are you birds here for a good time, or are those your wives?" Lon leads the quartet to a table and roughly announces, "There you are. Park the body!" When one of the party observes that Lon must not be familiar with Emily Post, he snarls, "Maybe I am, and maybe I ain't. Women is all alike for me. I never remember their names!"

When an obviously important couple arrives for the evening, Lon leads them to a table and barks, "Squat here!" Later, when a customer complains that a steak is not rare enough, Lon returns to the table with a completely raw side of beef. Although his scenes with and without Shemp are funny, his performance sometimes appears slightly labored. While adequate at situation comedy, he would never have been a candidate to become one of the Three Stooges. According to Patsy Chaney, Lon never liked slapstick anyway.

Chaney's next Universal release was the excellent serial *Riders of Death*

Chaney and Shemp Howard cavort in "San Antonio Rose" (1941).

Valley (1941). Kirby (James Blaine) and Davis (Monte Blue) attempt to form a miner's association in order to control all of the gold of Death Valley. Their only fear is Jim Benton (Dick Foran) and his riders: Pancho (Leo Carrillo), Tombstone (Buck Jones), Borax Bill (Guinn "Big Boy" Williams), and Smokey (Noah Beery, Jr.), who attempt to protect miners and prospectors in the Valley. Kirby and Davis, who appear to be respectable businessmen, are also in collusion with the notorious outlaw Wolfe Reade (Charles Bickford), who robs stages for extra income. After the Riders expose the miner's association scheme for what it is, Benton discovers that he and Mary Morgan (Jeanne Kelly) are co-heirs to a lost Aztec mine that the villains want to secure for themselves. The key henchman of the wrongdoers is Butch (Lon Chaney), who does his best to kill the Riders and secure the mine for his bosses.

Riders of Death Valley is probably one of the best Western serials of the forties. The cast is strong and the action unrelenting. With Charles Bickford as the main heavy, Lon effectively underplays as the cocky Butch. In fact, he is almost likable in some scenes, undoubtedly prompting Universal to cast him as the leading man in the later Western serial *Overland Mail*.

Lon's next Universal effort saw him as part of another strong cast in *Badlands of Dakota*. Bob Holliday (Broderick Crawford), rough-hewn dance hall owner in the newly settled Deadwood, South Dakota, sends his tenderfoot brother Jim (Robert Stack) to St. Louis to fetch his girlfriend, Anne (Anne Gwynne). Jim and Anne fall in love and marry on their way back to Deadwood. Before Bob learns of his loss, he casts off his former love interest, Calamity Jane (Francis Farmer), who continues to carry an angry torch.

When Jim and Anne arrive in Deadwood as man and wife, Bob joins up with local troublemaker and outlaw Jack McCall (Lon Chaney). He also has Jim appointed sheriff in order to hasten his demise. Having earned the confidence of Wild Bill Hickock, Jim somewhat reluctantly accepts the job. Wild Bill is shot in the back by McCall while holding eights and aces in a poker game, and Jim forms a posse to track McCall down. Using an Indian attack as cover, McCall and Bob attempt a bank robbery but are gunned down in the process by Jim and Jane. Custer's cavalry soon arrives to turn back the Indians and return Deadwood to normal.

While Lon carries off the role of McCall with appropriate menace, his supporting performance is overshadowed by the fine efforts of Crawford and Farmer, who easily walk away with top acting honors. The partnership of Chaney and Crawford in the film represented the beginning of a real-life friendship between the two. As hunting, fishing, and drinking buddies, they would provide Universal with a few headaches along the way. Of course, Crawford was the original Lennie in Broadway's *Of Mice and Men*.

When asked years later how he would compare his own Lennie to Lon's, Crawford replied, "He made it completely different from mine, and it was a damn fine role." Elaborating on their friendship, he continued:

> We went on a lot of hunting and fishing trips together. We'd go deer hunting, and he was a good cook all the way around. He enjoyed that. Our first picture together was *Badlands of Dakota*... It was a good picture, made in ten days.[1]

North to the Klondike (1942), Lon's first film after *The Wolf Man*, was a reunion with Brod Crawford and Evelyn Ankers. (The film was actually shot before *The Wolf Man* but released later.) Johnny Thorn (Broderick Crawford), a young mining expert, and his friend Klondike (Andy Devine) arrive at the settlement of New Haven to prospect for Nate Carson (Lon Chaney). Among the New Haven settlers are Mary Sloan (Evelyn Ankers) and her brother Ben (Roy Harris). Unknown to Thorn or the settlers, Carson has discovered a mine and plans to send them all away. When Thorn refuses to leave, Carson sends his henchmen to burn the settlers' winter supplies. Carson soon resorts to murder in order to protect the mine and break the will of the settlers. When Thorn's pals, Waterlily (Willie Fung) and his son Wellington Wong (Keye Luke), discover the secret mine behind a waterfall, Thorn knows for sure that Carson is the terrorist. With the settlers behind him, Thorn engages Carson in a monumental fist fight and eventually forces Carson to confess. At that moment, Dr. Curtis (Lloyd Corrigan), arrives by steamer with new supplies and a law officer.

North to the Klondike was based on a William Castle story suggested by Jack London's "Gold Hunters of the North." Critics saw it as a second-rate rip-off of *The Spoilers* (1942). Universal publicity drew the comparison, claiming that the climactic fistfight in *Klondike* rivaled a similar fist fight between Randolph

Scott and John Wayne in The *Spoilers*. Universal even claimed that Crawford and Chaney were coached by boxing experts in preparation for their screen confrontation and that during the filming itself, no punches were pulled. Whatever the truth is, Crawford failed to pull at least one punch which found its mark and chipped one of Lon's front teeth. The fight scenes were the first ones shot, which allowed Lon to keep the chipped tooth for the remainder of the film. The "wounded" actor rationalized keeping the chipped tooth, saying that his character would appear even nastier and that his buddy Crawford needed all the help he could get to look like a hero.

Chaney, Crawford, and Ankers got together on the set to shoot a photo for a Pepsi commercial, but in reality there was little love lost between Ankers and her male co-stars. Things got off on the wrong foot when Ankers was given Crawford's and Chaney's dressing room which they had nearly destroyed during one of their famous brawls. The two actors thought that they had lost their dressing room because the studio was trying to court Ankers. Although Chaney and Ankers would make a number of films together, matters escalated when the offended Crawford greeted Ankers on the set with a hearty, "Hi-ya, kid!" while slugging her in the arm with a good-natured jab. The blow immediately cramped Ankers's arm, sending her into tears. The tears, in turn, sent mascara into her eyes, creating an irritation which lasted for two days. When Chaney laughed at Ankers's misfortune, she lumped him in with Crawford as a bully boy. Unfortunately, the hard feelings remained throughout the many films in which Ankers and Chaney co-starred.

Asked about the famous Crawford-Chaney brawls, Brod recalled, "We kidded a lot, and kicked each other with cowboy boots on. We got some exercise, but we never hit each other in the face or anything."[2] Crawford recalled a prank involving a life-size cardboard cutout of Chaney as the Wolf Man:

> We got it out of my garage, went over to his house and put it in front of his door. We rang the bell and shined a flashlight on the picture. This was around 2:00 in the morning. He opened the door and stepped out with his hair all messed up. He jumped back, yelled, and we frightened the hell out of him![3]

On the set of *North to the Klondike*, as was his custom, Lon continued to cook and serve up gourmet food to his fellow cast members. In fact, much has been made of Lon's obsession with food. Keye Luke told Blackie Seymour that Chaney hid the equivalent of submarine sandwiches around the set in anticipation of breaks in the filming.[4] In a 1943 news item, Lon said:

> When I got some money, I bought me hundreds of cans and some apparatus for using them. I've canned foods of all kinds. I've gone out in the ocean and caught tuna fish and canned them. I've shot game and canned it. It makes me feel better to see all that food, because a fellow can never tell how long his luck's going to run in the movies.[5]

According to reports, Lon had several freezer-lockers full of frozen food between Los Angeles and San Diego.

The next Lon Chaney release was the Western serial *Overland Mail* (1942). Anyone watching Lon in his second starring role in a Western serial must be impressed by the poise, confidence, and skill that he had developed since his first. When Jim Lane (Lon Chaney) is sent to investigate an endless series of attempts to close down the Overland Mail Company, he rounds up two of his sidekicks, Sierra Pete (Noah Beery, Jr.) and Buckskin Bill Cody (Bob Baker), to help. When Barbara Gilbert (Helen Parrish), the daughter of the owner of Overland Mail arrives by stage, Lane has an additional reason to save the company. In the course of the action, Lon battles co-opted Indians, whites dressed as Indians, and just plain villainous henchmen, before identifying and overcoming the head heavy, oily Hank Chadwick (Noah Beery, Sr.), who had hoped to acquire a million-dollar mail contract upon Overland's demise.

As was the case with many serials, *Overland Mail* suffers from repetition. Still, Chaney's strong performance is ample proof that he could carry the leading man role in Westerns. Ironically, Lon wore a white shirt as the villain in *Riders of Death Valley*. Here he wears a black shirt and pants as the rugged hero.

After completing *Ghost of Frankenstein*, Lon appeared in an eleven-minute Universal short subject devoted to the war effort. The purpose of *Keeping Fit* (1942) was to convince Americans that they must maintain their physical health and stamina in order to perform their best on the job, thereby aiding U.S. war efforts on the home front. Most of the actors in the short appeared to portray themselves. When Robert Stack passes out while working in a factory, co-worker Brod Crawford calls for help. Later the doctor (Frank Morgan) warns Stack that he must eat right and keep fit if he is to continue working as hard as he has been. At a factory assembly, a fitness spokesperson introduces Louise Allbritton, who gives advice on how to prepare nutritious meals. To illustrate, Irene Hervey acts out the recommendations for the benefit of husband Dick Foran. The fitness spokesperson then recommends sports for exercise. To illustrate the point, Lon Chaney invites hammock-potato Andy Devine to a game of horseshoes. After seeing Andy pitch, Lon remarks, "As a horseshoe pitcher, you might make a good bowler." When Andy reveals that he used to bowl a pretty good game, Lon invites him to join a bowling team.

Lon's next nonseries picture was *Eyes of the Underworld* (1943), his first and only Universal foray into gangster films. When a gang of car thieves robs the war effort of needed metal and rubber, police chief Bryant (Richard Dix) tells officer Kirby (Joseph Crehan) that arrests must be made. Kirby, who is actually part of the crime ring, brings in an accomplice, Ed Jason (Don Porter) of the "State Bureau," to "investigate" Bryant. Part of Porter's task is to become romantically involved with Chief Bryant's girlfriend, Betty (Wendy Barrie). The gangsters are aware, although city officials are not, that Bryant once served a prison sentence before starting life over as a law enforcement officer.

Merlin (Edward Pauley), the head of the crime ring, hires a mobster from another city to allow himself to be captured by Bryant. Merlin then threatens to blackmail Bryant unless the chief frees him. Bryant refuses, but Kirby arranges the escape. Doctored tapes made by Kirby then implicate Bryant. When the police chief is jailed, his loyal chauffeur, Benny (Lon Chaney), abducts Hub Gelsey (Gaylord Pendleton), Merlin's driver, and makes him reveal the whole plot. Benny arranges for Bryant's escape, and the two arrive at the gang's garage just in time to stop their escape. After a torrid gun battle, justice prevails.

Led by an impressive cast and fashioned on a strong screenplay, *Eyes of the Underworld* emerges as a taut crime story. Watching Chaney as the slightly dimwitted chauffeur should help anyone understand why directors often wanted him to reprise Lennie. He is so perfect in such characterizations that the urge was undoubtedly hard to resist. Dix, Barrie, and others dominate most of the film, but the final ten minutes are all Lon's as he goes on a one man, barehanded rampage against the gang.

A sneer as Jim Lane in "Overland Mail" (1942).

Evidently Lon's reputation for uncontrolled strength followed him to the set of *Eyes of the Underworld*. Actor Marc Lawrence, who gets roughed up by Chaney in the finale, insisted that he and Lon work out all the details in advance. When asked why, Lawrence answered, "Are you kidding? He hurts people."[6]

Lon soon found himself in another Universal short subject designed to help the war effort: *What We Are Fighting For* (1943). While making his rounds at night, Jim (Samuel S. Hinds), a civilian air raid warden, cautions Bill (Lon Chaney) that the burning lamp in his living room violates dim-out regulations. Although Jim reluctantly agrees to comply, he quickly begins carping about civilian sacrifices: "The war! I'm getting fed up with the whole thing. All ya' do is 'Give us this, give us that'—pay taxes. What's all the sacrifice for? What *are* we fighting for anyway?"

To answer Bill's question, Jim walks him to the home of Mrs. Baxter (Osa Massen), a German refugee. Baxter relates to Bill how in Germany a knock at the door brings fear, how information is censored by the state, and how the Nazi soldiers steal food from their own people, causing the starvation deaths of small children. When the now patriotic Bill accidentally discovers a hidden crucifix, he says to Mrs. Baxter: "You don't have to hide your religion. This is America." The ten-minute short ends with an excerpt from a speech by Franklin Roosevelt, a waving American flag, and an appeal for war bonds.

Universal, who had disappointed Lon in 1939 by refusing to cast him in the title role of their remake of *The Hunchback of Notre Dame*, let him down a second time by reneging on a promise made in 1941 to cast him in the title role of their remake of his father's *Phantom of the Opera* (1943). Claude Rains got the part instead.

Under contract and powerless to alter fate, Lon undertook his next assignment, that of a psychopathic heel in the Western *Frontier Badman* (1943). Steve (Robert Paige), Jim (Noah Beery, Jr.), and Slim (Andy Devine) conclude an historic cattle drive northward along the Chisholm Trail into Kansas. In Abilene, they become aware that a mysterious middleman's stranglehold on the cattle market is driving up prices. Unknown to the heroes, the middleman is Ballard (Thomas Gomez), the owner of the local saloon. With the help of Chinito (Leo Carrillo), Steve and company work to uncover the mystery man's identity while Ballard's chief henchman, Chango (Lon Chaney), guns down one potential witness after another. Steve and Jim do finally identify Ballard as the unscrupulous individual that he is and form the Cattleman's Exchange to put his scheme out of business. When Steve finds himself about to be lynched because of a Ballard set-up, his girlfriend, Claire (Diana Barrymore), warns Chris (Anne Gwynne), who is Jim's love interest, to get help. At Chris's behest, Chinito, Steve's pals, and a herd of cattle storm the town, precipitating a full-scale shootout. When Jim runs out of bullets, Ballard sends Chango forward to finish him off. Claire slides a pistol down the bar to Jim, who shoots Chango. Ballard fires a bullet into Claire's arm and is in turn dropped by Jim. In the nick of time, Jim again turns his gun upon the wounded, but still deadly, Chango, finally ending the psycho's life with a slug to the midsection. In the final scene, Jim and Chris are united with Steve and Claire on a journey back to Texas.

Chaney steals a number of scenes as the sadistic Chango. As the action in the bar goes on around him, he strums his guitar while incongruously whistling "Beautiful Dreamer." Occasionally, he puts down the guitar, picks up his hat, and strides outside. A shot rings out, after which the killer reenters the bar and resumes his nonchalant serenade. In one scene, Gomez is trying to figure out how the heroes identified him as the middleman. "How could they have...?", he wonders. "Could Marvin, or Rawhide...?" "Naah," Lon snarls. "Too dead."

Although Robert Paige was uncomfortable in this, his first Western, saddle veteran Chaney made matters worse by continually teasing the star about his big "Texas style" hat. Many in the cast were already friends, however, and they turn in the usual solid performances that make *Frontier Badman* an exciting Western.

Universal then gave Lon a brief guest appearance in *Crazy House* (1943). When Olson and Johnson take over the studio to make an epic film, all craziness breaks loose in this musical comedy which features many star guests, including Basil Rathbone, Universal's Sherlock Holmes.

After *Crazy House*, Lon starred in one of the greatest horror films of the forties, *Son of Dracula* (1943). Eric Taylor wrote the screenplay based upon Curt Siodmak's outstanding story:

At their plantation, Dark Oaks, Colonel Caldwell (George Irving) and his daughter Katherine (Louise Allbritton) are preparing to entertain Count Alucard (Lon Chaney), whom Katharine had met in Budapest.

Katherine's fiancé, Frank Stanley (Robert Paige), suspicious of Alucard, discovers that the name is an alias, and her friend Doctor Brewster (Frank Craven) suspects that Alucard, whose name is "Dracula" spelled backward, is a vampire.

When Alucard arrives at Dark Oaks, he turns into a bat and drains the blood of Colonel Caldwell. Katherine, however, infatuated with the occult prospect of eternal life, marries Alucard.

Frank, jealous of Alucard, goes to Dark Oaks to confront the Count, fires a pistol at him, and watches the bullets pass through him without harm, killing Katherine. Later Dr. Brewster goes to Dark Oaks and finds Katherine alive and presumably well; but soon after, her body is found in the family vault at Dark Oaks.

Doctor Brewster calls in Professor Lazlo (J. Edward Bromberg) for consultation. Lazlo hypothesizes that Alucard is a vampire, a descendent of Dracula, or maybe even Dracula himself. Suddenly Alucard materializes from a mist that seeps under the door and warns Brewster and Lazlo to cease and desist.

Meanwhile, Katherine has also become a vampire. She reassumes human form and persuades Frank, who is in jail for her murder, to destroy Alucard and then join her in immortality. Frank escapes from jail, and burns Alucard's coffin. Unable to return to his resting place, the vampire is destroyed by the sunlight of the dawning day. Frank then destroys his beloved Katharine by setting fire to the house where she rests in her coffin.

Despite opinions to the contrary by Brunas, Brunas, and Weaver (and just about everyone else), the cast of *Son of Dracula* is nearly perfect. Probably the best performance in the picture is that of Louise Allbritton, whom many consider grossly miscast. Best known for her light comedies, Allbritton considered herself above the horror genre. Although she reportedly had difficulty with the part and cried on the set, her final product is exquisite. When she waxes on about metaphysical matters such as telepathy, she does not chew the scenery. Instead, the slight gleam in her eye complements the velvety distance in her voice. When mundane matters inconvenience her, the touch of impatience that crosses her lips and dulls her eyes enhances her performance as the otherworldly Katherine. She is sensual, both as the vampire and otherwise.

Also best-known in light comedy, Robert Paige is a rather unconventional, but wholly believable, leading man, especially after the mental shock accorded him by Allbritton's "death." Bromberg is much stronger here than in his and Chaney's *Pillow of Death*, and Frank Craven provides a homey, understated performance.

Praise for Chaney as Dracula has been both reluctant and long in coming. Critics have usually dismissed Chaney as physically miscast and simply not actor enough for the role, but in recent years he seems to be receiving his due. As Brunas, Brunas, and Weaver write:

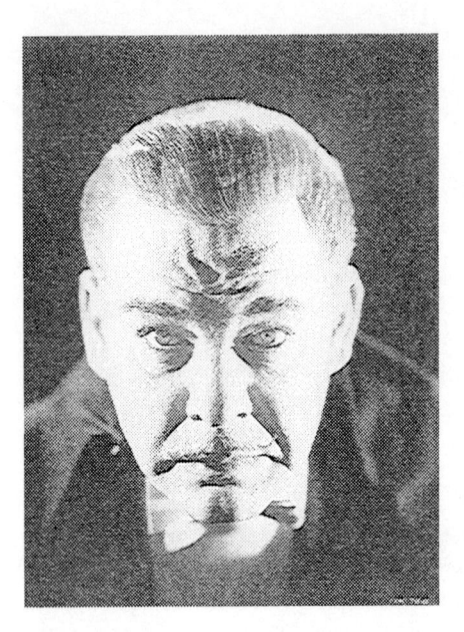

Chaney as Count Alucard in "Son of Dracula" (1943).

> The powerfully built but somewhat chubby Chaney cuts a more imposing physical presence than Lugosi [who also wanted the part]. He is particularly effective in his confrontation scene with Robert Paige. Subduing Paige in a vise-like grip and tossing him effortlessly aside, Chaney foreshadows Christopher Lee's superenergized interpretation of the character. Chaney's piercing, death-like stare as Paige bolts from the room is haunting.[7]

The most perceptive critic of Chaney's Dracula, however, is Michael Mallory, who correctly praises Chaney's Alucard as one of the actor's very best performances and provides convincing evidence for his contention:

> Rather than lurch or hulk, Chaney creeps very effectively, particularly in Alucard/Dracula's first scenes, and his voice, normally thick and dull, here takes on shades never heard before... John Carradine is usually credited with being the first actor to imbue the role of Dracula...with a sense of the erotic, but that honor should go to Chaney.... In a superb scene in which Dracula welcomes his bride home, the expression on Chaney's face as he slowly draws her into an embrace clearly indicates that *this* vampire has more on his mind than dinner!... Chaney's best moments in the picture come in the scene in which he discovers Dr. Brewster...sneaking around in the basement. We see a Dracula who is perfectly poised and in control, and condescendingly polite. But just under the surface seethes an ocean of menace, which surfaces slightly as the vampire orders Brewster to leave the house and never come back.[8]

Robert Siodmak, Curt's brother, directs the film with finesse, but Chaney's fine performance may have been attributable to his own high estimation of the character. In an interview, he compared Dracula to some of his other monsters such as the Frankenstein Monster, the Wolf Man, and the Mummy: "Dracula is certainly more potentially terrifying than those roles which required gruesome makeup. I feel there is no doubt that the mind's own sinister subtleties can be far more frightening than a semihuman beast."[9]

Unfortunately, though Lon demonstrates in *Son of Dracula* that he could play a monster different in temperament from Larry Talbot, no sequels were made with Chaney as the Count. Also unfortunate is the fact that *Son of Dracula* was not completed without another of Lon's "antics." At one point, undoubtedly drunk, he sneaked up behind Robert Siodmak and smashed a vase over the director's head. Supposedly, Chaney disliked "foreigners," a moniker he probably attached to colleagues of German descent such as Siodmak and Martin Kosleck. While Lon was evidently in a nasty mood at times during production, the humor often associated with him was present as well. In the film, of course, Dracula sometimes travels as a wisp of smoke. According to publicity, Lon at one point handed his wife Patsy a cigarette and a match, saying "Light up, dear, and see me in character."[10]

Why Universal stuck Chaney in the now-dated comedy *Ghost Catchers* (1944) is a mystery. He was at that time their biggest horror attraction as the Frankenstein Monster, the Wolf Man, the Mummy, and, most recently, Dracula. He had just appeared in the initial two films of the Inner Sanctum series, both of which were good. So why did Universal force him briefly into a bear costume to menace a comedy team? Perhaps it was a mild punishment for his embarrassing on-the-set hijinks in other pictures. Perhaps they thought the Chaney name would help draw members of their vast horror audience who might have been reluctant to shell out money for a musical comedy. My guess is that they simply never appreciated Lon as a talented actor and therefore never went out of their way to treat him like one. His frequent failure to carry himself with the appropriate dignity of a talented actor and his personal habits and erratic behavior that made his future at Universal a question mark also were probably part of the equation.

Lon apparently enjoyed making the picture. After all, he was again mucking around with his old pal Andy Devine, who trots about as a fellow gangster in a horse suit. Still, as a publicity interview shows, Lon was a bit testy and concerned over Universal's move:

> I had more fun than I've ever had in any picture I've ever worked in, but what it's going to do to my career is something else. We monsters should get together and form a union. The public comes to see us in a fantastic ghost, or mummy, or zombie, or Frankenstein, or Wolf Man picture, and we expect the audience to take us seriously. Thus far, they have. But now what can we expect when we let ourselves be cast in roles where the horror pictures are spoofed?[11]

Lon would get an answer to his question in 1948 when Universal would enlist his aid in the greatest horror picture spoof of all time, *Abbott and Costello Meet Frankenstein*.

Andy Devine as "the horse" and Lon as "the bear" in "Ghost Catchers" (1944).

Lon received even less screen time in his next picture, *Follow the Boys* (1944). Here he is on camera for a few moments playing himself as George Raft tries to organize USO shows and bond drive tours with Universal's contract players.

Chaney's next outing was *Cobra Woman* (1944), an offbeat costume fantasy starring Maria Montez and Jon Hall. Romu (Jon Hall) is preparing to marry Tollea (Maria Montez) when the latter is kidnapped and taken to Cobra Island by Hava (Lon Chaney), the tongueless guard of the Queen (Mary Nash). The Queen seeks Tollea's help in deposing Tollea's wicked twin sister, Nadja (Maria Montez), high priestess of the Cobra Cult, who brutally rules the island. With his young friend Sabu, Romu sails to Cobra Island to reclaim Tollea. Once there, he mistakes Nadja for Tollea. When the high priestess responds to his advances, Romu incurs the wrath of Nadja's second in command, Martok (Edgar Barrier). After several close escapes by Romu and his accomplices, Nadja falls from a palace window to her death and is impersonated by Tollea at the Cobra ceremony where Romu is to be sacrificed. Martok suspects the truth and orders Tollea to receive the bite of the cobra, as her sister was able to do without harm. Just as the cobra is about to bite Tollea, Hava instigates a riot that ends with the death of Martok and the return of island governance to the beneficent queen.

Critics have not been kind to *Cobra Woman* over the years. Pauline Kael, referring to its parodistic technicolor sets, called the film a "heavenly absurdity" and labeled the cast "impeccably lifeless."[12] The film is undoubtedly nothing more than juvenile escapism, but it is nevertheless entertaining on that level. It is humorous today to spot the veiled allusions to Nazi Germany in the wartime film. For example, the Queen complains that Nadja now rules because of her success in turning the island's inhabitants into religious fanatics. At the ceremony itself, the frenzied natives chant "King Cobra" in a cadence identical to "Heil Hitler," while raising their arms to resemble a striking cobra—and a Nazi salute.

Although his masquerade as a blind beggar in the opening scenes resembles some of his father's characterizations, Chaney's main purpose in the film is to present an imposing physical presence. Lon's big scenes consist of killing a guard with a full nelson and dispatching Edgar Barrier on a bed of spikes intended for Jon Hall. If Lon regretted the way the studio used him in *Cobra Woman*, the film brought sadness to him in another way as well. During production, Moose, his beloved German Shepherd, was hit by a car and killed.

After appearing for the last time as Universal's Kharis and after riding the sinking ship of the Inner Sanctum series with *Dead Man's Eyes*, Lon returned to comedy in *Here Come the Co-Eds* (1945), his first film with Abbott and Costello. On the lam from the law, Slats and Oliver (Bud Abbott and Lou Costello) go under cover as assistant caretakers at a woman's college. The head caretaker is "Strangler" Johnson (Lon Chaney), a former professional wrestler.

Chaney's considerable screen time is mostly spent in playing straight man to Lou Costello. In one scene, when Lou swallows a pair of dice, Lon and Bud shake him up physically and place him in front of a fluoroscope for a craps game. In another scene, Lou is hiding Peggy Moran under one of two twin beds when Lon arrives and decides to spend the night. Lou launches into a series of charades to distract Lon so Peggy can escape, even trying at one point to dance with the ex-professional wrestler. In escaping, Peggy knocks Lon's shoes

Lon with Abbott and Costello in "Here Come the Co-Eds" (1945).

off the window sill where he had left them. When Lon expresses suspicion, the shoes sail back into the room, knocking out both Lou and Lon, who sink to the floor together in mutual slumber. Later, Lou enters into what he thinks is a "fixed" wrestling match in order to raise money for the college. Unknown to him, however, the real Masked Marvel becomes ill and lets Strangler Johnson take his place. Already knowing a thing or two about wrestling, Lon donned the mask and did most of his own moves in the ring.

Chaney's comedy roles for Universal proved one thing: he did not possess any natural comedic gifts. He was not a naturally funny person, as were Shemp Howard and Lou Costello. He could play an adequate straight man, sometimes even a very good one, but Lon Chaney was no comedian. Any comedy generated had to come from the situation itself, not from the actor.

Before *House of Dracula* and *Pillow of Death* ended Lon Chaney's contract career at Universal, he played Grat Dalton in *The Daltons Ride Again* (1945), a run-of-the-mill "B" feature with an outstanding cast and the usual scenario:

Following the killing of his notorious brothers, Bob (Kent Taylor), Grat (Lon Chaney), and Ben (Noah Beery, Jr.), Emmett Dalton (Alan Curtis) goes on trial for his life in Coffeyville, Kansas. To please his sweetheart Mary (Martha O'Driscoll), Emmett agrees to tell the story of the tragic adventure which had started after a series of bank holdups and robberies.

In Emmett's recollections, he and his brothers, in flight from the law, rest

Patsy and Lon with Howard, the little boy they unsuccessfully tried to adopt in 1945.

their horses at Skeleton Creek, where they encounter McKenna (Thomas Gomez) and Wilkins (Walter Sande), the land crooks who had been murdering Kansas ranchers and then crushing the resistance of the victim's widows. The Daltons, after witnessing the cold-blooded killing of a friend at Skeleton Creek, agree to remain and protect his widow, Mrs. Walters (Virginia Brissac).

Meanwhile, Emmett falls in love with Mary, daughter of the militant newspaper publisher, Bohannon (John Litel). Now fighting for justice, the Daltons turn against McKenna and Wilkins.

The land renegades are defeated, but the Daltons are ambushed and, except for Emmett, wiped out. In the Coffeyville courtroom, Emmett is sentenced to life imprisonment, but Mary promises to wait for him, confident that someday he will be free again as a reward for his good conduct.

This film was a remake of Universal's *When the Daltons Rode* (1940), with Brian Donlevy as Grat. As is often the case, the earlier film was a cut above the remake. Chaney dispenses with the suave Donlevy characterization and sports the unshaven appearance of his brothers. In the remake, Chaney has little to do, but what he does do, he does well. In fact, he steals many of the scenes. Still, Universal was rapidly losing interest in him, and Lon would soon be a free-lancer without a contract.

During 1945 another disappointment occurred in Lon's life. It had become obvious to Lon and Patsy that they were going to have no children of their own. Lon's two sons from his previous marriage were nearly grown, and the financially secure actor wanted to adopt a child. As he explained at the time, "I only wish I had enough money to give countless deserving orphans a good home; the lousiest thing in this world is to grow up without love."

At that time, Lon became very fond of a little boy named Howard, whose parents worked on the Chaney ranch. The little boy was already part of a large family. When it came time for Howard's parents to move on to their next job, Lon suggested that they leave the preschooler with the Chaneys, during which time Lon would pay for the child's schooling, clothing, etc. If at the end of a year, the boy wanted to stay with the Chaneys, they would legally adopt him. If not, the Chaneys would send the boy back to his family. Howard's family apparently agreed, at which point the boy took up residence with Lon and Patsy. All went well until Howard's mother had second thoughts and made the unhappy Chaneys part with the child.

This adoption arrangement was rather odd in several respects. First of all, Lon wanted to adopt an unloved orphan, but Howard was not an orphan. Of course, Lon may have felt that Howard, as one of the youngest in a large family of migrant workers, was not receiving the attention and love he deserved. Still, the chances of such a trial adoption satisfying everyone would have been remote at best.

What is interesting, however, is the way that Lon describes the plight of an orphan. It is almost as if he has personally experienced what it is like to "grow up without love" and is determined to rescue other children from that same fate if he can. As an adult, Lon always expressed love and admiration for his father, but I wonder how confident he really was of his father's love. In interviews he speaks about how he was put out to live, to make his own way. Additionally, he grew up believing that his mother was dead, and though he was reunited with her and took care of her until she died, he never speaks of her in interviews. Insecurity of various kinds was Chaney's constant companion during his formative years and beyond, a fact which I believe shaped his personality and influenced, among other things, his desire to adopt.

Though Lon was apparently gentle with children, he was not always that way with women. According to Elena Verdugo, a story once circulated at Universal that Lon had sometimes physically abused his wife Patsy. "As the story goes," Verdugo said, "Patsy secretly took karate lessons. The next time Lon hit her, Patsy knocked him on his butt. After that he never laid a hand on her again. Of course, the story might not have been true."[13]

According to Robert Quarry, Lon definitely had a proclivity for violence against women. "When we were both at Universal," Quarry said, "Lon was having an affair with a young woman who booked films into the screening room. Sometimes after being with him, she would come to work wearing dark glasses to hide black eyes, or she would have bruises. One day I asked her, 'Why do you put up with it?' She said, 'He's very sweet when he's sober.' Of course, that wasn't very often."[14]

Chapter 9

Abbott and Costello Meet Frankenstein and Supporting Roles

With no studio contract, Lon cooled his heels until a call came from Paramount. The project was *My Favorite Brunette* (1947), a Bob Hope and Dorothy Lamour vehicle. The scenario provided Hope with one of his best pictures:

Ronnie Jackson (Bob Hope), a former private eye, sits in a San Quentin death cell, awaiting execution. As the time of the execution draws near, he tells his story to a newspaper reporter. It seems that he was not always the tough, hardboiled detective he appears to be.

In this account, although he is a baby photographer in San Francisco, Jackson has always wanted to be a detective like movie gumshoes Dick Powell, Humphrey Bogart, and Alan Ladd. One day the private detective next door asks Jackson to watch his office for a while.

A beautiful and mysterious woman, Carlotta Montay (Dorothy Lamour), mistakes Jackson for a real detective and hires him to find her uncle, the wealthy and invalid Baron Montay (Frank Puglia), who was kidnapped shortly after his arrival in the United States on a highly secret mission.

Jackson decides to play the role of detective and take the job. Carlotta provides him with a mysterious map which she says shows the location of a very valuable uranium mine. A sinister gang of foreign agents headed by Major Simon Montague (Charles Dingle) and including Karl (Peter Lorre), Dr. Landor (John Hoyt), and Willie (Lon Chaney, Jr.) want the map.

When the gang captures Jackson and subjects him to beatings and threats, he regrets having impersonated a detective and longs to return to his serene former life. Complicating matters, the gang also captures Carlotta. She and Jackson escape and precipitate a chase that ends in Washington, D. C., where the

Peter Lorre, Bob Hope, and Chaney in "My Favorite Brunette" (1947).

fleeing duo are helped by James Collins (Reginald Denny), a geologist friend of Baron Montay. Collins tells Jackson and Carlotta that they must notify the FBI immediately of the Baron's kidnapping.

When the gang finally catches up with Jackson and Carlotta, Collins is murdered by Karl, and Jackson is arrested convicted, and sentenced to death for the murder. Carlotta rescues him by obtaining evidence of Karl's guilt, along with enough evidence to convict the gang. Jackson gets a last minute reprieve, abandons his plans for being a private eye, and returns to the baby photography business.

Lon is described in publicity material as playing "a big, dumb mug who harasses Hope throughout the picture, a reportedly hilarious lampooning of the murder mysteries and chiller-thriller stories currently popular."[1] In other words, Lon is back in Lennie mode. And indeed he is. All the mannerisms, all the halting speech patterns, and all the confused frowns are present. Still, with his hair combed forward in a semi–Moe Howard cut, Lon's Willie has some legitimately funny scenes with Hope, such as the one in which he cracks walnuts with his eye lids. He also works well with Lorre, who is coldly amazed at his stupidity.

Lon could be proud that he was in a major comedy (one of director Elliott Nugent's favorite films) with a big budget and a top-notch cast, not to mention cameos by Alan Ladd and Bing Crosby. Still, he was basically lampooning his most serious work, a turn of events that had to hurt. The pain did not dissipate with his next performance, a 9½-minute short called *Laguna U.S.A.* (1947), in which he again does Lennie.

Lon's next film found him back in the dusty streets of the West. In *Albuquerque* (1948), he plays Merkil, a crooked sheriff, in a film that focuses upon the rebellion of a young man against his overly strict uncle. It was another good character actor role, and that seemed to be the direction in which Chaney's career was heading.

Lon's next film had to have been bittersweet. In a remake of *Sixteen Fathoms Deep* (1948), he played Dimitri, a middle-aged villain in the same scenario that had in 1934 seen him as the young virile hero (see Chapter 2). Although updated to post–World War II, the remake does not improve on the original. Lloyd Bridges provides both a running narrative and a performance prophetic of his future Mike Nelson characterization on television's "Sea Hunt," but he fails to infuse the role with the warmth and youthful optimism Chaney delivered in 1934. Arthur Lake, of "Blondie" fame, has a few good scenes as the comical, seafaring cook. Chaney is the soft-spoken, yet ruthless, heavy, showing early in the film that he is a conniving shyster.

The "startling Ansco color" doesn't enhance matters. Nor does the screenplay, which limps along at a mighty slow pace for an adventure film reputedly replete with "spine chilling thrills in the monster-ridden world beneath the sea." "Dull" is truly the most appropriate adjective.

In the period following his release from Universal, Lon also returned to the live theatre in the popular comedy *Born Yesterday*. Ironically, he was in a starring role essayed first by Broderick Crawford. In the play, Chaney assumes the role of Harry, a tough guy who begins life as a newspaper boy while collecting and stealing enough junk to finally buy senators in Washington. On his way to the top, the fast talking, racketeer junk dealer also picks up a blonde ex–chorus girl (Jean Parker), whom he treats as part of his collection. To increase his fortune, Harry opens offices in a magnificent hotel suite in Washington, D. C., and, with the help of his bought senators, he begins to take over all of the postwar scrap iron in the world. Because he is now moving in sophisticated circles, he decides to add some polish and social skill to both himself and his chorus cutie. But when he makes the mistake of hiring a liberal newshawk to remake Parker, his acculturated "alley cat" turns on him.

Both Chaney and Parker received good reviews for their work in the fast-paced comedy. Unfortunately for Lon, when *Born Yesterday* was adapted for the big screen in 1950, Brod Crawford reclaimed his starring role. Judy Holliday, who starred with Crawford during the play's original Broadway run, also returned for the film.

When *Born Yesterday* finished its run, Lon starred in a revival of *Of Mice and Men* on a Laguna stage. Just as Bela Lugosi could not escape Dracula, Lon could not escape Lennie. Still, film offers simply were not pouring in.

Unfortunately, Lon's next movie assignment did little to relieve his frustration. *The Counterfeiters* (1948) is an action tale in which a Scotland Yard cop (John Sutton) goes underground to capture a counterfeiting ring. Hugh Beaumont of later "Leave It to Beaver" television fame plays the lead heavy, and Lon, as Louie Struber, is reduced to delivering his third Lennie imitation in five films. Responding to Hollywood's proclivity for such typecasting, Lon later complained: "For three or four years, I couldn't get a job as anything but Lennie. It still haunts me. I get a call to play a sort of a dumb guy, and the director tells me not to play Lennie. But he's never happy until I play the part like Lennie, and he doesn't know why he likes it."[2]

In 1948, newly merged Universal-International Pictures found itself in a dire financial predicament. With bankruptcy staring him in the face, production chief William Goetz needed a hit, and he needed it fast. Abbott and Costello, Universal's top comedy team, were no longer at their peak of popularity, and rumor had it that their release might be near. Of course, the Universal monsters had run out of gas several years ago, and Goetz thought that they had given the studio a bad name anyway. Then producer Robert Arthur concocted the idea of a horror reunion which could include the Frankenstein Monster, Dracula, the Wolf Man, Kharis, Count Alucard, and the Invisible Man. Menaced by this well-worn crew would be Abbott and Costello. A script was written, but Costello promptly turned it down. Interest was rekindled, however, when producer Arthur offered the actor, who was in debt, a $50,000 advance on his percentage.

The final scenario of *Abbott and Costello Meet Frankenstein* (1948), though not including Kharis and Alucard, delivered all the other creatures:

Working their way to Florida as railroad baggage clerks, Chick Young (Bud Abbott) and Wilbur Brown (Lou Costello) deliver to McDougal's House of Horrors two crates containing the remains of Dracula (Bela Lugosi) and Frankenstein's monster (Glenn Strange). During the delivery, Dracula rises from his coffin and leads the Frankenstein Monster away. Wilbur witnesses the disappearance of the "corpses," but is unable to convince a doubting Chick of what he saw.

Joan Raymond (Jane Randolph), an insurance agent, pretends to fall in love with Wilbur in order to find out what happened to McDougal's exhibits. When Wilbur is convinced that no one is going to believe his story, a phone call arrives from London. On the line is Lawrence Talbot (Lon Chaney), who confides that he becomes the Wolf Man during cycles of the full moon. He explains that he has been following Count Dracula in order to prevent the vampire from transferring a new brain into the Frankenstein Monster. Chick thinks Talbot is slightly insane, but Wilbur has seen enough to encourage their joining forces.

At a masquerade ball, Wilbur is kidnapped by Dracula and a seductive woman named Sandra (Lenore Aubert), who happens to be Dracula's chief aide. The pair take Wilbur to a nearby island, where they prepare to place his harmless brain into the cranium of the Frankenstein Monster.

Chick and Talbot (the latter has arrived in America from London) realize Wilbur is in danger and go to the castle to rescue him. As he tries to free Wilbur from a gurney, Talbot is turned by the full moon into the Wolf Man. The Wolf Man chases Dracula off a balcony overlooking the sea, plunging after him. Meanwhile, Chick and Wilbur are leaving quietly when the Frankenstein Monster, powered by electric plasma, comes to life and stalks after them. They clamber into a rowboat and head for deep water as the Monster crashes through a burning pier to his destruction. Chick and Wilbur heave a sigh of relief, only to discover that their boat is being shared by a third party–the Invisible Man.

The film was a financial and critical success, easily emerging as the best horror-comedy ever made. The mixture works well, as the horror is played straight. Most Lugosiphiles rate Bela's performance as one of his best. Abbott and Costello provide one of their top outings, a move that reinvigorated their career, which quickly sank again as they kept meeting more monsters with markedly inferior results. Glenn Strange has more to do here than in his two previous Frankenstein films combined, which is the major factor why this Frankenstein Monster performance is his best. Lenore Aubert, Jane Randolph, and Frank Ferguson all contribute positively to this once-in-a-lifetime gem. As for Lon, he delivers another impeccable Lawrence Talbot interpretation, playing a perfect straight man to Lou Costello.

The studio resurrected the old publicity yarn about how the monsters in makeup were barred from the studio commissary during mealtimes because of their gruesome appearance. Lon played along with the gag and told a yarn about what happened when the three horror men walked into a restaurant instead: "We looked around and saw women turn green, full forks descend from mouths and waitresses practically spill their trays of food. At first it made us feel self-conscious, but then it became a joke, and we'd do it just to see the reaction."[3]

Reliable reports indicate that Abbott and Costello initiated a great deal of horseplay during production, especially pie fights, some of which enjoyed Lon's participation. On the negative side, however, the two comedians created a number of problems by going home and refusing to report for work for days at a time.

In retrospect, it appears that Lon Chaney was one of the most popular men on the set. When Glenn Strange broke his foot near the end of the film, Lon volunteered to don the Frankenstein Monster garb and play the scene in which the Monster tosses a stunt girl doubling for Aubert through the window. Lon's generosity saved the studio three days of lost shooting.

Director Charles Barton also remembered Lon fondly, but commented regretfully upon the actor's dark side:

He was a hell of a guy. We got along great.... He knew every take that he made. He really knew the character, and he didn't squawk about makeup. He was excellent.... Chaney was unpredictable. He could really hit the bottle sometimes. He was a Frankenstein when he was on the bottle.... But he wasn't really a bad boy.[4]

In the same interview, Barton also claimed that Lon engaged in a bit of ad-libbing with Costello in their hotel room scene.

Although so much wild fun surrounded the making of *Abbott and Costello Meet Frankenstein,* Lon almost died before the film was released. On the evening of April 22, 1948, following a serious argument with Patsy, Lon took 40 sleeping pills and retreated into his truck to die. His son Ron discovered the unconscious actor, who was rushed to Van Nuys Receiving Hospital in Burbank. Upon admittance, he was listed in critical condition, but in time he rallied and reunited with his distraught wife.

The Chaney family has never divulged the nature of the domestic argument that precipitated Lon's suicide attempt. According to Lon's grandson, Ron, the actor attempted suicide only on that one occasion, and this suggests that the argument came at a time when Lon's spirits were already quite low.

I believe that the years immediately following his release from Universal marked a turning point of sorts in Chaney's life and that the suicide attempt occurred while the actor was in the depths of a depression. Throughout his life Lon was a frequent victim of depression, and the one that descended upon him in 1947 and 1948 must have been quite severe. He had been the top horror actor at Universal Studios for most of a decade. He had been a star, a leading man. Before that he had immortalized himself as Lennie in *Of Mice and Men.* Yet he had never received the recognition or the mainstream parts he thought he had earned. His lack of a contract must have diminished his self-esteem considerably and reminded him of his years of struggle as a free-lance actor before 1940. Now, when studios did call, they usually wanted him to do yet another variation on Lennie. When Universal called, Lon must have considered the excellent *Abbott and Costello Meet Frankenstein* a silver bullet aimed straight at the heart of the character he considered his "baby."

Although Lon recovered from his suicide attempt, I think some part of him died that night—the part that still held out hope that he could establish himself as an important actor. By that time, he must have accepted his alcoholism. He also must have realized that he was to blame, at least in part, for his career's decline. As he himself was saying, "I am not an artist; I am a useful actor."[5] His father no longer stood before him as a receding horizon he simply could not reach. A Lon Chaney whose dreams had died left that hospital in 1948. He was a different man, less self-assuming. Because of his fears, he had sometimes acted in the past as though he hadn't really cared, but that was an act, perhaps one of his best performances ever. Now pain had really taught him no longer to care, at least not as he had before.

Following his final big screen performance as Larry Talbot, Allied Artists called him to appear in the light comedy *There's a Girl in My Heart* (1948), a Gay Nineties music hall romp which stars Elyse Knox, Lon's female interest from *The Mummy's Tomb*. This mediocre film chronicles the attempt of a slick ward-heeler (Lee Bowman) to acquire some New York City tenements for the purpose of building a sports arena. Lon appears as Bowman's dumb accomplice in yet another example of Lennie typecasting. Afterward, he went to work for Paramount in *Captain China* (1949), a film in which a strong cast is ultimately defeated by a listless scenario:

Charles S. Chinnough, known as Captain China (John Payne), sets sail drunk and heartsick over his fiancé's death. He passes out in his cabin only to find later that he is locked in. Upon breaking down the door, he finds his ship deserted and foundering during a storm. A passing steamer picks him up, adrift and badly injured. Ashore, China recovers and makes his way to Manila, where he learns he has been relieved of his command. That decision was due largely to false testimony provided by his former crew members, Brendensen (Jeffrey Lynn), Lynch (Lon Chaney), and Geech (John Qualen), who lied in saying that China ran his ship on the rocks.

When China learns that Brendensen has been given a captaincy, China books passage on his boat. Other passengers include Kim Mitchell (Gail Russell), traveling to meet her fiancé; a Dutch planter (Edgar Bergen) and his wife; a writer of mystery stories (Ellen Corby); crew members Lynch and Geech.

Confronted by China, Brendensen admits he was responsible for changing the course of China's ship but denies locking the captain in his quarters. China then realizes Lynch and Geech are the guilty ones.

A bloody fistfight ensues when Lynch makes a crack about a washed-up captain. Brendensen halts the altercation by pointing a gun at the combatants. Kim, who has watched the fight, is attracted by China's manly qualities, and they soon become intimate.

Keegan, a member of Brendensen's crew, warns Brendensen of an approaching typhoon and suggests they try to skirt it. The stubborn and incompetent Brendensen refuses to heed his advice. Later, as the typhoon gains force and threatens to capsize the ship, he is unable to manage the craft and is forced to call upon China for help.

During the storm, Lynch attempts to kill China, but he himself is crushed to death in the hold by a heavy packing crate loosened by the storm. China steers Brendensen's ship safely through the typhoon, and the grateful captain promises to clear him so that he will regain his command.

The relieved passengers are happy when they arrive safely in port. Kim's hometown fiancé is waiting for her at the dock. She starts down the gangplank to meet him but returns to Captain China when she realizes that it is really him that she loves.

Chaney has a meaty character part in *Captain China*, and he brings it off well. A large man, he is one of the few on board able physically to intimidate

Supporting Roles • 105

Chaney strikes a pose as John Colton in "There's a Girl in My Heart" (1949).

John Payne. In fact, Chaney's Lynch is the first in a long string of character roles in which Lon would menace the leading man. Paramount publicity especially played up two elements of the film, the typhoon and the fistfight between Chaney and Payne. The Chaney-Payne battle is one of the film's high points, but it doesn't rise above Lon's confrontation with Crawford in *North to the Klondike*. Publicity probably also stretched the truth in claiming that the prop boat's movements during the typhoon scenes were so real that Lon and the other cast members became ill, necessitating the use of sea-sick pills when shooting recommenced.

To coincide with the release of the film, National Comics Publications issued a comic book tie-in for *Captain China* under the title of *Feature Films*, No. 1. The March-April 1950 publication marked Chaney's first appearance in comic books. Introducing Lon as "Red Lynch, the most murderous menace who ever sailed the seven seas,"[6] the comic book highlights the fistfight, but has Lon washed off the ship by a wave rather than being crushed by a crate as in the film. At the end of the comic book is a feature titled "Meet the Stars" in which Lon is described as a screen "tough guy" who is "in private life...a swell fellow and one of the most popular Joes in Hollywood."[7]

Sometime between 1947 and 1949 (sources vary), a strange act of casting saw Lon Chaney star as Chester A. Riley in a television pilot of "The Life of Riley." The role had been made famous on radio in1943 by William Bendix, but when it came time to adapt Riley to the small screen, Bendix was busy with movie commitments. Lon landed the role, along with Rosemary DeCamp (as Peg) and Lanny Rees (as Junior). In the pilot episode, Riley finds $5 missing from the cookie jar and punishes Junior. Later Riley has to apologize when he discovers that he has unknowingly had the missing money all along.

Lon plays the stubborn, oafish, overreactive aircraft plant worker straight, as the situation comedy demands, adding dashes of Lennie throughout. Unfortunately, Lon was not naturally funny, a conclusion that should have been apparent to anyone watching his Universal comedies. He could deliver the laughs when playing straight man to Shemp Howard or Lou Costello, but he could not do so as the comedic center of attention. This fact must have soon become apparent to those in charge, because they quickly replaced Lon with the genuinely funny Jackie Gleason. While Lon's pilot was never shown on television, both Jackie Gleason (1949–1953) and William Bendix (1953–1958) went on to immortalize Chester A. Riley in American television history.

Having missed out on television sitcom stardom, Lon returned to big screen mediocrity in United Artists' *Once a Thief* (1950), a trifling film in which shoplifter June Havoc becomes romantically embroiled with Cesar Romero. Then he appeared in the tedious MGM drama *Inside Straight* (1951):

As a boy, Rip MacCool (Claude Jarmin, Jr.) sees his parents die of cholera on a trek from Kansas to Virginia City, leaving him with nothing except what he believes to be worthless shares of the Mona Lisa Mining Company stock. Aided by the kindly miner Shocker (Lon Chaney), he buries his parents himself and becomes fanatically obsessed at all costs to become rich and powerful.

In the year 1860 the now adult Rip MacCool (David Brian) arrives in San Francisco to enjoy the money and power he has accumulated. Shocker is still with him as his servant and bodyguard, and he makes another friend in Johnny Sanderson (Barry Sullivan), an idealistic ex-pug who wants to run a newspaper exposing the evils of the greedy speculators of the era. In the purchase of a San Francisco hotel, his first unscrupulous deal, Rip makes a bitter enemy of Ada Stritch (Mercedes McCambridge), a woman as shady and ambitious as he is.

As the years pass, Rip accumulates a fortune, a seat on the stock exchange, and a beautiful wife, Lily Douvane (Arlene Dahl), who has married him solely for his money and who, after the birth of their son John, gives Rip his freedom for the price of a million dollars. Totally consumed by the desire to make money, Rip neglects his son, putting the boy primarily in the care of Zoe Carnot (Paula Raymond), a French governess who serves as a substitute mother.

When a stock market crash destroys Rip's fortune, Zoe suggests a way for him to recoup his lost assets. But tragedy strikes again when Zoe gives birth to a baby girl and neither survives.

In the story's closing scenes, it is 1875, with San Francisco again on the brink of financial disaster and thousands of depositors facing ruin if a bank controlled by Ada Stritch fails. Rip can save the bank by putting up three million dollars. He forces Ada to let the answer hang on the fall of a poker card. But when the fateful gamble takes place, Ada comes out the winner and saves the bank. In the end, Rip discovers that money and power alone cannot make a person happy, and he decides at last to earn his son's affection and respect.

The story of Rip MacCool actually unfolds during the poker game, as one person after another takes a turn at revealing his or her experiences with the unsympathetic tycoon. Chaney once again adopts an Old World accent in his role as Shocker and gives one of the best performances in the picture. Unfortunately, the goings-on are largely unconvincing, and Lon has to settle again for a supporting role in a mediocre film.

Studio publicity for the film embellished Lon's childhood with the following tale: "Young Chaney first developed a taste for greasepaint at the age of four. Dressed in a Buster Brown suit, he led early film audiences in singing songs to slides while the projectionist switched reels."[8] Completely ignoring fact, the studio claimed that for *Inside Straight* Lon created his own makeup from his father's old wooden makeup case. Of course, union regulations had curbed such activity years ago.

Warner Bros. then put Lon to work in *Only the Valiant* (1951), an overly long but fairly interesting action picture emphasizing grace under pressure. When the highly respected Capt. Richard Lance (Gregory Peck) sends junior officer William Holloway (Gig Young) on a suicide mission against the Apaches, the post personnel believe he did it to eliminate the man who is competing with him for the love of Cathy Eversham (Barbara Payton), another officer's daughter. When Lance tries to explain that he was only carrying out the colonel's orders, even Cathy turns on him.

When an outnumbering Apache force approaches the post, Lance convinces the colonel to send him in charge of a seven-man guerrilla force to stall the Apaches until reinforcements can arrive. Lance deliberately chooses the men who despise him the most. Among that small force is Trooper Kebussyan (Lon Chaney), Sgt. Ben Murdock (Neville Brand), Cpl. Timothy Gilchrist (Ward Bond), Trooper Rutledge (Warner Anderson), and Trooper Onstot (Steve Brodie). Lance's patrol goes to the remains of a deserted fort. Upon arrival, several of Lance's troops attempt to take his life. When the Indians attack, however, the men, who prefer to survive, put their differences aside and stand together against the common foe. The Indians' final assault on the fort is repulsed by cavalry reinforcements with Gattling guns. Praised by all for his bravery, Lance returns to his fort as a hero and is reunited with Cathy.

Although script limitations hamper his role, Lon turns in a strong performance as the powerful, sullen Arab trooper who would like nothing better than to murder Gregory Peck. Indeed, the strong cast carries this otherwise mundane film and lifts it slightly above murky mediocrity.

In the interests of publicity, Lon granted an interview in which he traversed some of the old territory:

> Everybody expected the son with no acting experience to know what his father learned in thirty hard years on the stage and screen. I had always wanted to act, but while my father was alive, I preferred to keep busy at other things. And when I finally did become an actor, I was expected to play the kind of roles he made famous. So I did, and believe me, it was no easy task to wear those masks and body harness and what not—all to try to carry out the tradition set by my dad.[9]

But as Lon implied, he was beyond all of that at this stage and now considered himself merely a "useful actor."

RKO provided Lon his next role, that of Pinky, in a labored lampoon of gangster films called *Behave Yourself* (1951). Farley Granger and Shelley Winters portray a couple who have a dog wanted by gangsters. The dog, a Welsh terrier, has been trained as a go-between in a counterfeiting scheme. Comical murders abound as the miscast Granger and Winters wade through the proceedings. As Pinky, Lon has only a few scenes in which to display his wares as a dimwitted gangster in the Lennie mold. There are some laughs, but the overall product did nothing to enhance Lon's career or his reputation as an important actor. Much of what soon followed would do even less.

Lon then joined Raymond Burr and rejoined both Barbara Payton and director Curt Siodmak for a low-budget jungle horror called *Bride of the Gorilla* (1951). Lon delivers the opening narration over jungle footage:

> This is the jungle—lush, green, alive with incredible growth—as young as day, as old as time. I, Taro, Police Commissioner of Itman County, which borders the Amazon River, know it as well as any man will know it. Isn't it beautiful? But I have also learned that beauty can be... deadly, something terrifying, something of prehistoric ages when monstrous superstitions ruled the minds of men. Something that haunted the world for millions of years rose out of that verdant labyrinth. Let me tell you how the jungle itself took law into its own hands. This was Van Gelder Manor, built to stand against the searing sun, built to shelter generations of Van Gelders. Yet, it also has become prey to the powers of the jungle, that terrifying strength that rose to punish a man for his crime.

Trapped in a marriage of gratitude with her older husband, Klaus Van Gelder (Paul Cavanagh), Dina Van Gelder (Barbara Payton) is attracted to her husband's swarthy foreman, Barney Chavez (Raymond Burr). When Van Gelder fires Chavez, the latter slugs his former boss, allowing him to be killed by a poisonous snake. Unknown to Chavez, the deed is witnessed by an old native woman, Larina (Carol Varga), who is loyal to Van Gelder. Larina refuses to testify against Chavez at the inquest, but casts a spell upon the killer, turning him at night into a killer gorilla. The scenario also suggests that Chavez's conscience is as much a cause of his transformation as any jungle spell.

Investigating all of these suspicious goings-on is Taro (Lon Chaney), the county police commissioner, a jungle native with a university education. Chavez, who has by this time married Dina, comes under Taro's suspicion. The commissioner intimates to Dr. Viet (Tom Conway), who also loves Dina, that Chavez is probably the jungle demon the natives fear. When Viet laughs off such "superstition," Taro explains that his jungle experiences have taught him things that the university would never acknowledge as fact and that the jungle is going to bring Barney Chavez to justice. Soon justice does triumph when Chavez turns into the killer gorilla and abducts Dina into the jungle, where both perish in a shower of bullets. Taro then concludes his narration: "Like something that has been haunting the world for millions of years, the jungle has risen to punish Barney Chavez for his crime."

A stern pose as Commander Taro in "Bride of the Gorilla" (1951).

While *Bride of the Gorilla* ultimately languishes in the familiar zone of movie mediocrity, it does have its strengths. In fact, for a project shot in just seven days, it looks remarkably polished. Throughout the film, which rarely rises above the obvious, Burr and Payton provide a forbidden, smoldering sensuality. Tom Conway is quite at home as the "other man," and Lon Chaney is adequate as the police commissioner torn between two cultures. Sounding uncomfortable at times when delivering his lines, Lon does most of his acting with suspicious glances and scene-stealing gestures.

Fans of Chaney Jr. have always wondered why Lon was not assigned the werewolf-like role of Barney Chavez. After all, Siodmak's screenplay is fraught with lines reminiscent of *The Wolf Man*, and Burr seems a better choice for the role of Taro than Chaney.

According to Curt Siodmak, he switched the roles of Burr and Chaney simply "to avoid repeating *The Wolf Man*." While Siodmak discounts the following as an additional reason, a believable romance between the aging Chaney and the foxy Payton would have been difficult to pull off. Once again Lon was at a disadvantage due to casting. Of course, Raymond Burr was on the brink of horror film notoriety for his starring role in the American version of the Japanese monster classic *Godzilla* (1956). He was also poised for television stardom as "Perry Mason" (1957–1965). His screen paramour, Barbara Payton, was regrettably headed in the opposite direction. In 1954 she would star in an interesting Hammer Studios science fiction picture, *Four-Sided Triangle* (1954), but she died a degenerate alcoholic in 1967.

During production for *Bride of the Gorilla*, Raymond Burr developed an obvious dislike for Lon Chaney. Although Burr denied being homosexual, many observers consider him to have been so. Siodmak provided me with no details, but I think it was the chemistry between Burr and Chaney that led the director to the conclusion that Lon was a latent homosexual (see Chapter 14 for further discussion).

To help promote *Bride of the Gorilla*, Lon went on a scheduled ten day personal tour which was lengthened to an amazing four and a half months and forty-five hundred miles. Of the tour, Lon said: "What the people want, I discovered, was not for our Hollywoodites to appear in a theater and say, 'It's nice weather and I'm glad to be here.' The audience expects a real acting job when a movie personality appears on stage."[10]

From the jungle setting of *Bride of the Gorilla*, Lon trudged into his last film of 1951, an embarrassing run-of-the-mill costumer called *Flame of Araby*. Princess Tanya (Maureen O'Hara) sneaks away from the palace to avoid marrying one of two Corsican brothers, Borks (Lon Chaney) or Hakim (Buddy Baer). She meets and falls in love with Tamerlane (Jeff Chandler), a Bedouin sheik who is attempting to capture a wild black stallion. When Tamerlane finally secures his beloved horse, he vanquishes the Corsicans in a race and rides off into the desert with his admiring Tanya. Although the handsome pair of O'Hara and Chandler romp in suitably colorful settings, insipid dialogue and a preposterous scenario ultimately doom the project. Lon does little more than recite his sometimes stilted dialogue while assigning Christian slaves to this person or that or occasionally grunting in anger. Under the circumstances, his uninspired performance is understandable.

Probably happy to escape such trivial toil, Lon Chaney first appeared on the television screen in 1951. In many ways, the big screen had let him down. The small screen, then providing its initial competition against the movies, offered verdant territory for "useful actors." Ironically, Lon's first television appearance was as the Frankenstein Monster on NBC's "Colgate Comedy Hour," hosted by Abbott and Costello. Lon appears in two segments of the comedy-variety show. In the first, he portrays the Frankenstein Monster in a haunted house skit derived largely from *Abbott and Costello Meet Frankenstein*. Later, he returns as the Frankenstein monster to menace Lou at the end of a mock opera that concludes the show. This time Lon and Lou do a cute jig together.

Lon, wearing a Frankenstein Monster mask, along with the creature's usual garb, gives an uninteresting interpretation reminiscent of Glenn Strange's performance. Since Chaney never appears without the mask, anyone else of similar physical stature would have served equally well. Realistically, not much else was called for since the whole thing was just another spoof.

Lon ended 1951 with his second television appearance, a role in a "Cosmopolitan Theater" episode called "Last Concerto." As he slogged through one mediocre film role after another, Chaney could not have known that an angel of redemption was about to appear on his horizon in the form of a talented film producer/director named Stanley Kramer.

Chapter 10

Character Gems (1952–1955)

C haney's years as a free-lancer between 1947 and 1951 were difficult and discouraging. While he had come to grips with the reality of his career, he nevertheless hoped that good offers would occasionally surface. Fortunately for Lon and for the cinema itself, several excellent parts were soon to come.

Lon's first project of 1952 was *The Bushwackers*. When the Civil War ends, Jeff Waring (John Ireland), a former Confederate sergeant, vows "never to raise a gun against man again." While out seeking a peaceful town in which to live, he witnesses the burning out of a farmer and the killing of members of the man's family. Those responsible, led by ruthless killer Sam Tobin (Lawrence Tierney), pursue Waring, who eventually outwits them and arrives exhausted and alive in Independence, Missouri. There he is befriended by the owner of the local newspaper, Peter Sharpe (Frank Marlowe), and his daughter Cathy (Dorothy Malone). Taking a job on the newspaper, Waring finds himself drawn into the land war that he witnessed part of on his way to Independence.

Behind the killing and terror is Taylor (Lon Chaney), a cripple consumed with a lust for money and power, and his daughter Norah (Myrna Dell), who carries out his orders. Hoping to avoid violence, Waring leaves town but is taken prisoner when the trail he has chosen crosses Taylor's property. Realizing that an accomplice's slip of the tongue has tipped off Waring that he wants the land because of a proposed railroad, Taylor orders Waring shot. When the killers botch the job, Waring returns to town and reveals Taylor's railroad scheme to Sharpe, who plans to publish an editorial denouncing Taylor.

Taylor has Sharpe killed and plans a massacre for the same night to wipe out the homesteaders. Waring escapes from jail, where he has been placed by Marshall John Harding (Wayne Morris) at Taylor's request. Waring takes Sharpe's gun and organizes the resistance of the homesteaders, who launch a successful surprise attack against Taylor's massacre. Taylor and Norah are both killed and the bushwhackers wiped out, after which Waring and Cathy, convinced that peace has come to Independence, go to work on the next day's newspaper.

While reviews of this simply constructed Western were mixed, the cast clearly rises to the occasion. Former Academy Award nominee John Ireland is convincing as a pacifist army veteran, Dorothy Malone evokes sweetness and courage, and Myrna Dell is a slightly more feminine model of her monstrous father. As for Lon Chaney, *The Bushwackers* provides him his first chance to play an invalid, a challenge that he meets with striking success. Heavily made up to appear about sixty-five years old and shackled in a wheelchair, Lon's character rants and raves, almost bursting at times with the greed that drives him.

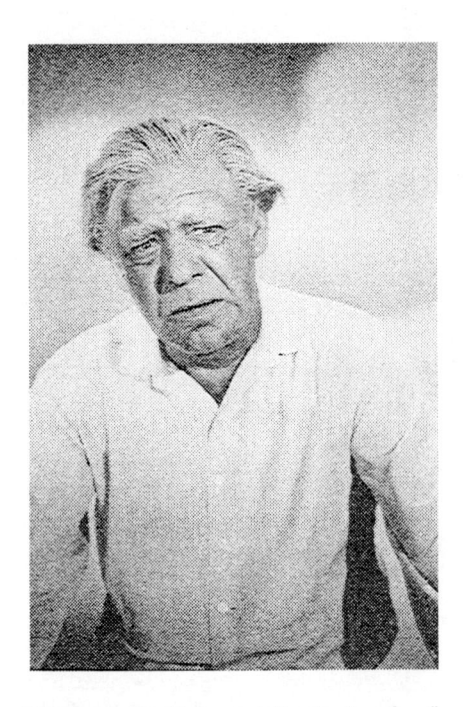

Chaney as Mr. Taylor in "The Bushwackers" (1952).

While Lon appears to have favorably impressed most co-workers during his career, he evidently rubbed actress Myrna Dell the wrong way. "He played my father in a film [*The Bushwackers*]," she said. "He wouldn't stand in the background for my close-ups, so I refused to stand in the background for his. I didn't like him!"[1]

At about this same time, however, Lon found himself in a low-budget Sam Katzman quickie called *Thief of Damascus* (1952), in which he plays Sinbad the Sailor. The jumbled scenario reduces the film to just another disappointing costume melodrama:

In the days of the *Arabian Nights*, Khalid, (John Sutton) is the despotic ruler of Damascus. His best general, Abu Andar (Paul Henreid), teams with Aladdin (Robert Clary), Sinbad (Lon Chaney) and Ali Baba (Philip Van Zandt) against Khalid. In response, Khalid orders the executions of the deposed sultan (Edward Colmans), his daughter, Princess Zafir (Helen Gilbert), and Sheherazade (Jeff Donnell), a lady of the harem. Andar and the insurgents enter the city hidden in large casks, and with the citizens of Damascus, they defeat Khalid in a street battle.

In *Thief of Damascus*, as in *Cobra Woman*, Lon's size is his only attribute used to advantage. Slogging through the affair, Lon is just part of the larger "Let's get this over with and in the can" attitude that the whole project exudes. There are a few well-staged battle sequences, but the real "thief" is Columbia Pictures, which took the movie-goers' money at the box office.

While Lon's next film was yet another Western, it was no ordinary Western. It was Stanley Kramer's *High Noon* (1952), probably the best film of its kind ever made. Carl Foreman's excellent scenario uses many of the familiar genre trappings but offers them up in unconventional ways:

The time is 1870. The place is Hadleyville, population around 400. In the past, Hadleyville had been terrorized by Frank Miller (Ian MacDonald) and his gang. But five years ago, Marshall Will Kane (Gary Cooper), backed up by half a dozen deputies, broke the Miller gang and arrested Miller for murder. Miller was sentenced to hang but was saved when influential friends in the territorial capital engineered a commutation of his sentence to life imprisonment. Now law and order have been so well established that Kane has only one deputy, Harvey Pell (Lloyd Bridges).

As the story opens, Will is marrying Amy (Grace Kelly) and giving up his job as sheriff to move to another town, where they plan to open a general store. As a Quaker, Amy opposes any form of violence. Suddenly, Ben Miller (Sheb Wooley), who is Frank's brother, Pierce (Bob Wilke), and Colby (Lee Van Cleef) ride into town and are recognized immediately by the townspeople. Shortly afterward, the stationmaster arrives at the courthouse where Will and Amy have just been married and announces that Frank Miller has been pardoned and that his three henchmen are awaiting his arrival on the noon train. It is now 10:40 A.M.

Will decides, much to Amy's dismay, that he must stay and face the Miller gang because the vengeful gunman will surely follow him wherever he goes. Will is convinced that he can raise a posse and defeat the gang, just as he did five years ago. Amy disagrees and leaves angrily, insisting it is no longer his business. As she waits at the hotel for the noon train, she meets Helen Ramirez (Katy Jurado), a fiery Mexican who has been a controversial figure in the town. Helen, who once had a romance with Will, cannot understand why Amy does not stand by her husband's side.

In an attempt to raise a posse, Will Kane visits every friend he has in town, but the people, who have grown soft and complacent over the last five years, all turn him down. When Kane interrupts a church service to ask for volunteers, the congregation decides that the marshall should simply leave town. Will, knowing that his four to one disadvantage means almost certain death, walks out without a word. It is now 11:44 A.M.

Harvey, Kane's jealous deputy, comes upon the marshall in the livery stable and tells him to leave town. When Will tells Harvey that he considers the young man too immature to be marshall, a fight ensues and Will emerges the battered victor.

It is twelve noon, and the first train whistle sounds. The town stops in hypnotic fascination, waiting. The second whistle blows, then the third. The train is stopping to discharge Frank Miller. Inside the marshall's office, Kane has finished writing his will. He steps outside just as Amy and Helen ride by on their way to the station. Arriving at the station, Helen and Amy board the train as Frank Miller steps down and greets his brother and Pierce and Colby.

Will Kane walks silently and alone up the deserted street, gun ready. Down a back street come the Millers, Pierce, and Colby, guns ready.

Suddenly gunfire blasts the stillness. Amy runs from the train and rushes back to the town. During the gun battle that follows, Will shoots three of the gang members, and Amy takes up arms to kill the fourth.

Then, as bodies lie in the street, the citizens of Hadleyville rush out to congratulate Will, but he will have none of it. Tossing his badge into the dust, he helps Amy into their buckboard, and the two ride off to begin their new life.

The film, which was released to critical accolades, garnered four Academy Awards: best actor (Gary Cooper), best song and best score (Dimitri Tiomkin–Ned Washington), and best editing (Elmo Williams and Harry Gerstad). Fred Zinneman directs expertly, staging camera angles that bring to life the dramatic implications of Foreman's screenplay.

Under Zinneman's guidance, Lon Chaney produces a memorable character gem as the town's soft-spoken, arthritic former marshall. With a pain-filled gesture of the hand, an anxious glance of the eye, and a tired voice of cynicism and resignation, Chaney carves out a top-flight character cameo.

In Lon's best scene, Will Kane arrives at the former marshall's house seeking help and advice:

Kane (Gary Cooper): You been my friend all my life. You got me this job. You made 'em send for me. Ever since I was a kid I wanted to be like you, Mart. You've been a lawman all your life.

Howe (Lon Chaney): Yeh...Yeh, all my life. It's a great life. You risk your skin catchin' killers and the juries turn 'em loose so they can come back and shoot at you again. If you're honest, you're poor your whole life, and in the end you end up dyin' all alone on some dirty street. For what? For nothin'. For a tin star.

Kane: Listen. The judge has left town, Harvey's quit, and I'm having trouble getting deputies.

Howe: It figures. It all happened too sudden. People gotta talk themselves into law and order before they do anything about it, maybe because deep down they don't care. They just don't care.... Get out, Will... get out.

Publicity states that Stanley Kramer chose Lon for the role based upon the actor's performance in *The Bushwhackers*, in which he also suffers from arthritis.[2] Indeed the makeup is similar in both films. For whatever reasons

Kramer chose Chaney, it was the beginning of a worthwhile collaboration that would infuse Lon's career with a shot of much needed dignity and respect.

So successful was the teaming of Chaney and Cooper in United Artists' *High Noon* that Warner Brothers signed both actors for another Western collaboration, *Springfield Rifle* (1952). This time, the results are unremarkable. During the Civil War, Major "Lex" Kearney (Gary Cooper), a Union officer, goes undercover with a band of rustlers to find out who is selling horses to the Confederates. One of the rustlers is Pete Elm (Lon Chaney), who suspects that Kearney is not what he appears to be. Besides being whipped by Cooper in a fistfight, Lon spends most of the film riding through colorful country and keeping a close eye on the protagonist.

As 1952 drew to a close, Chaney returned to Universal-International for yet another horror film. Sadly, *The Black Castle* shows how far both Universal and Lon had deteriorated in regard to the genre since the forties:

In order to find out why two of his close friends vanished during a hunting party with Viennese nobleman Count Von Bruno (Stephen McNally), English adventurer Sir Ronald Burton (Richard Greene) finagles an invitation to another hunting party on the Count's huge and forbidding estate in an effort to solve the mystery. Bruno is in fact pleased to draw Burton to the estate because the Englishman was the third of the trio who were unwittingly responsible for Von Bruno's failure to complete an unscrupulous ivory deal with African natives a few years earlier.

When Sir Ronald arrives at Von Bruno's castle, he falls in love with the Count's beautiful wife, Elga (Paula Corday), whom the Count had forced into marriage against her will. Evidence soon leads Sir Ronald to suspect that Von Bruno murdered his two friends. Realizing he is in danger, Sir Ronald tries to escape with Elga, but they are stopped by the Count and his hulking bodyguard, Gargon (Lon Chaney). Von Bruno tries to bury Sir Ronald and Elga alive, but the lovers are rescued by Dr. Meissen (Boris Karloff), who is stabbed to death for his trouble. Sir Ronald kills Von Bruno in self-defense, Gargon plunges to his death in a pool of alligators, and the lovers escape to freedom.

Neither the competent direction of Nathan Juran nor the presence of Boris Karloff and Lon Chaney can raise this film above the level of uninspired drivel. Stephen McNally is suitably sinister, however, as the nefarious hunter, undoubtedly suggested by Count Zaroff of The *Most Dangerous Game* (1932), and Richard Greene is the adequate British hero, a role he would fulfill admirably in his television series "Robin Hood" (1955–1969). Regrettably, Karloff and Chaney, from whom one would expect much, deliver little because of script limitations. Karloff, for instance, has only one line of dialogue in the first thirty-seven minutes, and poor Lon, saddled with a ridiculous puddingbowl haircut, mucks about completely mute for the entire film. While Karloff's screen time increases in the second half, its quality remains unremarkable. Likewise, Lon is simply called upon to scowl and appear physically intimidating.

Lon as Gargon in "The Black Castle" (1952).

Several explanations for the film's failure are possible. While the classic Universal horror films of both Chaney and Karloff were still in general rerelease, science fiction had replaced gothic horror as the audience's genre of choice. America was in the space age and was engaged in a cold war with a rival superpower. In addition, America was experiencing the flying saucer craze of the early fifties. As a result, such films as *Destination Moon* (1950), *Rocketship X-M* (1950), *The Thing from Another World* (1951), *Flight to Mars* (1951), and *The Man from Planet X* (1951) were appealing to the sophisticated tastes of a new generation. The space age had relegated the already tired bogeymen in cobwebbed castles to the realm of childhood myth. Karloff and Chaney were among those bogeymen.

In publicity for *The Black Castle*, Lon stated that he had turned down dozens of offers to recreate his famous father's roles because "My theory is that actors shouldn't be imitators of other actors, even in the case of their own parents."[3] While this may have been his view in 1952, it was clearly a case of revisionist history. Lon had been sorely disappointed at losing the starring roles in *The Phantom of the Opera* and *The Hunchback of Notre Dame* to other actors during the forties. After his 1948 suicide attempt, however, he apparently put all such hopes behind him and adopted the line he was expressing in 1952.

Reviews for the film were predictable. Among the most critical appeared in the *New York Times*: "Parents are specifically warned that an inordinate amount of needlessly sadistic action is to be seen in this aberration. Adults can pass it up on the grounds that it is a dull dud. To open Universal-International's "Black Castle" at any time is a mistake: to tender it to the public on Christmas Day is remarkably indiscreet."[4]

Also making the rounds at year's end was another Chaney offering: *The Battles of Chief Pontiac* (1952). Producer Jack Broder probably chose Chaney for the title role because of the actor's successful portrayal of an educated jungle native in Broder's *Bride of the Gorilla*. The film portrays Pontiac as a man of faith who believes that whites and Indians can live together peaceably.

On the frontier, tensions mount between the British and the Indians. The great Indian leader Pontiac (Lon Chaney), hoping to avoid war, sends for the chiefs of the tribes. At British headquarters, Sir Jeffery Amherst (Ramsey Hill), commander of the British forces, sends Colonel Von Weber (Barry Kroeger) with a detachment of Hessian mercenaries to relieve the garrison at Fort Detroit. Kent McIntyre (Lex Barker), a young Ranger lieutenant, rides to inform the fort that reinforcements are on the way. McIntyre, a friend of Pontiac, clashes with Von Weber, who considers all Indians brutal savages. When McIntyre insists that whites and Indians can coexist in peace, Von Weber counters that Indians understand only brute force.

At Pontiac's gathering, the tribes agree to fight for their land. As McIntyre marches through hostile territory, he sees a group of white prisoners with their Indian guards beside a river bank. One of the prisoners, a young woman named Winifred Lancaster (Helen Westcott), identifies herself to McIntyre as the daughter of the commander of Fort Sandusky, who was killed during an Indian raid. She is one of a party of prisoners being taken to Pontiac.

McIntyre allows himself to be taken prisoner and informs the braves that as Pontiac's blood brother, he demands to see the great chief. Pontiac is overjoyed to see him and agrees to hold a peace council with the whites. McIntyre also tells Pontiac that Winifred is pledged to him to prevent Hawkbill (Larry Chance), a hot-headed young brave, from forcing his attentions on her. Upon McIntyre's arrival at Fort Detroit, Major Gladwin (Roy Roberts) eagerly agrees to meet with Pontiac and discuss peace. To sabotage the peace process, Col. Von Weber, who is now in command, insults the Indian party when they appear at the fort and sends them gifts of smallpox-infected clothing and blankets.

When McIntyre becomes enraged at Von Weber's cruel treachery, the colonel places him under guard. Knowing that war will soon break out, McIntyre escapes and learns that Von Weber is unwittingly leading troops into an Indian ambush. Racing to halt the soldiers, he arrives too late and is wounded. Pontiac takes Von Weber prisoner, ties him to a stake, and wraps him in the pox-infected clothing he had sent to the Indians.

With Von Weber dead, the British and Indians agree to live in peace. Winifred is relieved to find McIntyre alive and recovered from his wounds. As the young lovers set out for a life together, Pontiac respectfully thanks his gods.

Factual only in the broadest sense, the film skirts the intriguing aspects of Pontiac's historical conspiracies and settles in as standard fare. The relationship between McIntyre and Winifred fluctuates between the ludicrous and the unbelievable. Von Weber, the Hessian leader, does a laughable, over-the-top Nazi impersonation, and though during the shooting, Lon actually lived in a tent among real Indians rather than at a hotel with the rest of the cast, the experience did not inspire an above average performance.

The product might have been good had it adhered more to historical accuracy, had it used a more imaginative director, had it relied less upon stereotypes, and had it switched the focus from McIntyre and Winifred to Pontiac. In other words, an entirely different film might have had possibilities.

Although the real Pontiac deserved better, Lon was apparently pleased, saying:

> It's a great part to play. Pontiac was a great leader and fought for peace between the Whites and the Indians. Being typed as the motion picture counterpart of a famous historical figure never did any actor any harm. [He points out Raymond Massey as Lincoln, Alexander Knox as Wilson, and Paul Muni as Pasteur as examples.]...They did alright [*sic*] by reliving history before the motion picture camera, and right now I'm thankful for the opportunity to bring Pontiac to the screen.[5]

In another context he added, "I've been trying for twenty-two years to play an Indian. This business has needed a good Indian for years—and I'd like to be it."[6]

Lon continued to perform on television in 1952. In January he was back in the role of the Monster on a "Tales of Tomorrow" version of "Frankenstein." Lon had some of his own ideas about how the Monster should look, so when he reported to Vincent J-R Kehoe's studio at 144 West 57th Street in New York, the makeup man rejected any temptation to recreate the Monster in the Universal mode and provided Chaney with a completely original look. The story itself was necessarily a severely truncated version of Mary Shelley's novel.

Over dinner at his Swiss castle, Victor Frankenstein (John Newland) tells his fiancée, Elizabeth (Mary Alice Moore), of his dream to create a "perfect man." Elizabeth's father laughs off the idea, but Elizabeth is disturbed. After his guests leave, Victor retires to his laboratory and brings his artificial man (Lon Chaney) to life. Victor's dream, however, is a nightmare–a bald, horribly scarred Monster who growls in rage and bewilderment while attempting to escape from the lab. Victor finally restrains the beast, but it breaks loose again and confronts little cousin William in the play room. When the Monster plays rough, the frightened boy angrily calls it ugly. The startled Monster quickly runs to a nearby mirror and grimaces at its hideous reflection. Going on a rampage, it kills the maid, but tumbles through a window into the lake after being shot repeatedly by the woman's husband. Convinced that the creature is dead, Victor confesses all to Elizabeth. Far from being dead, however, Victor's nemesis breaks into the castle. Using William and Elizabeth for bait, Victor lures the monster back into the lab, where he electrocutes it in a scene probably inspired by the finale of *The Thing from Another World*.

It is difficult to judge Chaney's performance in this production. Drinking heavily, he became confused and broke out a window with a chair during three separate dress rehearsals. On each occasion, or as the crew scurried to replace the window, Lon retired to the bar. Then Lon incredibly walked through the live broadcast believing it was the final dress rehearsal. The nearly hysterical director and crew watched helplessly as Lon carefully picked up and put down breakaway props that he was supposed to be smashing. Further confused, the actor cursed under his breath as he completed the laughable scenes. So mortified was Chaney upon learning of his error that it took him several weeks to recover emotionally.

Later in the year, Lon appeared on an episode of "You Asked for It." In response to a reader request, host Art Baker asks Lon to explain how his father achieved "that perfection in mimicry and pantomime." Lon replies:

> Well, pantomime to my father was just like A, B, C. Actually, Art, my father learned his ABCs in pantomime. The reason for that is that he was born of deaf mute parents. He learned his ABCs [signs them] that way. But, of course, like children always are, he had to learn words before he could learn his ABCs. So naturally, his parents taught him signs for words that would be fitting for a situation. Now, for instance, I imagine probably the first word they ever taught him was "love," for they had much in their hearts.

Chaney then demonstrates the signs for *love, hate,* and *fear,* explaining, "That is how my dad became such a great pantomimist."

As Baker shows scenes from *The Hunchback of Notre Dame,* Lon points out instances in which his father pantomimes such emotions as love, hate, frustration, determination, exaltation, and triumph. Lon finishes by informing Art that there are over three million deaf and dumb people in the United States and that there is a Silence Club in each major city. With evident enthusiasm, he exclaims how wonderful it would be if some person or organization would donate a television set to each of those clubs because of the great boon television would be for the deaf.

Chaney comes across as warm and sincere in this short piece. In addition, the brief insight he gives into his father's work is fascinating.

Lon's final 1952 television appearance was in a "Schlitz Playhouse of Stars" drama called "The Trial," which was filmed in Lon's favorite location, Mexico.

As a new year began, Lon found himself as Peg-Leg the Pirate in a United Artists time killer called *Raiders of the Seven Seas* (1953). Barbarossa (John Payne), a pirate, falls in love with a countess (Donna Reed) whom he has rescued. Lon then performed in a novelty short for Lippert called *Bandit Island* (1953), which was later incorporated into the full-length feature *The Big Chase*.

Always eager to return to serious drama, Lon accepted work under director Raoul Walsh in the kind of Huey Long takeoff that landed his pal Brod Crawford an Oscar. *A Lion in the Streets* (1953) tells the story of Hank Martin (James Cagney), a Southern swamp peddler, who runs for governor as a "man of the people." Among those who help him on his way up are Verity Wade (Barbara Hale), the wholesome school teacher whom he marries, and Jeb Brown, a yokel who believes in Martin to a fault. Of course corruption sets in, and Martin sells out to enhance his election chances. In doing so, he becomes entangled with Flamingo (Anne Francis), the town temptress. Worse than that, however, when his faithful follower Jeb is killed, Martin agrees to provide an alibi for the real murderer. When it becomes apparent that Martin is going to lose the election, he leads a mob to the State Capitol, where he is righteously shot to death by Jeb's widow (Jeanne Cagney). Lon Chaney received eighth billing as Spurge, Flamingo's father, a role for which he received good critical notices.

Lon's only television work in 1953 was a guest spot on "The Red Skelton Show," in which he shared the stage with horror compatriots Bela Lugosi and Peter Lorre. Needless to say, collectors and fans everywhere are waiting for a copy of that show to surface.

Lon's next portrayal was a small, unmemorable part in a jungle cheapie called *Jivaro* (1954). African trader Rio (Fernando Lamas) is pleasantly surprised when cool and beautiful Alice Parker (Rhonda Fleming) shows up at an Amazon trading post searching for her husband Tony (Brian Keith). It seems that he left for headhunter country more than a year ago to seek his fortune in gold. Rio, who falls in love with Alice, leads her to her husband, who has become a drunk. When Tony takes Alice, the two of them defenseless, on a safari deeper into Indian country, they fall under siege and are rescued in "cavalry fashion" by a band of saviors who arrive on foot rather than horseback.

In the film, which is obviously just another low-budget adventure yarn, Lon plays Pedro, a jocular shyster who puts a shady deal over on Rio. When the hero discovers he has been duped, he bides his time till he chances to encounter Chaney again. Rio initiates and wins a fistfight against his old buddy, after which the two shake hands and resume their friendship. For Lon, it is just another supporting role in another hackneyed film.

Speaking of hackneyed, Lon's next film, *The Boy from Oklahoma* (1954), revisits the tired theme of the friendly fellow who rides into a tough Western town and becomes sheriff. Will Rogers, Jr., is the title character, a pacifist sheriff who eventually establishes law and order and gets the girl, played by Nancy Olson. Despite the familiarity, director Michael Curtiz delivers a light, entertaining product with the help of Anthony Caruso, Merv Griffin, Wallace Ford, and Lon Chaney. Lon performs the role of town drunk Crazy Charlie with relish, much to the apparent amusement of Rogers and the others. The film served as the basis for the popular television series "Sugarfoot."

Continuing to work steadily, Lon was reunited with Bob Hope in a farcical romp titled *Casanova's Big Night* (1954). Although the film is a comedy, it manages to assemble an impressive congregation of actors associated with the horror genre: Basil Rathbone, John Carradine, Vincent Price, Raymond Burr, Henry Brandon, and, of course, Lon. Pippo Popolino (Bob Hope), a tailor's apprentice who masquerades as Casanova (Vincent Price), is hired by the Duchess of Genoa to test the fidelity of Elena DiGambetta (Audrey Dalton), who is engaged. In hopes of winning a share of the fee, Casanova's real valet (Basil Rathbone) and Francesca (Joan Fontaine), daughter of the local grocer, accompany Pippo on his mission.

Once in Venice, Pippo decides to abandon the assignment when he discovers that the engaged couple are really in love with each other. Matters become complicated, however, when the Doge of Venice (Arnold Moss) sees through the fraud and attempts to use it toward his own villainous ends. Pippo ends up in jail, is rescued by Francesca, and rushes toward the happy ending via an hilarious banquet and much swashbuckling.

Chaney plays Emo, Hope's cellmate, who arranges Bob's "escape" from prison. Bob gives his valuables to Lon and crawls through a "passage of escape" only to find himself in another cell with other prisoners who have fallen for the same ruse. While Lon has only a few minutes of screen time, he fills every second of it with gusto. At one point, he tips his hat to Lennie by repeating the old "pet a mouse" routine.

Lon's next project was a cops-and-robbers adventure called *The Big Chase* (1954). Rookie cop Pete Grayson (Glenn Langan) turns down a promotion to take a safer job with the Juvenile Department because his wife Doris (Adele Jergens) is expecting a baby. On patrol car duty, Pete chases a girl and three men: Kip (Lon Chaney), Brad Migs (Jim Davis), and Jim Bellows (Jay Lawrence), who have pulled a payroll robbery that Brad and Jim planned while in prison. At a railroad yard, police kill Kip in a gunfight. When the girl driving the getaway car is shot and her body dumped, an accomplice, Monty (Jack Daly), tells Lt. Ned Daggert (Douglas Kennedy) that the fugitives plan to reach Mexico by boat. Helicopter police locate the boat and force it back to shore,

Will Rogers, Jr., and Lon Chaney, Jr., in "The Body from Oklahoma" (1954).

and the fugitives are killed after a big chase. Pete then quickly heads for the hospital, where Doris has just born a daughter. The happy parents agree that Pete will accept that promotion to detective after all.

Although *The Big Chase* is only an average crime drama, Lon gives a strong performance, particularly in the shoot-out scenes that lead to his screen death. Grimacing with rage and half-insane with a desire for freedom, he gives a memorable portrayal as the mallet-wielding Kip. It is interesting to note that the film's star, Glenn Langan, would soon work as *The Amazing Colossal Man* (1957) for director Bert I. Gordon.

With his big chase completed, Lon took no rest but rushed headlong into another character role in the film *Passion* (1954). Embroiled in a land feud in old California, Juan Oberon (Cornel Wilde) pursues an agenda of revenge against those who massacred his wife and in-laws. Unfortunately, wooden dialogue, slow pacing, and one-dimensional characters keep this film from being anything like a precursor to Clint Eastwood. Lon, however, gives a good performance as Castro, a cowardly terrorist on Wilde's hit list. As one might guess, he dies in a knife fight with the hero.

Lon wrapped up 1954 with *The Black Pirates*, a bland account of pirates on a treasure hunt. Robert Clarke remembered working on the film with Lon: "It was fun. He referred to himself as 'the son of a good actor'–and then proceeded to have a big belt of booze [*laughs*]! But Lon was a fun-type man."[7]

Lon made several television appearances in 1954, one being a spot in a "Cavalcade Theatre" episode called "Moonlight School," with George Nader. He also filmed some unsold pilots with Rita Moreno that were later pieced together as two television movies. In the first, *Jack London's Tales of Adventure* (1954), Lon narrated and played an Alaskan trapper. The second, which played in 1955, was called *Flight from Adventure*.

Lon also starred in an episode of "The Whistler" titled "Backfire." Carl (Lon Chaney), an ex-convict, is hired by the wealthy Arnold Peirson (Dayton Lummis) as a chauffeur. Arnold makes it clear that he is relying on Carl to keep an eye on his flighty, unpredictable wife, Amy (Dorothy Green), who likes to go on wild drives and possibly have an affair or two on the side. While Arnold is away on an extended business trip, Carl falls in love with Amy, who uses him to help her conduct an affair with a piano player. Upon the eve of Arnold's return, Amy gives Carl the brush-off and reminds him that she will make trouble for him with the parole board if he becomes difficult. The angry chauffeur carries out a scheme to murder Arnold, and blames the crime on Amy. All goes according to plan until a surprise plot twist causes Carl's plot to backfire.

In 1955, Lon was reunited with Brod Crawford in a gritty jailbreak drama called *Big House, U.S.A.*:

Young Danny Lambert (Peter Votrian) runs away from camp in rugged northern Colorado and becomes the object of a statewide search led by the boy's wealthy father (Willis Bouchey). Unfortunately, Danny falls into the hands of Jerry Barker (Ralph Meeker), a shady character who hopes to hold the boy for a $200,000 ransom. Barker tells the boy to wait at the top of an abandoned lookout tower while he goes for help. Instead he makes the ransom call to Danny's father, collects the money, and buries most of it. In the meantime, Danny panics and stumbles from the tower to his death. When Barker returns, he throws the body off a cliff.

When the FBI arrests Barker with some of the ransom money on him, he claims that he never saw the boy and that he was simply taking advantage of the situation to get the $200,000. The FBI are unable to shake Barker's story, and he receives a sentence of five years in Casabel Island Prison for extortion.

Barker's cellmates are Rollo Lambar (Broderick Crawford), Alamo Smith (Lon Chaney), Benny Kelly (Charles Bronson), and Machine Gun Mason (William Talman). By this time the FBI have traced a connection between Emily Evans (Randy Farr), the nurse at Danny's camp, and Barker.

The five cellmates, led by Rollo, the ringleader who plans to kill Benny and dress him in Barker's clothes to throw off the police, execute a bold underwater escape from prison. The police, however, suspect a trick and head for North Carolina, where they think the convicts will come to recover the hidden ransom money. Falling into the police trap, Machine Gun is killed in a gun battle, and Rollo and Barker are caught and sentenced to die in the gas chamber. For her collusion with Barker, Emily is sent to a woman's prison.

Chaney made $3,500 for his work in the picture, which was shot in three weeks. His best line in the film comes as he observes Crawford applying artificial respiration to Ralph Meeker after the underwater prison break, all the while planning to kill him after being led to the loot. "Look at the Good Samaritan," he muses cynically, "fattenin' up the golden goose."

Lon lost a climactic fistfight to Brod Crawford in *North to the Klondike*. In *Big House, U.S.A.*, he gets shot by Brod, who then dumps him overboard a launch. Lon took it all good-naturedly, however, saying, "Wait'll I get him in the next picture. I'll even things up."[8] That next picture (*Not As a Stranger*) would come, and it would feature one of Lon's best performances, but once again, only Crawford would be alive at the end of the picture.

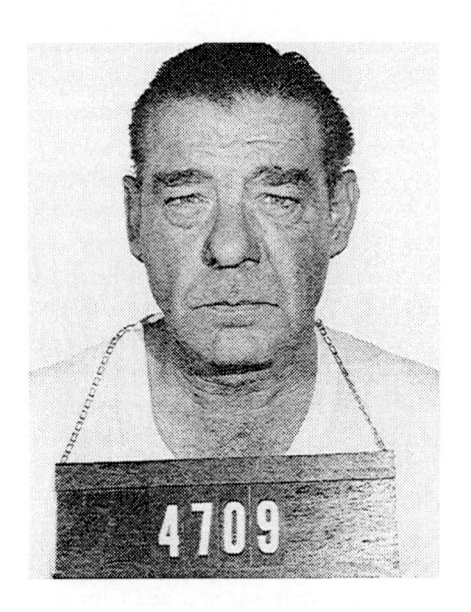

A mug-shot pose as Alamo Smith in "Big House, U.S.A." (1955).

Director Howard W. Koch retained warm memories of Lon:

> The first time I met him was when I was an assistant director at MGM, around 1949. He was being interviewed for a picture called *Across the Wide Missouri* (1951) with Clark Gable. They were casting for trappers. The role went to James Whitmore because he was under contract to MGM. Contract players were cheaper to get, and Lon was a free-lance actor.... Broderick Crawford gave us some problems during the making of the film because he drank a lot, vodka. But Lon's drinking never showed because he was good at covering that up. Some actors drink because it gives them courage.[9]

Before landing a character part in another fine film produced by Stanley Kramer, Lon walked through a run-of-the-mill Western called *The Silver Star*. Gregg (Earle Lyon) is a pacifist elected sheriff of a Western town. John W. Harmon (Lon Chaney), his defeated opponent, hires a trio of killers to put Gregg out of business. When retired marshall Bill Dowdy (Edgar Buchanan) shames the reluctant sheriff into strapping on a gun, the stage is set for a *High Noon*-style confrontation. Unfortunately, this film is no *High Noon*. Pedestrian direction and an uninterested cast sink it in the swamp of mediocrity.

Marie Windsor, who also appears in *The Silver Star*, told me in a 1991 telephone interview that while she was aware of stories concerning Lon's drinking, she never saw any problems during the shooting of that film.

Chaney and Robert Mitchum in "Not As a Stranger" (1955).

In *Not As a Stranger* (1955), Lon showed what he could do when given a part he respected. Produced by Stanley Kramer, it is the story of medical student Lucus Marsh (Robert Mitchum), whose drive for perfection alienates those around him. When Lucus's widowed father, Job Marsh (Lon Chaney), spends his son's inheritance on drink, Lucus marries a nurse, Kristina Hedvigson (Olivia de Havilland), whom he uses simply as a financial source for his medical school tuition. Lucus is unable to show compassion for anyone as he moves toward his goal of becoming a doctor, until the day that his own mistake causes the death of Dr. Runkleman (Charles Bickford), a man he had earlier accused of incompetency.

Not As a Stranger is a fine film. Other strong performances are delivered by Frank Sinatra as a medical student, Broderick Crawford as the head physician, and Gloria Graham as the seductress with designs on Mitchum. Lon appears in only one scene, but what a scene it is. When Mitchum realizes that his inheritance for medical school has been squandered by his drunken father, he goes to the old man's apartment for a confrontation. He walks into the dingy, ill-lit dwelling, examines an empty liquor bottle on the table, and opens a blind, at which point his father slowly emerges from an adjoining room:

Lucus (*Robert Mitchum*):	What did you do with it?
Job (*Lon Chaney*):	Luke, I...
Lucus:	What did you do with the money?
Job:	[*imploring*] Let me explain....
Lucus:	Was there any of it left? That was my mother's money, things she did without for me.
Job:	Please, Luke, please don't [*extends his hand toward Luke as if groping for understanding*]....
Lucus:	[*slaps down Job's hand and says with disgust*] You drunk!
Job:	I know what I am. Yes, I stole your money. But I'm not just an old man you left alone in this place. I'm a person, a human being. Your mother never understood that. You can't understand it. [*Lucus turns to go.*] You want to be a doctor. Ever since you were a kid you went running after them, just to carry their bags. I'm sorry, Luke. I don't think you'll ever make it. It isn't enough to have a brain. You have to have a heart. [*Lucus leaves without a response, and Job tosses back a glass of whiskey.*]

Although Chaney is killed off camera by a car after only one brief scene, that scene stands as one of his finest moments. Leaning in the doorway before emerging from a back room in his apartment, Lon's body projects the weakness of the alcoholic personality within, the physical portrait of a broken man in need of strength. Always underplaying, Lon begs for understanding with his watery eyes, his slumping body, his imploring hand, and his pathetic entreaties. All the while, Mitchum stares coldly and impassively with disgust. When Mitchum slaps down his hand, Lon pulls himself up, admits what he is, but suggests that his son lacks both self-understanding and compassion. Lon's almost defiant pouring of a drink as Mitchum is leaving expresses the self-affirmation of an authentic though weak human being, as well as a challenge to Mitchum to find himself before it is too late. Lon had played drunks before, and he would play them again, but never half so well as here.

Coming off his triumph as Job Marsh, Lon appeared in another small but impressive character role in *I Died a Thousand Times* (1955), a remake of Humphrey Bogart's *High Sierra* (1941).

While driving to meet up with the gang with whom he has planned a hotel robbery, Roy Earle (Jack Palance) meets and falls in love with Velma (Lori Nelson), a pretty, naive young girl with a clubfoot. Earle, expecting big money from the robbery, promises to finance an operation for her.

At the gang's headquarters, Earle meets Babe (Lee Marvin) and Marie (Shelley Winters). His mind on Velma, Earle remains aloof from the gang members and ignores Marie's romantic overtures. Earle's only friend is Pard, a mongrel dog whose previous three owners had met with violent deaths.

In the course of the hotel robbery, the plan goes wrong and one of the getaway cars goes over a cliff, killing all occupants except Mendoza (Perry Lopez), who is captured and exposes the entire operation to the police. Meanwhile, Earle, Marie, and Pard escape in the other car with the stolen jewelry and visit Velma, who is now recovered from the operation. Earle proposes marriage to her but is told she has a fiancé from Ohio.

Stunned and hurt, Earle makes Marie his girl, and they go into hiding. A newspaper story informs them of Mendoza's treachery, and they decide to split up temporarily. Later, when police corner Earle in the mountains, Marie hears of the chase over a radio and goes to the scene.

The sheriff urges Marie to tell Earle to surrender, but she refuses. When Earle calls "come up and get me" to the sheriff's demands, Pard recognizes his master's voice and runs to the mountain. Hearing Pard's bark, Earle rushes to the side of the cliff and is shot by a rifleman who has been deposited above him by a helicopter. Then, fulfilling the prophecy that all of Pard's masters will die violently, Earle staggers, falls down the mountainside, and dies.

Chaney plays Big Mac, the aging, dying mastermind behind the jewel caper. With an alcohol-induced bad heart, stomach trouble, and sick kidneys, Mac lies in bed belting down the hair of the dog that bit him. In justification of his continued drinking, Chaney explains, pouring a drink, "It's like the doc says. If I don't lay off of this stuff, it's gonna knock *me* off. But I'm gonna die anyway [*chuckles*]. So are you [*with disdain*]. So what! Nobody ever left this world alive [*holding up his glass*]. To your health, Roy."

That short explanation probably comes closer to revealing Lon's actual philosophy of life than anything else he did on the screen. In rapid succession, Job Marsh and Big Mac, undeveloped though they are, stand as a fairly accurate composite of Chaney the man. They also stand, along with his Martin Howe, as two gems of characterization worthy of recognition and respect.

Lon's last film of 1955 was *The Indian Fighter*, a big budget Western designed to showcase rising star Kirk Douglas and to introduce Elsa Martinelli.

On its way to Oregon in 1879, a wagon train is stopped by Sioux Indians at a small frontier fort and told that it cannot enter Indian territory. Fort Laramie sends Johnny Hawks (Kirk Douglas), a tough Indian fighter, to clear up the situation. Chief Red Cloud (Eduard Franz) tells Johnny that some white men led by Wes Todd (Walter Matthau) and Chivington (Lon Chaney) have been trading liquor to the Indians for gold. While Johnny settles the dispute, he meets Grey Wolf (Harry Landers), who avoids all white men. He also meets and falls in love with Red Cloud's fiery daughter, Onahti (Elsa Martinelli).

Todd and Chivington, young Tommy Rodgers (Michael Winkleman), and his widowed mother (Diana Douglas), who has matrimonial intentions, join the wagon train, and Johnny resumes his post as guide and guard.

Red Cloud's forces attack the fort when he learns that the unfair trading has been resumed and that his brother, Grey Wolf, has been killed in a brawl. When Johnny goes secretly to Onahti, she takes him to the gold mine, where he catches Todd and Chivington red-handed. Todd sets off an explosion which kills Chivington but he in turn is captured by Johnny.

Johnny turns Todd over to Red Cloud, and the prisoner is later killed trying to escape. Red Cloud ends his attack on the settlers when Johnny and Onahti reveal their plans to marry. The wagon train then safely rolls on its way through the Oregon hills.

Exciting and colorful, *The Indian Fighter* fulfills the expectations raised by its budget and cast. Although mentally a bit like Lennie, Lon's Chivington is a routine ruffian. In the scene in which Douglas escapes from camp to visit Martinelli, Lon follows him suspiciously to the edge of camp. Knowing he is being followed and knowing that Chivington is mentally dense, Douglas dodges his stalker in humorous fashion, leaving Lon slack-jawed and baffled.

Dell Comics issued a Movie Classic tie-in to coincide with the release of *The Indian Fighter*. It was the second time Chaney's image had appeared in comic book format.

Lon's only television performance in the busy year of 1955 was in a "Cavalcade Theatre" drama called "Stay on, Stranger," in which he co-starred with Edgar Buchanan. In the next seven years, except for an appearance in one more fine Stanley Kramer film, Lon's screen career would slide in quality with a string of low budget horror films. He would, however, produce a significant and impressive body of television work that deserves critical attention.

Chapter 11

Horror Films, Westerns, and Television (1956-1962)

I n 1956, Lon Chaney worked on location in Jamaica under the direction of W. Lee Wilder. The film was *Manfish*, based on "The Gold Bug" and "The Tell-Tale Heart" by Edgar Allan Poe. The screenplay by Joel Murcott maintains a mild suspense throughout:

A Scotland Yard official arrives in Jamaica to seek extradition of a criminal known as the "Professor." The Jamaican police chief says that extradition is impossible and explains why.

When Bianco (Vera Johns) threatens to confiscate the *Manfish*, Captain Brannigan's turtle boat, Swede (Lon Chaney), Brannigan's big, good-hearted, but slightly dumb "first mate" hunts for the captain. He finds Brannigan (John Bromfield) in a poker game and explains that he will lose the *Manfish* unless he pays the 300 pounds he owes Bianco. Brannigan, who is winning at cards, brushes off Swede and goes on playing.

That night, Brannigan confesses to Swede that he ended up losing at cards and doesn't even have enough money to buy a drink. He then begins a flirtation with a native girl named Alita (Tessa Prendergast), whom everyone considers the property of the Professor (Victor Jory), an older, bearded mystery man from another island. A native warns Brannigan to leave Alita alone because the Professor is "a little crazy." The Professor soon returns and starts trouble with Brannigan, but before a fight can erupt, the Professor is told to return to his own island. Before going, however, he vows that someday he will kill Brannigan.

The next day, Brannigan, Swede, and two swimmers are turtle fishing when Swede spots a shark. Brannigan dives in and saves the swimmers from the killer fish, but Swede makes the mistake of allowing the swimmers back on board before getting the captain's permission. When Brannigan rather unfairly upbraids Swede, the big dimwit apologizes but then explodes when

Chaney and John Bromfield in "Manfish" (1956).

Brannigan spits on the deck of the *Manfish*. Even though Brannigan did win the *Manfish* in a poker game, Swede considers the boat the only woman he has.

Suddenly the swimmers report finding a skeleton clutching a bottle. Brannigan dives in and brings up the bottle, which contains half of a coded map and a skull and crossbones ring similar to the one he saw on the Professor's hand the previous night.

Later Brannigan taunts Swede for being unable to read and tries to get his girl Mimi to translate the French code. Although she can translate the words, they make no sense because they represent only half the message. Brannigan returns to the boat, wakes Swede, and sets sail for the Professor's island.

After arriving at the island, Brannigan resumes his flirtation with the willing Alita but is interrupted by the arrival of the Professor. It seems that the Professor has been staying in the Caribbean for five years for no apparent reason. Brannigan suggests that the Professor has been staying there in order to find Brannigan's half of the coded map.

Equipped with an aqua lung, Brannigan dives under water to search the coral cove. Another swimmer appears and fires a deadly compressed air spear at him, barely missing. A fight ensues under water. When the two men surface, Brannigan finds his adversary to be the Professor. On shore, Alita hands Brannigan the other half of the map belonging to the Professor. As the

Professor is the only one who can decode the map, he and Brannigan are forced into an uneasy partnership, and both set out in the *Manfish* to dig up the treasure of the pirate Lafitte.

Soon the Professor has translated the French: "The dead man stares from the rocky peak. He guards the treasure that live men seek. Who finds the two rings will hold the key. One death head points, but the other can see. And a wise man walks backwards until he has learned the beginning and the end of the trail that has been joined." The Professor then explains that one must turn the map upside-down to find the treasure, which is on the island of Hispaniola. Realizing that Brannigan will kill him if he reveals enough for the captain to find the treasure alone, the Professor burns both halves of the map, telling the enraged Brannigan that holding the location of the treasure in his mind will be his "life insurance."

The *Manfish* anchors off Hispaniola and Brannigan, the Professor, and Swede row ashore, trek through the wilderness to the designated spot, and unearth an ancient treasure chest full of gold and jewels. Brannigan now conspires to kill the Professor but is thwarted when his wily "partner" produces from the treasure chest another map which will lead them to Lafitte's second treasure. As the Professor is the only one who can decode the map, Brannigan is again forced to cooperate.

While Swede is in town to sell some of the gold to finance a second treasure hunt, the Professor, gleeful that he can finally deliver on his threat, kills Brannigan with a compressed air spear, weighs the body down with compressed air tanks, and dumps it overboard. He also hides the treasure chest by tying it to the boat's propeller. Soon bubbles begin to rise to the surface from an opened valve on one of the air tanks. Swede returns, sees Brannigan's cap floating in the water amidst the air bubbles, and discovers his body.

The police arrest the Professor for the crime. As Swede, who now owns the *Manfish*, sails out to sea, the propeller cuts the rope to which the Professor had tied the treasure chest, and it sinks to the bottom of the sea.

Although set in Jamaica rather than South Carolina, the film retains a number of basic elements from Poe's story "The Gold Bug," in which two white men (one an eccentric) and a black servant decode a Captain Kidd map in order to find hidden treasure. Based loosely on the character of Jupiter, the black servant in "The Gold Bug," Swede has an I.Q. somewhere between low average and that of Steinbeck's Lennie. Although referred to in the film as dumb, stupid, illiterate, and brainless, he nevertheless possesses "a stubborn streak of decency." In fact, though again playing a dimwit, Chaney relies heavily on facial expression to create the only sympathetic role in the whole scenario. The Professor's horrified reaction to the rising bubbles from the submerged oxygen cylinder is suggested by a similar reaction by the narrator of Poe's "The Tell-Tale Heart." In that story, an unhinged young man fancies he hears the beating heart of the murder victim he has buried beneath the floor.

If there were only a few horror elements in *Manfish*, Chaney quickly returned to undiluted horror in *The Indestructible Man* (1956). The plot, that of an executed man transformed into an indestructible killer, bears a resemblance to Karloff's *The Walking Dead* (1936) and Chaney's own *Man-Made Monster* (1941).

The Butcher (Lon Chaney) goes to his death in the gas chamber at San Quentin, cursing three men who had crossed him: Squeamy Ellis (Marvin Ellis), Joe Marcellia (Ken Terrell), and Paul Lowe (Ross Elliott), Butcher's crooked mob attorney. When the Butcher dies without revealing the hiding place of the $6,000,000 stolen in an armored car holdup, a Los Angeles detective, Chasen (Casey Adams), watches the Butcher's former associates, particularly Eva Martin (Marian Carr), a burlesque dancer, with whom he soon falls in love.

In a secret experiment, Professor Bradshaw (Robert Shayne) restores the Butcher to life in the form of an indestructible man. Unimpressed by Bradshaw's devotion to science, the Butcher kills him and sets out in search of the three men who crossed him.

Killing a few people on the way, the Butcher returns to Los Angeles and disposes of Squeamy and Marcellia. Lowe, the attorney, learns of the Butcher's return and tips off the police. The Butcher kills Lowe and seeks safety in the vast Los Angeles storm drain system. Burned by police in the storm drain, he flees to a power station and is finally destroyed by a super electrical charge.

When questioned about the inspiration for the film, producer and director Jack Pollexfen replied that "*Man Made Monster* played no part in this picture. I wrote the first draft. Sue Bradford and Vy Russell, who get the screenplay credit ... helped on the second draft."[1] Pollexfen's disclaimer would be more believable if the narrator in the film did not refer to the Butcher as "this monster-made man."

While Chaney has dialogue early in the film, all of which he delivers with conviction, his character is rendered mute by Shayne's rejuvenating electricity. Thereafter he stalks his victims silently, his mouth grim with determination, his eyes squinting with rage. Perhaps these conditions were what led the *Monthly Film Bulletin* to accuse Chaney rather harshly of "playing his role with more energy than skill."[2]

Continuing to heap on the abuse, Ed Naha writes, "Dreadful gangster story is heightened in sheer futility by the ludicrous 'you are there' type narration describing the killer's moves as he makes them."[3] On the contrary, the documentary flavor adds a touch of realism that somewhat offsets the film's crudity. Unfortunately, aside from the narration, Chaney's performance in the early scenes, and satisfactory performances by his underworld prey, the film has little else to recommend it. As Bill Warren observes:

> Despite the presence of Lon Chaney, Jr., in the title role, *The Indestructible Man* is a flat, dull and unoriginal shocker, strictly bottom-of-the-double-bill fodder. [It played at the bottom of a double bill with *World Without End*.] ... Earlier in

the decade, no one would have bothered to produce a film as shoddy in concept as this one. But by 1956 science fiction and monster films had begun to repeat themselves. They were still drawing in money, but those made with more imagination and verve didn't make much more cash than quickies like this one. Hence the sad fact that the low-budget films late in the decade are inferior in most ways to those cheapies made at the beginning.[4]

Some charged that *The Indestructible Man* was the first of several films casting Chaney as a mute because the actor's drinking had impaired his ability to learn lines. Jack Pollexfen disagreed: "Chaney could handle dialogue reasonably well. Of course, a talkative monster would tend to be ridiculous. I found him intelligent, probably more so than many actors. He warned me before we started shooting, 'Don't make any changes in dialogue, or add new dialogue, after lunch!'—which he drank rather liberally."[5]

Soon Chaney again found himself under the direction of Reginald LeBorg. The project was *The Black Sleep,* a low budget picture with high budget intentions. LeBorg argued that the film should be made in color, but United Artists, which was funding the picture for Bel-Air Productions, would not loosen its grip on the purse strings. The studio did put forth enough funding to sign such horror fixtures as Basil Rathbone, Lon Chaney, Jr., Bela Lugosi, John Carradine, and Tor Johnson, but it would not meet Peter Lorre's asking price and replaced him with Akim Tamiroff. Because Chaney respected Howard Koch from their days on *Big House, U.S.A.* (1955), he told the producer, "Look, I'll do anything you want. I know you guys have no money—just tell me how much and I'll show up."[6] LeBorg assembled the actors, and they all walked through the script together. This is the plot they examined:

In 1870s England, Sir Joel Cadman (Basil Rathbone), a surgeon, seeks a cure for the strange brain disease afflicting his wife (Louanna Gardner). He prepares unwitting subjects for experimental brain surgery by administering to them an ancient drug called the "Black Sleep," which produces a state resembling death. A smooth-talking gypsy named Odo (Akim Tamiroff) supplies Cadman with victims.

When Gordon Ramsey (Herbert Rudley) is framed for murder and sentenced to die, Cadman uses the "Black Sleep" to induce a counterfeit death state and claims "the body." Upon being revived, the grateful Ramsey agrees to become one of Cadman's assistants. Soon, however, he becomes appalled at how the obsessed surgeon is coldly turning innocent people into mutants. Among them is Mungo (Lon Chaney), the father of a sweet young woman named Laurie (Patricia Blake), one of Cadman's unwitting assistants with whom Ramsey falls in love. The mutants, most of whom Cadman keeps confined in the basement, all hate the surgeon and await the day when they can escape and get revenge.

The mutants do finally escape and kill Mungo, Cadman, and his wife. Their distorted minds, however, send them after Laurie and Ramsey as well. The lovers are saved when the police arrive. The arrest of Odo, who confesses to the murder for which Ramsey was framed, allows Ramsey to return to London a free man.

The film was shot in only twelve days for a paltry $225,000. Despite being a throwback to the forties era, the film was financially successful. The performances are solid throughout, especially those of Tamiroff and Rathbone. The makeup is exceptional, and while the film drags a bit in the middle, it generally maintains an atmosphere true to its intentions. In retrospect, much credit for the film's minor success must go to LeBorg, who knew what he wanted and got it.

Chaney plays Mungo, Laurie's father, who has been reduced to a docile yet sometimes dangerous brute by a Cadman experiment. Bela Lugosi is Casimir, Cadman's mute servant, and John Carradine and Tor Johnson are among the mutants who escape and kill Mungo and Cadman.

We first see Chaney shortly after Cadman and Ramsey arrive at the former's castlelike estate only to have a screaming Laurie appeal to them for protection. In close-up, Chaney as Mungo shuffles toward her, hands grasping, his face a mask of hate. Only at the last moment is he calmed by nurse Daphne, the only person who can control him when the violent urge strikes. When driven to kill, Mungo is a cross between Kharis the Mummy and the Butcher of *The Indestructible Man*, neither of which are inspiring models. When in a subdued frame of mind (or mindlessness), Mungo just sits and stares.

For studio publicity, Chaney, noting that he wears less makeup than the other mutants, referred to himself comically as the "prettiest of the film's monsters." Director LeBorg, however, noted that Chaney's condition during production was anything but comic:

> It was like he had taken dope. He didn't take dope, but he had been drinking and it fit the part because he was supposed to be a goon. But I was sorry for him personally, because he was already forgetting and grunting and getting noisy and breathing hard. I made *The Mummy's Ghost* in the forties, and *The Black Sleep* was made about thirteen years later. But in his body, there was about twenty-five years' difference. With Chaney, I could see that he was dying because his voice was different and his face was bloated, and he was drinking quite a bit. He knew he was going, and he didn't care any more. When he did care, he wanted to be a great actor. He talked about it a number of times.[7]

Producer Koch, however, remembered Chaney in a very positive light: "Lon was also an amateur chef—he made the best chili in the world. If you loved his chili, he loved you. On the screen you always saw him as a horrible kind of guy, but in life he wasn't at all like that. He was anything *but*—he was a sweet, compassionate, wonderful man. He was great with me, and I was really crazy about him."[8]

Some animosity supposedly existed between Chaney and Bela Lugosi. Lugosi was probably disappointed that Chaney beat him out for the lead in

The Wolf Man (1941), even though Lugosi would have been grossly miscast in the role, and he was definitely upset when Universal gave Chaney the part of Dracula in *Son of Dracula* (1943). In any case, Chaney had no reason to envy Lugosi because "poor Bela" played second fiddle to him throughout the forties. No difficulty between them has ever been reported from the set of *Abbott and Costello Meet Frankenstein* (1948), perhaps because they were both playing the roles they made famous. LeBorg described the actors' relationship as he observed it on the set of *The Black Sleep* :

> There was–I won't say *hate*–but a rivalry going on between Chaney and Lugosi from the Universal days when they both played Dracula. You see, Lugosi was the great Dracula, but then something happened at Universal and they gave the part to Chaney [*Son of Dracula*]. There was a terrible rivalry between them before I even arrived at Universal. It came out on *The Black Sleep*: Chaney was sore at something Lugosi brought up and it nearly came to a fight. Chaney picked him up a little bit, but put him down—we stopped him. We kept them apart quite a bit.[9]

Patsy Chaney's description of the Chaney-Lugosi relationship was probably accurate: "They were very good friends. He liked Bela Lugosi. I met him first on the set of *The Wolf Man* and he was dressed as a gypsy. He was a fine actor and a nice man. If there was any resentment it was not on my husband's part. He also doubled for Lugosi on a picture. Lugosi was either ill or had injured himself."[10]

In all probability, the disgruntled Lugosi made some disparaging comment to a depressed and probably tipsy Chaney on the set of *The Black Sleep*. Known for sometimes getting physical when drunk, Chaney overreacted.

Lon returned to television in 1956 to perform in episodes of "The Climax" and "Studio 57." He also turned in one of his finest small screen performances, that of "The Golden Junkman" on "Telephone Time." Jules Samenian (Lon Chaney) works as a junkman for Mr. Constantin (Peter Brocco). When Jules' wife and two infant sons join him from the old country, she dies of influenza, leaving Jules to raise the boys. He wants the best for his sons and buys them a set of encyclopedias from which he encourages them to learn the knowledge of the world. He also works very hard and makes the junkyard a great success. As years pass, Jules becomes manager of the junkyard and opens up many new ones. Soon he is known as the Golden Junkman. His sons, Philip and Alexander (Corey Allen and Robert Arthur), do so well in school that Jules is able to send them to an upscale military academy. Alas, as the boys distinguish themselves academically and socially, they become ashamed of their ignorant father, whom they look upon as a peddler and a buffoon. Upon graduating from the military academy with honors, they finally tell him to his face that they are ashamed of him and want to live at the university rather than at home. Jules is angered and hurt, and though he continues to pay for his sons' education, he no longer writes to them or sees them. In the meantime, Jules memorizes

Chaney gave an outstanding performance with Peter Brocca in the "Telephone Time" episode "The Golden Junkman."

the encyclopedias and enrolls in college himself in order to make his sons proud. In a short time, he graduates at the top of his class. Mr. Constantin asks the sons to go someplace with him on the following evening without asking for explanations. When the boys comply, they find themselves at a banquet honoring their father for his academic achievement. Jules is now not only the biggest junkman in the state but also a bachelor of arts. The sons are embarrassed by their previous attitude, and the family is happily reunited. In "The Golden Junkman," Lon Chaney comfortably handles the Old World accent and gives a sincere and moving performance. His simple but powerful speech at the honors banquet is a very fine moment indeed. He handles his boisterous scenes expertly as he always does, but he also achieves the nuances necessary to pull off the more subtle scenes as well. Patsy Chaney later referred to "The Golden Junkman" as Lon's best television performance.

Also in 1956, Lon co-starred in the Canadian-American television series "Hawkeye and the Last of the Mohicans." Loosely based on characters from *The Last of the Mohicans* by James Fenimore Cooper, many of the 26 episodes in the series concern intrigues among the French, the British, and the Indians in upstate New York in the mid-eighteenth century. The plots range from average to silly, and the acting often leaves something to be desired, especially that of "star" John Hart. Hart had briefly replaced Clayton Moore as the Lone Ranger, but proved too wooden to carry the role. As Hawkeye, Hart's delivery is equally lifeless and unconvincing. Chaney's Chingachgook, the last of the Mohicans, moves comfortably among the various cultures and is a big, easygoing bear of a man unless riled. The series was successful with viewers of all ages because it satisfied the desire for situations similar to those of "The Lone Ranger." Syndicated television authority Hal Erickson did not care for the series, however, and pays Chaney a backhanded compliment: "You know you're in trouble with a series in which Lon Chaney, Jr., is the best actor."[11] It is interesting to note that the opening theme music of the pilot episode was the same as that used in Ed Wood's *Plan 9 from Outer Space* (1956).

Later in 1956, Chaney appeared again as an Indian. The film, *Daniel Boone, Trail Blazer*, concerns the attempt of Daniel Boone (Bruce Bennett) to move his family and other settlers from North Carolina to the stockade at Boonesborough, Kentucky. When the three-part caravan is attacked by the Shawnee, one contingent is wiped out, but Boone's group and another survive. In order to ensure the safety of the third group, led by his brother, Squire Boone, Daniel has to risk the ire of his Indian blood brother, Chief Blackfish (Lon Chaney). Daniel arrives too late to prevent the massacre of the third group, but he learns that his brother has been taken alive. Attempting to make peace, Blackfish and Boone send their own sons to bring Boone's delegates from the fort. Unfortunately, henchmen of the French renegade who arranged the Shawnee massacre waylay the young men and kill all but Blackfish's son, Running Deer. Boone has to flee the wrath of Blackfish and defend the fort against the Indians'

138 • *Lon Chaney, Jr.*

Chaney and Bruce Bennett in "Daniel Boone, Trail Blazer" (1956).

revenge. Boone knows he has to keep Running Deer alive until Blackfish can hear the truth. When Running Deer dies, Daniel uses the dead body to trick the killers into betraying their guilt. Blackfish, his faith in Daniel restored, kills the nefarious Frenchman and restores peace to the region.

This attractively mounted film almost overcomes its low budget. The Trucolor photography of Jack Draper brings the wilderness alive with beautiful and panoramic contrasts of deep red and rich green, the cast is generally effective, and there are stretches of engrossing excitement. Unfortunately, there are also stretches of dull exposition and unwelcome crooning. Publicity headlined the fact that "Lon Chaney sheds 'wolf' skin to play famous Indian chief."[12] Lon convincingly played several Indians in his career and brought nuances of difference to each performance, usually in the degree of humor exhibited.

Chaney was again in cowboy boots at the end of 1956 when he appeared in *Pardners*, one of the last comedy vehicles pairing Dean Martin and Jerry Lewis. In the film, Martin and Lewis are first seen as pioneer ranchers who die at the hands of raiders. Later they return as the grown children of their slain fathers. Lewis has grown into a Park Avenue tenderfoot who craves a little excitement, and Martin is the rancher who takes Lewis under his wing out West. Predictably, Lewis stumbles into the job of sheriff only to find that raiders are rampaging again. Chaney is part of this villainous band, which includes Lee Van Cleef, Jack Elam, Jeff Morrow, John Baragrey, and Bob Steele. As Whitey,

Lon's task is to threaten the comedy team with a pistol and lapse into Lennie-like bewilderment at Lewis's antics. Another day, another dollar. Despite the fact that *Pardners* is a musical comedy, the cast was no stranger to horror films: Lori Nelson (*Revenge of the Creature*, 1955), Lee Van Cleef (*The Beast from 20,000 Fathoms*, 1953, and *It Conquered the World*, 1956), and Jeff Morrow (*This Island Earth*, 1955, *The Creature Walks Among Us*, 1956, *The Giant Claw*, 1957, and *Kronos*, 1957). Agnes Moorhead, also in the cast, would go on to appear in several horror films from the late fifties to early seventies, including *The Bat* (1959), and *Hush, Hush, Sweet Charlotte* (1964).

About this time, Lon wrote his father's biography and sold it to Universal Pictures. The final product, *Man of a Thousand Faces* (1957), starred James Cagney as Lon Chaney and Dorothy Malone as Cleva. Roger Smith played the part of Creighton. Regrettably, from Lon Jr.'s perspective, the film altered many of the facts contained in the original script. As he had done in the past, Lon simply put the affair behind him and continued his film career.

Chaney's next screen outing, *The Cyclops* (1957), was a return to the horror genre. In the director's seat was Bert I. Gordon, who had just completed *The Beginning of the End* (1957), a film in which giant grasshoppers attack Illinois. Storywise, *The Cyclops* is a charmer:

Susan Winter (Gloria Talbot) organizes a search party to fly into a forbidden area of Mexico to look for her fiancé, who disappeared there three years ago. She brings with her Russ Bradford (James Craig), a scientist, Martin Melville (Lon Chaney, Jr.), who helps finance the expedition in hopes of finding uranium, and the pilot, Lee Brand (Tom Drake).

When their plane is forced down in a strange canyon, the expedition is menaced by giant animals whose growth never stops because of their overstimulated pituitary glands caused by an unusually high radiation emanating from the earth. Bradford theorizes that they, too, will start to grow unless they leave the area. Melville agrees, eager to leave in order to file a claim for the uranium, and no one except Susan believes that her fiancé will be found alive. In spite of increasing pressure to leave, the woman remains adamant that her search will eventually be successful.

Their difficulties mount when a hideous 50-foot Cyclops traps them in a cave. When the threatening creature shows signs of trying to remember something, Bradford realizes that Susan's search for her fiancé is over. Now a giant with a distorted brain, her fiancé has unfortunately found them first.

After two days and a night of terror during which the Cyclops kills Melville, the survivors escape the cave and try to reach the safety of their plane. The Cyclops is upon them before they can take off, and Bradford tries to decoy it away from the plane, which is vital to their escape. The creature corners Bradford on a mountain ledge, but before it can strike, the scientist throws a flaming spear into its eye.

As the mortally wounded monster stalks about blindly, Susan, Bradford and Drake fly out of the canyon to safety. The Cyclops now dead, Susan returns to civilization with the small consolation that she has at least learned her fiancé's fate.

Chaney is effective and believable as the impatient opportunist, especially when called upon to register panic, fear, or anxiety. Significantly, publicity material for the film hyped Chaney very little, referring to his famous father and generally just acknowledging his presence. Considering the film's subsequent reputation, perhaps Chaney would have preferred total anonymity. Bill Warren writes: "This dreary disaster is one of Gordon's worst films in all respects. It's tasteless in the makeup of the title character; it's dull, despite several action scenes; it's hopelessly unimaginative—the Cyclops is wounded in the traditional way for cyclopes. In fact, there is nothing whatever to recommend the film, not even as a curiosity piece."[13]

In truth, the film is not that bad. It is cheap, but the special effects are serviceable, though generally unimpressive, and the intrigues among the main characters sustain mild interest. The Cyclops is hideous, though overdone, and while his scenes are repetitious due to the low budget, he does inspire a minimal mixture of revulsion and pity. The key adjectives to describe *The Cyclops* are "unimaginative and unimpressive." Double billed with *Daughter of Dr. Jekyll*, which also stars Gloria Talbot, *The Cyclops* is "Average film fare with some nice visual whammies by Bert I. Gordon tossed in for good measure."[14]

As had long been his practice, Chaney drank throughout the project. Gloria Talbot recalled that this time Chaney was not drinking alone:

> Lon Chaney was a darling, darling man—but drunk as a skunk! ... I remember that all the scenes that took place on the Cesna were shot in a mock-up on a little tiny stage on Meltose that I think Bert Gordon rented for the day. Lon Chaney and Tom Drake were in the two front seats, and James Craig and I were in the back. Well, both Lon and Tom were absolutely *smashed*. James Craig was nipping a little, too, but nothing like what was going on in the front! And in this *h-o-t*, tiny mock-up I was getting blasted from the *fumes*! It was such close quarters that I was ingesting alcohol through my skin, I was getting absolutely stoned, and by the time we got out of there I was *weaving*.[15]

Still, Talbott's overall impression of Lon Chaney was very positive:

> Lon Chaney was just a dear, sweet man, with such a vulnerability that you wanted to wrap him in cotton and take him home. His mama came up to Bronson Canyon and brought him lunch, which I thought was dear, and brought him an air mattress. They blew it up, and he laid out in the sun and went to sleep on it! I thought that was charming. He was a bear of a man, but kind and sweet. I loved him.[16]

Chaney then went from that low budget and largely forgettable Bert I. Gordon film to what *Newsweek* called "A triumph! Hollywood's most distinguished movie of the year!"[17] The film was *The Defiant Ones* (1958), directed by Stanley Kramer. Chaney had, of course, impressed Kramer in the producer's

Chaney, Gloria Talbot, and James Craig in "The Cyclops" (1957).

earlier smash-hit *High Noon* (1952). Regarding Chaney, Kramer said, "He was very exact, a top-drawer character man and a wonderful actor. He was a big man with a lot of character in his face. He could control his emotions and always underacted. He wasn't too happy with monster movies and wanted to do legitimate character roles."[18]

The Defiant Ones was a very controversial film in the late fifties. The story concerns two escaped convicts (Tony Curtis and Sidney Poitier), one white and one black, shackled together as they flee from police and bloodhounds in the South. The two men detest each other because of their color, but the four-foot chain linking their wrists forces a grudged and explosive semicooperation. At one point they reach a settlement and are caught breaking into a storeroom. When Mac (Claude Akins) decides that the mob of townspeople should lynch the prisoners, a local named Big Sam (Lon Chaney) steps forward with an impassioned appeal:

> Big Sam: [*To Mac*] You just don't give a damn do you! [*To the mob*] All right. The rest of you big men... you want to lynch 'em, huh? You, Glover, you look anxious. [*Shoves the rope toward Glover*] Go ahead. Tie it around their necks. Go ahead. [*Takes an ax from another man's hands*] You want blood, huh? Well, here— chop 'em up! Go on! [*Picks up a torch from the fire*] You want to burn 'em. You want to burn 'em? Huh? [*Offering the torch to various men*] You want to burn 'em? Or do you want to burn 'em? Go on, burn 'em! Mac... [*Tossing the torch to Mac*].

Go on. Burn their eyes out! [*When Mac advances toward the prisoners with the torch, Big Sam knocks him unconscious with one punch.*] Now [*turning to the crowd*], any more big men?

Word then arrives that a townsperson injured by the prisoners is going to be all right. Big Sam sighs with relief, promises to deliver the prisoners to the law in the morning, and disperses the chastened mob. Instead, Sam actually frees the prisoners, revealing that he himself is an ex-convict who understands their plight.

While Chaney's screen time is brief, it is both powerful and memorable, another tribute to Stanley Kramer's ability to recognize quality as a producer and get the best out of an actor as a director. In his *Movie and Video Guide 1992*, Leonard Maltin specifically mentions Chaney's fine performance as a reason to view *The Defiant Ones*, which he accurately rates as a four-star film.

Undoubtedly, it was roles such as Big Sam that Chaney craved, but unfortunately, they were few and far between. Regardless, anyone familiar with Chaney's portrayals of Lennie, Martin Howe, Job Marsh, and Big Sam should have recognized that a quality actor was being wasted in low-budget Westerns and bad horror films.

Chaney closed out 1958 with work in a Western of little account titled *Money, Women, and Guns* (1958), a story about lawmen out to arrest killers and notify the victims' heirs of their inheritance. Lon's only television appearance that year was another guest spot on "The Red Skelton Show." This time he played a caveman in a comedy skit with Red.

In 1959, Chaney appeared in only two feature films, largely abandoning the big screen to star in eight television episodes and appear in a television series that would ultimately remain unsold.

His first job was in the series "The Rough Riders" in an episode called "An Eye for an Eye." After the Civil War, three former Union soldiers, the rough riders (Kent Taylor, Jan Merlin, and Peter Whitney), are riding west for California. They and Miss Johnston (Allison Hayes) and her shell-shocked brother are stopped by Pa Hawkins (Lon Chaney) and his three sons. Pa explains that since soldiers had burned his family off their property during the war, he hates all military men, regardless of their former affiliation. Hawkins orders everyone off his property and threatens to kill them if they do not obey. After managing to disarm the Hawkins family, the rough riders offer to accompany the Johnstons to their farm. The Hawkins men return for revenge later, and in the melee that follows, Pa is accidentally shot by one of his sons. Another son, relieved that the madness has at last ended, reflects that his pa "was driven mad by hate. Now he's at peace."

Chaney delivers a convincing performance as a man consumed by hate. It is enjoyable to see him share the screen with Allison Hayes, the 1950s science fiction icon who had starred the previous year in *Attack of the 50 Foot Woman* (1958). "Rough Riders" regular Kent Taylor would in the sixties and seventies appear in low-budget horror films such as *The Crawling Hand* (1963, with Allison Hayes), *The Day Mars Invaded Earth* (1964), and *Blood of Ghastly Horror* (1971, with John Carradine).

Chaney next appeared in an episode of "Rawhide" called "Incident on the Edge of Madness." Jesse Childress (Lon Chaney) is a big, powerful dimwit who on the cattle drive harbors a calf named Buttermilk. Against the advice and warnings of trail-boss Gil Favor (Eric Fleming), Childress is tricked by Warren Millett, an ex-Confederate officer, into joining a scheme to reestablish the Confederacy in Panama. Disillusioned when Millett's wife (Marie Windsor) fends off his advances after having led him on, Childress kills Millett and is shot in the stomach by another of Millett's recruits. He dies in the livery stable, wondering who is going to take care of Buttermilk when he is gone. Chaney is obviously doing Lennie again. The halting speech, the hand and fingers cupping the chin, and the baffled frown and dumb grin are all abundantly present. But as Marie Windsor explained to me in a 1991 telephone interview, "He [Chaney] liked the t.v. work. We all did. I think we were all glad to get it."[19]

Chaney's next small-screen outing was in the "Have Gun, Will Travel" episode "Scorched Feather." In it, Chaney plays William Ceilbleu, a drunkard whose son, part Indian and part white, is out to kill him. While dressed as a "white man," the young man hires Paladin (Richard Boone) to protect his father. Then, torn between two cultures, he dresses as an Indian and goes for the kill. Chaney provides a good character study as the tortured father.

Lon then made appearances in "G. E. Theatre" and "The Texan" before turning in a memorable performance as the "Black Marshall of Deadwood" in a fine entry from "Tombstone Territory." Sheriff Hollister (Pat Conway) and Harris Claibourne (Richard Eastham), editor of the *Tombstone Epitaph* newspaper, wonder why Taggert (Lon Chaney), the former Black Sheriff of Deadwood, is moving to Tombstone to set up a new life as a chicken rancher. Hollister fears that the Black Sheriff's presence will bring trouble from those he brutalized in the line of duty during his tenure as a peace officer. They soon discover that Taggert's hand is crippled, which ruined his effectiveness with a gun and forced his retirement from law enforcement. When villains out of Taggert's past arrive in Tombstone looking for revenge, Hollister tries to lock up the fearless sheriff for his own protection. When the bad guys get the jump on Hollister, the Black Sheriff, who has escaped from jail, barges into the room, stares down the marauders and, together with Hollister, beats the hell out of them. Chaney is perfect as the gruff, tough-as-nails ex-lawman.

Lon next guest-starred on the popular Western "Wanted: Dead or Alive," which featured Steve McQueen, star of *The Blob* (1958). Bounty hunter Josh Randall turns over killer Hunt Willis (Jack Kruschen) to a man pretending to be the sheriff's deputy (DeForrest Kelly). When Randall returns the next day for the bounty money, both the criminal and the "deputy" are gone. Lon Paulson (Lon Chaney), the real sheriff, explains that he was out of town the previous day, has no deputy, and knows nothing of what Randall is talking about. While Paulson is an effective red herring, it is he who finally saves Randall's life by shooting Hunt Willis when the bounty hunter wanders into an ambush. Afterward, the sheriff explains that Willis was his cousin. Still, as a man of the law, Paulson did what he had to do.

Chaney then guest-starred in an episode of "Adventures in Paradise" called "The Black Pearl." One Arm (Lon Chaney), a Tahitian trader, barters with a native for a newly harvested black pearl and hires Captain Troy (Gardner McCay) to take him as quickly as possible to a pearl marketing convention, where he hopes to become a rich man. Also on board the schooner are three individuals who covet the pearl: Mr. Reebley (Anthony Steel), Mr. Wagner (Kurt Kasznar), and Madame Solange (Patricia Medina). Soon after the schooner leaves Tahiti, someone on board pushes One Arm overboard into the jaws of a hungry shark. Captain Troy turns the boat around and heads for Tahiti and the Tahitian police. Another murder occurs before the killer meets his own death during an attempt to kill Troy. In the melee that follows, the black pearl rolls overboard into the ocean.

Chaney's One Arm is an unshaven, one-armed man with a somewhat wild demeanor. In his death scene, with his single arm flailing in the water, the hapless traitor battles for his life while those on board vainly attempt to save him from the jaws of death.

"Adventures in Paradise" was filmed on a 20th Century-Fox backlot, at about the same time as was *The Alligator People* (1959). In the latter feature film, Chaney is back in a supporting horror role. The plot concerns the tragic side-effects of some secret experiments:

Dr. Bennett (Douglas Kennedy) calls in his friend and colleague, Dr. Lorimer (Bruce Bennett), to hear the amazing story which his nurse, Jane Marvin (Beverly Garland), has told under hypnosis. Under drugs, Jane relates that she is really Joyce Webster, wife of Paul Webster, who disappeared on their wedding night.

In the hypnotic flashback, Joyce finally tracks her husband to a special private hospital in the Bayou country where Dr. Mark Wangate (George McCready) is conducting strange experiments on "alligator people," men and women who have been saved from death by a formula taken from the glands of alligators, but have started to turn into alligators themselves. Mannon, Dr. Wangate's hard-drinking, unshaven handyman, nurses a hatred for the omnipresent alligators because he once lost his hand to one of them. At the Bayou estate, he wears a hook where his hand had once been.

The experiments go awry, Mannon is killed by an alligator man, and Joyce's husband retires to the swamp to join his alligator brethren. As the story ends, the doctors debate whether to tell Jane of the dreadful experiences locked in her subconscious mind.

The Alligator People was conceived as the lower half of a double bill featuring Fox's *Return of the Fly* (1959). Although he was near the end of his life, director Roy Del Ruth (*The Maltese Falcon*, 1931) brought home a respectable product. Atmospheric photography and a more than competent cast overcome the film's ridiculous premise and unintentionally funny dialogue, lifting *The Alligator People* into the above average category.

Beverly Garland easily provides the film's best performance. A staple in fifties horror and science fiction films, she added a touch of class to such pictures as *The Neanderthal Man* (1953), *The Rocket Man* (1954), *It Conquered the World* (1956), *Not of This Earth* (1956), *Curucu, Beast of the Amazon* (1956), *Twice Told Tales* (1963), and *The Mad Room* (1969).

Others in the cast were also no strangers to horror and science fiction films: George Macready (*Soul of a Monster*, 1945, *The Monster and the Ape*, 1945, *Alias Nick Beal*, 1949, *The Human Duplicators*, 1965, *Dead Ringer*, 1964, *The Return of Count Yorga*, 1971, etc.); Bruce Bennett (*The Cosmic Man*, 1959); Richard Crane (*Mysterious Island*, serial, 1952, *The Neanderthal Man*, 1953, *The Devil's Partner*, 1958, and *House of the Damned*, 1963); Frieda Inescort (*Return of the Vampire*, 1943); and Douglas Kennedy (*The Amazing Transparent Man*, 1960).

Concerning Chaney's contribution, Bill Warren writes:

> Apart from Garland, the best performance in the film is Lon Chaney's, which is somewhat unusual for him at this point in his career, but he was well cast as Mannon. Totally out of his depth in roles requiring subtlety and reticence, Chaney always came into his own when playing larger-than-life louts. He's outrageously hammy in some scenes in *The Alligator People*, but it is in keeping with the character he plays. He relishes his comic big scene, when he's shooting at the gators, and has a good time hating them in the pickup trip from the depot to The Cypresses, running over a gator with great glee. The role of Mannon really seems crammed into the picture, just a device to keep the plot bubbling, but Chaney is great fun in the part.[20]

Warren is correct regarding the effectiveness of Chaney's performance, but he simply repeats the usual conventional wisdom when he dismisses Chaney's ability to handle subtlety and reticence. Warren apparently never saw, or simply chose to ignore, Lon's work in such films as *High Noon* and *Not as a Stranger*.

Publicity for the film did little to exploit Lon's presence. The pressbook simply notes that the film "marks the return of Lon Chaney to the sinister roles he has made famous in many of Hollywood's top monster and mobster films" and quotes Chaney as saying, "I was probably one of the very few 'Juniors' in the business who could not get started because my father was famous."[21]

It is interesting to note the similarities between Chaney's role in "The Black Pearl" episode of "Adventures in Paradise" and in *The Alligator People*. In *The Alligator People*, the unshaven Mannon, who lost his hand to an alligator, is finally killed by an alligator man. In "The Black Pearl," the unshaven One Arm, who has lost his arm to a shark, is finally killed by a shark. In fact, the two characters look alike, act alike, and are indeed one, demonstrating that on the Fox backlot, more than a little cross-fertilization went on between "The Black Pearl" and *The Alligator People*.

Beverly Garland enjoyed working with Chaney at Fox:

> I thought Lon Chaney was fabulous, fun and easy, and he certainly never drank on the set as far as I remember. It was fascinating to hear him talk about his dad and all the things he remembered about his father's career. He was a favorite person of mine. Maybe he worked with other people that made negative comments about him, but I just adored him and thought he was great.[22]

Lon left the United States on two occasions during 1959 to make films. One outing took him to Sweden to play in the framing devices of a television series called "13 Demon Street." Chaney's director from days gone-by, Curt Siodmak, conceived the series. Siodmak's friend, Leo Guild, convinced Herts-Lion Productions to shoot the series in Sweden. As each episode opens, the camera focuses on a house as a storm brews. The camera then enters the house and focuses on a strange, hirsute man (Lon Chaney). The man speaks toward the camera about the terrible crimes he has committed during his life and about how he is now condemned to remain in that house forever. The camera then tracks to the window and the show begins. Herts-Lion eventually showed Siodmak's twelve or thirteen episodes to CBS, which was underwhelmed. With an unsold and probably unsellable television series on their hands, Herts-Lion called in director Herbert L. Strock (*Gog*, 1954; *I Was a Teenage Frankenstein*, 1957; *Blood of Dracula*, 1957; *How to Make a Monster*, 1958; and *The Crawling Hand*, 1963) to reshoot three episodes as part of a horror anthology for theatrical release. The result was *The Devil's Messenger*, released in 1962. If the three episodes that make up the film are any indication, "13 Demon Street" was clearly inferior to such U.S. competition as "The Twilight Zone," "One Step Beyond," and "Thriller." The plot is pedestrian in every way:

In his subterranean abode, the Devil, (Lon Chaney) assigns newly arrived sinners to their fate. Selecting Satanya (Karen Kadler), a beautiful, sexy suicide, as his emissary to earth, the Devil instructs her to deliver entrapping devices to possible candidates for hell.

First, Satanya delivers a unique camera to a famous but lustful photographer in New York City. He rapes and kills a young, beautiful female occupant of one of his still-life subjects, a quaint old farmhouse in New England. Although the murder goes unsolved, the photographer (John Crawford) is driven to his own retribution—death by the repeated appearance of his victim's picture in his prize-winning photograph of the old farmhouse.

Revulsed by these satanical entrapment methods, Satanya begs the Devil to send her straight to hell. Instead, he promises to take her request to a special tribunal if only she will return to earth on another mission. Agreeing to the Devil's terms, Satanya goes to Torsholm, Sweden, and delivers a miner's pick to an anthropologist who discovers a beautiful woman trapped for millions of years in a glacier. When the anthropologist falls in love with his find, his passion leads to murder, and he is consigned to hell.

The Devil then gives Satanya the more pleasing assignment of tempting into perdition her former lover, whom she considers responsible for her suicide. In this instance, a crystal ball acts as the device of entrapment.

Once she and her lover arrive in hell, the Devil assigns them the task of delivering an envelope to the people of earth. With great glee, the Devil reveals that this envelope contains the formula for a five-hundred-megaton bomb. The people of earth deploy the bomb, and the human race is destroyed, leaving only a wandering black cat to face the future.

Despite the seedy production values of the film, or maybe in hopes of overcoming them, Herts-Lion hyped *The Devil's Messenger* with an attractive pressbook that featured a rare full-color cover. Unlike most other Chaney horror films of this era, the publicity material featured him prominently, rightfully reminding the public of his long, outstanding career in both films and television. Compared to the superior and even more offbeat *Carnival of Souls*, with which it was sometimes double billed, *The Devil's Messenger* registers as a barely passable, tedious disappointment.

As the Devil, Chaney sits without makeup and in shirt sleeves at a desk, thumbing through a revolving file of human sins. Grinning at the screams of tortured souls, he is a devil of whimsical demeanor, relishing his fallen angel status with sadistic glee. At one point, he cheerfully likens hell to "a big country club." Unfortunately, the "waiting room" of hell looks more like the interior of a dilapidated warehouse than the fearsome locality that Dante would have us imagine. One imagines that, for Chaney, the real hell was finding himself in this picture. Suggesting as much, director Siodmak recalled that Chaney was difficult during the filming: "Well, he was already deteriorating, believe you me. He was a drunk, an alcoholic."[23] Still, as Siodmak told me in a 1993 telephone interview, Lon's drinking did not interfere with his performance: "He needed a father figure on the set, so he took a bottle. 'You cannot drink on the set,' I told him. It was a bad example to set for all the others. 'Then I cannot work,' he said. I said 'Then go to your dressing room during lunch or whatever, but don't drink on the set.'"

The actor cooperated. Siodmak believes that Chaney wanted a father figure to tell him to stop drinking. In addition, he related that the actor was so troubled that he ran the bathtub faucet day and night in his hotel suite because it "calmed him."

Also in 1959, Chaney journeyed to Mexico to star in *La Casa del Terror* (The House of Terror), a horror comedy that also featured Mexican comedian Tin Tan. Lon plays a mummy revived by a mad scientist. When the bandages are removed and the corpse is returned to life, it turns into a werewolf. In 1965, producer Jerry Warren bought the film, cut out the comedy, and combined it with footage from a similarly butchered and badly dubbed Mexican film, *Attack*

Chaney as a mummy in "La Casa del Terror (Face of the Screaming Werewolf)" (1959/1965).

of the Mayan Mummy (1963). The result, a hodgepodge of a film called *Face of the Screaming Werewolf* (1965), had the following "plot":

A girl is regressed by hypnosis into a past life and reveals information leading to a hidden tomb. Archaeologists find two mummies in the tomb, one a Mayan mummy which comes to life and is destroyed. The other mummy (Lon Chaney) is later stolen by a jealous research scientist who performs life-giving operations on the body but fails due to a lack of high voltage.

After the doctor leaves the laboratory, an electrical storm supplies the required high voltage through lightning. The body rises from its slab and wanders to the window, only to encounter a full moon, whereupon it transforms into a snarling werewolf. The monster rages violently around the lab until it collapses from exhaustion. The doctor and his assistant then return and inject reviving drugs into the creature, after which it escapes from the lab and attacks women. A return to the lab leads to its death by fire.

Face of the Screaming Werewolf is a mess. Scenes of the girl under hypnosis drag on monotonously, and the added U. S. footage is poorly integrated. Then again, Jerry Warren has never been known for cinematic artistry.

Chaney wears clothes quite similar to those he wore as Larry Talbot during happier days at Universal. Once again he holds his face still as the slow dissolves turn him yet again into his creature of fame. Only one moment of intentional comedy remains. As Chaney chases a woman around her bedroom, he is startled by his own reflection in the mirror. Jerry Warren later commented upon Chaney's appearance in the film:

> I did work with him on *Face of the Screaming Werewolf,* and he was a trouper. He didn't like doing this kind of film; he didn't like being classified as a werewolf at all. After he did such a fine job in *Of Mice and Men,* he wanted to be Lon Chaney, not the sort of character whose face changed. But that's precisely what he had to do.... He did *not* like that, but in Hollywood, people do the things that they have to do.[24]

The film was double billed with another Warren abortion called *Curse of the Stone Hand,* an abysmal testament to chaos starring John Carradine.

An interesting item on *Face of the Screaming Werewolf* surfaced in Rudolph Grey's book *Nightmare of Ecstasy: The Life and Art of Edward Wood, Jr.*, wherein film editor Ewing Brown states that in 1957 director Wood shot footage of Chaney in werewolf makeup scaling the side of a highrise building as part of a promotional reel for an unsold screenplay. Of course, in *Face of the Screaming Werewolf,* Chaney scales a building in werewolf makeup just as Ewing describes. Was that footage used by Jerry Warren in the finale of his film? As I reported in "Bela Lugosi's Last Screen Rites," in *Filmfax* (no. 18, 1990), Ed Wood planned to use Chaney and Bela Lugosi in a film to be titled *The Ghoul Goes West,* or *The Phantom Ghoul.* Lugosi was to play a villain, Professor Smoke, and Chaney was to play Marty, the foreman of a dude ranch. Unfortunately (or fortunately, depending on your view of Ed Wood), proposed co-star Gene Autry pulled out of the project, finances dried up, Lugosi died, and the film was never made. Did Wood ever shoot footage of Chaney as a werewolf? In all probability, Ewing Brown is simply confusing Ed Wood with Jerry Warren, who probably shot the footage of Chaney as a werewolf in makeup for *Face of the Screaming Werewolf.* Either way, the answer is of relative unimportance. Still, it would be interesting to know for sure if Edward Wood ever actually directed Lon Chaney, Jr., even in a promotional reel.

As though *The Devil's Messenger* and *La Casa del Terror* were too much, Lon left the big screen almost entirely from 1960 to 1962 in order to essay character roles for television. His first prime-time appearance in 1960 was in a "Johnny Ringo" episode called "The Raffertys." In it, Sheriff Johnny Ringo (Don Durant) must track down Ben Rafferty (Lon Chaney), a man wrongly accused of murder, before a bounty hunter gets him first. Ringo gets a tip from a townsperson and heads for an isolated cabin where Rafferty's grown children keep watch. When the family gets the jump on him, Ringo convinces Ben to go back with him for trial rather than keep his family on the run. Ben agrees, and on the way back to town they foil an attempted ambush by the bounty hunter. Ben stands trial and is cleared by the jury, after which he and his family start a new life. Chaney gives this role all that it calls for, exhibiting the anger, bitterness, confusion, and sorrow to be expected of one in Ben Rafferty's circumstances.

Chaney next appeared in an untitled episode of "Lock Up." Upon arriving at a fishing lodge, Attorney Herbert L. Maris (MacDonald Carey) and Lt. Weston (John Ducette) discover that Joe, their friend and guide, has been arrested for the murder of his wife. Doubting that their friend committed the murder, Maris and Weston begin their own informal investigation. Because he adamantly refuses to consider alternative scenarios and suspects, Sheriff Davies (Lon Chaney) appears to be involved in some sort of cover-up. Maris and Weston discover that the sheriff's nephew was one of many men who had affairs with the murder victim. Shortly afterward, they find themselves dodging sniper fire. Sheriff Davies shoots the sniper, who indeed turns out to be his own nephew. Standing beside the body, the sheriff admits that he had suspected the boy but hoped his suspicions would prove wrong. Chaney's portrayal of the tortured sheriff is strong, multi-faceted, and believable. Displaying a charming grin and a bad case of down-home incorrect grammar, he creates tension as a man struggling to keep a lid on his own stress.

Later in the year, Lon appeared in an episode of "Bat Masterson" called "Bat Trap." This time out, the dapper Bat Masterson (Gene Barry) is hired to keep a shooting match on the up and up. Rance Fletcher (Lon Chaney), a bully accustomed to winning the matches by hook or by crook, quickly gets on the wrong side of Bat and loses a fist fight. When Fletcher must compete in the shoot on even terms, he shoots the young man who tied him in the preliminaries. He then sets a trap for Masterson in the hills outside of town, but Bat tricks Fletcher instead and saves the day. Again, Chaney portrays a version of the Western ruffian that he played so well.

Lon's next small-screen appearance in 1960 was in an episode of "Wagon Train" called "The Jose Morales Story." In this entry, members of a wagon train include a family of Quaker missionaries, Mr. Roak (Lon Chaney), and Bill Hawks, the wagonmaster. When Jose Morales (Lee Marvin) and his band of three Mexican marauders take control of the wagons, Morales, who thirty years previously had been part of Santa Anna's army, recognizes Roak as the man who deserted Travis at the Alamo. Roak, who has thus far appeared to be little more than a cynical ruffian, protests that as an immigrant to America he had nothing to die for at the Alamo and that he simply took Travis's word that anyone was free to leave before Santa Anna's charge. Hawks brands Roak a coward, but Morales stands up for his former enemy and points out that staying at the Alamo meant certain death. When Indians later corner the group in a small hovel, Roak insists on staying with his wounded friend Morales to fight a suicidal standoff against the Indians while the others escape. Returning to the scene to find Morales and Roak dead, Hawks realizes that he had misjudged Roak.

Chaney gives a touching performance as a man struggling for his honor. Two scenes are particularly memorable. In one, after Hawks criticizes him as being lower than dirt, Chaney provides a teary-eyed defense of his actions at the Alamo. In the second, he explains to Hawks how for thirty years he has searched for an ideal worth dying for, an ideal he has found in his doomed friend, Morales.

With the dawn of 1962, Chaney appeared in an episode of "Stagecoach West" called "Not in Our Stars." Stagecoach driver Simon Kane (Robert Bray) delivers passengers to a stopover station called Halfway House, where his young son David helps out. While attending to the horses, David is surprised by a man in the hayloft, who slips and injures himself as he falls. The disheveled stranger identifies himself as Ben Wait (Lon Chaney), a former bond slave in flight from his former "owner," Aaron Sutter (Jay C. Flippen), a single-minded fanatic who believes Wait killed his sister. Wait, who carries with him a copy of *Gray's Anatomy*, is taken in by Bray and given work at Halfway House. Shortly afterward, Wait uses his medical knowledge to save a young girl from snake bite when the drunken Dr. Ainsworth (Whit Bissell) proves incompetent. Sutter and his three sons soon arrive on the scene, hold the travelers at gunpoint, and begin a vicious flogging of Wait. After being rescued by Kane's partner, Luke Perry (Wayne Rogers), Wait explains how Sutter was wrong concerning his sister's death. The bullheaded Sutter is shot to death when he still attempts to exact revenge. In Ben Wait, Chaney is playing the kind of character he plays best. Some of the Lennie mannerisms are there, but Chaney gives a strong performance as the good-hearted ruffian.

Chaney's co-star, Whit Bissell, was a familiar face to horror film fans. Among his credits are such well-known titles as *I Was A Teenage Frankenstein* (1957) and *The Time Machine* (1960).

Chaney next played the leader of a renegade band of Union soldiers in an episode of "Klondike" called "The Hostages." Among the hostages the renegades take in their attempt to gain access to the bank vault are Goldie (Joi Lansing) and Kathy (Marie Blanchard). Series hero Mike Halliday (Ralph Taeger) overcomes one of the soldiers, dresses in the man's uniform, and subdues the renegade leader. Chaney's character is evil through and through. A clever man, he has an easygoing, throaty laugh that halts abruptly under the surge of sadistic impulses.

As though wishing to appear in every prime-time television Western, Chaney next co-starred in a "Zane Grey Theatre" episode called "Warm Day in Heaven," an entry that adds a touch of the supernatural to the typical oater. The impishly wicked Mr. Finn (Thomas Mitchell) mysteriously enters the town of Heaven, Arizona, and proceeds to interest the inhabitants in various business deals that eventually set townsperson against townsperson and turn Heaven into a hell. The town's jovial blacksmith, Michael Peters (Lon Chaney), becomes increasingly suspicious of Finn as he watches Heaven deteriorate. A killing that Finn indirectly causes finally helps Michael catch on that the "friendly" stranger is really the devil himself. Michael fires three bullets into Finn to prove that as the devil he cannot be harmed, but when Finn falls to the ground, the townspeople decide to lynch Michael on the spot. Just in the nick of time, a young boy discovers that Finn is only pretending to be dead. His ruse exposed, Finn rises from his prone position, flees from the crowd, and fades into invisibility. Wiser now, Michael and the people of Heaven return to their wholesome way of life. Although Thomas Mitchell is the episode's center of attention, Chaney virtually steals the show with his portrayal of the goodhearted common man.

Lon then appeared in episodes of the "The Deputy" and "Wagon Train" before abandoning the old West for the Miami Beach of "Surfside Six." In an episode called "Witness for the Defense," Lon is firmly back in the Lennie mold. Phil Compton harasses his ex-fiancée, Betty (Cathy Case), and her new boyfriend, Sandy (Troy Donohue), usually receiving a defensive punch from Sandy for his trouble. Compton's driver, Mike Polaski (Elisha Cook), plans to kill him and steal his diamond ring. To aid him in his plan, he engages the help of his dimwitted friend Tank Grosch (Lon Chaney), an ex-boxer who is taken in by Mike's promise of a yacht and years of pleasurable fishing. Tank hits Compton from behind and goes back to the car while Mike is supposed to be stealing the ring. Instead, Mike kills Compton and later tells Tank that the big guy's single blow was what killed the victim. Mike then puts stage two of his plot into action by implicating Sandy as the murderer. Series regulars Ken Madison (Van Williams) and Dave Thorne (Lee Patterson) then get on the case and try to find clues that can save the innocent Sandy. Mike next offers to reveal the real murderer to Sandy's father if the man will pay heavily for the information. When Mike gets the money, he implicates poor Tank, who really believes himself to be the murderer. During the ensuing trial, Mike cracks on the stand and admits that he set up Tank for the fall. Tank finally realizes that his "friend" has only been playing him for a sucker. Chaney as Tank Grosch is pure Lennie, Elisha Cook is the stand-in for George, and the fishing yacht fills in for the rabbits.

Echoing an observation made by Curt Siodmak, Elisha Cook, Lon's co-star in the "Surfside Six" episode, noted that the troubled actor still carried with him scars left by the elder Chaney. "He was a complex guy," Cook recalled, "always a little let down by the way his father had treated him."[25]

Lon then hit the road for his first appearance on "Route 66" in an episode entitled "The Mud Nest." When regulars Tod Stiles (Martin Milner) and Buz Murdock (George Maharis) turn off onto a side road and stop for gas in a rural village, the townspeople claim that Buz is part of the Colby family, probably the son of Dorothea Colby who left the town years ago while pregnant and never returned. Because Buz was an abandoned child, Tod encourages him to pursue the matter further. Tod insists that they drive out to the Colby place in hopes of unraveling the mystery of Buz's birth. As their car approaches the house, they are confronted by Mr. Colby (Lon Chaney), who insists that Buz fight his sons. When Buz defeats them, Colby acknowledges that Buz is probably indeed Dorothea's son because no one else could be that tough. Gathering what little information they can, Buz and Tod drive to Baltimore, where they are aided by a police lieutenant (Ed Asner). When Buz finally locates Dorothea Colby (Betty Field), she reveals that her son died shortly after birth and that Buz is really not a Colby. This is a well-wrought episode, typical of the general high quality of the "Route 66" series. While it reunites Chaney and Betty Field (*Of Mice and Men*), the two unfortunately share no scenes.

Lon made only one feature film in 1961, an unsatisfactory low-budget oddity called *Rebellion in Cuba*. Produced before the unsuccessful Bay of Pigs invasion and released only a few short months afterward, the film concerns a group of Americans who aid in the overthrow of Castro's Communist regime in Cuba. Among the rebel troupe are Ramon (Bill Fletcher), Julio (boxer Jake LaMotta), and Gordo (Lon Chaney). The location backdrop of the Isle of Pines is unfortunately the film's only concession to reality as we see a Cuba more resembling Nazi-occupied Europe than the island's actual postrevolution situation. As propaganda would dictate, all the Cuban citizens support the revolt and see it through to success. Both as an action film and as a treatment of a serious political subject, this work of producer and director Albert C. Gannaway fails in every way.

Chaney's first television stop in 1962 was an episode of "The Rifleman" appropriately titled "Gunfire." Marshall Micah Torrance (Paul Fix) and his deputies are nervous about holding the notorious Charlie Gordo (Lon Chaney) in their jail. Gordo boasts that, as in the past, his men will break him out and kill the lawmen. When family consideration prompts one deputy to turn in his badge, series centerpiece Lucus McCain (Chuck Connors) agrees to take his place. When the jailbreak occurs, it is Gordo and his men who end up dead under a shower of bullets. Although his screen time is limited, Chaney is competent in the relatively nondemanding role of the self-confident killer. Interestingly, Chaney finds himself with the same name in this Western television program that he had in the previous year's *Rebellion in Cuba*.

Chaney next joined John Russell in an episode of "Lawman" and participated from his San Fernando Valley home in a "Here's Hollywood" interview about his early career. Then came one of Lon's most memorable television shows: the Halloween season episode of "Route 66" called "Lizard's Leg and Owlet's Wing." Joining Lon were his two horror film compatriots Boris Karloff and Peter Lorre. Playing themselves, the three "horror men" check into the O'Hare Inn in Chicago under assumed names. Lorre informs the hotel staff that they represent the Society for the Preservation of Gerenuks (an endangered African antelope). As Lorre warns an incredulous listener, "If it can happen to the gerenuk, it can happen to you!" The real reason for the conference, however, is to discuss their response to a corporation that wishes them to star in a series of new horror films. Karloff believes that the old monsters are outdated and that the new films should focus on more contemporary horrors. Lorre and

Chaney, on the other hand, believe that the old monsters can still scare. "Real monsters –" as Lorre says, "no space creeps!" While the corporation secretary, Mrs. Baxter (Marita Hunt), is weird enough to feel right at home with the actors, she appears primarily interested in making a profit. At the same time the actors are conducting their deliberations, a busload of women headed by Lila Bain (Betsy Jones-Moreland) arrives for a convention of executive secretaries. Tod Stiles (Martin Milner) and Buz Murdock (George Maharis) are working at the hotel and are assigned as aides, Tod to the actors and Buz to the secretaries. Buz immediately becomes interested in a secretary named Molly (Jeannine Riley) who is pining because her boss apparently does not return her love. Tod convinces Lorre to conduct an experiment with the women in order to prove once and for all that the old monsters are still frightening. Carrying out the plan, Chaney, in Wolf Man makeup, soon barges into a room full of secretaries and frightens them immediately into a faint. Three of them, however, pass out at seeing Lorre out of makeup. Peter and Lon feel they have not completely proven their point, though, because Molly is not frightened at all by the Wolf Man, a fact that almost reduces Chaney to tears. In the meantime, Karloff works behind the scenes to unite Molly and her boss, after which she faints upon seeing Lorre, Chaney as the Wolf Man, and Karloff as the Frankenstein Monster. Boris is then convinced that Peter and Lon are right. As he says, "The power of all three of us in one picture–can you imagine it–almost too ghastly to contemplate!"

"Lizard's Leg and Owlet's Wing" is played completely for laughs, and, though Karloff is billed as the special guest star, Lorre steals the show. Lon appears to have the most fun as he capers about the hotel, growling and lunging at the ladies. In all, he appears in makeup as Kharis the Mummy, the Wolf Man, and as his father's Hunchback of Notre Dame.

By 1962, Karloff's key question of whether the old monsters could still scare had already been answered in the affirmative by Hammer Films. Following up on their very successful *Curse of Frankenstein* (1957) and *Dracula* (1958), Hammer revived other Universal monsters in *The Mummy* (1959), *Curse of the Werewolf* (1961), and *The Phantom of the Opera* (1962).

In retrospect, it is interesting to compare and contrast Lon's performances as the classic monsters with those of Hammer's Christopher Lee and Oliver Reed. Lon's Frankenstein Monster is such a different conception from Christopher Lee's in Hammer's *Curse of Frankenstein* that comparisons are difficult. Wearing an approximation of Karloff's monster makeup, Chaney is a stoic brute, usually passive, but capable of great power and destruction. Lee's monster, on the other hand, is a physically uncoordinated, emotionally and mentally confused creature who evokes sympathy much as a chained and confined animal would. In a move that also diminishes Lee's monster, Hammer's adaptation of Mary Shelley's classic focuses on Cushing's Dr. Frankenstein rather than on Lee's monster. Critics have always underrated Lee's monster. Still, even if the positive aspects of Lee's performance are fully considered, Chaney emerges superior.

The results are different, however, if we compare Chaney's performance as Dracula in *Son of Dracula* with that of Christopher Lee in Hammer's *Dracula*. While Chaney delivers a surprisingly good performance as the vampire, Lee's is simply one of the best ever. The latter's combination of Old World civility, dark sensuality, and animalistic power triumph over Chaney's comparatively narrow persona.

Due to matters largely beyond Lon's control, his Mummy clearly pales beside that of Christopher Lee in Hammer's *The Mummy*. Unlike Chaney's plodding, half-paralyzed monster, Lee's is agile, quick, and powerful. Blessed with the best mummy makeup ever devised, Lee is able to give a more complete performance than Chaney's makeup allowed. Lee's mouth, for example, a grim line, perfectly adapts to and accents the rage, sadness, and surrender skillfully projected by the actor's eyes.

Although Hammer's *Curse of the Werewolf* is not a remake of Universal's *The Wolf Man*, it is interesting to compare the lupine performances of Oliver Reed and Lon Chaney. The burly Reed makes a hideous and energetic werewolf, who, when in human form, is more frightened than pitiful, and more carnally inclined than the forties would allow Chaney to be. Reed's raw youth, flaring nostrils, and savage strength sustain a werewolf characterization as powerful in its own way as Chaney's. Both Reed and Chaney are superior to Henry Hull of Universal's *Werewolf of London*, who is more a seedy Mr. Hyde than a werewolf.

Chapter 12

The A. C. Lyles Years (1963–1965)

In the early 1960s, Roger Corman was the most successful horror film director in America. His financially successful "fast and furious" films for American-International Pictures in the 1950s included *The Day the World Ended* (1955), *It Conquered the World* (1956), *Attack of the Crab Monsters* (1956), *Not of This Earth* (1956), *The Undead* (1956), *She-Gods of Shark Reef* (1956), *Viking Women and the Sea Serpent* (1957), *War of the Satellites* (1957), *Teenage Caveman* (1958), *The Wasp Woman* (1959), and *A Bucket of Blood* (1959). In the early 1960s, however, he directed a series of films based on stories by Edgar Allan Poe that would bring him critical and financial success in both Europe and America: *The Fall of the House of Usher* (1960), *The Pit and the Pendulum* (1961), *The Premature Burial* (1961), *Tales of Terror* (1962), and *The Raven* (1963). Except for *The Premature Burial*, all featured Vincent Price.

In 1963, Corman directed a film based on *The Case of Charles Dexter Ward* by H. P. Lovecraft. The novel concerns eighteenth-century magician Joseph Curwen, who settles in the New World to carry out his experiments in necromancy and eternal life. His neighbors become frightened by his exploits and execute him. In the twentieth century, Curwen's distant descendent Charles Dexter Ward discovers that Curwen's associates are still attempting their experiments in Europe. Disaster results when Ward attempts to follow in Curwen's footsteps. Much to Corman's displeasure, the studio, unable to resist temptation to further exploit Edgar Allan Poe, insisted on calling the film *The Haunted Palace*, a title based on a poem which appeared in Poe's "The Fall of the House of Usher."

In this latest Corman project, Vincent Price was again cast as the lead, and Lon Chaney, Jr. (supposedly replacing Boris Karloff) landed an important supporting role. It would be the first and last film in which Price and Chaney would appear together. As if the pairing of Price and Chaney were not enough,

Chaney as Simon Orne in "The Haunted Palace" (1963).

screenwriter Charles Beaumont penned a motion picture scenario that is actually more eerie than the novel itself.

In the New England fishing village of Arkham, in the year 1765, the villagers are fearfully aware of strange events taking place at the palacelike mansion of Joseph Curwen (Vincent Price). One night they follow a young woman who walks as though she were in a strange trance to the mansion, where she participates in strange rites performed by Curwen from an occult text called *The Necronomicon*. Curwen is a sorcerer who imprisons young girls from the village and sacrifices them to strange creatures from another dimension.

Unwilling to put up with such activities in their midst, the villagers question Curwen and his woman, Hester Tillinghast (Cathy Merchant). When straight answers are not forthcoming, the frustrated villagers seize Curwen, tie him to a tree, and burn him alive as a warlock. Before he dies, he vows that he will return for revenge against the villagers, their children, and their children's children.

Over a century later, Charles Dexter Ward (Vincent Price) and his wife Ann (Debra Paget) arrive in Arkham by ship. When the descendants of the villagers who burned Curwen notice that Ward, an admitted ancestor of Curwen, bears a striking resemblance to the deceased warlock, their hostility is evident. Indeed, they fear that Curwen's curse has been fulfilled and that they will die according to the curse. As the Wards are on their way to take possession of the Curwen mansion, they encounter strangely deformed men, women, and children in the streets of Arkham.

Inside the mansion the Wards discover a painting of Joseph Curwen and notice its amazing resemblance to Charles. They also meet Simon Orne (Lon Chaney), who identifies himself as the caretaker and seems strangely familiar to Ward. When Ward looks again at the portrait, his personality and appearance change to resemble that of the warlock. From that time on, Ward wages a battle for his own soul but is often possessed by Curwen's more powerful spirit. Ward/Curwen is soon plotting with Orne and a warlock named Jabez Hutchinson (Milton Parsons) to restore Curwen to full power. Of course, these changes dismay Ann, who does not understand what is going on.

It seems that the mutants in the village are the results of the mating rites conducted by Curwen a century ago, as well as part of the fulfillment of his curse. The curse continues to fruition as several villagers are hideously burned to death. One night while Curwen has taken over Ward, Orne and Hutchinson unearth the coffin of Hester Tillinghast and prepare to bring her back to life.

The villagers decide that they must do what their ancestors did a century ago–destroy the warlock to save themselves. As Ward/Curwen is about to sacrifice Ann to a horrible creature conjured from a pit, the villagers storm the mansion and set it afire, rescuing Charles and Ann Ward in the process. Ward is no longer under Curwen's power. Or is he? As they watch the mansion perish, Charles' and Ann's faces seem to resemble those of Curwen and Hester.

The Haunted Palace has much to recommend it. With the opening scenes in the fog-bound New England village, Corman sustains the dark and brooding atmosphere of his earlier Poe efforts. Ronald Stein's rousing musical score is as foreboding as the lightning that cracks in the sky above Arkham, and Daniel Haller's art direction brings the village and the "haunted palace" to vivid life. The cast is uniformly effective. In supporting roles, Leo Gordon, Elisha Cook, and Frank Maxwell are particularly impressive.

Among the film's admirers was Judith Crist of the *New York Herald*, who wrote:

> The moral is that you can't keep a keen warlock down–and who would want to, when he's so debonair a chap as Price, telling an unwilling but admiring visitor to his torture chamber "Ah, yes, Torquemada spent many a happy hour here, a few centuries ago," and having so green-faced an assistant necromancer as Lon Chaney [Jr.], so lovely an 1875 wife as Debra Paget and so sexy a mistress as Cathy Merchent, who gets revivified merely by Price's reciting some fractured Latin over her coffin. The Torquemada line is almost worth the price of admission–but not quite.[1]

Corman respected Chaney's reputation as a horror man and used him accordingly. Early in the film, Paget, in close-up, is exploring a room of the mansion when she is shocked by a collision with Chaney. Later, Corman employs a similar technique as Price, in close-up, backs into Chaney, who is merely offering him his coat. Finally, Chaney emerges from the shadows to frighten Paget into a faint as she is going through the palace dungeon.

Shortly after making the film, Price remarked: "Lon Chaney is one of the most talented actors in films today. He has none of the high-class attitude of today's stars; in fact, he is undoubtedly one of the most unassuming men I ever had the pleasure of working with."[2] But years later Price recalled another side of Chaney: "He was very ill at the time. I had admired him enormously and wanted to meet him. He was not really very happy. I didn't really get to know him. I spent a lot of time with him, trying to talk with him and make him cheer up, but I couldn't do it."[3] *The Haunted Palace* did good business, earning AIP $1.3 million domestically and setting records in Australia, where Lovecraft's writings are very popular. But the film's success did little to resurrect Chaney's career as a top character actor.

In 1963, Lon starred with Paulette Goddard in *The Phantom*, a television pilot based on the exploits of Lee Falk's jungle hero, "the ghost who walks." Chaney, aided by vicious dogs, cruelly oversees a slave plantation. When the Phantom intervenes, Lon meets a fitting end. The pilot, however, remained unsold.

About this time Chaney reported to Los Angeles to star in Jack Hill's black and white oddity *Spider Baby* (1964). The film begins with Chaney "singing" the main theme to a sinister accompaniment over the credits:

> Fiends and ghouls and bats and bones,
> And teenage monsters in haunted homes...
> A ghost on the stair, a vampire's bite...
> Beware! There's a full moon tonight.
>
> Cannibal spiders creep and crawl,
> And boys and girls having a ball!
> Frankenstein, Dracula, and even the mummy
> Are sure to end up in somebody's tummy.
>
> Take a fresh rodent, some toadstools and weeds,
> And add an old owl and the young one she breeds.
> Mix in seven legs from an eight-legged beast
> And then you're all set for a cannibal feast.
>
> Sit round a fire with this cup of brew,
> A fiend and a werewolf on each side of you.
> This cannibal orgy is strange to behold–
> And the maddest story ever told!

While werewolves, vampires, and mummies have nothing to do with the plot, the song pays humorous homage to the monsters of Chaney's glory days at Universal and establishes *Spider Baby* as the offbeat gem that it is.

The film concerns a rare disease known as Merrye's Syndrome, which affects only members of the Merrye family, regressing them mentally to a pre-infantile state of savagery and cannibalism. In the Merrye mansion live three children, the only apparent survivors of the disease.

Elizabeth (Mary Mitchel), a teenager, dresses like a little girl and wears her hair in pigtails. Virginia (Jill Banner), also a teenager, fancies herself a spider to the point of eating insects and killing an occasional visitor. Ralph (Sid Haig), the oldest, is the most regressed. Trying to rear this brood is Bruno (Lon Chaney), the family chauffeur, who has made a vow to his boss, Titus Merrye, to protect the family.

Two distant cousins of Titus Merrye, Peter (Quinn Redeker) and Emily Howe (Carol Omhart), come to the mansion with their lawyer and his secretary in order take legal ownership of the mansion. Bruno is both desperate and compassionate as he tries to make life in the mansion seem normal. When he sends the children out to prepare dinner, they catch cats, insects, and who knows what else. Bruno passes off the dead cat as a rabbit and urges the guests to try Virginia's mushrooms ("She has an uncanny knack for picking only the non-poisonous varieties"). When Peter considers a helping of Virginia's slimy black stew, Bruno warns, "Oh, no sir! You wouldn't want any of that!" After Bruno explains to the guests that the children are forgoing rabbit because they are vegetarians, Ralph commences to gnaw at the remains, prompting Bruno to add illogically, "but Ralph is allowed to eat anything he catches." At one point when the dinner conversation turns to horror, one of the guests mentions the Wolf Man, and Chaney shudders with recognition.

The tension between the abnormal and the normal finally breaks down, and the totally regressed older members of the Merrye family rise from the recesses of the basement to wreak havoc. Bruno, realizing that the game is up, destroys the mansion, himself, and the children with sticks of dynamite. Only Peter, who is really a nice guy, and the secretary survive. In the closing scenes, after they have married, we see their young female offspring and realize that the Merrye syndrome has been passed on to yet another generation.

Producer Jack Hill noted, "Lon was just wonderful. I hadn't seen him in anything that well; it was a really good role for him. He played comedy, but he played it very straight and serious." As Jim Morton writes:

> Lon Chaney, Jr....is brilliant as Bruno.... *Spider Baby*'s visual impact may be attributed to Alfred Taylor, who gave this black comedy the chiaroscuro look of *film noir*; the shadows are deep and the lighting melodramatic. Except for a day-for-night chase scene, his cinematography is faultless. Throughout there are clever touches, when Elizabeth announces she has devised a plan for dealing with unwanted visitors, her face literally glows with malevolence.... As in most horror movies, the monsters (in this case, the children) are damned from the start; we know the kids are going to die. But death, when it comes, has no sting. It is met by the children with naive anticipation, and by Bruno with a shrug. The shrug sums up the prevailing philosophical attitude of *Spider Baby*—as Bruno says near the beginning of the film, "Nothing is very bad."[4]

The cast is nearly flawless. In fact, Chaney gives his best performance of the 1960s, and one of the five or six best of his career. Unfortunately, because of the history of the film, it has not received the recognition that it deserves. *Spider Baby* was financed by two men in the real estate business, Gil Lansky and Paul Monka. When the bottom fell out of the building business in the midsixties, the two went bankrupt and saw their film attached by creditors. After it sat in a lab for four years, David Hewitt acquired distribution rights and sent it around the country at the bottom half of double bills. Since it was a black-and-white film, he could not market it alone or as the main feature. Then, two years later (1970), he changed the title to *The Liver Eaters* and sent it around the drive-in circuit for hefty profits. The film is both frightening and funny, a truly unique addition to the horror film genre. As Morton writes, "It is macabre and grotesque, but in an offbeat, fun-loving way. In offering bizarre situations and weird ethical dilemmas the film rebuffs the simplistic response. Contradictory emotions abound."[5]

It was at this time that Chaney got his first offer from A. C. Lyles, a producer with an interesting Horatio Alger history. At the age of ten, Lyles was an usher at a Paramount theater in his home town of Jackson, Florida. After high school graduation, he landed a job as mail boy at Paramount Studios in Hollywood. After a successful year as mail boy he was promoted to the publicity department and later made director of advertising and publicity for the Pine-Thomas Company at Paramount. He then began producing "B" Westerns for which he hired veteran actors, many of whom were hard drinkers down on their luck. The idea of filling a film with old-timers was probably inspired by the success of television's "Burke's Law" (1963–1965), a mystery series in which familiar veterans played the suspects.

Chaney's first film for Lyles was *Law of the Lawless* (1964). Primarily because of television saturation, the "A" Western had largely disappeared by the late fifties and early sixties, but the genre could still occupy the lower half of a double bill. *Law of the Lawless* concerns Judge Clem Rogers (Dale Robertson), a former gunfighter who incurs the wrath of Big Tom Stone (Barton MacLane) when the judge sentences the big man's son to death. Big Tom tries to convince the townspeople to kill the judge, but his attempts all fail. Lon Chaney has the small role of Tiny. In his best scene, he slaps around Yvonne De Carlo and is knocked across a bed by Dale Robertson. A plethora of familiar faces occupy the screen throughout the film, more than compensating for the lack of action. Coincidently, Chaney finds himself in the film with William Bendix, who years earlier gained television fame as Chester A. Riley, the role Chaney was denied. In New York the film was second on the bill with *Robinson Crusoe on Mars*. *New York Times* critic Eugene Archer found it "inoffensive" but noted that the cast of oldsters "makes this frontier outpost look like an old folks home."[6] In 1964 Chaney flew to England's Shepperton Studios to star in *Witchcraft*. Producers Robert Lippert and Jack Parsons acquired the directorial services of Don Sharp, who had in 1962 directed the lauded Hammer film *Kiss of the Vampire*. Harry Spalding's screenplay was strong:

In the English countryside, a quarrel has smoldered between the Lanier and Whitlock families since the seventeenth century, when the Laniers buried a Whitlock woman alive as a witch and took over the Whitlock estate. For centuries the Whitlocks have sought revenge, and the Laniers have endeavored to discredit the Whitlocks by calling them a family of witches.

Now Morgan Whitlock (Lon Chaney) and his daughter Amy (Diane Clare) try to stop bulldozers sent by the Laniers to level former Whitlock land as part of a construction project. Bill Lanier (Jack Hedley) agrees not to disturb the Whitlock cemetery, but unknown to him, his partner, Miles Forrester (Harry Lineham), orders the bulldozers to continue. In the process, the machines overturn several gravestones and unearth the Whitlock dead. Morgan Whitlock rages at the desecration. Meanwhile, against the wishes of both families, Amy Whitlock and Todd Lanier (David Weston) plan to marry.

In the cemetery, Vanessa Whitlock, the witch buried alive centuries ago, rises from an overturned coffin. She and Morgan then use their supernatural powers against the Laniers. Soon members of the bewitched Lanier family begin meeting with fatal accidents.

One night Tracy Lanier (Jill Dixon) follows Amy into the family crypt and witnesses an occult rite performed by Vanessa and her witches. The witches discover Tracy and leave her drugged upon their altar. Meanwhile, Bill and Todd Lanier search the grounds for the missing girl and eventually discover her in the crypt. As they try to free her, the witches return with Morgan and Amy, forcing the Laniers to hide in a dark corridor. Later they escape.

With Bill and Tracy safe, Todd returns to the crypt to rescue Amy. Vanessa discovers him and tries to put him to death, but Amy pours oil on the witches and sets them afire. All the Whitlocks and witches are destroyed as Todd escapes through a smoke-filled tunnel. The girl he loves is gone, but at last his family is safe from the Whitlock curse.

Director Sharp was intrigued by the idea of making a present day witchcraft story. In fact, the opening scene establishes the basis of the conflict as the camera pans from a busy village street to the ancient Whitlock cemetery. With a small budget and a tight thirteen-day shooting schedule (David Pirie reports the schedule as twenty days), the crew often had to rely upon suggestion to get across the desired effect. While effectively filmed in black and white, *Witchcraft* nevertheless had the unenviable task of competing against the lavish, colorful horror of the Hammer Studio. It also had the misfortune of being double billed with one of director Terence Fisher's weaker efforts, *The Horror of It All* (1964), a horror farce starring Pat Boone. With the passage of the years, however, the suspenseful and atmospheric *Witchcraft* has rightfully established a loyal fan following. As David Pirie observes, it is "in many ways a remarkable little film, with a witch (Yvette Reece) almost up to Barbara Steele

Two scenes from "Witchcraft" (1964): *Top*: A noticeably heavier Chaney as Morgan Whitlock. *Bottom*: Chaney presides over the meeting of a witches' coven.

standards and with several extremely fine moments which utilize the possibilities of cinema cheaply and persuasively."[7]

Concerning Chaney's drinking, director Don Sharp said:

> Yes, he did drink a lot, but he was a very lonely man. He was such a nice man; kind, friendly. He was almost grateful when someone would spend ten minutes talking with him. One felt so sorry for him. I didn't know what happened in his life, but he was terribly lonely. He wanted to work, but as the morning went on, he started to drink and after lunch it was very difficult. But by the next morning, he would be so eager, so keen to do it right. He was a very sad man, indeed.[8]

While Chaney may have been depressed during the filming of *Witchcraft*, he provided the press with a typical Chaney response when asked about his opinion of witchcraft and black magic. "I don't believe in it at all," he responded. "This supernatural business may be great entertainment, but realistically it's just a lot of bunkum."[9] With *Witchcraft* in the can, Chaney received his second call from A. C. Lyles, whose new project was *Stage to Thunder Rock* (1964). Charles A. Wallace's screenplay stresses character over nonstop action. Sheriff Horne (Barry Sullivan), a retiring lawman, must bring to justice the sons of the man who raised him when he was orphaned as a child. He kills one but must retain custody over the other at a remote stagecoach station until the stage arrives. Complicating matters is the fact that the station is run by the parents (Lon Chaney and Anne Seymour) and daughter (Marilyn Maxwell) of Horne's prisoner. Horne was once the sweetheart of daughter Leah. Sam Swope (Scott Brady) adds tension to the mix as the gunman paid to see that Horne does not free his prisoner out of gratitude to the parents.

The film belongs to Sullivan, who is allowed to play a role with heart for a change. Again, Chaney is his competent self.

Lon next received third billing in Lyles' production of *Young Fury* (1965). Christian Nyby, who was credited with directing the science fiction classic *The Thing* (1951) and a plethora of "Perry Mason" television episodes was at the helm. Screenwriter Steve Fisher fashioned a Western to take advantage of the youth craze popular in American culture at the time. The story concerns Clint McCoy (Rory Calhoun), who returns to the town of his youth to make his last stand against the Dawson gang, a bunch of teenage hellions, with whom he once rode. Clint was banished from the town years ago for killing the lover of his wife, Sara (Virginia Mayo). Upon returning, he finds her working as the local saloon keeper. Dawson (John Agar) and his gang of teenagers arrive in town, and the shooting starts. Also present is Clint's son Tige (Preston Pierce), who hopes to see his father killed. Lon Chaney plays the bartender. Except for being roughed up a bit, he has little to do for his third billing. Agar, of course, was well known by science fiction fans for his starring roles in *Tarantula* (1955), *Revenge of the Creature* (1955), *The Mole People* (1956), *Daughter of Dr. Jekyll* (1957), *Brain from Planet Arous* (1957), *Invisible Invaders* (1959), and *Journey to the Seventh Planet* (1961).

Merry Anders, who appeared in *Young Fury*, remembered Lon as "a darling, kind, gentle man...who I think possibly wanted to seek the approval of his father, and who maybe never quite did receive the assurance from his dad that he was doing well." Again, we see evidence of the long shadow that Chaney Sr. cast over his son.

Lon then got the call to appear in another A. C. Lyles Western, *Black Spurs* (1965). R. G. Springsteen, who had been making "B" Westerns since the 1930s, was at the helm. The screenplay by Steve Fisher focuses on Santee (Rory Calhoun) who, against the will of his fiancée, Anna (Terry Moore), forsakes the rancher's life to become a successful bounty hunter. Angered when Anna marries someone else and leaves town, Santee drifts to the other side of the law and agrees to help Gus Kile (Lon Chaney, Jr.), the owner of a neighboring town, swing an easy-money scheme at the expense of the town of Lark. Lark is invaded by Santee, who takes orders from Henderson (Bruce Cabot) and the New Orleans madame, Sadie (Linda Darnell).

In this film, Lyles assembled a number of performers noted for their hard drinking, namely Chaney, Darnell, Cabot, and Richard Arlen. Along with Chaney, many in the cast had also starred in notable horror films: Darnell in *Hangover Square* (1945); Cabot in *King Kong* (1933); and Terry Moore in *Mighty Joe Young* (1949). Rory Calhoun was well known by Western fans as the star of the popular television series "The Texan" (1958–1960). He would go on to make a few horror films as well: *The Night of the Lepus* (1972) and *Motel Hell* (1980). This was the last film of Linda Darnell, who died shortly afterward when falling asleep with a lit cigarette.

About this time Chaney got an offer from producer Bill White to make a horror film called *The House of the Black Death* later re-titled *Blood of the Man Devil*. This time around Lon found himself part of a capable cast that included John Carradine. Unfortunately, with half the movie shot, everything began to unravel, and the inexperienced director could not keep control. Someone else took over the project and asked experienced horror film producer Jerry Warren if he could salvage the picture. Given Warren's track record, that was expecting a lot. Anyway, he accepted the challenge. Chaney's old buddy Reginald LeBorg was called in to direct a few second-unit scenes, and Warren went to work patching together something that could be released. The final product was a failure.

When a witch coven initiates a maid from the House of Desard, it tells her that all of the servants have left their employer, Andre Desard (John Carradine), and joined the cult. The maid agrees to uphold the attempts of her new master, Belial (Lon Chaney), to destroy Andre. Belial, a devil worshipper, is worried that a team of medical doctors is arriving to investigate the mysteries of the Desard house and to prove conclusively whether witchcraft is fact or fiction.

Belial's cult has called upon satanic demons to terrorize and kill members of the Desard family. The Satan worshipper has inducted servants of the Desard household into his cult in order to send them back to Andre as spies who can observe his movements and those of the medical team. Belial orders a member of his coven to cast a spell on Paul Desard, Andre's only son. The spell, perpetuated throughout nights of the full moon, brings death to Paul and grief to Andre, who knows that his son is a victim of witchcraft. Although Andre is Belial's real target, he is too strong to be attacked personally because of his own history as a practitioner of the black arts. Belial's next move is to call Andre's daughter Valerie to leave her father's house and join his coven.

Belial succeeds in luring Valerie to his altar of the Black Mass and turns her into a witch. Andre and one of the doctors rush to save her, but they are too late. Andre is successful, however, in destroying Belial.

The film's primary weakness is its plodding, talky screenplay. There are many references to werewolves, but this time Chaney is spared any transformation ordeals and does not in fact become a werewolf at all. Instead he skulks about in a robe and hood, occasionally removing the latter and subjecting the viewer to the rather ridiculous sight of Chaney wearing goat horns to emulate Satan. This was one of Lon's worst pictures to date and demonstrated the depths to which his career had fallen. As for John Carradine, film quality had been of little concern to him for well over a decade. One final observation is that Chaney and Carradine share no scenes. In most cases one would lament the oversight, but in this case, who cares?

After this forgettable foray into horror, Chaney returned to the Western genre to make three more films for A. C. Lyles, the first being *Town Tamer* (1965). From the snappy opening theme to the final shoot-out, this film is one of Lyles' best:

The life of gunfighter Tom Rosser (Dana Andrews) takes a tragic turn when a bullet fired at him by Lee Ring (Lyle Bettger) kills his wife (Coleen Gray) instead. The attempt on Rosser's life is only the first initiated by his mortal enemy, Kansas desperado Riley Condor (Bruce Cabot). Knowing that Condor was behind the plot that killed his wife, Rosser travels to White Plains, ostensibly to look over property, but actually to kill Condor.

On the way, Rosser meets Susan Tavenner (Terry Moore), who is traveling to meet her husband Guy Tavenner (De Forrest Kelley), Condor's supposed partner in a White Plains saloon. Condor soon discovers that Rosser is in town and realizes that his own henchmen, Honsinger (Richard Jaeckel), Ring, Tavenner, Sim Akins (Philip Carey), Flon (Roger Torres), and an aide (Don Barry), have little chance of overcoming the gunfighter, so he conceives a master plan to eliminate his nemesis once and for all. First he appoints Ring and Honsinger as deputies and arranges a fight between them and Rosser. After Rosser is arrested, Condor rigs the trial with Judge Murcott (Pat O'Brien). On another front, he plans to destroy the new railroad engineered by James Fenimore Fell (Barton Maclane), thus making the town untenable for progress.

Chaney as Belial in "The House of the Black Death" (1965).

When lawlessness ensues, a band of good citizens led by Leach (Lon Chaney), Fell, Dr. Kent (Richard Arlen), Davis (James Brown), and aides (Bob Steele and Richard Webb) decides to combat Condor's tactics. Meanwhile, Rosser has had a showdown with Condor and his cohorts, has been beaten once in a free-for-all with Flon, and has protected Susan from her drink-crazed husband and offered her continued protection.

Finally, the good citizen vigilantes try to take back the town but find themselves completely surrounded by Condor's gang. Rosser talks the citizens out of their plan, but as they withdraw, he goes to the saloon for a final showdown. Single-handedly he wipes out Condor and most of the gang, including Ring, who murdered his wife. As Guy Tavenner is also killed in the wild shoot-out, Rosser and Susan Tavenner are free to pursue their romantic interests.

Although again largely lost in the mix of Lyles' large cast of veteran actors, Chaney makes the most of his few good scenes, taking a bullet wound for law and order, but surviving to give Andrews and Moore his blessing. His presence adds to the proceedings and helps make *Town Tamer* an enjoyable walk down the West's memory lane.

Chaney quickly followed up with his second of three straight films for A. C. Lyles. *Apache Uprising* (1965) reunites many of Lyles' former stalwarts in another successful actioner.

Mustanger and trail boss Jim Walker (Rory Calhoun) is returning to

Lordsburg to pick up another herd of mustangs when he is jumped at night by two Apaches. Jim is saved when Bill Gibson (Arthur Hunnicut), a veteran scout and old friend, appears and helps him kill the attackers. Bill is shocked and hurriedly breaks camp when he learns that one of his victims is Deligo, son of Antone, chief of the fierce Tonto Apaches. Convinced that the Apaches are moving toward Apache Wells, Jim and Bill hope to reach the town first and warn the inhabitants. On the way, they fail to convince a cavalry patrol led by Captain Gannon (Richard Arlen) that a serious threat exists. Frustrated, they join the patrol headed for Apache Wells.

In Apache Wells, Mrs. Hawkes (Jean Parker) and a covey of outraged women are about to run out of town Janice MacKenzie (Corinne Calvet), a beautiful woman in distress. Simultaneously, Vance Buckner (John Russell), a renegade with a white man's price on his head and an Indian's price on his scalp, is plotting with two gunslingers, Jess Cooney (Gene Evans) and Toby Jack Saunders (De Forrest Kelley), to rob the Butterfield Stage of $80,000, killing all witnesses.

When the cavalry arrives in town with Jim and Bill, Jim takes an instant interest in Janice's welfare. Sheriff Ben Hall (Johnny Mack Brown), a cowardly bully, tries to use his position to push himself on Janice, but Jim pistol-whips him for his trouble.

That night, largely at the insistence of Hoyt Taylor (Robert H. Harris), district manager of the stage line, the Butterfield stagecoach thunders out of Apache Wells headed for Lordsburg. Jim volunteers to ride shotgun next to veteran stage driver Charley Russell (Lon Chaney). Also aboard are Janice, Taylor, Jess, Toby Jack, and Bill.

Another passenger is taken aboard when the travelers find Antone, chief of the Tontos, injured by a fall from a horse. Janice tends to the chief's wounds as best she can as the stage rumbles on. At the station, Chico Lopez (Robert Carricart) greets the strangers.

Just then, Vance Buckner bursts in the door with gun drawn. Jess and Toby Jack disarm the rest. Toby Jack kills Taylor in a double cross, then kills Bill because of an insult. During the turmoil, Jim and Janice escape to a nearby stable.

When a young Apache chief (Abel Fernandez), discovers Jim and Janice, the former explains that Chief Antone is being held prisoner inside the station by Buckner. He also convinces the Indian that the only way to save Antone is to let Buckner and Jess ride off with the money. After the Apaches agree and Buckner and Jess depart with the loot, Jim follows them. Discovering Jess shot in the back, he finds Buckner and wrestles him to the ground. When Jim is about to kill his foe, he decides that he cannot do so in cold blood. The Apaches step forward and claim Buckner, thereby ensuring the killer's painful death. Jim and Janice then reboard the Butterfield stagecoach and head safely for their destination.

The ending is rather chilling when one considers the reputation that Apaches had for torturing their captives, but considering the character of Buckner (John Russell), the audience sheds few tears in his defense. Chaney is effective as the good-natured Charlie Russell. The stage driver comes across as a man who smiles naturally but packs intestinal steel.

Apache Ambush was a reunion for Chaney and Jean Parker, their first and last film together since *Dead Man's Eyes* (1944). John Russell, of course, was well known to audiences as the star of the television series "Lawman" (1958-1960). Chaney and Russell would not appear in another film together until *Fireball Jungle* (1969). Corinne Calvet had recently made her first and only appearance in a horror film—*Bluebeard's Ten Honeymoons* (1960).

Chaney's third film in a row for A. C. Lyles was *Johnny Reno* (1966):

U.S. Marshal Johnny Reno (Dana Andrews), peacefully riding toward Stone Junction, becomes involved in a fierce gun battle when two fugitives, Ab (Dale Van Sickle) and Joe Connors (Tom Drake), mistakenly believe Reno is pursuing them. Reno kills Ab and captures Joe, who he soon learns is wanted for the murder of Ed Little Bear, son of Chief Little Bear. Joe denies he committed the murder, insisting he was framed. En route to Stone Junction, Reno saves Joe's life twice, once when a band of Indians tries to take justice into their own hands and once when the fugitive is shot in the arm by Wooster (Charles Horvath) during an ambush. Wooster escapes, but Reno sees the initials R.W. on the abandoned rifle.

Jess Yates (Lyle Bettger), the ruthless mayor of Stone Junction, is alarmed to see Joe riding back to the town, and beautiful Nona Williams (Jane Russell), operator of the saloon, is astonished to see the man to whom she was once engaged. Their relationship ended when Reno tried to help her brother escape from jail in the mistaken belief that he was innocent.

Sheriff Hodges (Lon Chaney) keeps Joe in jail until the trial in Kansas City. Yates' daughter Maria (Tracy Olson) tries to shoot Joe, but Yates stops her. He then introduces Reno to some of the town leaders, including Ned Duggan (Richard Arlen), Ed Tomkins (John Agar) and Reed (Robert Lowery). They offer Reno $10,000 to leave town without his prisoner, but he refuses. Yates tries to convince Reno with his fists, but the fight ends in the mayor's defeat.

Reno rides to Nona's ranch, and they patch up their relationship. Yates sends Wooster and Bellows (Chuck Hicks) to the ranch to keep Reno prisoner while the townspeople lynch Joe, but the marshal kills them and gets back in town in time to prevent the lynching. He also orders a reluctant and jittery Sheriff Hodges to collect the rifles that Yates has issued to the townspeople. The women and children are then sent out of Stone Junction, ostensibly to protect them from Indians eager to avenge the murder of Little Bear. Of course, Yates wants Reno dead to prevent his learning the secret of the murder.

The streets of Stone Junction soon become a battlefield of gunfire and exploding dynamite as Reno tries to save Joe from a torch-carrying mob.

Sheriff Hodges takes a fatal bullet while aiding the cause of justice. Knowing that the odds are greatly against them, Joe knocks Reno unconscious and surrenders with the condition that Reno can leave town alive. Yates agrees but immediately breaks his pledge, giving orders for both Reno and Joe to be hanged.

In the nick of time, Chief Little Bear (Paul Daniel) arrives on the scene with a band of Indians. The chief has learned from Tomkins that Yates ordered a henchman to kill his son. It seems that the mayor did not like the young Indian courting his daughter. A gun battle ensues and Reno shoots Yates. Afterward, he rides out to a campsite where Nona waits with the evacuated women and children. The two then ride off to begin a new life together.

While the dialogue is excellent, the plot is just too hackneyed to hold up. The cheap look and all too familiar characters drag the film down to "D" status. Chaney is believable as the sheriff, however; so are Tom Drake and John Agar. Still, this is Lyles' weakest product.

Chaney would make one more film for A. C. Lyles, but by this time the novelty of "spot the old-time stars" was wearing thin. Many of the parts taken by the veterans could have been carried off equally well by any troupe of competent performers. While hyping *Johnny Reno* Lyles said, "Westerns are ageless; ten years from now they will be as timely as they are today."[10] He could not have been more wrong. In 1968 when Lyles made his last "B" Western, the genre had virtually disappeared from both movies and television, and despite an occasional Clint Eastwood film and other one-shot efforts, no major comeback is in sight.

Unfortunately for Chaney, horror films were also continuing to evolve. Hitchcock's *Psycho* (1960) had given rise to a flock of well-executed psychological horror thrillers such as *Homicidal* (1961), *What Ever Happened to Baby Jane* (1962), *Hush...Hush, Sweet Charlotte* (1965), and *Repulsion* (1965). The Corman-Poe series had run its course, and Hammer was relying increasingly on sequels to its earlier hits. For whatever reason, except for an occasional low-budget backfire, few studios seemed interested in acquiring Chaney's services for any kind of horror film at all. Still, he remained popular with audiences familiar with his work. When asked why he thought horror films had such a mass appeal, Chaney replied, "I don't know, but I get a lot of fan mail from prominent people, doctors and lawyers for example. After all, is there anything more horrible than prizefights which have plenty of appeal, judging from the audience."[11]

Returning to television in 1966, Lon made semiregular appearances on the situation comedy "Pistols and Petticoats." The series, set in and around the town of Wretched, Colorado, in the 1870s, tells the story of the Hanks family, all of whom are quite adept with firearms. Ann Sheridan, Douglas Fowley, Ruth McDevitt, Carole Wells, and Gary Vinson headed up the regular cast. Lon played an Indian named Chief Eagle Shadow.

Lon next appeared in a wild and woolly episode of "The Monkees" called "Monkees in a Ghost Town." The rock-and-roll group the Monkees (Davey Jones, Peter Tork, Mike Nesmith, and Mickey Dolenz) runs out of gas while passing through a Western ghost town. They are quickly taken prisoner by two gangsters named George and Lennie (Len Lesser and Lon Chaney). The gangsters throw the Monkees in jail and await the arrival of the Big Man, with whom they are to split the proceeds from a robbery. It seems that the Big Man is dead, and the two are met instead by the Big Woman (Rose Marie). After much singing and gunfire, the Monkees capture the gangsters and turn them over to the police. This outrageous Monkees episode pokes fun at the gangster genre, the Western genre (particularly the television hit "Gunsmoke"), Bob Dylan, and of course, *Of Mice and Men*. Chaney, with a line inspired by his greatest role, says, "George, tell me how its gonna be when the Big Man gets here." In another scene inspired by his Lennie portrayal, Chaney reaches into his pocket for something and accidentally pulls out a mouse. Spoofing their tough guy roles in recurring gags, George says, "Lennie, give 'em your famous line." Chaney then frowns at the captives and growls, "You ain't goin' no place!" a line from both *Eyes of the Underworld* and *Frontier Badman*. All concerned give the impression of really enjoying themselves.

During the sixties, Lon was a celebrity guest at various Western film conventions. Newsman Roger Hurbert, who covered some of Lon's appearances, told me in a telephone interview of his surprise at Chaney's bad grammar and tendency to belch audibly in the company of others. As early interviews show, Lon's grammar could, when he cared, be meticulously correct. As the years passed, he adhered increasingly less to the social niceties.

In 1966, Chaney pulled himself together and made a triumphal guest-of-honor appearance at the Count Dracula Society to accept an award for lifetime achievement. Forrest J Ackerman recalled the evening:

> When his name was announced at the banquet I made the introductory speech about him. He then appeared on the stage, and he got a standing ovation, and that really turned him on. He said, "Would you like to see me do Lennie?" Everyone said yes, and he did Lennie. And he really had it down pat. He stood up there and he became that powerful figure from *Of Mice and Men*, and it brought tears to everybody's eyes to see how great he could be when he tried.[12]

Unfortunately, little future enjoyment and little enticement to be great lay in Chaney's stars. The shadows of a number of painful debilitating illnesses were closing in, and time was growing short.

Chapter 13

Exploitation, Decline, and Death (1966-1973)

T he last years of Lon Chaney's life were painful. Decades of hard drinking and heavy smoking had taken their toll. Besides arthritis, he also suffered from the following alcohol-related illnesses: 1. gout (an inflammatory condition of the joints caused by the imbalance in uric metabolism in the body); 2. beriberi (a vitamin B_1 deficiency characterized by partial paralysis of the extremities, anemia, and myocardiopathy [disease of the heart muscle]); 3. hepatitis (inflammation of the liver).[1]

Soon to come was the throat cancer that would ravage him and destroy his voice.

Along with a marked physical decline, Chaney also experienced a career decline. Never was that slump more evident than in *Dr. Terror's Gallery of Horrors* (1966), a low budget atrocity perpetrated by American General. Basing its title and anthology format on the British *Dr. Terror's House of Horrors* (1965), the company even goes so far as to name one of *Gallery*'s characters after Peter Cushing, one of the stars of *House*. Although top billing goes to John Carradine and Lon Chaney, the two stars are poorly utilized and are included only to lend a bad film some marquee value. As actor Ron Brogan recalled, "It was pretty much on the camp side–a phony thing. I completed my role, an inspector, in one day; I came in at eight o'clock and they gave me the script. We used the old actor's trick of having my lines with me on the set. Everything went so fast that you didn't have time to think."[2]

The film consists of five hopelessly clichéd stories, all introduced by John Carradine. In the first, "The Witch's Clock," Carradine plays a warlock intent on using a bewitched clock to bring back the dead. In the second, "King Vampire," the police search for a vampire who seems to know their every move in advance. In the third, "The Monster Raid," a man returns from the dead to take revenge on his unfaithful wife and her lover.

Chaney's segment, "The Spark of Life," is set in Scotland during the mid-1800s. Dr. Mendell (Lon Chaney), a former classmate of Dr. Frankenstein, enthusiastically theorizes that a dead body can be returned to life if all its cells are electrified. "Life is electrical by nature," he says, "but is electricity life?" Mendel is then called away (by a *phone* message in the mid 1800s). Curious to test the doctor's theory, two of his students, Dr. Cushing (Ron Doyle) and Dr. Sedgewick (Joey Benson), prepare a cadaver. When Mendell unexpectedly returns, they must invite the instructor to participate. When the cadaver revives, it identifies itself as executed mass murderer Amos Duncan (Vic McGee). The three medical men agree that Duncan must be returned to the dead. Mendell is chosen as the one to do the deed, but when the students return they find Mendell's body under the sheet where Duncan should have been. Suddenly, Duncan appears behind them, knife raised. The end.

The fifth and final story, "Count Alucard," steals the name of Chaney's character in *Son of Dracula*. If that were not bad enough, it employs a werewolf as part of the surprise ending. Actually, the segment is nothing more than a feeble attempt to parody elements of Hammer's *Horror of Dracula* (1958).

Ron Doyle recalled rehearsing four days at Chaney's North Hollywood home and observing Chaney on the set:

> He'd bring an ice chest with him that he said contained iced tea, which he would sip all morning. During lunch break he would suck up some more vermouth and then he'd go home. Chaney couldn't remember his lines, and all he could do was stand there and sweat.[3]

The "iced tea" Chaney drank was of course alcohol, and the combination of the booze and bad health made him a less than reliable performer. Chaney's close-ups are startling for the clarity they shed on his condition. Lacking makeup, he stands before the camera's cold eye as he really was–a bloated, blotched, alcohol-soaked shadow of his former self. By this time, of course, he had given up. A film was nothing more than another buck. Doyle recalled Chaney standing up once before a take and saying, "Okay, gentlemen, here we go with the same old shit."[4] At least the years of dissipation had not diminished his aesthetic judgment. Nor had it destroyed his love of the practical joke. Doyle explains: "We were doing a take, and I was supposed to look under a sheet at this dead body. Lon got under the sheet and I didn't know it. When I pulled it back Lon yelled, 'Aaarrr' and scared the hell out of me."[5]

All of the stories are dull, depending upon ineffectual surprise endings. The actors are wooden and unbelievable, the special effects are amateurish, and the screenplay is inept–all of which conspire to mar the final product. Even Chaney and Carradine at their best could not have rescued this mess. Significantly, neither actor attended the premiere.

Upon completion of the film, Chaney moved from his North Hollywood home to 26382 Palisades Drive, Capistrano Beach, California. He also made a very fine traditional Western, *Welcome to Hard Times* (1967). Based on the book by E. L. Doctorow, it stands up as one of Chaney's best Westerns.

The man from Bodie (Aldo Ray) is a "mad-dog killer" who ravages and burns the small, early Western community called Hard Times. When Will Blue (Henry Fonda) fails to stand up to him, he loses the respect of his woman, Molly Riordan (Janice Rule). After the bully leaves the town in ruin, the few survivors try to rebuild it. Jar (Keenan Wynn) settles down in the rebuilt community and constructs a saloon patronized by miners from the nearby hills. Although the community has experienced a moral disintegration as a result of its experience, things do eventually return to a semblance of order. But when the mines close down and the town is left relatively defenseless, the killer returns, and Will knows that he must rise to the occasion. While the plot sounds hackneyed, the strong cast and intelligent script lift the film above the commonplace. Chaney, billed thirteenth, plays Avery the bartender, a victim of the killer's binge in Hard Times. While it is a role that he could play in his sleep, it shows that he was still in demand when a studio needed a top-drawer character actor. Indeed he has several good scenes, the most memorable of which is also subtle. Very nervous behind the bar, Lon watches a girl come down the stairs as the mad dog killer smiles. Lon, who is drying glasses with a cloth, wipes the sweat from his neck with the cloth and continues to dry the rims of glasses with the same cloth. Unfortunately, *Welcome to Hard Times* would be his last quality film.

The next project was Woolner Brothers' *Hillbillys in a Haunted House* (1967), a sequel to their miserable *Las Vegas Hillbillies* (1966), which paired both Jane Mansfield and Mamie Van Doren. The title alone undoubtedly told Chaney all he needed to know: another day, another dollar, another waste of celluloid. The film attempts to exploit the then-current spy film craze by combining it with horror and country music, but the mix fails miserably. If Chaney doubted the seriousness of the project, a quick glance at the synopsis would have confirmed his darkest suspicions:

Driving on the way to the Nashville Jamboree, Country Western entertainer Woody Weatherby (Ferlin Husky), beautiful, blond singer Boots Malone (Joi Lansing), and their business manager, Jeepers (Don Bowman), are caught in a crossfire between police and spies. When the confrontation is over, the police tell them they can go on because the spies have been captured. All of this wrecks the nerves of Jeepers, who is already exhausted from overwork, so the trio decides to find a nice quiet place to stop for the night.

In a nearly deserted town, a gas station attendant directs them to a nearby abandoned mansion. Arriving there, they find the place rather forbidding, but since a storm is coming up, they decide to stay in spite of their fears. Woody sings a song to sooth Jeepers' nerves, but this brings a group of neighbors to investigate the sounds. The neighbors hang around long enough to sing a song and inform the trio that the house is haunted.

Exploitation, Decline, and Death (1966-1973) • 175

Chaney and John Carradine become involved in monkey business in "Hillbillys in a Haunted House" (1967).

When Woody, Boots, and Jeepers investigate, they are startled by sliding panels, dancing skeletons, and a huge gorilla. Their search for ghosts is interrupted by Madame Wong (Linda Ho), the owner of the house, and her bodyguard, Maximillian (Lon Chaney, Jr.). She agrees to let them spend the night in spite of the fact that they are trespassing.

From their headquarters in the cellar, Madame Wong and two scientists, Gregor (Basil Rathbone) and Dr. Himmil (John Carradine), carry out espionage activities against the United States by spying on a nearby missile base. To protect their cover, they have installed elaborate equipment to haunt the house and frighten away the idly curious.

At the missile base, Madame Wong and Maximillian shoot a collaborator and steal a secret rocket propellant formula. Jim Meadows (Richard Webb), agent for M.O.T.H.E.R (Master Organization to Halt Enemy Resistance), then enters the case and follows the spies back to the haunted house.

Meanwhile, a gorilla captures Boots and carries her into the cellar. Woody and Jeepers search for Boots and encounter Meadows, who thinks they are enemy agents. They convince the agent that they are indeed innocent singers by performing a tune. Then the three resume the search for Boots, whom the spies have mistaken for a M.O.T.H.E.R agent.

The spies throw Boots into an iron maiden and later discover that the formula they have stolen is fake. Knowing that their operation has been discovered, the spies try to flee. They are apprehended, however, by Meadows, with help from the singers and an unexpected real ghost. Jeepers, Woody, and Boots then drive on to Nashville in time for their big show at the Nashville Jamboree.

Only two of Chaney's scenes could by any stretch of the imagination be considered memorable. In the first, Chaney's snarling visage interrupts a Merle Haggard television broadcast. In the second, Chaney, wearing a white coat and possessing forged top secret clearance, makes his way through a scientific facility to pick up a secret rocket formula. Looking and acting more like the gangster that he is than a rocket scientist, he is stalled by a friendly maintenance man who wants to make conversation. The scene generates unintentional humor as Chaney irritably tries to extricate himself from the lowly pest while protecting his cover.

The making of *Hillbillys in a Haunted House* was not a happy experience for anyone. Joi Lansing was suffering from botched surgery that would eventually lead to her untimely death. Chaney, Rathbone, and Carradine must have remembered comparatively more fulfilling days—even those of *The Black Sleep*! As far as Chaney's performance is concerned, little was expected and little was given. The film was the last directorial outing of Jean Yarbrough, whose career began with Bela Lugosi's *The Devil Bat* (1941).

In August of 1967, a press release indicated that Lon was to replace R. G. Armstrong as the sheriff in *The Evil Gun*, which was then shooting in Durango, Mexico. When the film was released in 1968 as *Day of the Evil Gun*, Paul Fix was in the sheriff's role. Why Lon did not play the part is unknown. He loved Mexico, and unless something unexpected intervened, he surely would have followed through.

Chaney followed up *Hillbillys in a Haunted House* with *Buckskin*, his last traditional Western, as well as the last film he would make for A. C. Lyles:

Chaddock (Barry Sullivan), a frontiersman, has to accept the position of territorial marshal for Montana. The frontier is gone, his Indian wife is dead, and he must take the job to support his ten-year-old son, Akii (Gerald Michenaud).

When Chaddock and Akii arrive outside the town of Gloryhole, they meet the Cody family: Frank (Bill Williams), Sarah (Barbara Hale) and young Jimmy (Michael Larrain), one of seven homesteading families in the area that is preparing to move west to Oregon. It seems that a Rep Marlowe has bought land in the northern part of the valley and blocked off the water to the south, forcing the homesteaders to move so that he can open and run a mine. Chaddock promises to reopen the dam and convinces the Codys to stay.

Arriving in town, Chaddock and Akii find Sheriff Tangley (Lon Chaney) making his morning rounds. In the saloon, Chaddock meets Travis (Leo Gordon), who has lost to Rep Marlowe in a poker game all the money he had made after years of demanding labor. When Chaddock and Akii walk to the general store to get the boy bathed and outfitted for the new way of life, Rep Marlowe (Wendell Corey) and Patch (John Russell), a hardened gunman who wears a patch over one eye, enter the saloon.

Sheriff Tangley hurries in to inform Marlowe and Patch of Chaddock's arrival. Patch, who has had an altercation with Chaddock in the past, now looks forward to killing him. Marlowe, however, insists that they proceed cautiously because killing an outside lawman is serious business.

When key townspeople prove either unwilling or afraid to help Chaddock rid the area of Marlowe and Patch, he befriends Nora (Joan Caulfield), a former teacher fired by the citizens after she was assaulted in her bedroom one night by a group of miners. Because of her mistreatment, she has become an embittered saloon woman. Chaddock asks Nora to return to the classroom and teach his son. He then rides off to blow up Marlowe's dam.

A bloody gunfight ensues when Chaddock and Cody's young son meet the resistance of Marlowe's men. The dam falls, but the boy is killed and Chaddock is bitten by a rattlesnake. The marshal struggles back to the Cody ranch, where he is nursed back to health by the grieving family.

Knowing that Chaddock will soon return to town, Marlowe plans to have him met and killed by miners angered at the closing of the mine. When Chaddock arrives, he is surprised to find himself aided by the townspeople who had earlier turned him down. When the gunsmoke clears, Marlowe, Tangley, and several miners are dead, and Chaddock is wounded. Still, law and order has returned to Gloryhole, and Chaddock and his son are ready to begin a new life there.

Chaney receives fourth billing as the inept sheriff who finally works up the courage to do his duty, only to catch a fatal bullet for his trouble. Once again surrounded by veteran actors, he turns in his usual competent supporting performance.

In 1968, Universal compiled several episodes of the television series "Pistols and Petticoats" and released them as a television movie called *The Far Out West* (1968). Lon appears in the show as Chief Eagle Shadow, the character he played throughout the series.

On February 2, 1969, Boris Karloff passed away at the King Edward Hospital, Midhurst, Sussex. The second of the greatest horror stars of the thirties and forties was dead. Along with other celebrities, Chaney contributed some thoughts on Karloff for a memorial book by Forrest J Ackerman. Chaney's response was characteristic:

> They wanted me to go on television and talk about him but I had to turn them down because, to be honest, I didn't know him that well. And—you all know me—I'm not the gushy type. Just let me say that it was a pleasure to work with him—way back in '45 when we made *House of Frankenstein* together, and in '52 in *The Black Castle*—and some years later when we did that Route 66 stunt where I played my Dad's role of the Hunchback and Karloff was his own best creation,

the Frankenstein monster. I was glad to get to carry on his role in *Ghost of Frankenstein*, and like everybody else in show business, I guess we knew his death was to be expected, all the same it's sure hard to think of an actor like him gone after all the years he was active on the screen. He and I both got an award from the Count Dracula Society, and to all its members and the readers of this book, who I know will miss him most of all, let me say I'm sure it was a blessing to have so many people care about him at his age.

Rest in Peace, Boris Karloff.[6]

Chaney's next project was "A Stranger in Town" (1969), a feature for National Educational Television filmed in Brakettville, Texas. Shot under the auspices of the University of Texas, the project included a number of university students. As Chaney recalled, "I really had a ball with those kids."[7] Then he was reunited with John Russell in *Fireball Jungle* (1969). Exploitation producer George Roberts knew a good thing when he saw it. In 1967 he brought *The Weird World of LSD* to theater screens across the country. The hippie drug craze was hot, and Roberts exploited it. His philosophy of film production was simple: "You take handsome people, striking and exotic young actresses, combine with good actors and mix with just the correct blending of virility, sex and excitement."[8] With *Fireball Jungle*, he attempted to combine the psychedelic craze of the late sixties with the juvenile delinquency action formula of the 1950s. The plot synopsis says it all:

Cateye Meares (Alan Mixon), the vicious leader of a sadistic motorcycle gang, is charged by the Racing Commission with causing the death of another driver, Buzzy Cullen. Lack of evidence allows Cateye to go free, and he rejoins his hog-riders and their barracuda babes.

When Steve Cullen (Randy Kirby) appears at the tracks and begins winning races, Cateye and Marty (Steve Daniel) warn him to leave and later beat him up. Steve, racing under an assumed name, is really the brother of the murdered Buzzy Cullen. Bitterness intensifies between Steve and Cateye as the former attempts to learn the facts of his brother's death and falls in love with Ann Tracey (Nancy Donohue).

Cateye's fast life is actually backed by Nero (John Russell), a wealthy, underworld kingpin who uses the young hoodlum to supply his syndicate with stolen cars fenced through a junkyard operated by Sammy (Lon Chaney). Sammy wants out but feels too old to fight. When Steve is forced to join Nero's organization, he tries to give Sammy the courage to start a new life. Unfortunately, before that can happen, Cateye and his gang initiate a rumble at the junkyard and burn Sammy alive in his shack.

Furious over Sammy's death, Steve fights Cateye at the bikers' hangout, where Judy (Vicki Nunis), one of Cateye's barracudas, has been tortured for betraying the gang. Cateye's beating puts Steve in the hospital, but the young man recovers and challenges his nemesis to one last race. During the race, Cateye is killed. Steve has avenged the death of his brother.

As an exploitation film, *Fireball Jungle* delivers. On the positive side, Mears is effective in his role as a cruel smart-ass and steely-eyed Russell is chilling as Nero, the mob kingpin. On the negative side, Randy Kirby is a rather insipid hero and the comic relief scenes at the psychedelic bar where customers sit on toilet stools seem interminable.

With quivering jowls and rheumy eyes, Chaney turns in a short but moving performance as the pathetic junkman. At times he slips into broken English as though returning subconsciously to his excellent 1956 television role as "The Golden Junkman." The Chaney of 1969, however, is a stark enough contrast to the Chaney of 1956 to bring tears to one's eyes. In Chaney's best scene, Randy Kirby exhorts the tired and sick Chaney to screw up his courage, become a man again, and bring back the days when his junkyard was a source of pride. Buoyed up by the pep talk and momentarily filled with hope, Lon energetically rises with his broom as though to sweep away the past. As the screenplay would have it, however, he is burned alive only a few scenes later. Perhaps Chaney was aware of the parallels between the junkyard and his own career. While the film did nothing to enhance his reputation, the Tampa location provided Chaney the chance to get in some good fishing, health permitting.

Lon's next film project was another exploitation film. A good cut below *Fireball Jungle* in both taste and quality, it explores the violent potential of the "women's lib" movement. Filmed as *A Time to Run*, it was released in 1971 as *The Female Bunch*, a play on the title *The Wild Bunch* (1969). The film's central character, Grace (Jennifer Bishop), has assembled a gang of beautiful, disillusioned young women who hate men and society—in that order. At their hideout near the Mexican border, Grace's only laws are that she be accorded blind obedience and that the ranch be completely free of men. The women's lifestyle is one of alcoholism, drug abuse, and hedonistic abandon—not to speak of cruelty. When crossed by a man, they resort to such acts as a barbed wire hanging, a facial branding, a pitch-forking, and a horse-dragging.

Chaney plays Monty, an aged ex-stuntman and ranch groom who aids Grace in smuggling drugs across the border. When he begins to press Grace for a larger share of the smuggling profits and also forces his unwelcome attentions on her, she bashes him on the head with a hammer and sends him into the desert, dragged behind a wild horse. At the film's end, Monty returns, bloody but alive, just in time to shoot Grace and save a young couple from certain death at her hands.

The first thing one notices about Lon Chaney in this film is the obvious deterioration of his voice. Always gravel-voiced, he is now downright hoarse, evidence of the throat cancer that had begun its deadly advance.

Ad lines for the film include gems like these:
"They'll break your heart—or your head!"
"They rule men with whips and a branding iron!"

"Watch out for the female bunch! They'd just as soon kill you as kiss you...and they'll probably do both!"

"They treat their horses better than their men!"

In order to appeal to the morbidly curious, publicity material noted that several scenes were filmed at the Spahn Ranch in Chatsworth, California, home of the infamous Manson family. Other locations included Utah's Monument Park and the Valley of the Goblins, as well as Las Vegas.

Co-star Russ Tamblyn has never liked being reminded of the film. Chaney undoubtedly felt the same way about it at the time.

On October 10, Lon appeared on Johnny Carson's "Tonight Show." Shortly afterward he received a letter from fan and horror film memorabilia collector Gary Dorst. Lon's October 18 reply to Dorst reveals his plans at the close of 1969:

> Your very nice letter received and thank you very much. You write well–I'm never too busy to read a good letter.
>
> As you know from listening to the Johnny Carson show, I am in the process of compiling a pictorial anthology of my father's career and mine–when the book is published, it will contain several hundred photographs, covering over a hundred years of Chaneys in the world of entertainment. Quite a few persons have loaned photos for this project–we have reproduced them and returned the originals intact.
>
> I will be happy to autograph whatever you send me (personal, "to Gary")–and I wondered if you would do ME a favor. If there happens to be any pictures in the ones you send that we do not have for the book–would you mind if we made copies before returning them? It would be appreciated.
>
> In the event of our having to reproduce any of your material, there would be a slight delay in returning it–but you will get them back in the same good condition as you sent them–(and it shouldn't be more than a few weeks)–with the addition, of course, of my autograph as you requested.
>
> Let me know if this is agreeable–and I thank you very much.[9]

Dorst conducted what is believed to be Chaney's last full formal interview on November 20 and mailed him nine pieces of movie memorabilia, including posters from *Son of Dracula, Of Mice and Men, Ghost of Frankenstein, Man-Made Monster, One Million B.C.,* and *The Wolf Man*. Months passed without the posters being returned. After sending two queries, Dorst received the following reply dated February 20, 1970:

> After receiving your second letter about the return of the material that you had loaned me, I feel very badly because I have not written and returned the material sooner. As you know, I have been quite ill, and in the throes of writing my own book, so as you can well imagine the interval between rest periods for myself and writing consumes all my time. I am most appreciative of your efforts in every direction along these lines, and you have helped me immensely with just your good thoughts. As you can see, it is physically impossible for me to carry on a running correspondence at this time. Should there be any improvement, we can pick up where we left off.

Enclosed you will find all the posters and photographs that you sent me. Due to duplication, I have only made negatives from two posters. However, should the occasion arise that I need further help from you, I feel that you are a good enough friend that I may call upon you for assistance.... Re the expected publication date of my book, I am anticipating its release to coincide very nearly with Christmas, 1970.[10]

About this time, Forrest Ackerman, editor of *Famous Monsters of Filmland*, visited Chaney's home for an interview. Lon was interested in attaining Ackerman's help toward the completion of his book, but he was much less interested in volunteering information for Ackerman's interview. Forry recalled:

> He just wasted my time that afternoon. He just wanted to talk about fishing and other subjects that were not in the least bit rewarding in trying to find out anything about his career.... At any time I attempted to talk about his own career or his father's he would become very vague and uninterested. I asked where his father was buried and he said—"Oh, over there, somewhere." He didn't even know where he was pointing.[11]

Because of throat cancer and other illnesses, Chaney was in worse shape than anyone knew. Doctors performed surgery on the cancerous throat and removed half of his vocal chords. The safest procedure would have been complete removal, but Lon would not hear of it. After the surgery, he began a series of cobalt treatments. Under such conditions, the projected publication date for his book came and went.

Chaney's last film, *Dracula vs. Frankenstein* (1971), was almost never completed, not because of Chaney's health, but because of numerous production difficulties. The original production title was *Blood Freaks—The Blood Seekers*. Paul Lukus was to play the role that eventually went to J. Carrol Naish, that of a doctor who extracts blood from young women in order to rejuvenate his own aging body. Because the script was so bloody, Lukus decided not to participate. Broderick Crawford, set to portray the police detective, also bowed out. To accommodate the actors' schedules, shooting began before all the production elements were in place. When the rough cut was screened, production supervisor Sam Sherman realized that the film lacked punch and exploitation value. After toying with various possible repair scenarios, Sherman decided to add Dracula and the Frankenstein Monster to the mix. In reshooting elements of the film, an original motorcycle angle was greatly downplayed. Still, a prolonged series of reedits followed. When the producer decided to include a climactic battle between Dracula and the Frankenstein Monster, the title evolved from *Blood Freaks* to *Dracula vs. Frankenstein*.

Once the actors arrived on the set, it became clear to all concerned that Chaney and Naish were too sick to work. Actually, director Al Adamson hired them sight unseen, lured by the prospect of having the two legends appear together in his film. Also in the cast was Angelo Rossito, the dwarf who appeared with Bela Lugosi in *Spooks Run Wild* (1941) and *Scared to Death* (1947).

Also spicing up the whole affair were parts of the original laboratories created by Ken Strickfaden for *Frankenstein* (1931), *Son of Frankenstein* (1939), and *Flash Gordon* (1936).

The plot is quite convoluted:

In an old graveyard at midnight, Count Dracula (Zandor Vorkov) digs up the Frankenstein Monster (John Bloom) and kills the caretaker. Meanwhile, near an amusement park by the beach, Groton, the mad zombie (Lon Chaney), uses an axe to behead a young girl named Joan. Judith (Regina Carrol), Joan's sister, soon initiates a search for her missing sibling through Sgt. Martin (Jim Davis) of the Missing Persons Bureau.

Count Dracula discovers that Dr. Frankenstein (J. Carrol Naish), a relative of the infamous monster-maker, is using the name "Durea" and running a "House of Horrors" at the amusement pier. The museum is actually a front for the doctor's search for a blood serum capable of restoring youth and physical health. Groton and an evil dwarf named Grazbo (Angelo Rossitto) supply the doctor with young girls' bodies required for the experiments. Dracula wants the serum in order to extend his waking hours in the daytime. Dracula informs Dr. Frankenstein that he possesses the Frankenstein Monster. Predictably, the old man is eager to return the creature to full strength. Dr. Frankenstein also informs Dracula that he still has the lab equipment used by his infamous ancestor. The unholy partners soon strap the Monster to an operating table and revive it with electricity. Dr. Frankenstein then uses the 8-foot Monster to kill Dr. Beaumont (Forrest J Ackerman), who medically discredited him years earlier.

In her search for her sister, Judith teams up with a writer named Mike (Anthony Eisley), and together they pursue leads to Dr. Durea's museum. Durea, of course, denies any knowledge of Joan. Actually, the girl is one of Durea's living dead, confined in a glass coffin in the dungeon.

Later, while investigating the pier, Mike discovers the secret entrance to Dr. Frankenstein's lab. Judith and Mike enter and soon find themselves in the dungeon, where they are stopped by Dr. Frankenstein and Groton. The mad zombie chases Judith, and Mike pursues Dr. Frankenstein. The old man flees into the exhibit room of his chamber of horrors, fires a pistol at Mike, and is accidentally beheaded by his own guillotine.

Meanwhile, Groton chases Judith onto the roof, where the two are spotted by Sgt. Martin. As the mad zombie lunges at his prey, a bullet from Sgt. Martin's gun sends him to the pavement–dead. When Judith tries to descend the roof, Dracula puts her in a trance and prepares to make her the victim of the final blood serum experiment. The vampire takes her to a powerhouse and ties her to a railing platform high above the ground. Suddenly, the Frankenstein Monster arrives and begins walking down the long flight of stairs toward Judith. At that moment, Mike charges to the rescue with a lighted flare, which he uses to fend off the Frankenstein Monster. Blinded by the fire, the monster

· *Exploitation, Decline, and Death (1966-1973)* • 183

Axe in hand, Chaney totes back a victim in "Dracula vs. Frankenstein" (1971).

attacks Dracula, allowing Mike and Judith a chance to escape. Dracula quickly regains control, however, and burns Mike to death with a ray from his ring.

Dracula again takes possession of Judith, but this time the Monster expresses interest as well. The Monster and the king of the vampires engage in a death battle, which ends when Dracula literally tears the Monster limb from limb. Unknown to the victor, however, the sun is rising. Unable to return to his coffin in time, the Count perishes. Judith has survived the nightmare.

Needless to say, the final product is replete with problems. Regina Carrol gives the worst performance of her embarrassing career, the lighting during the final climactic battle of the monsters is inadequate, Zandor Vorkov is one of the worst Draculas in screen history, and big John Bloom projects no personality at all as the Frankenstein Monster. Despite these drawbacks, however, the film works at the exploitation level. Veteran composer William Lava's score is appropriately jarring, Strikfaden's lab greatly elevates the production values, and Rossito, Eisley, and Davis give adequate performances.

That brings us to a consideration of Naish and Chaney. This film, the last for both actors, was their first and only reunion since *Calling Dr. Death* and *House of Frankenstein* in the forties. Naish plays his role in a wheelchair, though he was not in reality confined to one. Struggling with ill-fitting dentures and not at all resembling the Naish of twenty-five years earlier, he is appropriate as the weary, aging, burned-out monster-maker. Unfortunately, his death scene is extremely clumsy due to poor directing and editing.

When asked how he got along with Chaney during shooting, Sam Sherman shed some disturbing light upon the actor's frame of mind at that time:

> I wasn't there for that, but I can pass on to you some of the things that I know from Denver Dixon. He had known Lon Chaney since the '30s and had worked in pictures with him. Denver told me that Chaney was dying from cancer of the throat and that he was constantly tired. He had to lie down between takes. He kept saying to Denver, "You and I are the only two left.... They're all gone.... I want to die now. There's nothing left for me; I just want to die." He kept saying that throughout the shooting of the movie. So we had a man who had been a heavy drinker, who had cancer, who was very ill. He was dying, *knew* that he was dying, and *wanted* to die. These certainly are *not* the elements that make up great acting in a movie![12]

Continuing in this sad vein, Russ Tamblyn recalled the scenes he and Chaney did together: "I don't remember much about it. We were down under a pier or something at night, and he was swinging an axe around. He was drunk; they had to hold him up. I just thought 'how sad.' He was in some of my favorite films when I was kid."[13] The late night shooting probably accounted for Lon's drunken state, as he had warned the director and producer, "Get everything you can out of me before 1 p.m. because after that I can't guarantee anything."[14] Still, the overall state of his health may have contributed to his having to be propped up.

As depressing as all of this sounds, Anthony Eisley observed another side of Chaney on the set. He recalls:

> He was probably the most fascinating man I had ever worked with. He was very, very ill then—he would have to lie down after every take—but to talk with him and to hear his stories was just incredible.... He spoke with a whisper, which is why they made his character a mute. You may recall that he and I had a little bit of a physical encounter in the picture. Lon was going to be doubled in that sequence, because he really was ill. Some time before they were supposed to do that sequence, he whispered to me that, once more before he—he didn't say *died*, but that's what he meant—he would really like to do a fight scene, and that they wouldn't let him do it. I thought, jeez, this guy has been around so long, he's a legend of a sort—why not give him his last wish? Back in my *Hawaiian Eye* days Bob Conrad and I had done a good portion of our own fights and so forth, so we knew the basic techniques. I went to Al Adamson and told him we could shoot this thing in really short cuts, and there was no reason that Chaney couldn't do it. So we did do the fight that way, and he was exhausted. The next day he came to the set and told me he'd gone home the night before and almost drowned in the bathtub, he was so tired—his wife had to wake him up! But he told me, "I'm so glad we did it, because that was the most fun I've had in ten years."[15]

Actually, Chaney turns in a commendable performance under the circumstances. The sadness of his appearance lies in the fact that he had so obviously deteriorated and was very sick. Of course, those who had followed his career were disappointed to see him in such a role. Still, when he assumes the baffled Lennie look and shakes his grimacing face and wild hair, he presents a ghastly apparition as Groton, the mad zombie. As the film makes clear, Groton himself is not in the best of health, and Chaney is appropriately frightening to the young audience that patronized and enjoyed the film. In keeping with his persona as Lennie gone mad, Chaney's role again calls for him occasionally to stroke a small animal, in this case a puppy.

In 1972, the ill Chaney received a visit from his lifelong friend, Broderick Crawford, who reported that Lon "was a pretty sick man by then, and had a lot of his insides taken out. But he didn't stay in bed. He was always up and moving around. He showed me quite a few stills for a book he was going to do [*A Century of Chaneys*]."[16]

Also about this time, Lon expressed the view that "They don't know how to make good horror films in Hollywood anymore. Boy, they really need me!"[17] He would often slam down his fist for emphasis when defending classic horror films against those of the late sixties and early seventies. As he aged, knowledge that those Universal horror films would probably be his lasting legacy must have increased his respect for them, and he was not afraid to say so.

In the May 1973 issue of *Famous Monsters of Filmland*, Forrest J Ackerman informed horror film fans of Chaney's ill health and encouraged them to send get well cards and fan letters: "Lon Chaney Jr. is a very sick man. 'I expect to be in the hospital till probably the end of April,' he said in a tired, weak, hoarse voice over the telephone.... The main thing is to let Lon know that thousands of you care, that he is not forgotten in his time of pain."[18]

The response was overwhelming. Soon afterward, Ackerman received a call from the grateful Chaney. "Say, young fellow," he said in his hoarse, gruff voice, "you sure been doing a great job for me. Want to thank you for all them letters I been getting. Really makes me feel good."[19] Unfortunately, not much else was making Lon feel good at this point. The cobalt treatments for cancer were taking an extreme toll. In addition to all the alcohol-related diseases mentioned earlier, he underwent a cataract operation and even resorted to acupuncture to escape his pain.

In his last days, Chaney received an offer to appear back East in a live-theater revival of *Arsenic and Old Lace*. Thoughts of the 3000-mile journey, the demands of a live theater schedule, and the nature of his illness should have persuaded him to decline the opportunity. Instead, he accepted, and resolving to use a throat microphone, he began learning his lines. Like his planned book, however, this last project would never come to fruition. On July 12, 1973, just six days after seeing his physician, he woke up to begin the last day of his life. Having felt comparatively fine all day, he suffered a heart attack and was pronounced dead at 4:30 P.M. He was 67.

In accordance with his wish to avoid funeral publicity, his body was donated as an anatomical specimen to the USC School of Medicine. A short while later, Patsy Chaney wrote an open letter to all his fans in care of Forrest J Ackerman and *Famous Monsters of Filmland.* It read:

> Thirty-six years of togetherness has been shattered by the ultimate end of us all–a failing heart.
>
> I cannot say that it was totally unexpected. The shadow of the end began to creep across our doorstep seven years ago–when Lon Chaney Jr. developed the same disease that had killed his father in 1930–cancer of the throat.
>
> Cobalt treatment eliminated the cancer–but there were many complications. In the end, I guess the Great Director needed another star performer in the Sky.
>
> We want to tell all of you wonderful people how great you are. Lon always insisted on signing all the autographs that he possibly could.
>
> He read your mail–and enjoyed all of it–the art work, the posters, the photographs–everything.
>
> Knowing that so many of you cared made him very happy. Thank you for caring.[20]

Chapter 14

The Summing Up

I t is difficult and possibly presumptuous for any human being to attempt with any confidence the assessment of another person's life. It is particularly difficult to assess the life of Lon Chaney, Jr., because so much of his private life has remained just that—private. His wife Patsy is deceased, but while she lived, she protected her husband from public scrutiny as many wives of alcoholics do. Lon himself granted interviews grudgingly and shunned personal publicity throughout his life. He preferred to let his films do the talking. While some have attempted to throw light upon Chaney's motivations, many of their conclusions are disputed. Nevertheless, I believe that a broad and accurate understanding of Lon Chaney, Jr., is possible.

As William Wordsworth wrote, "The child is father to the man." Unfortunately, comparatively little is known about the childhood of Lon Chaney, Jr., and some of that is disputed. When very young, he was obviously subjected to the arguments and tensions generated by his parents' professional struggles. He experienced separation from his mother and believed her dead. His busy father often sent the boy to live with others and was determined to harden him for the trials of life. While one of Lon Chaney, Jr.'s, grandsons reportedly doubts the story, Curt Siodmak's report of the beatings administered by Chaney, Sr. are probably true. Lon's early years were certainly anxiety-plagued.

Developmental psychology teaches that responses learned in early childhood guide and direct the adoption and practice of future behavior. Separation from his mother during his youth, uncertainty regarding his father's love, and frequent shifts in his early environment both hindered the boy's ability to trust the world around him and created insecurities that haunted him for the rest of his life. His alcoholism was in part the result of a history of such experiences. That his mother was treated for alcoholism increases the probability that Lon inherited addictive tendencies common in children of alcoholics.

Research shows that the only characteristic common to the backgrounds of most problem drinkers is personal maladjustment. A number of investigators have identified alcohol as a means of relieving anxiety, depression, and other unpleasant feelings that Lon experienced. Some investigators hypothesize that alcoholism is a learned behavior, the result of repeatedly using the drug successfully as a sedative. Since problem drinkers know no other stress-reducing behaviors, alcohol use grows and becomes their habitual coping strategy.

Aggravating the above factors was his father's legendary status within the film world. Despite Patsy Chaney's claim to the contrary, Lon *was* dominated throughout his life by the memory of Lon Chaney, Sr. He loved and respected his father, but he did not consider his love reciprocated. That is why he sought a father figure throughout his adult life. Director Reginald LeBorg was one such father substitute. Lon called him "Pappy" and vowed that they would do great things together. When the director left the Inner Sanctum series, Lon was angered and hurt. In his mind, another father had deserted him. Curt Siodmak was a later father substitute. Lon wanted his "father" to stop him from drinking on the set of *The Devil's Messenger*, and director Siodmak played the role. Before their quarrel, Lon even called Bela Lugosi "Pop."

At least until 1948, Lon competed against the memory of Chaney, Sr., attempting not only to emulate him but to surpass him. Although he later denied it, he fought hard to play some of the roles made famous by his father. Born Creighton Chaney, he was at first too proud to accept the moniker of Lon Chaney, Jr., even when it was obvious that such a move would advance his film career. Instead, he wanted to achieve fame on his own. He finally did agree to change his name to Lon Chaney, Jr. But when Universal dropped "Jr." from his billing, he fought to retain it, probably because—even during his peak at Universal—he never felt himself his father's equal.

Insecurity haunted Lon in other ways as well. Consider his neurotic compulsion to horde food. The experience of literally going hungry must have fed his general distrust and fear, a fear shared by his father as a result of the latter's experience with the vicissitudes of the actor's life. Later in life he exhibited some of the coarse behavior and feelings of inadequacy, isolation, and depression typical of longtime heavy drinkers.

Lon's alcoholism is important in the context of this book because it was so much a part of the man and because it harmed his professional career. It was alcoholism and alcohol-induced escapades of an embarrassing nature that prompted Universal to rein in Chaney's career and leave him without a contract in 1946. Thereafter, he was rarely hired by those in charge of major productions.

Why did Lon attempt suicide in 1948? As I have explained, he was subject to depression, and the late forties constituted one of the lowest periods of his life. Still, the nature of the family quarrel that drove him over the brink of endurance remains undivulged. Lon's survivors are understandably disinclined to open such private family matters to public scrutiny, especially since the knowledge would shed no light upon his acting career.

Was Lon also a latent homosexual? Curt Siodmak thinks so and points to Lon's troubled relationship with his father as a probable cause. In a series of phone conversations in 1993, however, Blackie Seymour of Pentegram Library suggested to me another interpretation of what Siodmak might have sensed. Seymour told me that in his research into Universal Pictures, and in preparation for a possible biography of Lon Chaney, Jr., he interviewed Brod Crawford, Reginald LeBorg, Andy Devine, and Dick Foran. According to Seymour, all of these men said Lon was distrustful of women. They said that when the opposite sex was present, Lon would be one of the boys, but at a certain point, he would back off, grow quiet, and effectively discourage any intimacy. Seymour concluded from these interviews that Lon distrusted women largely because of his early separation from his mother and because of the failure of his first marriage. Such an interpretation is clearly defensible. I have already suggested that certain developmentally important experiences instilled in him a general distrust of life. Lon's distrust of women as described by his friends is consistent with that assessment.

At least part of Curt Siodmak's suspicion that Lon was homosexual stems from the fact that Raymond Burr took a dislike to the actor during the making of *Bride of the Gorilla*. Although he won't say what it was, Siodmak sensed something in the chemistry between the two that led him to his conclusions about Lon's sexual nature. Still, it is clear that Burr's dislike could have stemmed from other reasons.

Lon's grandson Ron told me in a 1993 telephone conversation that he considers the charge of latent homosexuality groundless. Except in the interest of biographical accuracy, it probably does not matter either way.

Given all that has been said, what was the nature of Lon's relationship with his wife Patsy? She stood by him through all their trials and protected him till the end—and beyond. My impression is that Patsy developed all the coping strategies common to wives of alcoholics. She was, in essence, his caretaker and possibly a surrogate mother. All research on the subject indicates that families containing alcoholics are not well-adjusted, happy units. The Chaneys were probably no exception. As Leo Tolstoy wrote, "Happy families are all alike; every unhappy family is unhappy in its own way." Perhaps that is where we should leave our assessment of the Chaneys.

While Lon was a very troubled man, we should acknowledge his many positive qualities. Unhappy with his 4-F status during World War II, he worked hard for the war effort in any way that he could. He genuinely liked children and apparently empathized with those he deemed unfortunate. Almost everyone who knew Chaney liked him, and he had an active sense of humor. He performed many acts of kindness for which he expected no reward. He expressed interest in directing a film, but never actively pursued the possibility. An "average guy" in many ways, he enjoyed playing cards and watching sports on television, especially boxing. His favorite reading consisted of Zane

Grey westerns. Chaney did not enjoy watching his own films, preferring the work of Paul Muni instead. But most important in the positive sense, he left behind a body of work that continues to entertain audiences everywhere.

Lon Chaney, Jr., is indeed an enduring icon of American popular culture. Like Karloff's Frankenstein Monster and Lugosi's Dracula, Lon's Wolf Man is a unique characterization, an immortal part of American cinematic history. We must respect Lon all the more because his success did not come easily. While he never overcame his personal demons, he rose above their destructive influence to carve out an impressive acting career spanning thirty-nine years. Because he lacked natural acting ability, he had to work hard to master his craft, but work hard he did. As a horror star, it is true that his skill never quite equaled that of Lon Chaney, Sr., Boris Karloff, and Peter Cushing. It is also true that he lacked the charisma of Bela Lugosi; unlike Lugosi, his presence alone could not save a bad film. Still, he belongs in the company of such major contributors to the horror genre as Vincent Price, Christopher Lee, and Peter Lorre. In fact, his Wolf Man is eclipsed only by Karloff's Frankenstein Monster and Lugosi's Dracula as the most culturally significant horror characterization of all time.

Ultimately, Lon's reputation as a major star rests upon five films: *Of Mice and Men, The Wolf Man, Son of Dracula, Frankenstein Meets the Wolf Man,* and *Strange Confession.* His fine work in *One Million B.C., Man-Made Monster, The Ghost of Frankenstein, Calling Dr. Death,* and *Spider Baby* solidifies his reputation. The fact that he also played the Mummy would qualify him for a lifetime achievement award in the horror genre.

Indeed, Lon was correct when he said near the end of his life that the horror genre really needed him. The seventies and beyond have been dismal decades for horror as directors spew forth films based upon a strip-show mentality. As Jerome Bixby, author of *It! The Terror from Beyond Space* and many other highly regarded screenplays, explains:

> The face stays the same, I think. Styles and cosmetics change. We've had fine older horror films.... Due to advanced film techniques, the newer breed can be more effective in some ways; yet often the older devices, right down to black and white film, can deliver more clout. It's easier to be undifferentiated in black and white, to only imply, which is the essence of true horror. Today's latest spotlighting transformation scene, man into ravening kangaroo, is hyped with a year's advance publicity, analyses of makeup and hardware, photos. Thus when you finally see it you're already brimming with expectant admiration for technical achievement...but are you frightened? In horror as in sex, it's what you don't see or barely see that is most exciting.... Add a whole new genre, which couldn't have been made under previous standards, the splatter flicks.... Cut-'em-ups are a return to burlesque, a sweating wait for the next boob (cut throat) to be disclosed, and the next, and the next, redundantly, predictably. Pratfall horror.... Good films will always boil down to good stories, despite any amount of visual whammies—and the pendulum swings.[1]

Lon was correct in saying that the genre required literate stories of the type written by Curt Siodmak and characters that spoke to the human condition, such as his Lawrence Talbot. Perhaps that is why, in his later years, he wrote his own screenplay called *The Gila Man*, which has yet to be published.

But Lon was more than a leading man (or monster). He was also a top-drawer character actor. His three performances for Stanley Kramer are easily his best, but there are many others of exceptional quality. In addition, now that television is finally receiving the critical attention it deserves, perhaps Lon's small-screen legacy will become better known and more appreciated.

For years, rumor has suggested the imminent publication of the long-awaited *A Century of Chaneys*, the book Lon was completing at the time of his death. According to Ron Chaney, Lon's grandson, the newly organized Chaney Enterprises is preparing the book for publication, as well as planning other strategies for preserving and enhancing the reputation of Lon Chaney, Jr. Perhaps we will finally see Lon's screenplay of *The Gila Man* and other items of interest presumed lost.

In many ways, Chaney Enterprises has arrived at a most opportune time. Until recently, film pundits have looked upon Chaney's career with haughty disdain, assessing him simply as the untalented son of a film legend. Against this assessment, all the actors and actresses I have interviewed sincerely opined that Lon was a fine actor who remains unaccountably underrated. Indeed, the tide is finally shifting in favor of Lon Chaney, Jr., as adventurous critics brave the shoals of conventional wisdom in reassessing the career of the man aptly dubbed "the screen's master character creator."

Notes

Preface
(pages 1-3)

1. Philip di Franco, ed., *The Movie World of Roger Corman* (New York: Chelsea House, 1979), p. 31.
2. Carlos Clarens, *An Illustrated History of the Horror Film*, (New York: Capricorn Books, 1967), p. 101.

Chapter 1. The Early Years (1906-1931)
(pages 4-9)

1. Forrest J Ackerman, "Lon Is Gone." *Famous Monsters of Filmland,* 103 (1973): 28.
2. Calvin Beck, *Heroes of the Horrors* (New York: Collier Books, 1975), p. 226.
3. Ibid., pp. 226-227.
4. Robert G. Anderson, *Faces, Forms, Films: The Artistry of Lon Chaney* (New York: Castle Books, 1971), p. 23.
5. Beck, *Heroes*, p. 227.
6. John Brosnan, *The Horror People* (New York: St. Martin's, 1976), p. 18.
7. Tom Weaver, *Interviews with B Science Fiction and Horror Movie Makers* (Jefferson, N.C.: McFarland, 1988), p. 304.
8. Michael B. Blake, "The Man Behind the Thousand Faces," *Filmfax* 38 (1993): 47.
9. Beck, *Heroes*, p. 228.
10. Ibid.
11. Ibid.

Chapter 2. Learning His Craft (1931-1938)
(pages 10-23)

1. Calvin Beck, *Heroes of the Horrors* (New York: Collier Books, 1975), pp. 228-29.
2. Ibid.
3. Helen Louise Walker, "Second Generation?" *Modern Screen* (July 1932): 75.
4. Ibid., pp. 75, 105.

5. Ibid., p. 105.
6. Ibid.
7. Ibid.
8. Ibid.
9. Beck, *Heroes*, p. 229.
10. "Tonight Show," October 8, 1969.
11. Beck, *Heroes*, p. 230.
12. Ibid., p. 231.
13. Ibid.

Chapter 3. Of Mice and Men *(1939-1940)*
(pages 24-31)

1. Calvin Beck, *Heroes of the Horrors* (New York: Collier Books, 1975), p. 232.
2. Ibid.
3. Ibid.
4. Ibid., p. 234.
5. Ibid., p. 235.
6. B. Gelman Jackson, "The Life Story of Lon Chaney, Jr." *Monster Fantasy* 1, no. 4 (1975): 28.
7. *Of Mice and Men* (pressbook, 1939), p. 14.
8. Beck, *Heroes*, p. 235.

Chapter 4. Man-Made Monster *and* The Wolf Man *(1941)*
(pages 32-41)

1. Michael Brunas, John Brunas, and Tom Weaver, *Universal Horrors* (Jefferson, N.C.: McFarland, 1990), p. 246.
2. William K. Everson, *Classics of the Horror Film* (Secaucus, N.J.: Citadel Press, 1974), p. 152.
3. *The Atomic Monster* (pressbook, undated rerelease of *Man-Made Monster*), p. 3.
4. *The Atomic Monster*, p. 3.
5. Brunas, Brunas, and Weaver, *Universal Horrors*, p. 269.
6. Lloyd Mayer, "Son of Chaney: The Story of Lon Chaney, Jr." *Monster Magazine* 1, no. 4 (1975): 23.
7. *New York Times*, December 22, 1941.
8. Donald C. Willis, *Horror and Science Fiction Films II* (Metuchen, N.J.: Scarecrow, 1982), p. 437.
9. Brunas, Brunas, and Weaver, *Universal Horrors*, pp. 271-72.
10. R. H. W. Dillard, "Drawing the Circle: A Devolution of Values in Three Horror Films," *The Film Journal* 5 (1973): 6-35.
11. Ibid., p. 20.
12. Blackie Seymour, *Living Legend of Lon Chaney* (Worcester, MA.: Pentegram, 1966), p. 2.
13. Gregory William Mank, *It's Alive* (San Diego: A. S. Barnes, 1981), p. 100.
14. Dillard, "Drawing the Circle," p. 23.

Chapter 5. The Frankenstein Series
(pages 42-58)

1. "An Interview with Lon Chaney, Jr." *Castle of Frankenstein*, 10 (1966): 26.
2. Lon Chaney, Jr., Preface to Philip J. Riley, ed., *The Ghost of Frankenstein* (Absecon, N.J.: MagicImage Filmbooks, 1990), pp. 8-9.
3. Denis Gifford, *A Pictorial History of Horror Movies* (London: Hamlyn, 1973), pp. 136, 139.
4. "Interview with Jack Pierce," *Monster Mania* (October 1966): 13.
5. *Hollywood Reporter*, March 2, 1942.
6. *Motion Picture Herald*, March 7, 1942.
7. *New York Times*, April 4, 1942.
8. William K. Everson, *Classics of the Horror Film* (Secaucus, N.J.: Citadel, 1974), pp. 51-52.
9. Blackie Seymour, *Living Legend of Lon Chaney* (Worcester, MA: Pentegram, 1966), p. 26.
10. Michael Brunas, John Brunas, and Tom Weaver, *Universal Horrors* (Jefferson, N.C.: McFarland, 1990), p. 290.
11. Ibid., p. 288.
12. Leonard Wolf, "Frankenstein: a Selected Filmography" in *The Ultimate Frankenstein*, ed. Byron Priess (New York: Dell, 1991), p. 322.
13. Ralph Bellamy, Introduction, in Philip J. Riley (ed.) *The Ghost of Frankenstein* (MagicImage Filmbooks: Absecon, N.J., 1990) p. 17.
14. Blackie Seymour, *Living Legend*, p. 26.
15. Leonard Wolf, "Frankenstein," p. 323.
16. Brunas, Brunas, and Weaver, *Universal Horrors*, p. 342.
17. Gregory William Mank, *It's Alive* (San Diego: A. S. Barnes, 1981), p. 123.
18. Ibid., p. 117.
19. Scott Allen Nollen, *Boris Karloff* (Jefferson, N.C.: McFarland, 1991), p. 474.
20. *House of Frankenstein* (pressbook, 1944), p. 3
21. Brunas, Brunas, and Weaver, *Universal Horrors*, p. 475.
22. Mank, *It's Alive*, pp. 136-137.
23. Don Glut and Bob Burns, "Special Interview: Glenn Strange," *Modern Monsters* 4 (1966): 16.
24. Mank, *It's Alive*, p.131.
25. Brunas, Brunas, and Weaver, *Universal Horrors*, p. 523.
26. Ibid.
27. Glut and Burns, "Glenn Strange," p. 18.
28. Jack Gourlay, "Lon Chaney, Jr., Part Two," *Filmfax* 21 (1990): 74.

Chapter 6. The Mummy Series
(pages 59-67)

1. Michael Brunas, John Brunas, and Tom Weaver, *Universal Horrors* (Jefferson, N.C.: McFarland, 1990), p. 321.
2. *New York Times*, July 1, 1944.
3. Jack Gourlay and Gary Dorst, "Lon Chaney, Jr." *Filmfax* 20 (1990): 58.
4. Brunas, Brunas, and Weaver, *Universal Horrors*, p. 431.
5. Calvin Beck, *Heroes of the Horrors* (New York: Collier Books, 1975), p. 226.
6. *The Mummy's Ghost* (pressbook, undated rerelease), p. 2.

7. *New York Times*, May 31, 1945.
8. Brunas, Brunas, and Weaver, *Universal Horrors*, p. 482.
9. Don G. Smith, "Tid-Bits of Terror: Horror Gleanings," *Midnight Marquee* 38 (1989): 31.
10. Don Leifert, "Virginia Christine," *Filmfax* 21 (1990): 79.
11. Blackie Seymour, "Pentegram Revues," *Classic Images*, 153 (1988): 57.
12. Brunas, Brunas, and Weaver, *Universal Horrors*, p. 496.

Chapter 7. The Inner Sanctum Series
(pages 68–80)

1. *New York Times*, February 12, 1944.
2. Michael Brunas, John Brunas, and Tom Weaver, *Universal Horrors* (Jefferson, N.C.: McFarland, 1990), p. 396.
3. Ibid.
4. *Calling Dr. Death* (pressbook, 1953 rerelease), p. 1
5. *Reader's Digest*, March 1946, p. 63.
6. *New York Times*, April 1, 1944.
7. Brunas, Brunas, and Weaver, *Universal Horrors*, p. 404.
8. *Dead Man's Eyes* (pressbook, 1944), p. 2.
9. Brunas, Brunas, and Weaver, *Universal Horrors*, p. 492.
10. Ibid., p. 494.
11. Ibid., p. 496.
12. Ibid., p. 512.
13. Ibid., p. 531.
14. Blackie Seymour, "Pentegram Revues," *Classic Images*, 129 (1986): 37.

Chapter 8. Son of Dracula and Others (1941–1946)
(pages 81–97)

1. Jack Gourlay and Gary Dorst, "Lon Chaney, Jr." *Filmfax* 20 (1990): 56.
2. Ibid.
3. Ibid.
4. Blackie Seymour, telephone interview, December 2, 1992.
5. Michael Brunas, John Brunas, and Tom Weaver, *Universal Horrors* (Jefferson, N.C.: McFarland, 1990), p. 513.
6. Blackie Seymour, "Pentegram Revues," *Classic Images* 120 (1985): 61.
7. Brunas, Brunas, and Weaver, *Universal Horrors*, p. 384.
8. Michael Mallory, "Frankenstein and Dracula Meet the Critics," *Scarlet Street* 8 (1992): 33.
9. Calvin Beck, *Heroes of the Horrors* (New York: Collier Books, 1975), p. 257.
10. *Son of Dracula* (pressbook), p. 2.
11. *Ghost Catchers* (pressbook, 1944), p. 4.
12. Pauline Kael, *5001 Nights at the Movies* (New York: Henry Holt, 1991), p. 143.
13. Elena Verdugo, conversation with author, July 21, 1995.
14. Robert Quarry, conversation with author, July 23, 1995.

Chapter 9. Supporting Roles
(pages 98-110)

1. *My Favorite Brunette* (pressbook, 1947), p. 19.
2. B. Gelman Jackson, "The Life Story of Lon Chaney, Jr.," *Monster Fantasy* 1, no. 4 (1975): 32.
3. *Abbott and Costello Meet Frankenstein* (pressbook, 1948), p. 4.
4. Jack Gourlay, "Lon Chaney, Jr., Part Two," *Filmfax* 21 (1990): 69.
5. B. Gelman Jackson, "The Life Story," p. 32.
6. *Feature Films* 1 (1950): 2.
7. Ibid., p. 44.
8. *Inside Straight* (pressbook, 1951), p. 3.
9. *Only the Valiant* (pressbook, 1951), p. 15.
10. Calvin Beck, *Heroes of the Horrors* (New York: Collier Books, 1975), pp. 268-69.

Chapter 10. Character Gems (1952-1955)
(pages 111-128)

1. Don G. Smith, "Tid-Bits of Terror: Horror Gleanings," *Midnight Marquee*, 38 (1989): 31.
2. *The Bushwackers* (pressbook, 1952), p. 6.
3. *The Black Castle* (pressbook, 1952), p. 6.
4. *New York Times*, December 26, 1952.
5. *The Battles of Chief Pontiac* (pressbook, 1952), p. 5.
6. B. Gelman Jackson, "The Life Story of Lon Chaney, Jr.," *Monster Fantasy* 1, no. 4 (1975): 32.
7. Tom Weaver, *Interviews with B Science Fiction and Horror Movie Makers* (Jefferson, N.C.: McFarland, 1988), p. 81.
8. *Big House, U.S.A.* (pressbook, 1955), p. 10.
9. Jack Gourlay, "Lon Chaney, Jr., Part Two," *Filmfax* 21 (1990): 69.

Chapter 11. Horror Films, Westerns, and Television (1956-1962)
(pages 129-155)

1. Tom Weaver, *Interviews with B Science Fiction and Horror Movie Makers* (Jefferson, N.C.: McFarland, 1988), p. 280.
2. Bill Warren, *Keep Watching the Skies!*, vol. 1 (Jefferson, N.C.: McFarland, 1982), p. 280.
3. Ed Naha, *Horrors: From Screen to Scream* (New York: Avon Books, 1975), p. 140.
4. Warren, *Keep Watching*, pp. 280-281.
5. Weaver, *Interviews*, p. 281.
6. Ibid., p. 212.
7. Bernie O'Heir, "Interview with Reginald LeBorg," *Cinemacabre* 7 (1988): 33.
8. Weaver, *Interview*, p. 212.
9. Ibid., p. 242.
10. Jack Gourlay and Gary Dorst, "Lon Chaney, Jr.," *Filmfax* 20 (1990): 53.
11. Hal Erickson, *Syndicated Television: The First Forty Years, 1947-1987* (Jefferson, N.C.: McFarland, 1989), p. 29.
12. *Daniel Boone, Trail Blazer* (pressbook, 1956), p.4.
13. Warren, *Keep Watching*, pp. 333-34.

198 • Notes–Chapters 12, 13

14. Naha, *Horrors*, p. 59.
15. Weaver, *Interviews*, pp. 334–35.
16. Ibid., p. 334.
17. *The Defiant Ones* (pressbook, 1958), p. 9.
18. Jack Gourlay, "Lon Chaney, Jr., Part Two," *Filmfax* 21 (1990): 74.
19. Marie Windsor, telephone interview, October 25, 1991.
20. Warren, *Keep Watching*, p. 220.
21. *Return of the Fly/The Alligator People* (pressbook, 1959), p. 2.
22. Weaver, *Interviews*, p. 166.
23. Ibid., p. 310.
24. Ibid., p. 378.
25. Gregory William Mank, *Karloff and Lugosi: The Story of a Haunting Collaboration* (Jefferson, N.C.: McFarland, 1990), p. 236

Chapter 12. The A. C. Lyles Years (1963–1965)
(pages 156–171)

1. Ed Naha, *The Films of Roger Corman* (New York: Arco, 1982), p. 174.
2. Calvin Beck, *Heroes of the Horrors* (New York: Collier Books, 1975), p. 276.
3. Steve Biodrowski, David Del Valle, and Lawrence French, "Vincent Price: Horror's Crown Prince," *Cinéfantastique* (January 1989): 59.
4. Jim Morton, "Spider Baby," in *Incredibly Strange Films* #10 (San Francisco: V. Vale and Andrea Juno, 1988), p.182.
5. Ibid.
6. *New York Times*, August 27, 1964.
7. David Pirie, *A Heritage of Horror* (New York: Equinox Books, 1973), p. 117.
8. Bruce Hallenbeck, "The Making of *Kiss of the Vampire*," *Little Shoppe of Horrors* 10-11 (1990): 52.
9. *Witchcraft* (pressbook, 1964), p. 1.
10. *Johnny Reno* (pressbook, 1965), p. 5.
11. Beck, *Heroes*, p. 277.
12. John Brosnan, *The Horror People* (New York: St. Martin's, 1976), p. 25.

Chapter 13. Exploitation, Decline, and Death (1966–1973)
(pages 172–186)

1. L. Ann Mueller, M.D., and Katherine Ketcham, *Recovering: How to Get and Stay Sober* (New York: Bantam Books, 1987), pp. 56-57.
2. Jack Gourlay, "Lon Chaney, Jr., Part Two," *Filmfax* 20 (1990): 71.
3. Ibid., p. 72.
4. Ibid.
5. Ibid.
6. Forrest J Ackerman, *Boris Karloff: The Frankenscience Monster* (New York: Ace Books, 1969), p.16.
7. Jack Gourlay and Gary Dorst, "Lon Chaney Jr.," *Filmfax* 20 (1990): 52.
8. *Fireball Jungle* (pressbook, 1969), p. 2.
9. Lon Chaney, Jr., letter to Gary Dorst, October 18, 1969.
10. Lon Chaney, Jr., letter to Gary Dorst, February 20, 1970.
11. John Brosnan, *The Horror People* (New York: St. Martin's, 1976), p. 25.

12. Tom Weaver, "Sam Sherman," *Filmfax* 27 (1991): 88.
13. Russ Tamblyn, interview with author, August 15, 1992.
14. Brosnan, *Horror People*, p. 23.
15. Tom Weaver, *Interviews with B Science Fiction and Horror Movie Makers* (Jefferson, N.C.: McFarland, 1988), pp. 138-39.
16. Gourlay and Dorst, "Lon Chaney, Jr.," p. 56.
17. Gregory William Mank, *It's Alive* (San Diego: A. S. Barnes, 1981), p. 170.
18. Forrest J Ackerman, "Cheer for Chaney!" *Famous Monsters of Filmland* 98 (1973): 40.
19. Brosnan, *Horror People*, p. 26.
20. Forrest J Ackerman, "Lon Is Gone," *Famous Monsters of Filmland* 103 (1973): 40.

Chapter 14. The Summing Up
(pages 187-191)

1. Don G. Smith, "Jerome Bixby," *Fangoria* 25 (1983): 44-45.

Filmography

Films

THE TRAP (1922)
Chaney's hands were supposedly used in this silent film.

BIRD OF PARADISE (RKO, 1932)
Credits: Directed and produced by King Vidor; screenplay by Wells Root, Wanda Tuchoo, and Leonard Praskins.
Cast: Dolores del Rio, Joel McCrae, John Haliday, Richard "Skeets" Gallagher, Bert Roach, and Creighton Chaney (as Thornton).

GIRL CRAZY (RKO, 1932)
Credits: Directed by William A. Seiter; produced by William LeBaron; screenplay by Tim Whelan, Herman J. Mankiewicz, Edward Welch, and Walter De Leon.
Cast: Bert Wheeler, Robert Woolsey, Eddie Quillan, Dorothy Lee, Mitzi Green, Kitty Kelly, Arline Judge, and Creighton Chaney (as a chorus dancer).

THE MOST DANGEROUS GAME (RKO, 1932)
Credits: Directed and produced by Irving Pichel and Ernest B. Shoedsack; screenplay by James Creelman, from the short story by Richard Connell.
Cast: Joel McCrea, Fay Wray, Robert Armstrong, Leslie Banks, Hale Hamilton, Noble Johnson, and Creighton Chaney (in a small role edited from film).

THE LAST FRONTIER (RKO, 1933), twelve-chapter serial
Credits: Directed by Spencer Bennett and Thomas L. Storey; produced by Fred McConnell.
Cast: Creighton Chaney (as Tom Kirby), Dorothy Gulliver, Francis X. Bushman, Jr., Joe Bonomo, Mary Jo Desmond, and Slim Cole.

LUCKY DEVILS (RKO, 1933)
Credits: Directed by Ralph Ince; produced by David O. Selznick; screenplay by Ben Markson and Agnes Christine Johnson.
Cast: William Boyd, Dorothy Wilson, William Gargan, Bruce Cabot, and Creighton Chaney (as Frankie Wilde).

SCARLET RIVER (RKO, 1933)
Credits: Directed by Otto Brower; produced by David Lewis; screenplay by Harold Shumate.
Cast: Tom Keene, Dorothy Wilson, Creighton Chaney (as Jeff Todd), Betty Furness, Roso Ates, and Edgar Kennedy.

SON OF THE BORDER (RKO, 1933)
Credits: Directed by Lloyd Nosler; produced by David Lewis; screenplay by Wellyn Totman and Harold Shumate.
Cast: Tom Keene, Edgar Kennedy, Julie Haydon, David Durand, and Creighton Chaney (as Jack Breen).

THE THREE MUSKETEERS (Mascot, 1933), twelve-chapter serial
Credits: Directed by Armand Schaefer and Colbert Clark; screenplay by Norman Hall, Colbert Clark, Ben Cohn, and Wyndham Gittens.
Cast: Jack Mulhall, Raymond Hatton, Frances X. Bushman, Jr., John Wayne, Ruth Hall, Creighton Chaney (as Armand Corday), and Noah Beery, Jr.

SIXTEEN FATHOMS DEEP (Monogram, 1934)
Credits: Directed by Armand Schaefer; produced by Paul Malvern; screenplay by Norman Houston.
Cast: Sally O' Neil, Creighton Chaney (as Joe Bethel), Russell Simpson, Maurice Black, Jack Kennedy, and George Regas.

GIRL O' MY DREAMS (Monogram, 1934)
Credits: Directed by Raymond McCarey; produced by William T. Lackey; screenplay by Waldemar Young, based on a play by David Belasco.
Cast: Mary Carlisle, Sterling Holloway, Eddie Nugent, Arthur Lake, Creighton Chaney (as Don Cooper), Gigi Parrish, and Tommy Dugan.

THE LIFE OF VERGIE WINTERS (RKO, 1934)
Credits: Directed by Alfred Santell; produced by Pandro S. Berman; screenplay by Jane Murfin.
Cast: John Boles, Ann Harding, Helen Vinson, Frank Albertson, Creighton Chaney (as Hugo McQueen), Sara Haden, Ben Alexander, and Edward Van Sloan.

THE SHADOW OF SILK LENNOX (Commodore, 1935)
Credits: Directed by Ray Kirkwood (co-director Jack Nelson); produced by Ray Kirkwood; screenplay by Norman Springer.
Cast: Creighton Chaney (as Silk Lennox), Dean Benton, Marie Burton, Jack Mulhall, and Eddie Gribbon.
Note: Rereleased as *Case of the Crime Cartel*.

CAPTAIN HURRICANE (RKO, 1935)
Credits: Directed by John S. Robertson; screenplay by Joseph Lovett, based on the novel *The Taming of Zenas Henry* by Sara Ware Bassett.
Cast: James Barton, Helen Westley, Helen Mack, Gene Lockhart, Douglas Walton, Helen Travers, and Creighton Chaney (as Helen Westley's newlywed brother).

THE MARRIAGE BARGAIN (Hollywood Exchange, 1935)
Credits: Directed by Albert Ray; screenplay by Betty Laidlaw and Bob Lively.
Cast: Creighton Chaney (as Bob Gordon), Edmund Breese, Audrey Ferris, Francis McDonald, Fern Emmett, Vic Potel, and Tommy Bond.

A SCREAM IN THE NIGHT (Commodore, 1935)
Credits: Directed by Fred Newmeyer; produced by Ray Kirkwood; screenplay by Norman Springer.
Cast: Creighton Chaney (as Jack Wilson and Butch Curtain), Zarah Tazil, Manuel Lopez, Shelia Terry, Philip Ahn, and John Ince.

HOLD 'EM YALE (Paramount, 1935)
Credits: Directed by Sidney Lanfield; produced by Charles R. Rogers; screenplay by Paul Gerard Smith and Eddie Welch, from a story by Damon Runyon.
Cast: Patricia Ellis, Caesar Romero, Larry Crabbe, William Frawley, Andy Devine, and Creighton Chaney (as football player, unbilled).

ACCENT ON YOUTH (Paramount, 1935)
Credits: Directed by Wesley Ruggles; produced by Douglas MacLean; screenplay by Herbert Fields and Claude Binyon.
Cast: Sylvia Sidney, Herbert Marshall, Phillip Reed, Holmes Herbert, Catharine Doucet, Astrid Allwyn, Ernest Cossart, Donald Meek, and Creighton Chaney (as Chuck).

THE ROSEBOWL (Paramount, 1936)
Credits: Directed by Charles Barton; produced by A. M. Botsford; screenplay by

Marguerite Roberts, based on the novel *O'Reilly of Notre Dame* by Francis Wallace.
Cast: Eleanor Whitney, Tom Brown, Larry "Buster" Crabbe, William Frawley, Benny Baker, and Creighton Chaney (as a football player).

THE SINGING COWBOY (Republic, 1936)
Credits: Directed by Mack Wright, produced by Nat Levine, screenplay by Dorrell and Stuart McGowan.
Cast: Gene Autry, Smiley Burnette, Lois Wilde, and Lon Chaney, Jr. (as Martin).

UNDERSEA KINGDOM (Republic, 1936), twelve-chapter serial
Credits: Directed by "Breezy" Reeves Eason and Joseph Kane; produced by Nat Levine; screenplay by John Rahtmell, Maurice Geraghty, Oliver Drake, and T. Knight.
Cast: Ray "Crash" Corrigan, Lois Wilde, Monte Blue, William Farnum, Lon Chaney, Jr. (as Hakur), Boothe Howard, C. Montague Shaw, Lee Van Atta, Smiley Burnette, and Raymond Hatton.

ACE DRUMMOND (Universal, 1936), thirteen-chapter serial
Credits: Directed by Cliff Smith and Ford Beebe; produced by Barney Sarecky and Ben Koenig; screenplay by Wyndham Gittens, Ray Trampe, and Norman Hall.
Cast: John King, Jean Rogers, Noah Beery, Jr., Lon Chaney, Jr. (as Ivan), Russell Wade, and House Peters, Jr.

THE OLD CORRAL (Republic, 1936)
Credits: Directed by Joseph Kane; produced by Nat Levine; screenplay by Sherman Lowe and Joseph Poland.
Cast: Gene Autry, Smiley Burnette, Hope Manning, Sons of the Pioneers, Cornelius Keefe, and Lon Chaney, Jr. (as Garland).

KILLER AT LARGE (Columbia, 1936)
Credits: Directed and produced by Cecil B. De Mille; screenplay by Harold Shumate.
Cast: Mary Brian, Russell Hardie, George McKay, Thurston Hall, Henry Brandon, Betty Compson, and Lon Chaney, Jr. (as wax museum guard).

CHEYENNE RIDES AGAIN (Victory, 1937)
Credits: Directed by Bill Hill; produced by Sam Katzman.
Cast: Creighton Chaney (as Girard).

MIDNIGHT TAXI (Fox, 1937)
Credits: Directed by Eugene Ford; produced by Milton Feld; screenplay by Lou Breslow and John Patrick.
Cast: Brian Donlevy, Frances Drake, Alan Dinehart, Sig Rumann, Gilbert Roland, Harold Huber, Paul Stanton, and Lon Chaney, Jr. (as Erikson).

SECRET AGENT X-9 (Universal, 1937), twelve-chapter serial
Credits: Directed by Ford Beebe; screenplay by W. Gittens, N. S. Hall, R. Trampe, and L. Swanbacker.
Cast: Scott Kolk, Jean Rogers, Monte Blue, Henry Brandon, Lon Chaney, Jr. (as Maroni), Ed Parker, Tom Steele, and Eddy C. Waller.

THAT I MAY LIVE (Fox, 1937)
Credits: Directed by Allan Dwan; produced by Sol M. Wurtzel; screenplay by Ben Mardson and William Conselman.
Cast: Rochelle Hudson, Robert Kane, J. Edward Bromberg, Jack La Rue, Frank Conroy, and Lon Chaney, Jr. (as an engineer).

ANGEL'S HOLIDAY (Fox, 1937)
Credits: Directed by James Tinling; produced by John Stone; screenplay by Frank Fenton and Lynn Root.
Cast: Jane Withers, Robert Kent, Joan Davis, Sally Blane, Harold Huber, Frank Jenks, Ray Walker, John Qualen, and Lon Chaney, Jr. (as Eddie).

SLAVE SHIP (Fox, 1937)
Credits: Directed by Tay Garnett; produced by Darryl F. Zanuck; screenplay by Sam Hellman, Lamar Trotti, and Gladys Lehman, from a story by William Faulkner based on a novel by George S. King.

Cast: Warner Baxter, Wallace Beery, Elizabeth Allan, Mickey Rooney, George Sanders, Jane Darwell, Joseph Schildkraut, and Lon Chaney, Jr. (as a laborer, unbilled).

BORN RECKLESS (Fox, 1937)
Credits: Directed by Mal St. Clair; produced by Sol M. Wurtzel; screenplay by John Patrick, Robert Ellis, and Helen Logan.
Cast: Rochelle Hudson, Brian Donlevy, Barton MacLane, Robert Kent, Harry Carey, Pauline Moore, and Lon Chaney, Jr. (as a garage mechanic, unbilled).

WILD AND WOOLY (Fox, 1937)
Credits: Directed by Albert Werker; produced by John Stone; screenplay by Lynn Root and Frank Fenton.
Cast: Jane Withers, Walter Brennan, Pauline Moore, Carl "Alfalfa" Switzer, Jack Searl, Berton Churchill, Douglas Fowley, and Lon Chaney, Jr. (as Dutch).

THE LADY ESCAPES (Fox, 1937)
Credits: Directed by Eugene Forde; produced by Leslie Landau; screenplay by Don Ettlinger, from a play by Eugene Helta.
Cast: Gloria Stuart, Michael Whalen, George Sanders, Cora Witherspoon, Gerald Oliver-Smith, and Lon Chaney, Jr. (as a reporter, bit part).

ONE MILE FROM HEAVEN (Fox, 1937)
Credits: Directed by Allan Swan; produced by Sol M. Wurtzel; screenplay by Lou Breslow and John Patrick.
Cast: Claire Trevor, Sally Blane, Douglas Fowley, Fredi Washington, Joan Carol, Ralf Harolde, and Lon Chaney, Jr. (as a cop, unbilled).

THIN ICE (20th, 1937)
Credits: Directed by Sidney Lanfield; produced by Darryl F. Zanuck; screenplay by Boris Ingster and Milton Sperling, from the play *Der Komet* by Attila Obok.
Cast: Sonja Henie, Tyrone Power, Arthur Treacher, Taymond Walburn, Joan Davis, Sig Rumann, Alan Hale, and Lon Chaney, Jr. (as an American reporter, unbilled).

WIFE, DOCTOR, AND NURSE (Fox, 1937)
Credits: Directed by Walter Lang; produced by Raymond Griffith; screenplay by Kathryn Scola, Darrell Ware, and Lamar Trotti.
Cast: Loretta Young, Warner Baxter, Virginia Bruce, Jane Darwell, Sidney Blackmer, Maurice Cass, Elisha Cook, Jr., and Lon Chaney, Jr. (as a chauffeur).

LIFE BEGINS IN COLLEGE (Fox, 1937)
Credits: Directed by William A. Seiter; produced by Harold Wilson; screenplay by Karl Tunberg and Don Ettlinger, from a series of stories by Darrell Ware.
Cast: The Ritz Brothers, Joan Davis, Tony Martin, Gloria Stuart, Fred Stone, Nat Pendleton, and Lon Chaney, Jr. (as Gilks).

CHARLIE CHAN ON BROADWAY (Fox, 1937)
Credits: Directed by Eugene Forde; produced by John Stone; screenplay by Charles Belden and Jerry Cady, based upon the character created by Earl Derr Biggers.
Cast: Warner Oland, Keye Luke, Joan Marsh, J. Edward Bromberg, Douglas Fowley, Harold Huber, and Lon Chaney, Jr. (as a desk man).

SECOND HONEYMOON (Fox, 1937)
Credits: Directed by Walter Lang; produced by Raymond Griffith; screenplay by Kathryn Scola and Darrel Ware.
Cast: Tyrone Power, Loretta Young, Stuart Erwin, Claire Trevor, Marjorie Weaver, Lyle Talbot, J. Edward Bromberg, and Lon Chaney, Jr. (as a reporter, unbilled).

THIS IS MY AFFAIR (Fox, 1937)
Credits: Directed by William S. Seiter; produced by Darryl F. Zanuck; screenplay by Allen Rivkin and Lamar Trotti, based on the novel *The McKinley Case* by Melville Crossman.
Cast: Robert Taylor, Barbara Stanwyck, Victor McLaglen, Brian Donlevy, Sidney Blackmer, John Carradine, and Lon Chaney, Jr. (offscreen voice).

LOVE AND HISSES (Fox, 1937)
Credits: Directed by Sidney Lanfield; produced by Darryl F. Zanuck; screenplay by Curtis Kenyon and Art Arthur.
Cast: Walter Winchell, Ben Bernie, Simone Simon, Bert Lahr, Joan Davis, Dick Baldwin, and Lon Chaney, Jr. (as an attendant, unbilled).

LOVE IS NEWS (Fox, 1937)
Credits: Directed by Tay Garnett; produced by Harold Wilson and Earl Carroll; screenplay by Harry Tugend and Jack Yellen.
Cast: Tyrone Power, Loretta Young, Don Ameche, Slim Summerville, Dudley Digges, George Sanders, Jane Darwell, Elisha Cook, Jr., and Lon Chaney, Jr. (as a newsman, unbilled).

CITY GIRL (Fox, 1937)
Credits: Directed by Alfred Werker; produced by Sol M. Wurtzel; screenplay by Frances Hyland, Robin Harris, and Lester Ziffren.
Cast: Phyllis Brooks, Ricardo Cortez, Robert Wilcox, Douglas Fowley, Chick Chandler, and Lon Chaney, Jr. (as a gangster, unbilled).

CHECKERS (Fox, 1937)
Credits: Directed by H. Bruce Humberstone; produced by John Stone; screenplay by Lynn Root, Frank Fenton, Robert Chapin, and Karen DeWolf.
Cast: Jane Withers, Stuart Erwin, Una Merkel, Marvin Stephens, Andrew Tombes, June Carlson, and Lon Chaney, Jr. (as a man at the race track, unbilled).

HAPPY LANDING (Fox, 1938)
Credits: Directed by Roy Del Ruth; produced by Darryl F. Zanuck; screenplay by Milton Sperling and Boris Ingster.
Cast: Sonja Henie, Don Ameche, Cesar Romero, Ethel Merman, Jean Hersholt, and Lon Chaney, Jr. (as a newspaper reporter, unbilled).

SALLY, IRENE, AND MARY (Fox, 1938)
Credits: Directed by William S. Seiter; produced by Darryl F. Zanuck; screenplay by Harold Tugend and Jack Yellen, based on the play by Edward Sowling and Cyril Wood.
Cast: Alice Faye, Tony Martin, Fred Allen, Jimmy Durante, Joan Davis, Gregory Ratoff, and Lon Chaney, Jr. (as a cop, unbilled).

WALKING DOWN BROADWAY (Fox, 1938)
Credits: Directed by Norman Foster; produced by Sol M. Wurtzel; screenplay by Robert Chapin and Karen DeWolf.
Cast: Claire Trevor, Phyllis Brooks, Leah Ray, Dixie Dunbar, Jayne Regan, and Lon Chaney, Jr. (in an unbilled bit part).

MR. MOTO'S GAMBLE (Fox, 1938)
Credits: Directed by James Tinling; produced by John Stone; screenplay by Charles Belden and Jerry Cady, based on the character created by John P. Marquand.
Cast: Peter Lorre, Keye Luke, Dick Baldwin, Lynn Bari, Douglas Fowley, Maxie Rosenbloom, Ward Bond, and Lon Chaney, Jr. (as Joey).

JOSETTE (Fox, 1938)
Credits: Directed by Allan Dwan; produced by Gene Markey; screenplay by James Edward, from a play by Paul Frank and Georg Fraser, from a story by Ladislaus Vadnai.
Cast: Don Ameche, Simone Simon, Robert Young, Joan Davis, Bert Lahr, Paul Hurst, William Collier, Sr., Tala Birell, and Lon Chaney, Jr. (as a boatman).

PASSPORT HUSBAND (Fox, 1938)
Credits: Directed by James Tinling; produced by Sol M. Wurtzel; screenplay Karen de Wolf and Robert Chapin.
Cast: Stuart Erwin, Pauline Moore, Douglas Fowley, Joan Woodbury, Robert Lowery, and Lon Chaney, Jr. (as Bull).

ALEXANDER'S RAGTIME BAND (Fox, 1938)
Credits: Directed by Henry King; produced by Darryl F. Zanuck; screenplay by Kathryn Scola and Lamar Trotti.

Cast: Tyrone Power, Alice Faye, Don Ameche, Ethel Merman, Jack Haley, Jean Hersholt, Helen Westley, John Carradine, and Lon Chaney, Jr. (as a photographer).

SPEED TO BURN (Fox, 1938)
Credits: Directed by Jerry Hoffman; produced by Otto Brower; screenplay by Robert Ellis and Helen Logan.
Cast: Michael Whalen, Lynn Bari, Marvin Stephens, Henry Armetta, Chick Chandler, Sidney Blackmer, and Lon Chaney, Jr. (as a racetrack mug).

STRAIGHT, PLACE, AND SHOW (Fox, 1938)
Credits: Directed by David Butler; produced by Darryl F. Zanuck; screenplay by M. M. Musselman and Allen Rivkin, from a play by Damon Runyon and Irvin Caesar.
Cast: The Ritz Brothers, Richard Arlen, Ethel Merman, Phyllis Brooks, George Barbier, Sidney Blackmer, and Lon Chaney, Jr. (as a chauffeur).

SUBMARINE PATROL (FOX, 1938)
Credits: Directed by John Ford; produced by Darryl F. Zanuck; screenplay by Rian James, Darrell Ware, and Jack Yellen.
Cast: Richard Greene, Nancy Kelly, Preston Foster, George Bancroft, Slim Summerville, John Carradine, Joan Valerie, Maxie Rosenbloom, Ward Bond, Robert Lowery, and Lon Chaney, Jr. (as a sailor, unbilled).

ROAD DEMON (Fox, 1938)
Credits: Directed by Otto Brower; produced by Jerry Hoffman; screenplay by Robert Ellis and Helen Logan.
Cast: Henry Arthur, Joan Valerie, Henry Armetta, Tom Beck, Jonathon Hale, Bill (Bojangles) Robinson, and Lon Chaney, Jr. (as a race racketeer).

JESSE JAMES (Fox, 1939)
Credits: Directed by Henry King; produced by Darryl F. Zanuck; screenplay by Nunnally Johnson.
Cast: Tyrone Power, Henry Fonda, Nancy Kelly, Randolph Scott, Henry Hull, Slim Summerville, J. Edward Bromberg, Brian Donlevy, John Carradine, John Russell, Jane Darwell, Charles Middleton, and Lon Chaney, Jr. (as a bearded outlaw in Jesse's gang).

UNION PACIFIC (Paramount, 1939)
Credits: Directed and produced by Cecil B. De Mille; screenplay by Walter de Leon.
Cast: Barbara Stanwyck, Joel McCrea, Akim Tamiroff, Robert Preston, Lynn Overman, Brian Donlevy, Anthony Quinn, Stanley Ridges, Evelyn Keyes, Regis Toomey, and Lon Chaney, Jr. (as a bearded train passenger).

FRONTIER MARSHAL (Fox, 1939)
Credits: Directed by Allan Dwan; produced by Sol M. Wurtzel; screenplay by Sam Hellman, based on a book by Stuart N. Lake.
Cast: Randolph Scott, Nancy Kelly, Cesar Romero, Binnie Barnes, John Carradine, Edward Norris, Ward Bond, and Lon Chaney, Jr. (as Pringle).

CHARLIE CHAN IN THE CITY OF DARKNESS (Fox, 1939)
Credits: Directed by Herbert I. Leeds; produced by John Stone; screenplay by Robert Ellis and Helen Logan, from a play by Gina Kaus and Ladislaus Fodor, based on the character created by Earl Derr Biggers.
Cast: Sidney Toler, Lynn Bari, Richard Clarke, Harold Huber, Pedro de Cordoba, Dorothy Tree, Leo Carroll, and Lon Chaney, Jr. (as Pierre).

OF MICE AND MEN (United Artists, 1939)
Credits: Directed and produced by Lewis Milestone; screenplay by Eugene Solow, from the novel by John Steinbeck; music by Aaron Copland.
Cast: Burgess Meredith, Betty Field, Lon Chaney, Jr. (as Lennie), Charles Bickford, Roman Bohnen, Bob Steele, Noah Beery, Jr., Oscar O'Shea, Granville Bates, and Leigh Whipper.

ONE MILLION B.C. (United Artists, 1940)
Credits: Directed by Hal Roach and Hal Roach, Jr., and D. W. Griffith; screenplay

by Mickell Novak, George Baker, and Joseph Frickert.
Cast: Victor Mature, Carole Landis, Lon Chaney, Jr. (as Akhoba), Nigel de Brulier, John Hubbard, Jean Porter, and narrated by Conrad Nagel.

NORTHWEST MOUNTED POLICE (Paramount, 1940)
Credits: Directed and produced by Cecil B. De Mille; screenplay by Alan LeMay, Jesse Laskey, Jr., and C. Gardner Sullivan.
Cast: Gary Cooper, Paulette Goddard, Madeleine Carroll, Preston Foster, Robert Preston, George Bancroft, Lynn Overman, Akim Tamiroff, and Lon Chaney, Jr. (as Shorty).

BILLY THE KID (MGM, 1941)
Credits: Directed by David Miller; produced by Irving Asher; screenplay by Gene Fowler.
Cast: Robert Taylor, Brian Donlevy, Ian Hunter, Mary Howard, Gene Lockhart, and Lon Chaney, Jr. (as "Spike" Hudson).

MAN-MADE MONSTER (Universal, 1941)
Credits: Directed by George Waggner; screenplay by Joseph West (George Waggner), based on the story "The Electric Man" by Harry J. Essex, Sid Schwartz, and Len Golos; music by Hans Salter.
Cast: Lon Chaney, Jr. (as "Dynamo" Dan McCormick), Lionel Atwill, Anne Nagel, Frank Albertson, and Samuel S. Hinds.
Note: Rereleased in 1953 by Realart Pictures as *The Atomic Monster*.

TOO MANY BLONDES (Universal, 1941)
Credits: Directed by Thornton Freeland; produced by Joseph G. Sanford; screenplay by Maxwell Shane and Louis S. Kaye.
Cast: Rudy Vallee, Helen Parrish, Lon Chaney, Jr. (as Marvin Gimble), Jerome Cowan, Shemp Howard, and Iris Adrian.

SAN ANTONIO ROSE (Universal, 1941)
Credits: Directed by Charles Lamont; produced by Ken Goldsmith; screenplay by Hugh Wedlock, Jr., Howard Snyder, and Paul Gerard Smith.
Cast: Jane Frazee, Robert Paige, Eve Arden, Lon Chaney, Jr. (as Jigsaw Kennedy), Shemp Howard, and Richard Lane.

RIDERS OF DEATH VALLEY (Universal, 1941), fifteen-chapter serial
Credits: Directed by Ford Beebe and Ray Taylor; screenplay by Sherman Lowe, George Plympton, Basil Dickey, and Jack Connell.
Cast: Dick Foran, Leo Carrillo, Buck Jones, Charles Bickford, Lon Chaney, Jr. (as Butch), Noah Beery, Jr., "Big Boy" Williams, and Glenn Strange.

BADLANDS OF DAKOTA (Universal, 1941)
Credits: Directed by Alfred E. Green; produced by George Waggner; screenplay by Gerald Geraghty; music by Hans Salter.
Cast: Broderick Crawford, Hugh Herbert, Robert Stack, Richard Dix, Frances Farmer, and Lon Chaney, Jr. (as Jack McCall).

THE WOLF MAN (Universal, 1941)
Credits: Directed and produced by George Waggner; screenplay by Curt Siodmak; music by Hans Salter.
Cast: Lon Chaney, Jr. (as Lawrence Talbot), Claude Rains, Warren William, Ralph Bellamy, Patric Knowles, Evelyn Ankers, Maria Ouspenskaya, Bela Lugosi, and Fay Helm.

NORTH TO THE KLONDIKE (Universal, 1942)
Credits: Directed by Earl C. Kenton; screenplay by Clarence Upson Young, Lou Sarecky, and George Bricker, based on a story by William Castle, from "Gold Hunters of the North" by Jack London.
Cast: Broderick Crawford, Lon Chaney, Jr. (as Nate Carson), Evelyn Ankers, Andy Devine, Lloyd Corrigan, Willie Fung, and Keye Luke.

OVERLAND MAIL (Universal, 1942), fifteen-chapter serial

Credits: Directed by Ford Beebe and John Rawlins; screenplay by Paul Huston.
Cast: Lon Chaney, Jr. (as Jim Lane), Helen Parrish, Noah Beery, Jr., Don Terry, Bob Baker, and Noah Beery.

GHOST OF FRANKENSTEIN (Universal, 1942)
Credits: Directed by Earl C. Kenton; produced by George Waggner; screenplay by W. Scott Darling.
Cast: Lon Chaney, Jr. (as the Frankenstein Monster), Sir Cedric Hardwicke, Bela Lugosi, Ralph Bellamy, Lionel Atwill, Evelyn Ankers, and Janet Ann Gallow.

KEEPING FIT (Universal, 1942), eleven-minute short
Credits: Directed by Arthur Lubin; screenplay by Paul Huston.
Cast: Robert Stack, Broderick Crawford, Frank Morgan, Louise Allbritton, Irene Hervey, Andy Devine, Dick Foran, and Lon Chaney, Jr. (as himself).

THE MUMMY'S TOMB (Universal, 1942)
Credits: Directed by Harold Young; screenplay by Griffin Jay and Henry Sucher.
Cast: Lon Chaney, Jr. (as Kharis), Dick Foran, John Hubbard, Elyse Knox, Wallace Ford, Turhan Bey, and George Zucco.

EYES OF THE UNDERWORLD (Universal, 1943)
Credits: Directed by Roy Williams Neill; produced by Ben Pivar; screenplay by Michael L. Simmons and Arthur Straun.
Cast: Richard Dix, Wendy Barrie, Lon Chaney, Jr. (as Benny), Lloyd Corrigan, Don Porter, Billy Lee, and Marc Lawrence.
Note: Rereleased by Realart Pictures in 1951 as *Criminals of the Underworld*.

FRANKENSTEIN MEETS THE WOLF MAN (Universal, 1943)
Credits: Directed by Roy William Neill; produced by George Waggner; screenplay by Curt Siodmak; music direction by Hans Salter.
Cast: Lon Chaney, Jr. (as Lawrence Talbot), Patric Knowles, Ilona Massey, Lionel Atwill, Bela Lugosi, Maria Ouspenskaya, Dennis Hoey, Don Barclay, and Dwight Frey.

WHAT WE ARE FIGHTING FOR (Universal, 1943)
Credits: Directed by Erle C. Kenton; screenplay by Paul Huston.
Cast: Lon Chaney, Jr. (as Bill), Samuel S. Hinds, and Osa Massen.

FRONTIER BADMEN (Universal, 1943)
Credits: Directed by Ford Beebe and William McGann; produced by Ford Beebe; screenplay by Gerald Geraghty and Morgan B. Cox.
Cast: Robert Paige, Anne Gwynne, Noah Beery, Jr., Diana Barrymore, Leo Carrillo, Andy Devine, Thomas Gomez, Frank Lackteen, William Farnum, and Lon Chaney, Jr. (as Chango).

CRAZY HOUSE (Universal, 1943)
Credits: Directed by Edward F. Kline; produced by Erle C. Kenton; screenplay by Robert Lees and Frederic L. Rinaldo.
Cast: Ole Olsen and Chic Johnson, Cass Daley, Patric Knowles, Martha O' Driscoll, Leighton Noble, Thomas Gomez, Percy Kilbride, Hans Conreid, Leo Carrillo, Andy Devine, Robert Paige, Lon Chaney, Jr. (as a guest star), Basil Rathbone, and Nigel Bruce.

SON OF DRACULA (Universal, 1943)
Credits: Directed by Robert Siodmak; produced by Ford Beebe; screenplay by Erik Taylor, from an original story by Curt Siodmak; music by Hans Salter.
Cast: Lon Chaney, Jr. (as Count Alucard), Louise Allbritton, Robert Paige, Evelyn Ankers, Frank Craven, J. Edward Bromberg, and Samuel S. Hinds.

CALLING DR. DEATH (Universal, 1943)
Credits: Directed by Reginald LeBorg; screenplay by Edward Dein.
Cast: Lon Chaney, Jr. (as Dr. Mark Steele), Patricia Morison, J. Carrol Naish, Ramsay Ames, David Bruce, Fay Helm, and Holmes Herbert.

WEIRD WOMAN (Universal, 1944)
Credits: Directed by Reginald LeBorg;

produced by Ben Pivar; screenplay by Brenda Weisberg, based on the novel *Conjure Wife* by Fritz Leiber, Jr.
Cast: Lon Chaney, Jr. (Professor Norman Reed), Anne Gwynne, Evelyn Ankers, Ralph Morgan, Elisabeth Risdon, Lois Collier, and Elizabeth Russell.

GHOST CATCHERS (Universal, 1944)
Credits: Directed by Edward F. Cline; produced by Edmund L. Hartmann; screenplay by Edmund L. Hartmann.
Cast: Ole Olsen and Chic Johnson; Gloria Jean, Martha O'Driscoll, Leo Carrillo, Andy Devine, and Lon Chaney, Jr. (as the bear).

FOLLOW THE BOYS (Universal, 1944)
Credits: Directed by Edward Sutherland; produced by Charles K. Feldman; screenplay by Lon Breslow and Gertrude Purcell.
Cast: George Raft, Vera Zorina, Grace McDonald, Charles Grapewin, Charles Butterworth, Ramsay Ames, W. C. Fields, Marlene Dietrich, Orson Welles, and Lon Chaney, Jr. (as himself).

COBRA WOMAN (Universal, 1944)
Credits: Directed by Robert Siodmak; produced by George Waggner; screenplay by Gene Lewis and Richard Brooks.
Cast: Maria Montez, Jon Hall, Sabu, Edgar Barrier, Mary Nash, Lois Collier, Samuel S. Hinds, Moroni Olson, and Lon Chaney, Jr. (as Hava).

THE MUMMY'S GHOST (Universal, 1944)
Credits: Directed by Reginald LeBorg; produced by Joseph Gershenson; screenplay by Griffin Jay and Henry Sucher; music by Hans Salter.
Cast: Lon Chaney, Jr. (as Kharis), John Carradine, Robert Lowery, Ramsay Ames, Barton MacLane, George Zucco, and Frank Reicher.

DEAD MAN'S EYES (Universal, 1944)
Credits: Directed by Reginald LeBorg; produced by Ben Pivar; screenplay by Dwight V. Babcock.
Cast: Lon Chaney, Jr. (as Dave Stuart), Jean Parker, Paul Kelly, Acquanetta, Thomas Gomez, and Jonathan Hale.

HOUSE OF FRANKENSTEIN (Universal, 1944)
Credits: Directed by Erle C. Kenton; produced by Paul Malvern; screenplay by Edward T. Lowe, based on a story by Curt Siodmak; music by Hans Salter.
Cast: Boris Karloff, Lon Chaney, Jr. (as Lawrence Talbot), John Carradine, J. Carrol Naish, Elena Verdugo, Anne Gwynne, Peter Coe, Lionel Atwill, and Glenn Strange.

THE MUMMY'S CURSE (Universal, 1944)
Credits: Directed by Leslie Goodwins; produced by Ben Pivar; screenplay by Bernard L. Schubert.
Cast: Lon Chaney, Jr. (as Kharis), Peter Coe, Virginia Christine, Kay Harding, Dennis Moore, Martin Kosleck, Kurt Katch, Addison Richards, and Holmes Herbert.

HERE COME THE CO-EDS (Universal, 1945)
Credits: Directed by Jean Yarbrough; produced by John Grant; screenplay by Arthur T. Horman and John Grant.
Cast: Bud Abbott and Lou Costello, Peggy Ryan, Martha O'Driscoll, June Vincent, Lon Chaney, Jr. (as Johnson), and Donald Cook.

THE FROZEN GHOST (Universal, 1945)
Credits: Directed by Harold Young; produced by Ben Pivar; screenplay by Bernard L. Schubert and Luci Ward.
Cast: Lon Chaney, Jr. (as Alex Gregor), Evelyn Ankers, Milburn Stone, Douglass Dumbrille, Martin Kosleck, Elena Verdugo, and Tala Birell.

STRANGE CONFESSION (Universal, 1945)
Credits: Directed by John Hoffman; produced by Ben Pivar; screenplay by M. Coates Webster, based on the story "The Man Who Reclaimed His Head" by Jean Bart [Maria Antoinette Sarlabous].
Cast: Lon Chaney, Jr. (as Jeff Carter), Brenda Joyce, J. Carrol Naish, Milburn Stone, Lloyd Bridges, Addison Richards, and Mary Gordon.

Note: Rereleased by Realart Pictures in 1953 as *The Missing Head*.

THE DALTONS RIDE AGAIN (Universal, 1945)
Credits: Directed by Ray Taylor; produced by Howard Welsch; screenplay by Roy Chanslor, Paul Gangelin, and Henry Blankfort.
Cast: Alan Curtis, Kent Taylor, Lon Chaney, Jr. (as Grat Dalton), Noah Beery, Jr., Martha O'Driscoll, Jess Barker, Thomas Gomez, and Milburn Stone.

HOUSE OF DRACULA (Universal, 1945)
Credits: Directed by Erle C. Kenton; produced by Paul Malvern; screenplay by Edward T. Lowe.
Cast: Lon Chaney, Jr. (as Lawrence Talbot), John Carradine, Martha O'Driscoll, Lionel Atwill, Onslow Stevens, Jane Adams, Ludwig Stossel, and Glenn Strange.

PILLOW OF DEATH (Universal, 1945)
Credits: Directed by Wallace Fox; produced by Ben Pivar; screenplay by George Bricker.
Cast: Lon Chaney, Jr. (as Wayne Fletcher), Brenda Joyce, J. Edward Bromberg, Rosalind Ivan, Clara Blandick, George Cleveland, and Wilton Graff.

MY FAVORITE BRUNETTE (Paramount, 1947)
Credits: Directed by Elliott Nugent; produced by Daniel Dare; screenplay by Edmund Beloin and Jack Rose.
Cast: Bob Hope, Dorothy Lamour, Peter Lorre, Lon Chaney, Jr. (as Willie), John Hoyt, Charles Dingle, and Reginald Denny.

LAGUNA U.S.A. (Columbia, 1947), 9½-minute short
Cast: Lon Chaney, Jr. (as Lennie).

ALBUQUERQUE (Paramount, 1948)
Credits: Directed by Ray Enright; produced by William Pine and William Thomas; screenplay by Gene Lewis and Clarence Upson Young, based upon the novel by Luke Short.

Cast: Randolph Scott, Barbara Britton, George "Gabby" Hayes, Lon Chaney, Jr. (as Murkil), and Russell Hayden.

SIXTEEN FATHOMS DEEP (Monogram, 1948)
Credits: Directed by Irving Allen; produced by James S. Burkett and Irving Allen; screenplay by Max Trell and Forrest Judd, based on the story "Sixteen Fathoms Under" by Eustace L. Adams.
Cast: Lon Chaney, Jr. (as Dimitri), Arthur Lake, Lloyd Bridges, Eric Feldary, Tanis Chandler, John Qualen, Ian MacDonald, and Dickie Moore.

THE COUNTERFEITERS (20th, 1948)
Credits: Directed by Peter Stewart; produced by Maurice H. Conn; screenplay by Fred Myton and Barbara Worth.
Cast: John Sutton, Doris Merrick, Hugh Beaumont, Lon Chaney, Jr. (as Louie Struber), and George O'Hanlon.

ABBOTT AND COSTELLO MEET FRANKENSTEIN (Universal, 1948)
Credits: Directed by Charles T. Barton; screenplay by Robert Lees, Frederic Rinaldo, and John Grant.
Cast: Bud Abbott and Lou Costello, Lon Chaney, Jr. (as Lawrence Talbot), Bela Lugosi, Glenn Strange, Lenore Aubert, Jane Randolph, Frank Ferguson, and Vincent Price (as voice of the Invisible Man).

THERE'S A GIRL IN MY HEART (Allied Artists, 1949)
Credits: Directed and produced by Arthur Dreifuss; screenplay by Arthur Hoerl and John Eugene Hasty.
Cast: Lee Bowman, Elyse Knox, Gloria Jean, Peggy Ryan, Lon Chaney, Jr. (as John Colton), and Ray McDonald.

CAPTAIN CHINA (Paramount, 1949)
Credits: Directed by Lewis R. Foster; produced by William H. Pine and William C. Thomas; screenplay by Lewis R. Foster and Gwen Bagni.
Cast: John Payne, Gail Russell, Jeffrey Lynn, Lon Chaney, Jr. (as Red Lynch), Edgar Bergen, and Michael O' Shea.

ONCE A THIEF (United Artists, 1950)
Credits: Directed and produced by W. Lee Wilder; screenplay by Richard S. Conway.
Cast: Cesar Romero, June Havoc, Marie McDonald, Lon Chaney, Jr. (as Gus), and Iris Adrian.

INSIDE STRAIGHT (MGM, 1951)
Credits: Directed by Gerald Mayer; produced by Richard Goldstone; screenplay by Guy Trosper.
Cast: David Brian, Arlene Dahl, Barry Sullivan, Mercedes McCambridge, Paula Raymond, Claude Jarman, Jr., and Lon Chaney, Jr. (as Shocker).

ONLY THE VALIANT (Warner Bros., 1951)
Credits: Directed by Gordon Douglas; produced by William Cagney; screenplay by Edmund H. North and Harry Brown, based on a novel by Charles Marquis Warren.
Cast: Gregory Peck, Barbara Payton, Ward Bond, Gig Young, Lon Chaney, Jr. (as Trooper Kebussyan), Neville Brand, Jeff Corey, Warner Anderson, and Steve Brodie.

BEHAVE YOURSELF (RKO, 1951)
Credits: Directed by George Beck; produced by Jerry Wald, Norman Krasna, and Stanley Rubin; screenplay by George Beck.
Cast: Farley Granger, Shelley Winters, Margalo Gilmore, William Demarest, Francis L. Sullivan, Lon Chaney, Jr. (as Pinky), Sheldon Leonard, and Elisha Cook.

BRIDE OF THE GORILLA (Realart, 1951)
Credits: Directed by Curt Siodmak; produced by Jack Broder; screenplay by Curt Siodmak.
Cast: Barbara Payton, Lon Chaney, Jr. (as Commander Taro), Raymond Burr, Tom Conway, Paul Cavanagh, Carol Varga, and Paul Maxey.

FLAME OF ARABY (Universal-International, 1952)
Credits: Directed by Charles Lamont; produced by Leonard Goldstein; screenplay by Gerald Drayson Adams.
Cast: Maureen O'Hara; Jeff Chandler, Maxwell Reed, Susan Cabot, Lon Chaney, Jr. (as Borks), Buddy Baer, and Richard Egan.

THE BUSHWACKERS (Realart, 1952)
Credits: Directed by Rod Amateau; produced by Larry Finley; screenplay by Rod Amateau and Thomas Gries.
Cast: John Ireland, Wayne Morris, Lawrence Tierney, Dorothy Malone, Lon Chaney, Jr. (as Mr. Taylor), Frank Marlowe, and Myrna Dell.

THIEF OF DAMASCUS (Columbia, 1952)
Credits: Directed by Will Jason; produced by Sam Katzman; screenplay by Robert E. Kent.
Cast: Paul Henreid, John Sutton, Jeff Donnell, Elena Verdugo, Helen Gilbert, and Lon Chaney, Jr. (as Sinbad).

HIGH NOON (United Artists, 1952)
Credits: Directed by Fred Zinneman; produced by Stanley Kramer; screenplay by Carl Foreman.
Cast: Gary Cooper, Thomas Mitchell, Lloyd Bridges, Katy Jurado, Grace Kelly, Otto Kruger, Lon Chaney, Jr. (as Martin Howe), Henry Morgan, Ian MacDonald, and Lee Van Cleef.

SPRINGFIELD RIFLE (Warner Bros., 1952)
Credits: Directed by Andre de Toth; produced by Louis F. Edelman; screenplay by Charles Marquis Warren and Frank Davis.
Cast: Gary Cooper, Phyllis Thaxter, David Brian, Paul Kelly, Lon Chaney, Jr. (as Pete Elm), and Philip Carey.

THE BLACK CASTLE (Universal-International, 1952)
Credits: Directed by Nathan Juran; produced by William Alland; screenplay by Jerry Sackheim.
Cast: Stephen McNally, Richard Greene, Paula Corday, Boris Karloff, and Lon Chaney, Jr. (as Gargon).

THE BATTLES OF CHIEF PONTIAC (Realart, 1952)
Credits: Directed by Felix Feist; produced by Irving Starr; screenplay by Jack De Witt.
Cast: Lex Barker, Helen Westcott, Lon Chaney, Jr. (as Chief Pontiac), Berry Kroeger, and Roy Roberts.

RAIDERS OF THE SEVEN SEAS (United Artists, 1953)
Credits: Directed and produced by Sidney Salkow; screenplay by John O'Dea and Sidney Salkow.
Cast: John Payne, Donna Reed, Gerald Mohr, Lon Chaney, Jr. (as Peg Leg), Anthony Caruso, and Henry Brandon.

BANDIT ISLAND (Lippert, 1953), novelty short in 3-D.
Cast: Lon Chaney, Jr. (as Kip).

A LION IN THE STREETS (Warner Bros., 1953)
Credits: Directed by Raoul Walsh; produced by William Cagney; screenplay by Luther Davis.
Cast: James Cagney, Barbara Hale, Anne Francis, Warner Anderson, John McIntire, Jeanne Cagney, Lon Chaney, Jr. (as Spurge), and Onslow Stevens.

JIVARO (Paramount, 1954)
Credits: Directed by Edward Ludwig; produced by William H. Fine and William C. Thomas; screenplay by Winston Miller.
Cast: Fernando Lamas, Rhonda Fleming, Brian Keith, Lon Chaney, Jr. (as Pedro), Richard Denning, and Rita Moreno.

THE BOY FROM OKLAHOMA (Warner Bros., 1954)
Credits: Directed by Michael Curtiz; produced by David Weisbart; screenplay by Frank Davis Miller, based on a *Saturday Evening Post* story by Michael Fessier; music by Max Steiner.
Cast: Will Rogers, Jr., Nancy Olson, Lon Chaney, Jr. (as Crazy Charlie), Anthony Caruso, Wallace Ford, Clem Bevans, and Merv Griffin.

CASANOVA'S BIG NIGHT (Paramount, 1954)
Credits: Directed by Norman Z. McLeod; produced by Paul Jones; screenplay by Hal Kanter and Edmund Hartmann.
Cast: Bob Hope, Joan Fontaine, Basil Rathbone, Audrey Dalton, Hugh Marlowe, Arnold Moss, John Carradine, John Hoyt, Hope Emerson, Robert Hutton, Lon Chaney, Jr. (as Emo), Raymond Burr, and Vincent Price.

THE BIG CHASE (Lippert, 1954)
Credits: Directed by Arthur Hilton; produced by Robert L. Lippert, Jr.; screenplay by Fred Freiberger.
Cast: Glenn Langan, Adele Jergens, Lon Chaney, Jr. (as Kip), Douglas Kennedy, and Jay Lawrence.

PASSION (RKO, 1954)
Credits: Directed by Alan Dwan; produced by Benedict Borgeaus; screenplay by Beatrice A. Dresher and Josef Leytes.
Cast: Cornel Wilde, Yvonne De Carlo, Raymond Burr, Lon Chaney, Jr. (as Castro), Rodolfo Acosta, and Anthony Caruso.

THE BLACK PIRATES (Lippert, 1954)
Credits: Directed by Allen Miner; produced by Robert L. Lippet, Jr.; screenplay by Fred Freiberger and Al C. Ward.
Cast: Anthony Dexter, Martha Roth, Lon Chaney, Jr. (as Felipe), Robert Clarke, and Victor Mendoza.

BIG HOUSE, U.S.A. (United Artists, 1955)
Credits: Directed by Howard W. Koch; produced by Aubrey Schenck; screenplay by John C. Higgins.
Cast: Broderick Crawford, Ralph Meeker, Reed Hadley, William Talman, Lon Chaney, Jr. (as Alamo Smith), and Charles Bronson.

THE SILVER STAR (Lippert, 1955)
Credits: Directed by Richard Bartlett; produced by Earle Lyon; screenplay by Richard Bartlett and Ian MacDonald.
Cast: Edgar Buchanan, Marie Windsor, Lon Chaney, Jr. (as John Harmon), Earle

Lyon, Richard Bartlett, Barton MacLane, and Morris Ankrum.

NOT AS A STRANGER (United Artists, 1955)
Credits: Directed and produced by Stanley Kramer; screenplay by Edna and Edward Anhalt, based on the novel by Morton Thompson.
Cast: Robert Mitchum, Olivia de Havilland, Frank Sinatra, Gloria Grahame, Broderick Crawford, Charles Bickford, Myron McCormick, Lon Chaney, Jr. (as Job Marsh), Jesse White, Harry Morgan, Lee Marvin, Virginia Christine, Whit Bissell, and Mae Clarke.

I DIED A THOUSAND TIMES (Warner Bros., 1955)
Credits: Directed by Stuart Heisler; produced by Willis Goldbeck; screenplay by W. R. Burnett.
Cast: Jack Palance, Shelley Winters, Lori Nelson, Lee Marvin, Gonzalez Gonzalez, and Lon Chaney, Jr. (as Big Mac).

THE INDIAN FIGHTER (United Artists, 1955)
Credits: Directed by Andre de Toth; produced by William Schorr; screenplay by Frank Davis and Ben Hecht.
Cast: Kirk Douglas, Walter Matthau, Diana Douglas, Walter Abel, Elsa Martinelli, Lon Chaney, Jr. (as Chivington), Eduard Franz, and Alan Hale.

MANFISH (United Artists, 1956)
Credits: Directed and produced by W. Lee Wilder; screenplay by Joel Murcott, based on "The Tell-Tale Heart" and "The Gold Bug" by Edgar Allan Poe.
Cast: Victor Jory, Lon Chaney, Jr. (as Swede), John Bromfield, Barbara Nichols, and Vincent Chang.

THE INDESTRUCTIBLE MAN (Allied Artists, 1956)
Credits: Directed and produced by Jack Pollexfen; screenplay by Vy Russell and Sue Bradford; music by Albert Glasser.
Cast: Lon Chaney, Jr. (as Charles Benton), Casey Adams, Robert Shayne, Marian Carr, Ross Elliott, Kenneth Terrell, Marvin Ellis, and Stuart Randall.

THE BLACK SLEEP (United Artists, 1956)
Credits: Directed by Reginald LeBorg; produced by Howard W. Koch; screenplay by Reginald LeBorg and John C. Higgins; music by Les Baxter.
Cast: Basil Rathbone, Bela Lugosi, Lon Chaney, Jr. (as Mongo), Akim Tamiroff, John Carradine, Tor Johnson, Herbert Rudley, George Sawaya, and Sally Yarnell.
Note: Rereleased by Carl Releasing Corporation in 1963 as *Dr. Cadman's Secret*.

DANIEL BOONE, TRAIL BLAZER (Republic, 1956)
Credits: Directed by Albert C. Gannaway and Ismael Rodriguez; produced by Albert C. Gannaway; screenplay by Tom Hubbard and Jack Patrick.
Cast: Bruce Bennett, Lon Chaney, Jr. (as Chief Blackfish), Faron Young, Ken Dibbs, Damian O'Flynn, and Jacqueline Evans.

PARDNERS (Paramount, 1956)
Credits: Directed by Norman Taurog; produced by Paul Jones, screenplay by Sidney Sheldon.
Cast: Dean Martin and Jerry Lewis, Lori Nelson, Jeff Morrow, Jackie Loughery, John Baragrey, Agnes Moorhead, and Lon Chaney, Jr. (as Whitey).

THE CYCLOPS (Allied Artists, 1957)
Credits: Directed, produced, and written by Bert I. Gordon.
Cast: Lon Chaney, Jr. (as Martin Melville), James Craig, Gloria Talbott, and Tom Drake.

THE DEFIANT ONES (United Artists, 1958)
Credits: Directed and produced by Stanley Kramer; screenplay by Nathan E. Douglas and Harold Jacob Smith.
Cast: Tony Curtis, Sidney Poitier, Theodore Bikel, Charles McGraw, Lon Chaney, Jr. (as Big Sam), and King Donovan.

MONEY, WOMEN, AND GUNS (Universal-International, 1958)
Credits: Directed by Richard Bartlett; produced by Howie Horowitz; screenplay by Montgomery Pittman.
Cast: Jock Mahoney, Kim Hunter, Tim Hovey, Gene Evans, Tom Drake, and Lon Chaney, Jr. (as Art Birdwell).

LA CASA DEL TERROR (Diana-Des Fuentes-Azteca, 1959)
Credits: Directed by Gilberto M. Solares; screenplay by Gilberto M. Solares and Juan Garcia.
Cast: Lon Chaney, Jr. (as a mummy/werewolf), Tin Tan.

FACE OF THE SCREAMING WEREWOLF (Associated Distributors Pictures, 1959)
Credits: Directed and produced by Jerry Warren; screenplay by Jerry Warren and Alfred Salimar.
Cast: Lon Chaney, Jr. (as a mummy/werewolf), Landa Varle, Raymond Gaylord, and D. W. Barron.
Note: Producer Jerry Warren combined footage from *La Casa del Terror* and *Attack of the Mayan Mummy* to make this film.

THE ALLIGATOR PEOPLE (20th Century-Fox, 1959)
Credits: Directed by Roy Del Ruth; produced by Jack Leewood; screenplay by Orville H. Hampton.
Cast: Beverly Garland, Bruce Bennett, Lon Chaney, Jr. (as Mannon), George Macready, Frieda Inescort, and Richard Crane.

REBELLION IN CUBA (International Film Distributors, 1961)
Credits: Directed and produced by Albert C. Gannaway; screenplay by Frank Graves and Mark Hanna.
Cast: Bill Fletcher, Jake LaMotta, Lon Chaney, Jr. (as Gordo), Sonja Marrero, and Dan Gould.

THE DEVIL'S MESSENGER (Herts-Lion, 1962)
Credits: Directed by Herbert L. Strock; produced by Kenneth Herts; screenplay by Leo Guild.
Cast: Lon Chaney, Jr. (as the Devil), Karen Kadler, Gunnel Brostrom, Michael Hinn, Tammy Newmara, John Crawford, Jan Blomberg, Ralph Brown, Ingrid Bedoya, Bert Johnson, Eve Hossner, and Chalmers Goodlin.

THE HAUNTED PALACE (AIP, 1963)
Credits: Directed and produced by Roger Corman; screenplay by Charles Beaumont, based on the poem "The Haunted Palace" by Edgar Allan Poe and the novella *The Case of Charles Dexter Ward* by H. P. Lovecraft; music by Ronald Stein; art direction by Daniel Haller.
Cast: Vincent Price, Debra Paget, Lon Chaney, Jr. (as Simon Orne), Leo Gordon, Elisha Cook, Jr., John Dierkes, Harry Ellerbe, Barboura Morris, and Bruno Ve Sota.

SPIDER BABY (American General, 1964)
Credits: Directed produced, and written by Jack Hill.
Cast: Lon Chaney, Jr. (as Bruno), Carol Ohmart, Quinn Redecker, Mantan Moreland, Jill Banner, Mary Mitchell, and Sid Haig.
Note: Rereleased in 1970 as *The Liver Eaters*.

LAW OF THE LAWLESS (Paramount, 1964)
Credits: Directed by William F. Claxton; produced by A. C. Lyles; screenplay by Steve Fisher.
Cast: Dale Robertson, Yvonne De Carlo, William Bendix, Bruce Cabot, Barton MacLane, John Agar, Richard Arlen, Kent Taylor, and Lon Chaney, Jr. (as Tiny).

WITCHCRAFT (20th Century-Fox, 1964)
Credits: Directed by Don Sharp; produced by Robert Lippert and Jack Parsons; screenplay by Harry Spalding.
Cast: Lon Chaney, Jr. (as Morgan Whitlock), Jack Hedley, Jill Dixon, Viola Keats, Marie Ney, David Weston, and Yvette Rees.

STAGE TO THUNDER ROCK (Paramount, 1964)
Credits: Directed by William F.

Claxton; produced by A. C. Lyles; screenplay by Charles Wallace.
Cast: Barry Sullivan, Marilyn Maxwell, Scott Brady, Lon Chaney, Jr. (as Harry Parker), Keenan Wynn, and John Agar.

YOUNG FURY (Paramount, 1965)
Credits: Directed by Chris Nyby; produced by A. C. Lyles, screenplay by Steve Fisher.
Cast: Rory Calhoun, Virginia Mayo, Lon Chaney, Jr. (as Ace, the bartender), John Agar, Richard Arlen, William Bendix, Preston Pierce, Robert Biheller, and Marc Cavell.

BLACK SPURS (Paramount, 1965)
Credits: Directed by R. G. "Bud" Springsteen; produced by A. C. Lyles; screenplay by Steve Fisher.
Cast: Rory Calhoun, Terry Moore, Linda Darnell, Scott Brady, Lon Chaney, Jr. (as Kile), Bruce Cabot, and Richard Arlen.

HOUSE OF THE BLACK DEATH (Medallion, 1965)
Credits: Directed by Harold Daniels; produced by William White; screenplay by Rich Mahoney.
Cast: Lon Chaney, Jr. (as Belial), John Carradine, Tom Drake, Andrea King, Sabrina, George Andre, and Katherine Victor.
Note: Rereleased in 1966 as *Blood of the Man-Devil*.

TOWN TAMER (Paramount, 1965)
Credits: Directed by Leslie Selander; produced by A. C. Lyles; screenplay by Frank Gruber, based on his novel.
Cast: Dana Andrews, Terry Moore, Pat O'Brien, Lon Chaney, Jr. (as Mayor Charlie Leach), Bruce Cabot, Lyle Bettger, Coleen Gray, Barton MacLane, Richard Arlen, Richard Jaeckel, Philip Carey, and Sonny Tufts.

APACHE UPRISING (Paramount, 1966)
Credits: Directed by R. G. "Bud" Springsteen; produced by A. C. Lyles; screenplay by Harry Sanford and Max Lamb.
Cast: Rory Calhoun, Corinne Calvet, John Russell, Lon Chaney, Jr. (as Charlie Russell), Gene Evans, Richard Arlen, Arthur Hunnicut, De Forrest Kelley, George Chandler, Johnny Mack Brown, Jean Parker, and Don Barry.

JOHNNY RENO (Paramount, 1966)
Credits: Directed by R. G. "Bud" Springsteen; produced by A. C. Lyles; screenplay by Steve Fisher.
Cast: Dana Andrews, Jane Russell, Lon Chaney, Jr. (as Sheriff Hodges), John Agar, Lyle Bettger, Tom Drake, Richard Arlen, and Robert Lowery.

DR. TERROR'S GALLERY OF HORRORS (American General, 1966)
Credits: Directed and produced by David L. Hewitt; screenplay by Gary Heacock, David Prentiss, and Russ Jones.
Cast: Lon Chaney, Jr. (as Dr. Mendel), John Carradine, Rochelle Hudson, Ron Doyle, Roger Gentry, Vic McGee, Gray Daniels, and Mitch Evans.
Note: Television title: "Return from the Past."

WELCOME TO HARD TIMES (MGM, 1967)
Credits: Directed by Burt Kennedy; produced by Max E. Youngstein; screenplay by Burt Kennedy.
Cast: Henry Fonda, Janice Rule, Keenan Wynn, Janis Paige, John Anderson, Warren Oates, Fay Spain, Edgar Buchanan, Aldo Ray, and Lon Chaney, Jr. (as Avery, the bartender).

HILLBILLYS IN A HAUNTED HOUSE (Woolner Brothers, 1967)
Credits: Directed by Jean Yarbrough; produced by Bernard Woolner; screenplay by Duke Yelton.
Cast: Ferlin Husky, Joi Lansing, Don Bowman, John Carradine, Lon Chaney, Jr. (as Maximillian), Linda Ho, and Basil Rathbone.

BUCKSKIN (Paramount, 1968)
Credits: Directed by Michael Moore; produced by A. C. Lyles; screenplay by Michael Fisher.

Cast: Barry Sullivan, Joan Caulfield, Wendell Corey, Lon Chaney, Jr. (as Sheriff Tangley), John Russell, Barbara Hale, Barton MacLane, Bill Williams, and Richard Arlen.

FIREBALL JUNGLE (Americana, 1969)
Credits: Directed by Jose Priete; produced by G. B. Roberts; screenplay by Harry Whittington.
Cast: John Russell, Lon Chaney, Jr. (as Sammy), Randy Kirby, Alan Mixon, Chuck Daniel, Nancy Donohue, and Vicki Nunis.

THE FEMALE BUNCH (Burbank International, 1971)
Credits: Directed by Al Adamson and John Cardos; produced by Raphael Nussbaum; screenplay by Jale Lockwood and Brent Nimrod.
Cast: Russ Tamblyn, Jennifer Bishop, and Lon Chaney, Jr. (as Monty).

DRACULA VS. FRANKENSTEIN (Independent International, 1971)
Credits: Directed by Al Adamson; produced by Al Adamson and John Van Horn; screenplay by William Pugsley and Samuel M. Sherman; special effects by Ken Strickfaden.
Cast: J. Carrol Naish, Lon Chaney, Jr. (as Groton, the mad zombie), Zandor Vorkov, Russ Tamblyn, Jim Davis, Anthony Eisley, Regina Carrol, Angelo Rossitto, and John Bloom.

Television Performances

"THE LIFE OF RILEY" (unaired pilot, 1947 or 1949)

"COLGATE COMEDY HOUR" (1951)
Format: comedy, variety; Network: NBC; Running Time: 60 minutes.

"COSMOPOLITAN THEATER" (November 6, 1951)
Format: dramatic anthology; Title: "Last Concerto"; Network: DuMont; Running time: 60 minutes.

"TALES OF TOMORROW" (January 18, 1952)
Format: science fiction anthology; Title: "Frankenstein"; Network: ABC; Running Time: 30 minutes.

"YOU ASKED FOR IT" (1952?)
Format: audience participation; Network: ABC; Running Time: 30 minutes.

"SCHLITZ PLAYHOUSE OF STARS" (September 25, 1952)
Format: dramatic anthology; Title: "The Trial"; Network: CBS; Running Time: 30 minutes.

"THE RED SKELTON SHOW" (October 27 [?], 1953)
Format: comedy, variety; Network: CBS; Running Time: 30 minutes.

"THE WHISTLER" (1954)
Format: suspense anthology; Title: "Backfire"; Network: syndicated; Running Time: 30 minutes.

"JACK LONDON'S TALES OF ADVENTURE" (unaired pilot, 1954)
Mutual-Pathé apparently turned the footage into a television movie of the same title.

"CAVALCADE THEATER" (May 18, 1954)
Format: dramatic anthology; Title: "Moonlight School"; Network: ABC; Running Time: 30 minutes.

"CAVALCADE THEATER" (May 3, 1955)
Format: dramatic anthology; Title: "Stay On, Stranger"; Network: ABC; Running Time: 30 minutes.

"FLIGHT FROM ADVENTURE" (1955, unsold series)
American Releasing apparently turned the footage into a television movie of the same title.

"MASQUERADE PARTY" (1955)
Format: quiz/audience participation; Network: ABC; Running Time: 30 minutes.

"CLIMAX" (January 26, 1956)
Format: dramatic anthology; Title: "Secret of River Lane"; Network: CBS; Running Time: 60 minutes.

"TELEPHONE TIME" (April 8, 1956)
Format: dramatic anthology; Title: "The Golden Junkman"; Network: CBS; Running Time: 30 minutes.

"STUDIO 57" (August 12, 1956)
Format: dramatic anthology; Title: "Ballad of Jubal Pickett"; Network: DuMont; Running Time: 30 minutes.

"HAWKEYE AND THE LAST OF THE MOHICANS" (1957)
Format: adventure series; Network: syndicated; Running Time: 30 minutes. Lon Chaney, Jr. co-starred as Chingachgook in the show's 26 episodes.
International Television Corporation compiled episodes from the television series to create four feature films: *Along the Mohawk Trail, Redmen and the Renegades, Long Rifle and the Tomahawk,* and *Pathfinder and the Mohican.*

"CLIMAX" (September 19, 1957)
Format: dramatic anthology; Title: "Necessary Evil"; Network: CBS; Running Time: 60 minutes.

"TARGET" (1958)
Format: suspense anthology; Network: syndicated; Running Time: 30 minutes.

"THE RED SKELTON SHOW" (1958)
Format: comedy, variety; Network: CBS; Running Time: 30 minutes.

"TRUTH OR CONSEQUENCES" (1958)
Format: quiz/audience participation; Network: NBC. Running Time: 30 minutes.

"THE ROUGH RIDERS" (January 15, 1959)
Format: Western series; Title: "An Eye for an Eye"; Network: ABC; Running Time: 30 minutes.

"RAWHIDE" (February 6, 1959)
Format: Western series; Title: "Incident on the Edge of Madness"; Network: CBS; Running Time: 60 minutes.

"NUMBER 13 DEMON STREET" (1959)
This was an unsold horror anthology series consisting of at least 14 episodes, all filmed in Sweden.

"HAVE GUN, WILL TRAVEL" (February 14, 1959)
Format: Western series; Title: "Scorched Feather"; Network: CBS; Running Time: 30 minutes.

"GENERAL ELECTRIC THEATER" (February 22, 1959)
Format: dramatic anthology; Title: "Family Man"; Network: CBS; Running Time: 30 minutes.

"THE TEXAN" (March 9, 1959)
Format: Western series; Title: "No Love Wasted"; Network: CBS; Running Time: 30 minutes.

"TOMBSTONE TERRITORY" (June 12, 1959)
Format: Western series; Title: "The Black Marshal from Deadwood"; Network: ABC; Running Time: 30 minutes.

"WANTED: DEAD OR ALIVE" (October 10, 1959)
Format: Western series; Title: "The Hostage"; Network: CBS; Running Time: 30 minutes.

"ADVENTURES IN PARADISE" (October 12, 1959)
Format: adventure series; Title: "The Black Pearl"; Network: ABC; Running Time: 60 minutes.

"LOCK-UP" (1960)
Format: dramatic series; Network: syndicated; Running Time: 30 minutes.

218 • *Filmography*

"JOHNNY RINGO" (March 3, 1960)
Format: Western series; Title: "The Raffertys"; Network: CBS; Running Time: 30 minutes.

"BAT MASTERSON" (October 13, 1960)
Format: western series; Title: "Bat Trap"; Network: NBC; Running Time: 30 minutes.

"WAGON TRAIN" (October 26, 1960)
Format: Western series; Title: "The Jose Morales Story"; Network: NBC; Running Time: 60 minutes.

"STAGECOACH WEST" (February 7, 1961)
Format: western series; Title: "Not in Our Stars"; Network: ABC; Running Time: 60 minutes.

"KLONDIKE" (February 13, 1961)
Format: adventure series; Title: "The Hostages"; Network: NBC; Running Time: 30 minutes.

"ZANE GREY THEATER" (March 23, 1961)
Format: Western anthology; Title: "A Warm Day in Heaven"; Network: CBS; Running Time: 30 minutes.

"THE DEPUTY" (April 15, 1961)
Format: Western series; Title: "Brother in Arms"; Network: NBC; Running Time: 30 minutes.

"WAGON TRAIN" (May 24, 1961)
Format: Western series; Title: "The Chalice"; Network: NBC; Running Time: 60 minutes.

"SURFSIDE SIX" (October 23, 1961)
Format: detective series; Title: "Witness for the Defense"; Network: ABC; Running Time: 60 minutes.

"ROUTE 66" (November 10, 1961)
Format: adventure series; Title: "The Mud Nest"; Network: CBS; Running Time: 60 minutes.

"THE RIFLEMAN" (January 15, 1962)
Format: Western series; Title: "Gunfire"; Network: ABC; Running Time: 30 minutes.

"LAWMAN" (January 28, 1962)
Format: Western series; Title: "Tarnished Badge"; Network: ABC; Running Time: 30 minutes.

"HERE'S HOLLYWOOD" (Summer, 1962)
Format: interview; Running Time: 30 minutes.

"ROUTE 66" (October 26, 1962)
Format: adventure series; Title: "Lizard's Leg and Owlet's Wing"; Network: CBS; Running Time: 60 minutes.

"THE GUNSLINGER" (1961)
Format: Western; Network: CBS; Running Time: 60 minutes.

"RAWHIDE" (January 18, 1963)
Format: Western series; Title: "Incident at Spider Rock"; Network: CBS; Running Time: 60 minutes.

"HAVE GUN, WILL TRAVEL" (February 16, 1963)
Format: Western series; Title: "Cage at McNab"; Network: CBS; Running Time: 30 minutes.

"EMPIRE" (March 26, 1963)
Format: Western series; Title: "Hidden Asset"; Network: NBC; Running Time: 60 minutes.

"THE PHANTOM" (1963 pilot for unsold series)

"ROUTE 66" (October 11, 1963)
Format: adventure series; Title: "Come Out, Come Out, Wherever You Are"; Network: CBS; Running Time: 60 minutes.

"ROUTE 66" (April 24, 1964)
Format: adventure series; Network: CBS; Running Time: 60 minutes.

"PISTOLS AND PETTICOATS" (1966–1967)
Format: situation comedy series; Network: CBS; Running Time: 30 minutes. Lon Chaney, Jr., played Chief Eagle Shadow on a semiregular basis.

In 1968, Universal compiled several episodes of "Pistols and Petticoats" to create a television movie called *The Far Out West*. Lon appears in that compilation.

"THE MONKEES" (October 24, 1966)
Format: situation comedy, musical series; **Title:** "Monkees in a Ghost Town"; **Network:** NBC; **Running Time:** 30 minutes.

"THE PAT BOONE SHOW" (1967)
Format: variety; **Running Time:** 90 minutes.

"STAR CLOSE-UP" (1968)
Format: interview; **Network:** British Broadcasting Company; **Running Time:** 30 minutes.

"A STRANGER IN TOWN" (1969)
Format: telefeature **Network:** National Educational Television.

"THE TONIGHT SHOW" (October 8, 1969)
Format: variety; **Network:** NBC; **Running Time:** 90 minutes.

"WHAT'S NEW?" (1971)
Network: National Educational Television; **Title:** "The Children's West."

Television Commercials: Chaney appeared in a television commercial for Procter and Gamble's Bold Detergent in 1967, and he appeared as a cop in a Pontiac truck commercial called "The Chain Gang" with Henry Branden in 1969.

Note: Evidence exists that Lon did a skit with Milton Berle and Frank Sinatra, probably on "The Milton Berle Show," but I cannot verify the year and date.

Other references incorrectly list the "Wagon Train" (NBC, 10/26/60) episode "The Colter Craven Story" as one of Chaney's television credits.

At his death, Lon left a television credit list which is both incomplete and inaccurate. On that list, however, are the following probable episode titles for which I cannot trace the television programs:
"Passing Parade" (1955)
"Border Patrol" (1959)
"The Big Sleep" (1959)
"Escape" (1960)
"Address: Hell" (1961)
"First Impressions" (1962)

Therefore, Lon may have made seven television appearances in addition to the 59 listed above in the filmography.

Selected Bibliography

Ackerman, Forrest J. "Lon Is Gone." *Famous Monsters of Filmland* 103 (1973).
Beck, Calvin. *Heroes of the Horrors.* New York: Collier Books, 1975.
Brosnan, John. *The Horror People.* New York: St. Martin's Press, 1967.
Brunas, Michael, John Brunas, and Tom Weaver. *Universal Horrors: The Studio's Classic Films, 1931-1946.* Jefferson, N.C.: McFarland, 1990.
Chaney, Lon, Jr. Preface to *The Ghost of Frankenstein*, Philip J. Riley, ed. Absecon, N.J.: MagicImage Film Books, 1990.
"A Chip Off the Old Block?: The Career of Lon Chaney, Jr." *Movie Monsters* 1, no. 4 (1975).
Clarens, Carlos. *An Illustrated History of the Horror Film.* New York; Capricorn Books, 1967.
Gifford, Dennis. *A Pictorial History of Horror Movies.* London: Hamlyn, 1973.
Gourlay, Jack, and Gary Dorst. "Lon Chaney, Jr." *Filmfax* 20 (1993).
Gourlay, Jack. "Lon Chaney, Jr., Part Two." *Filmfax* 21 (1990).
Hoffman, Eric L. "The Wolf Man." *Monsterland* 16 (1987).
"An Interview with Lon Chaney, Jr." *Castle of Frankenstein* 10 (1966).
Jackson, B. Gelman. "The Life Story of Lon Chaney, Jr." *Monster Fantasy* 1, no. 4 (1975).
"Lon Chaney, Jr." *World of Horror* 8 (1975).
Mank, Gregory William. *It's Alive.* San Diego: A. S. Barnes, 1981.
Mayer, Lloyd. "Son of Chaney: The Story of Lon Chaney, Jr." *Monster Magazine* 1, no. 4 (1975).
Seymour, Blackie. *Living Legend of Lon Chaney.* Worcester, MA.: Pentegram, 1966.
Sheppard, Don. "Chaney: Champion of Chills." *Mad Monsters* 8 (1964).
Sielski, Mark L. "Lon Chaney, Jr.: Remembering the Wolfman." *Monsterland* 7 (1986.)
Walker, Helen Louise. "Second Generation?" *Modern Screen* (July 1932).

Index

Page numbers in bold indicate photographs.

Abbott, Bud 58, 93, **94**, 101, 102, 110
Abbott and Costello Meet Frankenstein 91, 101–103, 110, 210
Abbott and Costello Meet the Mummy 65
Accent on Youth 202
Ace Drummond 20, 203
Ackerman, Forrest J 15, 171, 177, 181, 182, 185, 186
Acquanetta 73, 74
Across the Wide Missouri 124
Adams, Casey 132
Adams, Jane 56
Adamson, Al 181
Adrian, Iris 81
"Adventures in Paradise" 144, 145, 217
Agar, John 164, 169, 170
Akins, Claude 141
Albertson, Frank 34
Albuquerque 100
Alexander's Ragtime Band 205–206
Alger, Horatio 161
Alias Nick Beal 145
Allbritton, Louise 86, 89, 90
Allen, Corey 135
Allied Artists Studios 103
The Alligator People 144–146, 214
The Amazing Colossal Man 122
The Amazing Transparent Man 145
American General Pictures 172
American-International Pictures 156, 159

Ames, Ramsey 61, 68
Anders, Mary 165
Anderson, Warner 107
Andrews, Dana 166, 167, 169
Angel's Holiday 203
Ankers, Evelyn 35, 36, 37, 38, 43, 47, 55, 72, 73, 74, 75, 76, 84, 85
Apache Uprising 167–169, 215
Archer, Eugene 161
Arden, Eve 82
Arlen, Richard 165, 167, 168, 169
Armstrong, R. G. 175
Arsenic and Old Lace (play) 185
Arthur, Robert 101, 135
The Atomic Man see *Man-Made Monster*
Attack of the Crab Monsters 156
Attack of the 50 Foot Woman 142
Attack of the Mayan Mummy 148, 214
Atwill, Lionel 32, 34, 35, 43, 45, 47, 50, 78, 79
Aubert, Lenore 101, 102
Autry, Gene 19, 149

"Backfire" 123
Badlands of Dakota 83–84, 207
Baer, Buddy 110
Baker, Art 119
Baker, Bob 86
Bandit Island 120, 212
Banning, Jill 160
Baragrey, John 138

224 • Index

Barker, Lex 117
Barrie, Wendy 86, 87
Barrier, Edgar 93
Barry, Don 166
Barry, Gene 150
Barrymore, Diana 88
Barrymore, John 32
Barton, Charles 102-103
The Bat 139
"Bat Masterson" 150, 218
"Bat Trap" 150
Battles of Chief Pontiac 117-118, 212
The Beast from 20,000 Fathoms 139
Beaumont, Charles 157
Beaumont, Hugh 100, 101
"Beautiful Dreamer" 88
Beck, Calvin 8
The Beginning of the End 139
Beery, Noah, Jr. 83, 86, 88, 94
Beery, Noah, Sr. 15, 86
Behave Yourself 108, 211
Bel-Air Productions 133
"Bela Lugosi's Last Screen Rites" 149
Bellamy, Ralph 35, 36, 42, 47
Ben-Hur 13
Bendix, William 106, 161
Bennett, Bruce 137, **138**, 144, 145
Benson, Joey 173
Benton, Dean 17
Bergen, Edgar 104
Bettger, Lyle 166, 169
Bey, Turhan 59
Bickford, Charles 26, 83, 125
The Big Chase 120, 121-122, 212
Big House, U.S.A. 123-124, **124**, 133, 212
Billy the Kid 31, 207
Bird of Paradise 12, 201
Birell, Tala 75, 76, 77
Bishop, Jennifer 179
Bissell, Whit 151
Bixby, Jerome 190
The Black Castle 115, **116**, 117, 177, 211
Black Friday 32
"Black Marshall of Deadwood" 143
"The Black Pearl 144, 145, 146
The Black Pirates 122, 212
The Black Room 18
The Black Sleep 133-135, 176, 213
Black Spurs 165, 215

Blaine, James 83
Blake, Patricia 133
Blanchard, Marie 151
Blandick, Clara 79
The Blob 143
Blood Freaks—The Blood Seekers see *Dracula vs. Frankenstein*
Blood of Dracula 146
Blood of Frankenstein see *Dracula vs. Frankenstein*
Blood of Ghastly Horror 143
Blood of the Man-Devil see *House of the Black Death*
Bloom, John 182, 183
Blue, Monte 83
Bluebeard's Ten Honeymoons 169
Bogart, Humphrey 98, 126
Boles, John 15
Bond, Ward 107
Boone, Pat 162
Boone, Richard 143
Boris Karloff (book) 52
Born Yesterday (play) 100
Bouchey, Willis 123
Bowman, Don 174
Bowman, Lee 104
The Boy from Oklahoma 121, **122**, 212
Boyd, William 13
Bradford, Sue 132
Brady, Scott 164
The Brain from Planet Arous 164
Brand, Neville 107
Brandon, Henry 20-21, 121
Bray, Robert 151
Breese, Edmund 19
Brian, David 106
Brian, Mary 20
The Bride of Frankenstein 45, 46, 50
Bride of the Gorilla 108-110, **109**, 117, 211
Bridges, Lloyd 79, 100, 113
Brissac, Virginia 96
Brocco, Peter 135, **136**
Broder, Jack 117
Brodie, Steve 107
Brogan, Ron 172
Bromberg, J. Edward 79, 89, 90
Bromfield, John 129
Bronson, Charles 123
Brown, James 167
Brown, Johnny Mack 168

Brown, Phil 72
Bruce, David 68
Bruce, Virginia 32
Brunas, John 34, 45, 49, 56, 60, 76, 78, 79, 80, 89, 90
Brunas, Michael 34, 45, 49, 56, 60, 76, 78, 79, 80, 89, 90
Buchanan, Edgar 124, 128
A Bucket of Blood 156
Buckskin 176–177, 215
"Burke's Law" 161
Burn, Witch, Burn 73
Burr, Raymond 108, 109, 121, 189
Burton, Marie 17
Bushman, Francis X. 13, 15
The Bushwackers 111–112, 112, 114, 211

The Cabinet of Dr. Caligari 1
Cabot, Bruce 15, 165, 167
Cagney, James 120, 139
Cagney, Jeanne 120
Calhoun, Rory 164, 165, 167
Calling Dr. Death 68–70, 69, 79, 183, 190, 208
Calvet, Corinne 168, 169
Canutt, Yakima 13
Captain China 104–105, 210
Captain Hurricane 202
Carey, Macdonald 150
Carey, Philip 166
Carillo, Leo 83, 88
Carnival of Souls 147
Carr, Marian 132
Carradine, John 24, 51, 53, 55, 56, 58, 61, 62, 121, 133, 134, 143, 149, 165, 166, 172, 173, 175, 175, 176
Carricart, Robert 168
Carrol, Regina 182, 183
Carroll, Madeleine 31
Carson, Johnny 180
Caruso, Anthony 121
La Casa del Terror 147–149, 148, 214
Casanova's Big Night 121, 212
Case, Cathy 152
The Case of Charles Dexter Ward (novel) 156
Case of the Crime Cartel see *The Shadow of Silk Lennox*
Castle, William 84

The Cat People (1942) 38
Caulfield, Joan 177
"Cavalcade Theatre" 122, 128, 216
Cavanagh, Paul 108
CBS Radio 31
CBS (television) 146
A Century of Chaneys 185, 191
Chance, Larry 117
Chandler, Jeff 110
Chaney, Cleva 4–6, 8–9, 139, 140
Chaney, Creighton Tull see Chaney, Lon, Jr.
Chaney, Dorothy (Hinckley) 8, 21
Chaney, Lon, Jr. attempt to adopt a child 95, 96–97; birth 4; changes name to Lon Chaney, Jr. 23; death 185; dislike of foreigners 91; divorce 21; drinking 16, 41, 44, 54, 55, 56–57, 61, 62, 63, 64, 66–67, 77, 80, 84, 91, 102, 119, 122, 124, 133, 134, 135, 147, 164, 172, 173, 184, 188; illnesses 172, 173, 179, 185; latent homosexuality 40–41, 109, 189; marriage to Dorothy Hinckley 8; marriage to Patsy Beck 21; opinion of slapstick comedy 82; patriotism 71, 79; relationship with father 39–40, 43, 97, 103, 152, 165, 187, 188; suicide attempt 103, 117, 188; violence against women 97
Chaney, Lon, Sr. 2, 4–10, 35, 40, 41, 54, 119, 139, 190
Chaney, Lon III 8, 54
Chaney, Patsy (Beck) 21, 22, 26, 37, 80, 82, 91, 95, 96, 103, 135, 185, 187, 189
Chaney, Ronald 8, 54, 103
Chaney, Ronald II 103, 189, 191
Chaney Enterprises 191
Charlie Chan in the City of Darkness 24, 206
Charlie Chan on Broadway 204
Checkers 205
Cheyenne Rides Again 203
Christine, Virginia 65, 66, 66–67
City Girl 205
Clare, Diane 162
Clarens, Carlos 3
Clary, Robert 112
Classic Images 62
Classics of the Horror Film 35

Cleveland, George 79
"Climax" 135, 217
Cobra Woman 92, 113, 209
Codee, Ann 66
Coe, Peter 51, 54, 65, 66
"Colgate Comedy Hour" 110, 216
Collier, Lois 72, 73
Colmans, Edward 112
Columbia Studios 113
Commodore Pictures 16, 18
Conjure Wife 71, 73
Connors, Chuck 153
Conway, Pat 143
Conway, Tom 108, 109
Cook, Elisha 152, 158
Cooper, Gary 31, 113, 114, 115
Cooper, James Fenimore 137
Copland, Aaron 27
Corby, Ellen 104
Corday, Paula 115
Corey, Wendell 177
Corman, Roger 1, 3, 156, 158, 159, 170
Corrigan, Lloyd 84
Corrigan, Ray "Crash" 20
The Cosmic Man 145
"Cosmopolitan Theater" 110, 216
Costello, Lou 58, 93, 94, 94, 101, 102, 103, 106, 110
"Count Alucard" 173
Count Dracula Society 171, 178
The Counterfeiters 101, 210
Cowan, Jerome 81
Crabbe, Larry "Buster" 12
Craig, James 139, 140, 141
Crane, Richard 145
Craven, Frank 89
Crawford, Broderick 24, 83, 84, 85, 86, 100, 105, 120, 123, 124, 125, 181, 185
Crawford, John 146
The Crawling Hand 143, 146
Crazy House 89, 208
The Creature Walks Among Us 139
Crehan, Joseph 86
Criminals of the Underworld see *Eyes of the Underworld*
Crist, Judith 158
Crosby, Bing 99
Cup of Gold 29
The Curse of Frankenstein 2, 154

Curse of the Stone Hand 149
Curse of the Werewolf 154–155
Curtis, Alan 94
Curtis, Tony 141
Curtiz, Michael 3, 121
Curucu, Beast of the Amazon 145
Cushing, Peter 2, 154, 172, 190
The Cyclops 139–140, **141**, 213

Dahl, Arlene 106
Dalton, Audrey 121
The Daltons Ride Again 94, 96, 210
Daly, Jack 121
Daniel, Paul 170
Daniel Boone, Trail Blazer 137–138, **138**, 213
Daniels, Steve 178
Darling, W. Scott 42, 47
Darnell, Linda 165
Daughter of Dr. Jekyll 140, 164
Davis, Jim 121
The Day Mars Invaded Earth 143
Day of the Evil Gun 176
The Day the World Ended 156
Dead Man's Eyes 73–75, **76**, 93, 169, 209
Dead Ringer 145
DeCamp, Rosemary 105
De Carlo, Yvonne 161
The Defiant Ones 140–142, 213
de Havilland, Olivia 125
Dein, Edward 70
Dekker, Albert 71
Dell, Myrna 111, 112
Dell Comics 128
Del Ruth, Roy 145
De Mille, Cecil B. 3
Denning, Richard 55
Denny, Reginald 98
"The Deputy" 152, 218
Desmond, William 13
Destination Moon 116
The Devil Bat 176
The Devil's Brood 51
The Devil's Messenger 146–147, 149, 214
The Devil's Partner 145
Devine, Andy 84, 86, 88, 91, **92**, 189
Dillard, R. H. W. 38, 41
Dingle, Charles 98

Dix, Richard 86, 87
Dixon, Jill 162
Dr. Cadman's Secret see *The Black Sleep*
Dr. Terror's Gallery of Horrors 172–173, 215
Dr. Terror's House of Horrors 172
Doctorow, E. L. 174
Dolenz, Mickey 171
Donlevy, Brian 31, 96
Donnell, Jeff 112
Donohue, Nancy 178
Donohue, Troy 152
Dorst, Gary 180
Douglas, Diana 128
Douglas, Kirk 127, 128
Doyle, Ron 173
Dracula (1931) 15, 32
Dracula (1958) 154, 155; see also *Horror of Dracula*
Dracula vs. Frankenstein 181–185, 183, 216
Drake, Oliver 20, 21
Drake, Tom 139, 140, 169, 170
Draper, Jack 138
Ducette, John 150
Dumbrille, Douglas 75, 76
Durant, Don 149
Dylan, Bob 171

Earp, Wyatt 24
Eastham, Richard 143
Eastwood, Clint 122
Edwards, Edgar 29
Eisley, Anthony 182, 183, 184
Elam, Jack 138
Elliott, Ross 132
Ellis, Marvin 132
"Empire" 218
Englund, Robert 2
Erickson, Hal 137
Everson, William K. 35, 45
The Evil Gun see *Day of the Evil Gun*
"An Eye for an Eye" 142
Eyes of the Underworld 86–87, 171, 208

Face of the Screaming Werewolf 148–149, 214
Falk, Lee 159

The Fall of the House of Usher 156
"The Fall of the House of Usher" (short story) 156
Famous Monsters of Filmland 181, 185, 186
The Far Out West 177, 219
Farmer, Francis 83, 84
Farnum, William 65, 66
Farr, Randy 123
Feature Films (comic book) 105
The Female Bunch 179–180, 216
Ferguson, Frank 102
Fernandez, Abel 168
Ferris, Audrey 19
Ferris Hartman's Comic Opera Company 5, 6
Field, Betty 26, 27, 153
Fielding, Edward 73
The Film Journal 38
Filmfax 149
Fireball Jungle 169, 178–179, 216
Fisher, Steve 164, 165
Fisher, Terence 162
Fix, Paul 153, 176
Flame of Araby 110, 211
Flash Gordon 182
Fleming, Eric 143
Fleming, Rhonda 120
Fletcher, Bill 153
"Flight from Adventure" 123, 216
Flight to Mars 116
Flippen, Jay C. 151
The Fly (1956) 2
Flynn, Errol 67
Follow the Boys 92, 209
Fonda, Henry 174
Fontaine, Joan 121
Foran, Dick 59, 83, 86, 189
Ford, Wallace 25, 59, 121
Foreman, Carl 113
Foster, Preston 31
Four-Sided Triangle 109
Fowley, Douglas 170
Fox Studios 23
Fraff, William 79
Francis, Anne 120
Frankenstein (1931) 12, 15, 32, 182
"Frankenstein" (television broadcast) 118
Frankenstein Meets the Wolf Man 2, 47–51, 49, 52, 190, 208

Franz, Eduard 127
Frazee, Jane 81
Friday the 13th 1
Frontier Badman 88, 171, 208
Frontier Marshall 24, 206
Frozen Ghost 67, 75-77, 77, 209
Fung, Willie 84

Gable, Clark 124
Gallow, Janet Ann 42
Gannaway, Albert C. 153
Gardner, Louanna 133
Garland, Beverly 144, 145, 146
"G. E. Theatre" 143, 217
Gerstad, Harry 114
Ghost Catchers 91, 92, 209
The Ghost of Frankenstein 42-47, **43**, 86, 178, 180, 190, 208
The Ghoul Goes West 149
The Giant Claw 139
The Gila Man 191
Gilbert, Helen 112
Girl Crazy 12, 201
The Girl in the Kimono (play) 5
Girl o' My Dreams 15, 16, 202
Gleason, Jackie 106
Goddard, Paulette 159
Godzilla 109
Goetz, William 101
Gog 146
"The Gold Bug" 129, 131
"Gold Hunters of the North" 84
"The Golden Junkman" 135-137, **136**, 179
Gomez, Thomas 73, 88, 96
Goodwins, Leslie 66, 67
Gordon, Bert I. 122, 139, 140
Gordon, Leo 158, 176
Graham, Gloria 125
Granger, Farley 108
Gray, Coleen 166
Green, Dorothy 123
Greene, Richard 115
Grey, Rudolph 149
Grey, Zane 190
Griffin, Merv 121
Griffith, D. W. 30, 31
Guild, Leo 146
"Gunfire" 153
Gunnison, Grace 73

"The Gunslinger" 218
"Gunsmoke" 171
Gwynne, Anne 51, 72, **74**, 83, 88

Haig, Sid 160
Hale, Barbara 120, 176
Hale, Jonathan 73
Hall, Jon 92, 93
Haller, Daniel 158
Hammer Studios 2, 109, 154, 155, 161, 162, 170, 173
Hangover Square 165
Happy Landing 205
Hardie, Russell 20
Harding, Ann 15, 16
Harding, Kay 65
Hardwicke, Cedric 42, 47
Hardy, Oliver 30
Harris, Robert H. 168
Harris, Roy 84
Hart, John 137
Hastings, Hazel 6
The Haunted Palace 156-159, **157**, 214
"Have Gun, Will Travel" 143, 217, 218
Havoc, June 106
"Hawaiian Eye" 184
"Hawkeye and the Last of the Mohicans" 137, 217
Hayes, Allison 142, 143
Hedley, Jack 162
Helm, Fay 36
Henreid, Paul 112
Here Come the Co-Eds 93-94, **94**, 209
"Here's Hollywood" 153, 218
Herts-Lion Productions 146, 147
Hervey, Irene 86
Hewitt, David 161
Hicks, Chuck 169
High Noon 31, 113-115, 124, 141, 145, 211
High Sierra 126
Hill, Jack 159
Hill, Ramsay 117
Hillbillys in a Haunted House 174-176, **175**, 215
Hinds, Samuel S. 34, 87
Hitchcock, Alfred 170
Ho, Linda 175

Hoffman, David 68
Hohl, Arthur 75, 76
Hold 'Em Yale 19, 202
Holliday, Judy 100
Hollywood Exchange 19
Hollywood Reporter 44
Homicidal 170
Hope, Bob 98, 99, **99**, 121
Horror and Science Fiction Films II 38
Horror of Dracula 2, 173; see also *Dracula* (1958)
The Horror of It All 162
Horvath, Charles 169
"The Hostages" 151
House of Dracula 53, 54, 55-58, **57**, 94, 210
House of Fear (1939) 32
The House of Frankenstein 51-55, **53**, 56, 59, 65, 177, 183, 209
The House of Terror see *The Face of the Screaming Werewolf*
House of the Black Death 165-166, **167**, 215
House of the Damned 145
The House of the Seven Gables 32
The House on Haunted Hill 2
How to Make a Monster 146
Howard, Moe 99
Howard, Shemp 81, 82, **83**, 94, 106
Hoyt, John 98
Hull, Henry 155
The Human Duplicators 145
The Human Robot 32, 33
The Hunchback of Notre Dame (1923) 8, 119
The Hunchback of Notre Dame (1939) 24, 25, 88, 117
Hunnicut, Arthur 168
Hunt, Marita 154
Hurlbert, Roger 171
Hush, Hush, Sweet Charlotte 139, 170
Husky, Ferlin 174

I Died a Thousand Times 126-127, 213
I Was a Teenage Frankenstein 146, 151
"Incident on the Edge of Madness" 143
The Indestructible Man 132-133, 134, 213

The Indian Fighter 127-128, 213
Inescort, Frieda 145
Inside Straight 106-107, 211
Invisible Invaders 164
The Invisible Man 15
The Invisible Man Returns 32
The Invisible Woman 32
Ireland, John 111, 112
Irving, George 89, **89**
It Conquered the World 139, 145, 156
It! The Terror from Beyond Space 2, 190
Ivan, Rosalind 79

"Jack London's Tales of Adventure" 123, 216
Jaeckel, Richard 166
Jarmin, Claude, Jr. 106
Jergens, Adele 121
Jeske, John 9
Jesse James 23, 206
Jivaro 120, 212
Johnny Reno 169-170, 215
"Johnny Ringo" 149, 218
Johns, Vera 129
Johnson, Chic 89
Johnson, Tor 133, 134
Jones, Buck 83
Jones, Davey 171
Jones-Moreland, Betsy 154
Jory, Victor 121
"The Jose Morales Story" 150-151
Josette 205
Journey to the Seventh Planet 164
Joyce, Brenda 77, 79
Jurado, Katy 113
Juran, Nathan 115

Kadler, Karen 146
Kael, Pauline 93
Karloff, Boris 2, 3, 12, 15, 18, 19, 32, 35, 36, 42, 43, 44, 45, 46, 48, 50, 51, 52, 53, **53**, 55, 56, 57, 58, 59, 60, 115, 116, 132, 153, 154, 156, 177-178, 190
Kasznar, Kurt 144
Katch, Kurt 66
Katzman, Sam 112
Keene, Tom 14

Keeping Fit 86, 208
Kehoe, Vincent J-R 118
Keith, Brian 120
Kelly, DeForest 143, 166, 168
Kelly, Grace 113
Kelly, Jeanne 83
Kelly, Paul 73
Kennedy, Douglas 121, 144, 145
Killer at Large 20, 203
King, Henry 23
King, John 20
King Kong (1933) 15, 31, 165
King of the Jungle 12
"King Vampire" 172
Kirby, Randy 178, 179
Kiss of the Vampire 161
"Klondike" 151, 218
Knowles, Patrick 35, 36, 48, 50
Knox, Alexander 118
Knox, Elyse 59, 60, 104
Koch, Howard W. 124, 133, 134
Kosleck, Martin 65, 67, 75, 76, 77, 91
Kramer, Stanley 110, 113, 114, 124, 128, 140, 141, 142, 191
Kroeger, Barry 117
Kronos 139
Kruschen, Jack 143

Ladd, Alan 98, 99
The Lady Escapes 204
Laguna, U.S.A. 100, 210
Lake, Arthur 100
Lamas, Fernando 120
LaMotta, Jake 153
Lamour, Dorothy 98
Landers, Harry 127
Landis, Carole 29
Lane, Richard 81
Langan, Glenn 121, 122
Lansing, Joi 151, 174, 176
Lansky, Gil 161
The Last Frontier 12-13, 201
The Last of the Mohicans (book) 137
Las Vegas Hillbillies 174
Laugh, Clown, Laugh 8
Laughton, Charles 24, 25
Laurel, Stan 30
Lava, William 183
Law of the Lawless 161, 214

"Lawman" 153, 169, 218
Lawrence, Jay 121
Lawrence, Marc 87
"Leave It to Beaver" 101
LeBorg, Reginald 63, 73, 74, 75, 133, 134, 165, 188
Lee, Christopher 2, 90, 154, 155, 190
Lee, Lila 19
Leiber, Fritz, Jr. 71
Lesser, Len 171
Lewis, Jerry 138, 139
Lewton, Val 38
Life Begins at College 204
"The Life of Riley" (television pilot) 105, 216
The Life of Vergie Winters 15, 202
Lincoln, Abraham 118
Lineham, Harry 162
A Lion in the Streets 120, 212
Lippert, Robert 161
Lippert Studios 120
Litel, John 96
"Little Red Caboose Behind the Train" (song) 5
The Liver Eaters see *Spider Baby*
"Lizard's Leg and Owlet's Wing" 153-154
"Lock Up" 150, 217
London, Jack 84
"The Lone Ranger" 137
Long, Huey 120
Lorre, Peter 2, 98, 99, **99** 120, 133, 153, 154, 190
The Lost World 29, 31
Love and Hisses 205
Love Is News 205
Lovecraft, H. P. 156, 159
Lowery, Robert 61, 169
Lucky Devils 13, 201
Lugosi, Bela 2, 3, 15, 18, 19, 28, 32, 35, 36, 42, 45, 47, 48, 52, 55, 58, 90, 100, 101, 102, 120, 133, 134-135, 149, 181, 190
Lugosi, Bela, Jr. **49**, 102
Luke, Keye 84, 85
Lummis, Dayton 123
Lyles, A. C. 161, 164, 165, 166, 167, 169, 170, 176
Lynn, Jeffrey 104
Lyon, Earle 124

McCambridge, Mercedes 106
McCay, Gardner 144
McCready, George 144, 145
McDevitt, Ruth 170
McDonald, Ian 113
McGee, Vic 173
MacLane, Barton 161, 166
McNally, Stephen 115
McQueen, Steve 143
McRae, Joel 12
The Mad Monster 55
The Mad Room 145
Madsen, Bill 30
Maharis, George 152, 154
Mallory, Michael 90
Malone, Dorothy 111, 112, 139
The Maltese Falcon (1931) 145
Maltin, Leonard 142
The Man from Planet X 116
The Man in the Cab 32
Man of a Thousand Faces 139
The Man Who Reclaimed His Head 78
Manfish 129-132, 130, 213
Man-Made Monster 2, 33, 34-35, 132, 180, 190, 207
Mank, Gregory William 50
Mansfield, Jayne 174
A Marriage Bargain 19, 202
Martin, Dean 138
Martinelli, Elsa 127
Marvin, Lee 127, 150
"Masquerade Party" 217
Massen, Osa 87
Massey, Ilona 48, 50, 51
Massey, Raymond 118
Matthau, Walter 127
Mature, Victor 29
Maxwell, Frank 158
Maxwell, Marilyn 164
Mayo, Virginia 164
Medina, Patricia 144
Meeker, George 73
Meeker, Ralph 123, 124
Merchant, Cathy 157, 158
Meredith, Burgess 26, 27
Merlin, Jan 142
MGM Studios 31, 106, 124
Michenaud, Gerald 176
Midnight Taxi 203
Milestone, Lewis 3, 25, 27
Milner, Martin 152, 154

The Missing Head see *Strange Confession*
Mr. Moto's Gamble 205
Mitchell, Mary 160
Mitchell, Thomas 151
Mitchum, Robert 125, 125, 126
Mixon, Alan 178
The Mole People 164
Money, Women, and Guns 142, 214
Monka, Paul 161
"The Monkees" 170-171, 219
"Monkees in a Ghost Town" 171
Monogram Pictures 34
Monroe, Marilyn 3
The Monster and the Ape 145
"The Monster Raid" 172-173
Montez, Maria 92
Monthly Film Bulletin 132
"Moonlight School" 122
Moore, Clayton 137
Moore, Dennis 65
Moore, Mary Alice 119
Moore, Terry 165, 166, 167
Moorhead, Agnes 139
Moose (Lon Chaney's German Shepherd) 51, 60, 93
Moran, Peggy 93
Moreno, Rita 122
Morgan, Frank 86
Morgan Ralph 72, 73
Morison, Patricia 68, 69, 69, 70, 79
Morris, Wayne 111
Morrow, Jeff 138, 139
Morton, Jim 160
Moss, Arnold 121
The Most Dangerous Game 12, 115, 201
Motel Hell 165
Motion Picture Herald 44
Movie and Video Guide 1992 142
"The Mud Nest" 152
Mulhall, Jack 17
The Mummy (1932) 15, 59
The Mummy (1959) 154, 155
The Mummy's Curse 52, 54, 64-67, 66, 209
The Mummy's Ghost 61-64, 62, 64, 75, 134, 209
The Mummy's Hand 59, 60
The Mummy's Tomb 59-61, 104, 208
Muni, Paul 118, 190

Murder by Television 18
Murders in the Rue Morgue (1932) 15
My Favorite Brunette 98, 99, **99**, 210
The Mysterious Dr. R 32
The Mysterious Island (1952) 145

Nader, George 122
Nagel, Anne 34
Naha, Ed 132
Naish, J. Carrol 51, 53, 68, **69**, 70, 77, 78, 79, 181, 182, 183
Nash, Mary 93
National Educational Television 178
The Neanderthal Man 145
Nelson, Lori 126, 139
Nesmith, Mike 171
New York Herald 158
New York Times 37, 45, 61, 65, 69, 117, 161
Newland, John 119
Newsweek 140
Night of the Lepus 165
Nightmare of Ecstacy: The Life and Art of Edward Wood, Jr. 149
A Nightmare on Elm Street 1, 2
Nollen, Scott 52
North to the Klondike 84–85, 105, 124, 207
Northwest Mounted Police 31, 207
Not as a Stranger 124–126, **125**, 145, 213
"Not in Our Stars" 151
Not of This Earth 145, 156
Nugent, Elliott 99
Nunis, Vicki 178
Nyby, Christian 164

O'Brien, Pat 166
O'Brien, Willis 30
O'Driscoll, Martha 55, 56, 94
Of Mice and Men (film) 3, 25–29, **28**, 31, 35, 55, 103, 149, 153, 171, 180, 190, 206
Of Mice and Men (play) 24, 84, 100
O'Hara, Maureen 110
The Old Corral 19, 203
The Old Dark House (1932) 15
Olson, Nancy 121

Olson, Ole 89
Olson, Tracy 169
Omhart, Carol 160
Once a Thief 106, 211
One Mile from Heaven 204
One Million B.C. (1940) 29–31, **30**, 180, 190, 206–207
"One Step Beyond" 146
O'Neill, Sally 15
Only the Valiant 107, 211
Otterson, Jack 44
Ouspenskaya, Marie 35, 36, 48, 50
Overland Mail 83, 86, 87, 207–208

Paget, Debra 157, 158, 159
Paige, Robert 82, 88, 89, 90
Palance, Jack 126
Paramount Pictures 12, 31, 98, 104, 161
Pardners 138–139, 213
Parker, Eddie 58
Parker, Jean 73, 100, 168, 169
Parrish, Helen 81, 86
Parson, Milton 158
Parsons, Jack 161
Passion 122, 212
Passport Husband 205
Pasteur, Louis 118
"The Pat Boone Show" 219
Patterson, Lee 152
Pauley, Edward 86
Payne, John 104, 105, 120
Payton, Barbara 107, 108, 109
Pearl Harbor 37
Peck, Gregory 107
Pendleton, Gaylord 87
Pentegram Library 45, 189
"Perry Mason" 109, 164
"The Phantom" 159, 218
The Phantom Ghoul 149
The Phantom of the Opera (1925) 8, 35
The Phantom of the Opera (1943) 88, 117
The Phantom of the Opera (1962) 154
Pierce, Jack 37, 44, 45, **64**
Pierce, Preston 164
Pillow of Death 78, 79–80, 94, 210
Pine-Thomas Company 161
Pirie, David 162
"Pistols and Petticoats" 170, 177, 218

The Pit and the Pendulum (1961) 156
Pivar, Ben 68
Plan 9 from Outer Space 137
Poe, Edgar Allan 129, 131, 156, 170
Poitier, Sidney 141
Pollexfen, Jack 132, 133
Pontiac 117, 118
Poor Jake's Demise 6
Porter, Don 86
Powell, William 69, 98
The Premature Burial 156
Prendergast, Tessa 129
Presley, Elvis 20
PRC 34
Price, Vincent 2, 32, 121, 157, 158, 159
Psycho 170
Puglia, Frank 98

Qualen, John 104
Quarry, Robert 97
Quiz Kids 63

"The Raffertys" 149
Raft, George 92
Raiders of the Seven Seas 119, 212
Rains, Claude 35, 36, 38, 78
Randolph, Jane 101, 102
Rathbone, Basil 32, 89, 121, 133, 176
The Raven (1935) 19, 32
The Raven (1963) 156
"Rawhide" 143, 217, 218
Ray, Aldo 174
Raymond, Paula 106
Rebellion in Cuba 153, 214
"The Red Skelton Show" 120, 142, 216, 217
Redeker, Quinn 160
Reece, Yvette 162
Reed, Donna 120
Reed, Oliver 155
Rees, Lanny 105
Regas, George 15
Regina Theatre 32
Reicher, Frank 61, 62-63
Repulsion 170
Return from the Past see *Dr. Terror's Gallery of Horrors*
The Return of Count Yorga 145

Return of the Fly 145
The Return of the Vampire 145
Revenge of the Creature 139, 164
Richards, Addison 65
Riders of Death Valley 82-83, 86, 207
"The Rifleman" 153, 218
Riley, Jeannine 154
RKO Studios 10, 11, 12, 13, 14, 16, 23, 24, 25, 108
Roach, Hal 29, 30
Road Demon 206
The Road to Mandalay 18
Roberts, George 178
Roberts, Roy 117
Robertson, Dale 161
"Robin Hood" 115
Robinson Crusoe on Mars 161
The Rocket Man 145
Rocketship X-M 116
Rodan the Flying Monster 2
Rogers, Wayne 151
Rogers, Will, Jr. 121, 122
Romeo and Juliet 29
Romero, Cesar 106
Roosevelt, Franklin 88
Rose Marie 171
The Rosebowl 202-203
Rossito, Angelo 181, 182, 183
"The Rough Riders" 142, 217
"Route 66" 152, 153-154, 218
Rudley, Herbert 133
Rule, Janice 174
Russell, Elizabeth 72, 73
Russell, Gail 104
Russell, Jane 169
Russell, John 153, 168, 169, 177, 178, 179
Russell, Vy 132
Ruth, Roy Dell 3

Sally, Irene, and Mary 205
Salter, Hans J. 35, 53
San Antonio Rose 81-82, 83, 207
Sande, Walter 96
Scared to Death 181
Scarlet River 13, 133
"Schlitz Playhouse of Stars" 120, 216
Scott, Randolph 84-85
A Scream in the Night 17, 18, 202
"Sea Hunt" 100

Second Honeymoon 204
Secret Agent X-9 203
Selznik, David O. 10
Seymour, Anne 164
Seymour, Blackie 45, 47, 62-63, 76, 80, 85, 189
The Shadow of Silk Lennox 16-17, 202
Sharp, Don 161, 164
Shayne, Robert 132
She-Gods of Shark Reef 156
Shelley, Mary 118
Shepperton Studios 161
Sheridan, Ann 170
Sherman, Sam 181, 184
The Silver Star 124, 212-213
Simon and Schuster 68
The Singing Cowboy 19, 203
Siodmak, Curt 7, 35, 36, 38, 40-41, 47, 50, 51, 89, 90, 108, 109, 146, 147, 152, 187, 188, 189, 191
Siodmak, Robert 90, 91
Sixteen Fathoms Deep (1934) 15, 202
Sixteen Fathoms Deep (1948) 100, 210
Skelton, Red 142
Slaughter, Todd 56
Slave Ship 203
Smith, Roger 139
Sobol, Louis 31
Son of Dracula 50, 68, 89-91, **90**, 135, 155, 173, 180, 190, 208
Son of Frankenstein 32, 45, 46, 50, 182
Son of Kong 32
Son of the Border 14, 201
Soul of a Monster 145
Spalding, Harry 161
"The Spark of Life" 173
Speed to Burn 206
Spider Baby 15, 159-161, 190, 216
The Spoilers 84, 85
Spooks Run Wild 181
Springfield Rifle 31, 115, 211
Springsteen, R. G. 165
Stack, Robert 86
Stage to Thunder Rock 164, 214
"Stagecoach West" 151, 218
"Star Close-Up" 219
"Stay On, Stranger" 128
Steel, Anthony 144
Steele, Barbara 162
Steele, Bob 26, 27, 138, 167
Stein, Ronald 158

Steinbeck, John 26, 29, 131
Stevens, Onslow 55, 56
Stone, Milburn 75, 76, 79
Stossel, Ludwig 56
Straight, Place, and Show 206
Strange Confession 77-79, 190, 209
Strange, Glenn 52, 53, 53, 55, 56-58, 101, 102, 110
"Stranger in Town" 178, 219
Strickfaden, Ken 182, 183
Strock, Herbert L. 146
"Studio 57" 135, 217
Submarine Patrol 206
"Sugarfoot" 121
Sullivan, Barry 106, 164, 176
"Surfside Six" 152, 218
Sutton, John 100, 112

Talbot, Gloria 139, 140
Tales of Terror 156
"Tales of Tomorrow" 118, 216
Talman, William 123
Tamblyn, Russ 180, 184
Tamiroff, Akim 133, 134
Tarantula 164
"Target" 217
Taylor, Alfred 160
Taylor, Eric 42, 89
Taylor, Kent 94, 142
Taylor, Robert 31
"Telephone Time" 135-137, **136**, 217
"The Tell-Tale Heart" 129, 131
Teenage Caveman 156
Teresa of Avila 28
Terrell, Ken 132
"The Texan" 143, 165, 217
The Texas Chainsaw Massacre 2
That I May Live 203
There's a Girl in My Heart 104, **105**, 210
Thief of Damascus 112-113, 211
The Thing from Another World 116, 119
Thin Ice 204
"13 Demon Street" 146, 217
This Island Earth 139
This Is My Affair 204
Thomas, Bernard B 79
The Three Musketeers 15, 202
The Three Stooges 82
"Thriller" 146

Tierney, Lawrence 111
The Time Machine 151
A Time to Run see *The Female Bunch*
Tin Tan 147
Tiomkin, Dimitri 114
Tolstoy, Leo 189
"Tombstone Territory" 143, 217
"The Tonight Show" 180, 219
Too Many Blondes 81, 82, 207
Tork, Peter 171
Torres, Roger 166
Town Tamer 166–167, 215
The Trap 201
"The Trial" 120
"Truth or Consequences" 217
20th Century-Fox 144, 145, 146
Twice Told Tales 145
"The Twilight Zone" 146
Tyler, Tom 32, 59, 60

Ullman, Emil 32
The Undead 156
The Undersea Kingdom 20, 203
The Unholy Three 8
Union Pacific 24, 206
United Artists Studios 25, 27, 106, 133
Universal Studios 15, 19, 32, 33, 34, 35, 36, 100, 101, 105, 115, 116, 135, 139, 148, 159, 188
Universal-International Studios 32–97, 101, 115, 117
Universal Television 177

Vallee, Rudy 81
Van Cleef, Lee 113, 138, 139
Van Doren, Mamie 174
Van Sickle, Dale 169
Van Sloan, Edward 15
Van Zant, Philip 112
Varga, Carol 108
Verdugo, Elena 52, 53, 54, 75, 76, 97
Vidor, King 3
Viking Women and the Sea Serpent 156
Vinson, Gary 170
Vorkov, Zandor 182, 183
Votrian, Peter 123

Waggner, George 35, 45

"Wagon Train" 150, 152, 218
Walker, Helen Louise 10
The Walking Dead 132
Walking Down Broadway 205
Wallace, Charles A. 164
Walsh, Raoul 3, 120
"Wanted: Dead or Alive" 143–144, 217
War of the Satellites 156
"A Warm Day in Heaven" 151
Warner Bros. Studios 106, 115
Warren, Bill 132, 140, 145
Warren, Jerry 147, 148, 149, 165
Washington, Ned 114
The Wasp Woman 156
Wayne, John 15
Weaver, Tom 34, 45, 49, 56, 60, 76, 78, 79, 80, 89, 90
Webb, Richard 167, 175
Weird Woman 71–73, 74, 75, 208–209
The Weird World of LSD 178
Welcome to Hard Times 174, 215
Welles, Orson 24
Wells, Carole 170
The Werewolf of London 36, 37, 155
Westcott, Helen 117
Weston, David 162
West Side Story 20
What Ever Happened to Baby Jane? 170
"What's New?" 219
What We Are Fighting For 87–88, 208
When the Daltons Rode 96
"The Whistler" 123, 216
White, Bill 165
Whitmore, James 124
Whitney, Peter 142
Wife, Doctor, and Nurse 204
Wild and Wooly 204
The Wild Bunch 179
Wilde, Cornel 122
Wilder, W. Lee 129
Wilke, Bob 113
Williams, Bill 176
Williams, Elmo 114
Williams, Guinn "Big Boy" 83
Williams, Van 152
Williams, Warren 35, 36
Willis, Donald C. 38
Wilson, Woodrow 118
Windsor, Marie 121, 143

Winkleman, Michael 127
Winters, Shelley 108, 127
Witchcraft 161–164, **163**, 214
"The Witch's Clock" 172
"Witness for the Defense" 152
Wolf, Leonard 46, 48
The Wolf Man 2, 35–41, **40**, 42, 47, 50, 109, 135, 155, 180, 207
Wood, Edward Jr. 137, 149
Wooley, Sheb 113
Wordsworth, William 187
Wray, Fay 12
Wybrow, Eric 35
Wynn, Keenan 174

Yarborough, Barton 43
Yarbrough, Jean 176
"You Asked for It" 119, 216
Young Fury 164–165, 214–215
Young, Gig 107
Young, Harold 75

"Zane Grey Theatre" 151, 218
Zinneman, Fred 3, 112
Zucco, George 51, 55